More praise for

THE MILLIONAIRES

"It's the kind of book that is both entertaining and thought-provoking and there are no loose ends, no unfinished plot lines. It has a clear message and focus. It's literature, and serious readers will want to tackle it."
—*The Advocate* (Baton Rouge)

"[There are] flashes of absolutely brilliant prose. . . . This is a story of the New South, and of the politics, the financial shenanigans, and the competitive mind games that bring wealth and power to a handful of determined men. [Majors's] description of the beautiful Appalachian mountains is a plus."
—*Midwest Book Review*

"Remarkable and very timely . . . the story of two small-town brothers who rise to dangerous big-city heights is as big and ambitious as the physical book itself."
—*Bookpage*

"Majors's depiction of a Tennessee evening is reminiscent of James Agee's hypnotic *Knoxville: Summer of 1915.*"
—*New York Times*

"Since the new rich often get short shrift in fiction . . . Mr. Majors's approach is actually refreshing. . . . Giving us profligate bankers who borrow badly, *The Millionaires* is a timely work."
—*Wall Street Journal*

"A deftly rendered look at the modern South and contemporary America. . . . Scenes that require it burst at the seams with Majors's poetry."
—*Anniston Star*

"An engrossing story about ambition and integrity. . . . Majors deserves ample applause for his storytelling and character-drawing skills."
—*Raleigh News and Observer*

THE
MILLIONAIRES

Other books by Inman Majors

Wonderdog
Swimming in Sky

THE
MILLIONAIRES

A Novel of the New South

INMAN MAJORS

W. W. NORTON & COMPANY

NEW YORK   LONDON

This book is dedicated to Joe Inman Majors,
who gave the kettle time to boil

For information about permission to reproduce selections from this book,
write to Permissions, W. W. Norton & Company, Inc., 500 Fifth Avenue,
New York, NY 10110

For information about special discounts for bulk purchases, please contact
W. W. Norton Special Sales at specialsales@wwnorton.com or 800-233-4830

Manufacturing by RR Donnelley, Bloomsburg
Book design by Dana Sloan
Production manager: Anna Oler

Library of Congress Cataloging-in-Publication Data

Majors, Inman.
The millionaires / Inman Majors.—1st ed.
p. cm.
ISBN 978-0-393-06802-3 (hardcover)
1. Brothers—Fiction. 2. Millionaires—Fiction. 3. Bankers—Fiction.
4. Politicians—Fiction. 5. Banks and Banking—Fiction. 6. Political
corruptions—Tennessee—Fiction. 7. Tennessee—Fiction. I. Title.
PS3563.A3927M55 2009
813'.54—dc22   2008041518

ISBN 978-0-393-33727-3 pbk.

W. W. Norton & Company, Inc.
500 Fifth Avenue, New York, N.Y. 10110
www.wwnorton.com

W. W. Norton & Company Ltd.
Castle House, 75/76 Wells Street, London W1T 3QT

1 2 3 4 5 6 7 8 9 0

All the switchmen knew by the engine's moans

That the man at the throttle was Casey Jones

—THE BALLAD OF CASEY JONES

The

Candidate

1978

They were playing poker in the back room of the Clearwater Country Club bar, the last survivors of the member-guest tournament that had ended earlier that day. They sat at the poker table, dressed still in their colorful golfing shirts and pants, an assortment of half-filled drinks scattered among their piles of chips, laughing and swirling cards in the otherwise empty clubhouse. Behind them the bartender's tip jar would soon have to be replaced with an empty one. And twice already the waitress had gone to her purse to deposit a stack of the crisp bills that seemed to come from a burgeoning and inexhaustible source. For these were cash men, with long leather wallets designed for the inside of a suit jacket, and they couldn't be bothered with the smaller denominations.

A hawk's-eye view during the daylight hours would have shown eighteen fairly well-manicured fairways, with only the occasional unrepentant clump of crabgrass, the odd bare spot here or there where shade proved too abundant or puddles lingered beyond their due. Even a generous viewer would have described the course as hilly, set as it was in the aftermath of that tectonic shifting of plates that created the Appalachian Mountains blue and brooding in the distance. The members called it the Billy Goat. As in, we're riding the Billy Goat after lunch. And only a few young members or very fit members would ever think to walk it. Golf cart accidents occurred approximately one to the month, usually a teenager showing out or a senior who'd lost his command of the wheel.

Six men sat around the poker table, though it is the Cole brothers who consistently draw the eye, the Cole brothers who are our primary concern. Earlier that day this same group had driven the Billy Goat like bats out of hell when out of view of the golfers they didn't know. Had raced down the fairways and skidded around winding corners. Had, often, allowed two wheels of the cart to leave terra firma while maneuvering to be first to arrive at the tee box. Yes, new rules. Honors on the box no longer went to low score on the previous hole, but more simply, more efficiently, to the cart that arrived, wheels smoking and smelling of discarded rubber, first. J. T. Cole's rule change. The least golfer of the bunch, the least patient with the pace of the game, with any pace not exclusively hell-bent-for-leather. The least patient with an antiquarianism like honors on the tee. Yes, to hell with that. And who on the course will be first to offer J.T. an etiquette lesson?

The members of the Clearwater Country Club, when entertaining guests from out of town, specifically guests from large cities out of town, even more specifically when entertaining guests from the northern industrial region of the country, would say, we're a *country* country club. And would smile when saying this, would chuckle, perhaps. An old line, a well-worn line. A line to say, before you could, you the guest from out of town, before you could think it, because you would think it, that we know we're podunky, we know you're not supposed to drive your golf cart like that, we know that no one in their right mind would place a golf course on this poor excuse for a ski slope.

In short, a line to say, we know our place. Do not add vanity and ridiculous pride to our very real, our undisguisable, provincialism. We know what we are. And we know that we are not much.

And the guest from out of town, particularly those not familiar with this region's long tradition of self-deprecation, this region's storied tradition of beating the outsider to the punch, might often feel more comfortable after hearing such a remark. Might often think, well, at least they know.

But let us not be fooled. Beneath that self-deprecation, beneath that veneer of humility, lies, and lies very close to the surface, a quiet but red-hot smoldering. For these members love their country club. Have laughed here and drunk here and danced here, too close sometimes, with the wives and husbands of their friends. Have come here for New Year's and Fourth of July and Wednesday night before Thanksgiving. For bridge and Rotary and Lions Club. And their children have grown up around the pool, have gone from warming the kiddie pool to long and lean jackknives off the board, have borrowed golf carts with spiderwebs in the ball holder from old widow ladies who can't yet bear to sell their husband's cart and raced these same carts down those steep hills with girls who've been sunning, oiled and lemon-juiced, by the pool all day and now sit drinking beer and boasting about god knows what on the sixteenth green, the farthest from the clubhouse and the darkest and the quietest, with only the hum of the cicadas and the tree frogs and the crack and hiss of a beer can being popped.

So when the members of Clearwater Country Club show you the swimming pool, brand-new and big as any anywhere, there will be no more apologies. And no more apologies or false humility for the rest of the day or weekend. And those who will be invited back will compliment the high dive and the buffet spread at dinner. For this *country* country club is, ultimately, the sign and symbol of these member families' social and economic progress, the progress of the family line in perpetuity. Yes, count them now among the leisure class, a leisure not a one of their forbears had the first minute of. So yes. A word to the wise. Remove the high hat when in the presence of another man's leisure.

The men playing seven-card stud had not a high hat among them on this Saturday night, despite their money and the fact that one of their group, Roland Cole, was a prime candidate for governor of the state. Roland Cole and his brother J.T. were the guests here, down for the day from Glennville, and they were being hosted in the grandest local style by the brass of the Clearwater Community Bank.

All of them, tossing chips in their loose and luxurious manner, sported sunburned faces and necks and arms from their day on the course. Scorched. Red as beets. In the recent past, their fathers and grandfathers had earned these same peculiar markings behind a plow, behind the backside of a mule. But the markings were virtually identical, excepting the variable of short versus long sleeves, and virtually identical in their peculiarity, more peculiar still when undressed and standing in front of a wife for bed-bath-lovemaking, the whitest white and the reddest red in such vivid and humorous contrast.

One walking in to this scene from Atlanta or New York City or perhaps even the city of Glennville just fifty miles up the road and seeing these men with their sunburned skin and their drinking and their boisterous conversations might be tempted to use that oldest of descriptions for white males of the southern region of the United States. Or to top it off with a final condescension. *Rednecks with money.* None of these men would be surprised to hear themselves described as such and they suspected, correctly, that the phrase was whispered often and perniciously whenever they attended functions of the higher caste in the city fifty miles up the road. More often than not what was whispered was the coded shorthand version of the moniker above. *New money.*

But to use the phrase about these particular men would be ungenerous and essentially inaccurate. We'll not now go into the shadings and delineations of the white southern male, though such a study would seem necessary at times. Let's say this and move on: there are as many variations of this brand of *Homo sapiens*, southern white male, as there are of any other. If you believe that all northern white males are the same, that all African-Americans are the same, all Japanese, all Sri Lankans, then you will perhaps doubt this statement. Fair enough.

I'll see your twenty, said J. T. Cole. And let's bump it twenty more.

They folded quickly and with little comment, tossing their cards without ceremony in front of them or to the discard pile in the middle of the table.

And then the call was back to the player who'd first raised the stakes, whose bet had just been called and then raised. This bettor, Roland Cole, Democratic candidate for governor, eyed his brother's cards spread out flippantly before him.

Said Roland: You're awful proud of those two sevens.

I like em fine, said J.T., taking one and straightening it a bit for Roland's perusal.

Roland eyed his own cards. A pair of threes up top and a king kicker in the hole. J.T. had him beat showing. Little chance J.T. had another pair or the third seven. If he had, he'd have bet lower and tried to milk the pot along awhile. And the fourth seven had been burned earlier in the hand.

You don't seem to think much of my threes, said Roland.

I like your threes fine, said J.T. Mine are just four bigger is all.

Roland smiled at his brother, two years older and three full sheets to the wind. Not just brother, but founding partner in their banking empire that now included eighteen banks and savings and loans in the region and more to come. He wondered if J.T. had even looked at his, Roland's, cards. More times than not, he just played his own hand, bet a hand what he thought it was worth, then let the chips fall where they may. Likely as not, J.T. hadn't even noticed the pair of threes until he'd mentioned them.

Are we gonna call Teague or not? said J.T.

We're in the middle of a hand, said Roland.

I can do two things at once, said J.T., motioning toward the waitress for another round. Sometimes three or four. Just wake me up when you decide if you're gonna bet or not.

Roland smiled. Wondered, not for the first time, how many hours he'd spent consciously or subconsciously studying the man across from him. Hell, I must have been studying him from the first day. Popped out crying, saw this big disinterested head somewhere out of the corner of my eye, and school was in session, forty-two years' worth. Roland smiled again and looked at his older brother.

What are you smiling about over there? said J. T. Cole.

I never taught you a damn thing, did I?

Not that I recall, said J.T.

Not even one thing?

I thought you might have said something about liking a quick pace in a card game and not a lot of yapping.

Bet's twenty, you say?

And has been for five minutes.

At times like these Roland felt a little guilty about knowing he was going to win the hand before he'd actually won it. It was like knowledge one shouldn't have. A feel. He had a good feel for money, Roland did, and a good feel for people. He could catch a vibe and just know. How and why other people couldn't read J.T. like he could had proved an elusive mystery through the years, but if historical perspective was worth anything, you could count on the following truisms: introspective J.T., humbled J.T., quietly confident J.T. was unbeatable. Would hunker down and bring it all day long. J.T. running high, wide, and handsome, like now, distracted, semi-drunk, overconfident and flirting with the waitress, well, that was another story.

I'll call and raise you a hundred, Roland said.

A hundred?

One hundred.

Little brother's trying to get my attention, I believe, said J.T.

Roland smiled.

That's a lot of cattle feed.

That's a quarter of the way to a new pair of boots, Roland said smiling.

With this, J.T. raised his leg up on the table. You're only an eighth of the way to these, he said. Elk skin.

Fine boots, J.T., said a couple of the men at the table.

I'm thinking after this hand I'll be wearing those out of here, said Roland.

You just might do that, said J.T. But you'll be stuffing some cotton in the toes if you don't want blisters.

Ah, thought Roland, here we go. Physicality. Size twelves versus size tens. He'll call and raise a hundred. Hell, maybe two hundred. And he was going to lose. And be pissed off. And thinking this, Roland felt the odd, thrilling mixture of pride and sorrow that had accompanied every victory over his older brother since childhood. And how rare those victories had been. J.T. had shown him no mercy. How much shit he'd eaten. Less rare, those victories now, but how long did those childhood rivalries and histories last? Eternally? And how often now did he even get J.T.'s best game anymore? Why did J.T. seem to take so little pleasure in his own victories over him? And then the answer. Oh yes. Guilt. And now guilt and older sibling arrogance battling it out on the far end of the table. He'll raise three hundred, maybe more.

Did I ever tell you about the merits of a quick pace to a poker game? said Roland.

J.T. smiled. Took his drink from the waitress and slid her a ten-dollar note in the bargain. I'll just call, he said, looking around the table at the other men. Little brother over there has got his jaw set.

Roland smiled, appreciating exceptions that prove rules. Perhaps J.T. was not riding quite so high-wide-handsome after all. Perhaps. But goddam, life was interesting. It was interesting and if you didn't think so, tough luck for you, you weren't paying enough attention.

And now the final card, tossed face down with low altitude and tight velocity from across the table. A good dealer, this Johnny Boy, with a quick pace and easy on the table talk. The card? A nice fat king to go with his twin brother in the hole.

And just after he peeked at the king, he'd looked up to see J.T. smiling at him, saying with his eyes, *you liked that one, didn't you, little brother?*

And yes, thought Roland, that is why I study my brother. For his predictability is unpredictable. And there is reason to play the game after all.

Sevens are still tall, said the dealer.

We gonna call Teague tonight or not? J.T. said.

Table talk, said Roland.

You want to win this election or not?

Roland smiled. Why don't you just fold, big boy?

I'll bet two hundred and a call to Teague, said J.T., looping his chips high in the air. The chips landed and clacked and spilled in an arrogant manner and J.T. took a casual sip from his drink.

This time Roland didn't smile. He looked at his cards on the table. Peeked at the second king in the hole to see that it hadn't morphed suddenly into a jack or a deuce. Baited? Yes. It was too damn late at night to call a man like Teague. And this group and this setting, well, it wasn't Teague's cup of tea either. Just wait till Monday to call. No difference now as then.

Said J.T.: Richie here went to school with him, you remember? Didn't you, Richie? Richie would make the call, ain't that right, buddy?

Sure, said Richie, slight of build and checking his watch every ten minutes. President of the Clearwater bank and nervous as hell about church in the morning, no doubt. This hosting session already more than he bargained for. And again. Sure, J.T. I'd call him. He's up. And he's not a person to get upset about a thing like that.

Thank you, Richie, said Roland. What time is it again?

Richie consulted the familiar watch, seemed momentarily relieved that the matter of time was finally on the table, as it were. Business is business and a banking man has to do these golfing and poker things, but sometimes enough was enough. Ten till eleven, he said.

Roland thanked him. Thought, why not just go home? Who's going to stop you? So they razz you for a minute about breaking up the game. Who gives a shit? Miserable here for the last two hours and hell to pay when you get home. Long Sunday for old Rich, he'd wager.

Said Roland: I'll call and raise two hundred, your cowboy boots, and the condition that Richie be allowed to go home.

So if I win, Richie has to call Teague and stay till he gets here?

That's right, said Roland.

If I lose, you get my boots and Richie goes home.

Yes. Plus, I think you ought to have to wear your golf shoes the rest of the night and on the ride home tomorrow.

Well hell yes, said J.T. Of course. Only other shoes I got.

He won't come out this time of night, said Richie.

Yes he will, said J.T.

I'll call him, but I can't stay out till four in the morning, said Richie.

Let's call that a negotiation point, said J.T. But have a little faith. You might be walking out the door and home to the little lady in just a minute here.

Richie eyed the cards on the table, then against all odds and semblance of self-discipline checked his timepiece again. Yes, still on his wrist. Yes, still fucked at home. As J.T. began taking off an elk-skin boot to place on the pile of chips on the table, Roland thought suddenly and precisely, simultaneous *p-ling* of arrow fired and *plunk* of tip on target: The drunk bastard's got the third seven.

You've got the seven, said Roland.

That I do.

Last card?

J.T. smiled and removed his boot from the table. Flipped the magic seven out of the hole and spun it skidding across the table toward the worried man and his twitching watch. Richie, you know where that phone is?

Teague pulled out of the long circular driveway, gleaming white and ghostly under the fluorescent lanterns that lined the drive. Past crisp and rectangular boxwoods neat as bales of hay. The glowing drive revealed a house in an affluent neighborhood in the western section of the city of Glennville. The house sat on four acres of white-fenced pasture and another acre more of immaculate lawn, enough property to build twelve or so of his neighbors' homes, and swimming pools to boot. The house sat sideways to the Boulevard, so townspeople driving by often took a moment as they passed to look at the high white fence surrounding the pool, often to see a brown body paused briefly over the lattice for a moment, suspended against the hazy blue sky, diving board nowhere in sight, invisible launching pad, then the body gone again into the silent splash of a lazy summer day by the pool. Others still, were no bodies being launched skyward, might stop for a moment to ponder the three white horses grazing in the pasture. Incongruity would be the word that the driver bent his mind toward, for a half mile up the road awaited more of the neon-afflicted concrete that this respite of horses and flying bodies had broken for just a moment. And after the driver passed, the image that lingered in the mind was jumbled but reassuring: white house/white lattice/white fence/white horses. And had Teague turned to face his house as he pulled onto the Boulevard at eleven-thirty on this summer night, he would have seen the same image of glowing whiteness, unassuming and unassailable.

But he didn't turn. He fiddled with the radio. Tried to get comfortable. Fumbled about in the glove compartment for his prescription bottle. Found it. Popped the dosage dry-mouthed. Where it hung up in his throat. He hacked around a bit. Worked up some saliva. Cursed his chiropractor. Cursed that damn sack of feed he should have let the boy lift. Swallowed again. Smoothly this time. Rolled, slowly, his neck. Wondered what those hick bankers were going to offer.

INT: AN EMPTY RESTAURANT KITCHEN—NIGHT

Metallic UTENSILS and stove eyes and silvery refrigerators. The fluorescent GLOW from the overhead lights is interrupted by pockets of SHADOWS near the utility closet and the deep sinks in the back. The shadows drift across the walk-in cooler, meshing with the thin vibrato hum of the lights. Then a thinner sound, faint but incessant: a MOTH wildly, crazily flickering its milk-colored wings against the lights. In the half-light by the manager's locked door: J.T. and the WAITRESS in a white dress shirt, black vest, and name tag. They are not yet touching, but that seems to be in the cards. J.T.'s posture is that of one slightly affected by drink. The waitress's drink tray gently taps against the office door.

> J.T.
> Damn you're good-looking.

> WAITRESS
> (pleased but noncommittal)
> Well thank you.

> J.T.
> I'm not just saying that. You look like you ought to be
> in New York or somewhere.

> WAITRESS
> (laughing)
> Now what would I be doing in New York or
> somewhere?

> J.T.
> (smiling at the weakness of the offered line)

Hell if I know. Modeling. Acting. Running a business.
No offense, but I can't figure why someone like you is
hustling drinks in a backwoods joint like this.

WAITRESS
What's a nice girl like you doing in a place like this?

J.T.
(smiling)
I never said you were a nice girl.

The waitress laughs despite herself. At this cue, J.T. moves a bit closer and
places his hand on the hand that is tapping the office door with the tray.

J.T.
You going straight home after work?

THE SQUEAK of a door checked midway halts the conversation. The
couple's faces are seen in shadowy silhouette.

BARTENDER (O.S.)
(not caring for this chore)
Mr. Cole? Mike Teague is here. Your brother asked me
to let you know.

CUT TO:

THE SWINGING BAR DOOR
(BEAT)
And then we hear:
A MUFFLED WHISPER FROM THE KITCHEN.
A WOMAN LAUGHING QUIETLY.
THE SOUND OF COWBOY BOOTS ON TILES.

CUT TO:

Richie checking his watch and offering his seat to J.T.

Said J.T.: Nah, Big R. You keep your seat. Us young fellows don't mind standing.

Next to Richie sat his old high school buddy, Mike Teague, who wondered just how the sallow fellow, sallow even as a youngster, came to be keeping such company. Too fast for you, old Rich. Ought to be back at home with Sylvia entering hour two of your snoring-for-volume contest.

Richie gave a tired smile and sipped from his glass of ginger ale. He said: You're keeping late hours these days, Teague.

Only for old friends, said Teague, putting a hand on Richie's shoulder and pushing around in a bowl of mixed nuts.

Roland sat at the bar, smiling amicably but not talking much. Beside him were his hosts from the Clearwater bank. Minor players in the action, thought Teague, if any kind of players at all. They talked among themselves and seemed waiting to do some kind of favor for the brothers Cole. Now J. T. Cole strode to the jukebox in search of the right atmosphere. Little question he'd played some ball in his day, one form or another. Teague guessed they were about the same age, though both the brothers appeared a bit younger than their years, as did Teague himself. Keep the weight off in your thirties, his father had told him, and you'll be home free the rest of the way.

Another fellow, whose name Teague never really caught, with red hair and a pink golf shirt, joined J.T. over the musical selections. This was Cut Worm Morris, the Cole brothers' hometown friend and business partner. But at this moment Teague wasn't thinking about the redhead or the other minor players in the room or even about the somewhat pitiable ways of small-town bankers and their obsession with trying to land any big fish that comes their way.

No, what he was thinking about was the same thing that had

occupied the greater part of his mind during the fifty-mile drive down from Glennville, and that was this: he'd have to flip-flop these bumpkin brothers. Treat J.T., the well-known raconteur, like the polished man he suspected he was when dining with his more sophisticated clients. Conversely, he would treat Roland, the sophisticated one, the one less bucolic in manner, to some of the rawer elements in his repertoire. He'd seen these tight-as-tick brother combos all his life, especially the country ones, and knew that in a social situation they resorted to type, resorted to some sibling dynamic forged long ago over pitchfork and slop jar. In short, get J.T. by himself and he's less likely to don the cowboy boots in the clubhouse and play the implied bullyboy. And Roland without J.T. would be leading the way on nips from the bottle and waitress flirtation. So the thing to do was to play to the side that neither brother got to show when the two of them were together. To do so would discombobulate the quarry and show a crafty insight into the nature of all things human.

The other thing he'd decided was to ask for the moon.

Mr. Teague, said Roland, I'd just like to say that it was definitely not my idea to call you at this late hour.

He lost a bet in a poker game, said J.T. from the jukebox. I'm afraid to say we were wagering over your presence.

Well now I feel a little cheap, said Teague.

J.T. approached the group at the bar, the beginning strains of an old country song at his back. We've heard a lot about you, Mr. Teague, he said. But the one word we never heard was cheap.

Teague smiled. You mean this isn't just a social call?

It is as far as I'm concerned, said Roland.

Teague ordered a second whiskey from the bartender. He knew that for all the lead-taking J.T. was doing, any real decisions about this business would have to come from Roland.

Richie, said Roland, you ready to hit the road? We're about to start infringing on your hospitality.

If it's all the same, I believe I will call it a night, said Richie, fumbling around in his pocket and craning his neck to avoid looking at the timepiece on his wrist.

Said J.T.: Richie, Richie, Richie. How are we going to make a good impression on your pal here without your steady hand to guide us?

I'm afraid it's too late for that, said Teague, looking now at Roland. I already think you boys are a bunch of horse's asses.

Setting, yes, setting and a quick update. For time has passed like invisible ink into air, into another tense. Country music still and always. J.T. as lone DJ, with only nodding recognition to requests from Cut Worm. Richie, long gone. Received his meal of hot tongue and cold shoulder and now snoozing away, hosting duties bequeathed to his younger colleague, Johnny Boy. Waitress drinking vodka tonics with triple limes from a wine glass. A touch of class, yes, the vessel and the multiple bits of citrus. Fights the scurvy to boot. Limes, that is. Equals derivation of limey. Again, limes. British sailors sucking them down like lozenges. Bartender drinking behind the bar and moving casually about his cleanup duties, thoughts of certificates of deposit and compounding interest, a snowball rolling down-hill, dancing in his head. Having a good time. Big night on the tip jar and good fun to boot. Nice fellows, the Coles. No putting on of airs, as the old folks say. The remaining men sit in a semicircle facing out from the bar, looking when the fancy strikes at the illuminated pool outside, looking at it through the large picture window that reflects their smoky images and the wooden plaques for past champions of the club behind them.

Said J.T.: We know Montgomery is going to be tough to beat. Any fool can tell you that.

Yes, he'll be tough to beat, said Teague. That's safe to say.

Our campaign manager basically thought it was a lost cause. That's why he's no longer our campaign manager.

Teague took a sip of his drink. He smiled and said: In general, you'd prefer your campaign manager to wait just a bit longer before throwing in the towel.

Exactly, said J.T. If there's one thing I can't stand, it's a front-runner.

He pointed out Teague's nearly empty glass to the bartender and twirled his finger for another round for everyone at the bar.

J.T. said: The rumor on the street is that you gave Montgomery the idea for the Whistle-Stop Tour when he was running against Hart, but he decided against it. And that he's been kicking himself for the last four years for not listening to you. Thinks it cost him the election in '74. Is that true?

Montgomery's usually not one to second-guess himself like that, said Teague smiling.

But you did give him the idea?

Yes, said Teague. But you can't blame me for the engineer's cap. Or the overalls either. He came up with those on his own this go-round.

The mention of the train apparel, grey-and-white-striped and paired with a rustic denim shirt, was met with a series of groans and stage-whispered threats. The railroading ensemble was proving a persistent image on the local news. See the smiling Republican speak at one small depot after another. Watch as he smiles and waves his engineer's cap from the caboose on departure. Cut to smiling anchorman. News plus home-spun angle, don't you know. Local news in a nutshell. The plan, Teague's plan five years prior, was a steam locomotive tour of the state, east to west, mountains to Mississippi River. A marketing coup to be sure. The Back to Basics Whistle-Stop Tour. Overalled man of the people, you see, the press eating it up with a spoon.

Said J.T.: Would you have any interest in working for a man who's actually worn overalls to work in? I mean real work, without any cameras present? Or do you work exclusively for the doctors' sons of the state?

I prefer to work for winners, said Teague. But if the money's right, the money's right.

The money will be right, said J.T. Don't you worry about that. You just tell us how to beat this urban railroader.

Hold on just a minute, said Roland, standing up from his barstool. I believe I have a say in this too. The first thing I'd like to ask is who all you've represented.

Teague ticked off the politicians he'd assisted: a large number of state senators, the occasional state representative from a large district or with especially deep pockets. U.S. congressmen. A U.S. senator, now dead.

And of course Montgomery, their Republican opponent for the governor's office.

Said Teague: That doesn't include the corporations I've worked with. And I also keep my lobbyist license current for when the right job comes along. That's how I got started. As a lobbyist.

Said Roland with a smile: And tell me again what people pay you for doing?

That's a good question, said Teague. I guess to achieve their aims. Some of that involves presentation, or marketing. The face you show to the public. Some of it is public relations. A good deal of it just involves strategizing, how best to handle a specific scenario.

Teague smiled. I give advice.

Roland looked at him, but didn't tip his hand one way or another. Finally he said: Well, the next thing I want to hear is if you actually think I have a chance to win. If you don't, we're just wasting money.

The current governor isn't helping you any, said Teague. He's muddying the water for every Democrat in the state.

Hell, we knew that, said Roland. And we're supposed to meet Governor Hart later this month for a Democratic fundraiser in Jackson.

I'll give you this one for free, said Teague. That's one event I'd skip. Until this election is over, you don't need to be within a hundred miles of Governor Hart.

So there is something to that pardon business? We've been hearing about it for a month now.

Teague smiled but didn't reply.

You've heard it?

Maybe a little, said Teague. Some of my pals in Nashville just keep saying if you've got a relative in prison, now might be a good time to get them out.

Roland ran a hand through his thick brown hair. How good's your information?

Pretty good, I'd say. How's yours?

Hit or miss.

He going to get caught? asked J.T.

Could, said Teague. If you've heard it and I've heard it, you've got to wonder who else has.

Caught before the election?

They'll get him before or not at all would be my guess, said Teague. No fun for the TBI to take down a guy who's already out of office. If it's coming, it's coming in the next four months or so. Fifty-fifty proposition, I'd say.

We're dead in the water if he's indicted, said J.T. There's enough people already who think me and Roland are making our money a little too quick and easy. Be easy to paint us with the same brush.

Speak for yourself, said Roland. I've got no connection with Governor Hart.

Democrats are as Democrats do, said Teague. You couldn't get a Republican elected dogcatcher after Watergate.

Okay, so if Hart gets busted, we're done, said Roland. What I want to know is if we're done anyway. Frankly, I've got other things on my plate besides losing an election.

To be honest, said Teague, it's the other things on your plate that I'm most interested in. But I can help with this election. Like you said, Montgomery would have beat Hart in '74 if he'd listened to me.

About the Whistle-Stop Tour?

But not the cap or overalls, remember.

Invective en masse regarding the Republican engineer.

So why didn't Montgomery keep you on? said the man called Johnny Boy.

Teague looked at him closely for the first time all evening, this youngest of the hosting crew from Clearwater. Shrewder than one would first surmise. A bit tired of the Clearwater nightlife and wondering what the big city might have to offer a young man with a little change in his pocket. And now asking the question the Coles would have wanted to ask. Shows initiative. Shows I'll do the dirty work, boys, so you don't have to. Can sniff the money falling off the truck and blowing in the wind. All you got to do is follow behind and pick it up. More than enough for everyone.

Teague smiled now at Johnny Boy, who was doing his damnedest

either side. And oh the saps, the sappy sappy saps, who were now piddling along behind some baler loaded down with hay, stuck in the past, stuck on the old two-lane highway heading east at forty miles per hour.

He popped a Coke, enjoying the crisp clean tearing of metal, the subsequent *aah* of carbonic release, and layered his tongue with two packets of dry headache powder. This was washed down with a mammoth swig from the can. Best thing there was for a headache. Other than a Bloody Mary and an unacrobatic roll in the hay. But not today. Had to turn and burn. But the thought of the hotel room in the wee morning hours, the blurry and mutual physicality of it, sustained him now. Good gal. And God bless her. Again he considered stopping to see if his sunglasses were in the golf bag. Then decided to hell with it and rolled on down the road, toward the home place and his folks and Corrine and the kids.

An odd vantage point on the exterior of this scene, namely a large blue automobile speeding down an unopened highway, was had by a boy out walking his bird dog pup. The dog was an English setter, the breed his grandfather had trained to stand point before a covey of quail, for nigh five decades. The boy had it in his mind to train this pup. His grandfather was dead now and his father had no interest in hunting or dogs. But the boy had read several books on the subject and queried a few locals, inexpert locals, granted, about getting started. He knew from his grandfather that the greater portion of finding the covey and pointing was instinctual. He knew as well that it was better to have a dog that roamed too far than one that was always underfoot. This he knew directly from his grandfather. The grandfather believed that you could always train a far-ranging dog back to your sights, even the wildest, most scatteredbrained-seeming ones. For most of the good ones, when young, do roam wild and free and too fast and have minds of their own that you don't want to break too quickly or too completely. More than anything you didn't want to stem this unfettered love of the hunt or the innate confidence in their own ability. The young dogs, however, who were forever underfoot, who stayed at heel throughout the day, were never any good, at least as hunting dogs. Might make a good dog to play with the kids and nothing wrong with that. Might even breed a good dog out of one of these nonroamers, couldn't always tell. But if they were young and underfoot, you wouldn't ever teach them to roam. It just wasn't in their nature.

So these were the things the boy had been thinking before he heard the blue Cadillac zipping from the west like one great whoosh of air being released from a large balloon. He carried a pellet gun to get the dog used to the instrument and had walked in the pose of a future hunter to the edge of the family property, the other two-thirds of which had been forcibly bought by the state, *eminent domain*, for this sleek slab of concrete. He stood fifty feet above the road, behind a makeshift Tennessee Highway Department wooden fence, and watched the first car he'd ever seen on this road, save those of the construction bosses, speed like something from the future over this surreal landscape of red clay and abandoned machinery, the colorful machines like massive sci-fi spiders and ants below. And as the car raced past and beyond, growing quickly and ever smaller against the hazy blue sky, but never quite disappearing, the din of the whoosh receding, receding but never completely abating, the aboriginal automobile hum stuck in his ears and brought on a number of complicated feelings.

After a bit, he turned to walk back to the house. The pup was off somewhere and it took the boy a while to find him. But he walked on back to the house all the same.

All through church she'd done her best to find the solitude within. Of course the kids were raising all kinds of hell, grabassing and knocking about in the pew. And Mrs. Cole with her sideways glances and prim rectitude, a premeditated study in how one and one's family should comport themselves in the house of the Lord. And the soloist on Shall We Gather at the River, Mary Akers, J.T.'s girlfriend when they'd broken up for a summer in high school, fatted up some but not quite enough. And Mrs. Cole's look of languid dolor as Mary sang. All of that had been quite enough to prevent the finding of solitude within, so now, back at the Coles' house, helping Mrs. Cole and Sis and Roland's wife Libby prepare dinner, she forgot the notion of inner peace and gave herself over completely to the ways and means by which she would ream J.T. a new one. And in so doing, she found herself more relaxed, more naturally in her element, than she'd been in days.

When she came out to the back yard where the tables were set up, carrying two baskets of rolls, she found the old man, Mr. Cole, sitting under a shade tree and watching the grandkids whack unceremoniously at various skittering and careening croquet balls. Stitches were soon to be in order, the mallets flying as they were, but that was someone else's business. Damned if she was taking a kid to the emergency room on a Sunday afternoon.

The boys are running a little late today, the old man said, getting up from his lawn chair and taking one end of a folded plastic tablecloth.

Uh-huh, said Corrine, placing the baskets on the ground and grabbing the other end of the tablecloth. Together they spread it over the card tables that had been set up as a makeshift buffet.

Kind of was expecting them to roll in last night.

Yep, said Corrine, yanking the tablecloth about and firing a look at her middle child, who had just missed braining Roland and Libby's youngest with a baseball cut at the ball. The boy nodded and moved out of range of both of his cousins. If he were to kill anyone, he best keep it in the immediate family.

There's some rope up in the barn if you want me to help string him up when he gets here, the old man said.

When Corrine turned to look at him finally, he was smiling and coming over to her. Got a good ax too, he said, placing a quick patting hand on her shoulder. Those boys ain't worth a damn sometimes.

With this came the sudden, angry tears. She wiped hastily at them with a paper napkin, hating as she had since childhood that her anger lay so close to the surface, that her anger often was expressed in this manner. To shed tears of sadness or joy was one thing. That she didn't mind. But to be angry to the point of hostility, and then to have that powerful feeling, that strong feeling, accompanied by tears, so weak-looking and stereotypical, so easily misunderstood by others, well that was simply intolerable. And had been since her memory began.

I swear, Mr. Cole, there's no telling what I might have said or done.

The old man nodded. He said, rope or ax, you just let me know.

Corrine gave a quick scornful laugh and recovered her bearings. She said: I just get so mad sometimes.

I know, I know. They're my sons, but that doesn't mean I agree with everything they do.

Corrine nodded but said nothing more.

I think of you like a daughter, said the old man. And I've always been proud of having you in the family. I hope you know that.

With this came more tears, but different than before. She walked over to Mr. Cole and gave him a quick, awkward hug. Then she walked over to her car in the driveway, though there was nothing there she needed.

The old man sat in his chair on the carport and watched his grandchildren at play, chasing and rolling against a backdrop of old silver maples whose leaves flipped green to silver in the inconstant breeze. He looked out over the farm and remembered his own children when small. Whacking at trees and raising Cain. Perhaps he should have laid the strap a few more times like his own father did to him. But that was as likely to make them more rebellious as less. And it was too late for overdue strappings or for anything else. Better or worse, the boys were on their own.

So what to make of the old man, Sunday shirt rolled to the elbows, coat and tie forsaken, who looks out over the farm and the children playing in a kind of hazy slow motion before him?

He is looking out over a freshly mowed yard that runs seamlessly into the green of a new field of corn. And on past the old barn to the other fields set in great rectangular grids, and past them, to the far woods and the mud-crusted service road and the modern barn which gleams clean and sterile and efficient under a sun taut as a kite in a strong, steady breeze.

He is thinking of his own father, who looked him up and down after the big growth spurt of sixteen, the first leap into the physical side of manhood, and said: *If it takes me getting the rifle and filling you with holes, that's what it will be before you ever whip my ass.* And knowing, as his father said it, that his father loved him. And that his father would never want to do such a thing. But that he would. And was that the reason he was so sparing of the rod with his own sons? That pride and temper and hierarchical streak?

And the complicated feelings that come from the warning, lifetime in nature, against taking up arms against your father, for that's what it was, a warning, telling him, *don't get ideas. Crossing the physical boundary of manhood does not give you the privilege of crossing all boundaries. I.e., there are limits to your masculinity, there are limits to your newfound physicality.* And what was complicated, now as much as ever, is how those words and that notion were comforting as well. But how was it comforting? Not then. Then, it was scary as hell. Later, when he was a father with his own children and the man with the threat got to play grandfather. And he realized, at forty or so, that *he* was now the man with the threat, implied or otherwise, and that primal and barbaric as it sounds he was the sole defender of his children and his wife and himself. And yes, his father too. And with that realization came the weight of responsibility, for he knew, strange as it seems in this modern world, modern even when his kids were small, that when you got down to it, it's still man versus man, who's better you or me, who's stronger. And the crazy, innate pressure of that, if in fact you were a physical presence, and he was, was enough to wear you down, enough to make you mean if you didn't watch it.

And now he wonders why he and his father and his sons see the world this way.

What in their pride and insecurity makes for such an unrefined look at men and mankind.

And why he is thinking of whipping asses on the Lord's Day with the voices of lovely grandchildren pitched and twittering like little birds on the lawn and his boys whom he loves soon to arrive.

The pastor's sermon was on charity. He'd read from First Corinthians.

He sits waiting for the tardy arrival of his grown sons to the farm, wondering why the media, after some brainwashing from the first campaign manager, began calling it the old home place. When it was simply a farm, which was what he and everyone in the family had called it since he first bought it in 1934.

Why would going to visit the old home place get more votes than going to visit the farm?

But at the end of the day, what matter nomenclature?

What matter what a thing is called when you have been tied to that thing, body and soul, for forty-plus years?

And where, after so many years, did the land stop and you begin?

But what a nice plot of land to be tied to.

And what a truly lovely summer day.

And the unusual summer fog that lay on the farm early this morning.

And Queenie's brush of nails against the screen door to be let in.

And Esther about the kitchen dressed for church save her stockings, which are hot in the old kitchen, and humming, as she always does, Bringing in the Sheaves.

Esther:

The times before the children were born and amorous outdoor adventures.

How it takes a crafty and veteran mind to hold simultaneously Granny in the kitchen and teen bride in the hayloft.

Late teens, for those keeping score.

And the squalls of childbirth in yonder back window like a faint and cinematic din in the memory, lacking the nails-against-chalkboard pitch and volume of reality, echoic and sentimental, the skinned squirrel of delivery, pinched and red-faced, replaced by a fat and cherubic angel on the lap of a young mother, young breasts high as before.

And the day of Roland's birth:

Who did not care to leave the womb. Two weeks late on Thanksgiving Day and Jet Peters out in the truck waiting to go quail hunting like they have every Thanksgiving since boyhood. Dressing for the cold, saying, *come on child, come on. One way or another you're coming, so come on, so I can go.* A crisp and cold November, the ground frozen and crunchy underneath, and you can just smell those quail. And Jet's dogs whining in the trunk, aching for the hunt. And Duke and Little Pearl pacing about their pen, moaning and anxious, have seen the shotgun and shells go in the trunk, have heard the crunch of boots on ground, and now the whine of Jet's dogs.

Best go on, Jet. This little one can't seem to make up his mind about joining us.

You can smell the quail.

Well hell yes I know you can smell the quail.

Jet smiled and put the truck in gear and rattled down the rutted dirt drive that would not be paved for two decades hence.

And twenty minutes later, out popped Roland.

And now four-plus decades of having to live down wanting to go hunting on your son's birthday.

And now, thinking of his son's delayed arrival, the mind moves in another direction:

The smell of the counter girl, some kind of vanilla perfume, before he had to let her go.

The counter girl's hips in the grey fitted skirt.

The triangular day with Esther at the booths, and him at the register, and the girl at the counter. And Esther, without saying a word, informed him that she was no hypotenuse.

And was it normal to recall, vividly, forty years later, vanilla perfume and a fitted grey skirt?

Of course, J.T. really did need his ass kicked.

And this thought leading to:

The fact of the grandchildren's lacking not a thing materially, lacking not a thing that a child could want.

Except perhaps:

More of their fathers.

There was never enough of the fathers.

Or never exactly the right kind.

And he and Roland with so little need to talk, so like were their minds.

And J.T. with his dukes up from the beginning, some sense of other from brother and father. All the years of being described like Esther's folks. Folks saying, *I believe he's more like the Blacks. And that one*—pointing at Roland—*he's a Cole through and through. Pick him out as a Cole if I came across him in Nome, Alaska.*

And Libby's daddy who died when she was nine.

And Corrine's daddy run off to a whiskey bottle.

And Esther's daddy, the petty tyrant, the petty, meddling tyrant, run off to the afterlife not a minute too soon for anyone.

And Sis with no daddy nor mother either until she came to live with them. The women from the church dropping by the house to tell them of the baby left in the sanctuary and no idea where she came from. And after they left, Esther saying: Well, what do you think?

I was waiting on you.

You like babies.

Yes, I do.

Well, one more mouth to feed won't make any difference.

All right. Fine. I'm all for it.

And the baby coming to live with them that very evening, a baby who seemed never to cry, and such dark unblinking eyes. How attentive the boys were, how excited by the new addition, reaching again and again into the crib to have their fingers clutched by the tiny, firm hand.

But now the breeze picks up, and the mind moves to:

The glide of wind through corn, scratchy then smooth

The sudden and humorous plopping of the unseen frog into a pond

The gentle flickering of lightning bugs over this same field of corn the night before

And why do the lightning bugs fly higher early in the summer?

And why would God make mosquitoes?

And speaking of:

God. How could such a concept be denied?

Big Bang? Nothing from nothing? Counterintuitive at best.

And no afterlife? A one-act play? A sudden start. A sudden and final cessation?

Arguments against:

The seasons, for one.

Another:

Little Pearl's blood in Queenie at this moment. Little Pearl in Queenie. Queenie there and Little Pearl there, in some form, in the blood, four generations later.

Could see Little Pearl's eyes in there at times.

And the grandchildren in the yard. Eyes looking back like looking in a mirror. And their recognition of it too, the odd moment, of blue eye to blue eye and no separation, like one set of eyes simultaneously flickering.

The helicoptering of sugar maple seedlings. And the wild redbuds on the edge of the fields. And the stiff baby pinecones buried to the neck, digging through the winter ground for a foothold.

Oh, how he hated to cut down a wild tree, a volunteer tree, sent, one night, unseen to that spot by the wind.

And the ghostly comforting Indians at night, in the wind, in the corn most of all.

And the milkweed and the dandelion scattered willy-nilly, the sheer insistence on perpetuation of that scorned and weedy life.

And the blood in him now, in the grandchildren, running, alive, for as long as there has been blood, from the beginning, Adam and Eve or monkey grandparents on the vine. The blood in his veins swinging on a vine or participant in the fall from grace.

And what a nice word, is grace.

Teague on Board

Roland left the car with the parking attendant and walked back out of the underground garage, walking briskly in black wing tips that caught the sun, the shoes glimmering black against the white of the new sidewalk that ran along the side and front of his new building. He'd entered this way twelve of the fifteen days the First Bank of Glennville had been open. The other three were raining.

It was a damn awesome sight, the building, from any angle or vantage point you might choose for the viewing. Standing on Franklin Street, Roland's angle was straight up, like looking at a plane overhead. What he saw were twenty-nine stories of green mirrors on a shiny, rectangular tower, the mirrors catching and reflecting the sun's light and sending it in darting rays across the shadowed and dreary downtown below. Was there a better phrase than dwarfing the skyline? Obliterating the skyline? Inventing a skyline?

Inventing an actual city was more like it.

Behind him, the cars tooted their horns and men in suits, women in high heels, gawked up at his building. He didn't have to turn and see to know this. The first week of its opening a policeman's incessant whistle had punctuated every workday. He'd been assigned especially to that corner of Franklin and Brooks to keep motorized and pedestrian traffic in motion and out of physical contact with one another, the pedestrians walking backward without thinking off the curb and into the street to take in the whole of the view.

Roland worked his neck and smiled as he did so. The neck had been stiff for two weeks and when he complained about it to Libby, she'd merely pointed up to the sky and imitated a rube on his first openmouthed trek to the big city. Now he watched the people entering the lobby through the revolving door, many of whom glanced at him first before entering, a few smiling and waving. Turning back toward the traffic and looking down Franklin, he tried to remember what this corner had looked like three years before. Try as he might, the image was lost in the memory of jackhammer rattle and current skyscraper gleam. Standing here, he noticed the slight descent of Franklin Street down to the Market Square, and, again, the shadowed and dingy and old-fashioned-looking department stores and law offices and three-story banks that were his neighbors. He thought back to his awe of this street, the buildings, the twelve-story Lewis House Hotel, the urbanity of the men in their suits, when as a boy he and the family would come in from Henry City for Christmas Shopping at Jaeger's Department Store. On those occasions, he'd always felt vaguely uncomfortable, the new shoes not just right in the city, the haircut a little shorter than the norm, and had stuck close to J.T.'s hip as they window-shopped and studied the movie posters behind glass and J.T. talked in his normal speaking voice as if not the least ashamed of being country.

Smiling at the self-conscious and sensitive youth that was his former incarnation, he strolled now past the outdoor water fountains spraying their clean-looking streams and thought if time allowed he'd like to have a drink in the Lewis House bar, like the old days when he and Libby and J.T. and Corrine had first moved to town. He went through the revolving doors and thought of the kids at the opening, going round and round like a carnival ride, and then past Charles, the shoeshine guy in the corner, who stood and clacked his brushes two quick entrepreneurial times as Roland passed.

Tomorrow, said Roland over his shoulder: I can still see my reflection in these.

The shoeshine guy nodded and sat back down, whistling an old standard Roland couldn't immediately place. And the clean, high-ceilinged lobby, with the comfortable chairs and the oversized plants and light streaming in from all directions. On the other side of the security desk was the bank proper, the main branch, and he caught a glimpse of people already in line waiting for one of the ten tellers on duty. All of this, the lighted lobby, the comfortable chairs, the plants at a hundred dollars a pop, made him feel suddenly rich and settled. In fifty years, this lobby would have that lived-in, rich feel that the Lewis House did before it let itself go. And thinking this, he felt, for lack of a better word, historic.

He'd made it past the security desk without having to chitchat, a bad habit, that chitchat, but running for office made a man see voters everywhere he looked. He'd be glad when that was over no matter how the election shook out. He stood waiting at the elevator, watching the trio of elevators race from the ninth and fifteenth and twenty-third floors, still more than a little awed by this building that was his own.

Excuse me, said a voice over his shoulder.

Chitchat, thought Roland. I jinxed myself thinking I'd made a clean getaway.

He turned, expecting to see the security man or one of the staff from the help desk. Instead he saw a worn blue jean work shirt and an unfamiliar face, one bearded and intent.

Yes, said Roland smiling. What can I do for you?

The man shoved a wad of leaflets, wrinkled and worried over, into Roland's hand. I'd like you to read these, he said, dark eyes flat and unblinking.

Thank you, said Roland, sticking the leaflets under his arm and glancing up toward the flashing floor numbers above the elevators.

They're about the Expo.

Ah, said Roland.

I'm with the Glennville Citizens' Group.

The elevator arrived not a moment too soon and several sharply dressed men and women got out. Roland waited with hand on door for everyone to disembark, then, with a nod and pleased-to-meet-you to the man beside him, he stepped into the brass-gleaming elevator. He pushed the button for the twenty-ninth floor and thought, I'll be damned, as the concerned citizen boarded the elevator as well.

The man made no movement toward pushing a button, but simply leaned against the wall opposite Roland and eyed the golden leaflets. Roland hoped that someone else would hop on, but no one did, and as the elevator doors began to close, he briefly considered going for security. But the doors closed and the elevator began its ascent. Roland looked to the man and considered that he might have to pummel him into submission. He hoped not. He was wearing his favorite suit.

Are you going to read those, Mr. Cole?

I'm not sure, Mr. . . .

Ginkowski. Lionel Ginkowski.

Well, Mr. Ginkowski, you may know that I'm a little busy at present. I'm trying not to lose a gubernatorial election.

I know what you're running for.

Well, said Roland smiling, can I count on your vote then Mr. Ginkowski?

No, you cannot.

I'm sorry to hear that, said Roland, glancing down at the leaflets and hoping, strangely, that the citizen would lunge at him. He'd not had the urge to throttle someone in a good long while, and frankly he'd missed the sensation. He wondered how the press would spin it. Self-defense, obviously. Couldn't hurt in this neck of the woods, in the entire state for that matter. Show the wispy train conductor who was tough on crime. It was a moment, lost in his comic-violent revelry, before he took in the caption of the leaflet he'd been looking at: *Glennville Taxpayers Getting the Shaft*.

As the door opened on his floor, Roland tried to hand the leaflets back to the man. I don't agree with your position, Mr. Ginkowski, he said. And I'd hate to waste your literature that you've spent good money getting printed up.

No, keep it, the man said, standing with his foot in the groove of the elevator door. Apparently he wanted to follow Roland out of the elevator and continue this conversation, such as it was, in the privacy of Roland's office.

Sir, I simply do not have the time. To read these. Or to continue this conversation. You really need to be talking to the vice president of the Expo Commission. He handles all of the day-to-day affairs.

Your vice president has been giving us the runaround for over a week now. We've decided to speak with you directly.

As I said, I don't handle day-to-day affairs.

You're the moneyman. You're the capital.

Roland smiled. He saw out of the corner of his eye that the receptionist was looking toward them.

We want a public debate, said Lionel Ginkowski. We want a referendum on the city bond issue.

I suggest you contact city council then. I'm just a banker at present. And the office I'm running for is statewide. The bond issue is a local one.

You're the moneyman. You're the capital.

Roland stepped out of the elevator without looking again at the man. Over his shoulder the man was shouting, I smell a rat. And I think you, Mr. Cole, are a crook.

Roland saw the receptionist's eyes widen and heard the office sounds of typewriter, telephone conversation, adding machine, go silent. He stepped back toward the elevator and grabbed the man by his shirtfront. As he did so, the man's foot was dislodged from the elevator groove and the door began to shut behind them. Without looking, he smacked a handful of buttons behind him and backed the man into the corner of the elevator. What did you say?

I think the people are getting screwed.

That's not what you said. I'd like to hear what you said up there in front of my office staff.

The man remained silent, pinned against the back wall and offering no resistance. The elevator door opened behind Roland. The man's eyes widened, as if hoping someone would join them. But no one did.

Why don't you repeat your earlier phrase? Roland said, his hand feeling the brisk whiskers of the man's beard.

The people are getting screwed, said Lionel Ginkowski against the pleasant beep of the elevator door closing in the background, the nearly imperceptible whir of the elevator cable on its descent.

Roland pulled the man toward him briefly to get a firmer grip of his shirt then pushed him back against the wall. Already the logical side of his brain had begun to talk in his inner ear about running for governor, about running a business, about adults physically confronting other adults. But this voice was nothing against the white-hot anger that flooded his brain and made his eyes narrow to two flashing slits.

Said Roland: What the people are getting, if we do get Expo, is a world-class event. One that will bring more free publicity to this one-horse town than they've had in the past hundred years. What the people are getting, if the old money farts in this town and the pissant tightwads like yourself will get out of the way, is about fifteen million visitors dropping about three hundred million dollars in this area.

The door opened and a young lawyer Roland had met the week before got on. The lawyer greeted Roland and pushed the button for the ground floor before he noticed that one man in the elevator had his hands, essentially, around another man's neck. The lawyer's eyes goggled a bit. Oh, he said, excuse me.

You're fine, said Roland. I'm just giving this man a quick civic lesson.

The door to the elevator shut again and the young lawyer stared a hole in the door, breathing audibly through his mouth. Roland spoke now in a clipped, even tone, saying, and what the people are getting, my friend, is a whole new downtown and an untold number of new jobs. That, my friend, is what the people will get.

With this, Roland let go of the man's shirt, but didn't step away. The man straightened his shirt, rubbed his neck and chin in a reflective manner, unfazed, undeterred. So you say.

So says an independent consulting firm.

Independent? said Ginkowski smiling.

That's right.

If the Expo is all that you say it is, I'm sure the people of Glennville are reasonable enough to see its merits. Let's put it to a vote.

The elevator stopped again at a floor, the last floor of the buttons randomly popped when Roland reentered the elevator. Roland glanced up for a moment. Fifteenth floor. No one got on. Glanced at the young lawyer memorizing the buttons on the wall. Take it to city council, said Roland, walking out of the elevator.

You own city council.

Roland stood outside the elevator and slowly turned his head to look back in. He expected the man to be wearing an ironic smile or to have a defiant set to his jaw. But the man's face was as flat as his intonation.

If that's the case, Roland said, I guess you're shit out of luck.

Then the elevator door was closing and Roland made his way down an unfamiliar hall. He had not yet learned the nature of business of all of his building's tenants, and now walked past a row of partitioned cubicles, an accounting firm perhaps, a few startled workers looking at him as he passed. He made it to the emergency exit without being greeted and began his fourteen-story walk up the stairs to his office and his ten o'clock meeting with Teague.

Teague stood at the enormous picture windows in the state-of-the-art penthouse conference room. Plush carpeting. Wet bar. Refrigerator. Stylish framed black and white photos of Glennville landmarks from the early years of this twentieth century. The entirety of this corner of the building was glass, from floor to ceiling, and natural light was abundant.

Teague stood now, a few feet back from the windows, looking out over the place of his birth. In the far distance, the mountains slept in hazy and stoic green, making Teague feel, as they always did from a distance, comforted if slightly claustrophobic. They were just there, infinitely, immovably, irretractably there. It was hard not to feel like a boy in their presence. Not necessarily immature like a boy. Just innocent. I.e., lacking knowledge. Teague smiled at that notion, then felt the forced weight of the irony he'd foisted on his repose and checked the smile.

And when, he wonders, did I get so cynical?

His eyes moved away from the mountains, though they never really left the mind of a Glennvillean—they were always in the background, always in the subconscious. He looked now at the steep foothills and the county roads and neighborhoods that dotted them, for this area felt less like a proper valley than a minor continuance, a glissando, of the mountains behind them. Closer to the city, small farms dotted the landscape in various shades of green and yellow and coppery brown, rectangular tiles sloping this way and that according to the land. Gradually the houses became more clustered and the roads dense with strip malls veining off in a crazy and unplanned fashion. It was this area where Teague searched for his boyhood home on the other side of the river, but he could not spot it amid the unkempt sprawl. Nor could he pinpoint the locale of his old high school, long gone to annexation and the wrecking ball.

He remembered his dream of the night before, his high school girlfriend outside by the red brick of the gym and Teague, grown Teague, skulking among the cars in the parking lot, not wanting to be seen, feeling tired and jaded against the wavy shine of her hair.

The image of the bright hair, lighting the red brick of the old gym, lingered and was not to be shaken. My god, he thought, my daughter is almost her age now.

Below him the big river snaked like a strand of brown yarn through hills and farms and urbanity. A wide grey barge, loaded down with something in squat barrels, seemed to be losing its battle of inertia with the sluggish water. The slow shadow of a cloud passed over the stately old Douglass Street Bridge and then the new Municipal Bridge that had taken its place one hundred yards down. Four shells from the university's crew team zipped down river a mile or so ahead of the barge, looking like yellow dragonflies in their jerking and stop-start motion. Above the shells, looming in shadowed concrete above the river, the gargantuan saucer of the university's football stadium.

Then the sound of impatient feet treading down the carpeted hall toward the conference room, a residue of murmur and yes sirs trailing in its wake.

I grabbed a guy in the elevator, Roland said, entering the room.

Good morning, said Teague.

Did you hear me? I just grabbed some guy in the elevator.

I heard you. Good morning.

Goddammit good morning. Now what are we going to do about it?

Roland sat down at the conference table and Teague moved away from the windows, away from nostalgia and high school dreams. Much better, he thought, pulling out a chair opposite Roland. Action, yes. Action was what the mind demanded, the sane and restful mind.

Who was the guy? said Teague. And why did you grab him?

One of those clodhoppers from the Citizens' Group. The ones who want the referendum. He said some things that were out of line.

Teague nodded. The steam was coming out of Roland's ears. He wasn't surprised that Roland had a temper, more politicians than not would blow a gasket quicker than the average Joe. Most, however, managed to do so in private.

Said Teague: If he's just talking about Expo or the referendum, you've just got to take it. You've been around long enough to know that.

Roland stood up from the table, paced a few steps, then stopped in front of the leather chair he'd been sitting in. No, he said, this guy made it personal.

Was he crippled?

No.

Old?

No.

Underage?

No.

Mentally incompetent?

Maybe. But not obviously so.

A minority?

No.

Smaller than you?

No.

Unemployed?

I don't think so. He looked like a carpenter or construction worker, that line of work.

Did he cow down or hold his ground?

Held his ground. Except for the thing that set me off. He didn't say that again.

So any man who would actually call himself a man would have reacted the same way to what the guy said? Excepting of course rational men running for statewide election?

Roland smiled.

I'd say you're fine. It's just like high school. You never had to worry about the guy who would stand his ground, even if you ended up knocking the holy shit out of them. They can sleep nights knowing they didn't turn tail. It's the ones you think you got beat, the ones who back down that you've got to worry about. Those are the ones who will run to the teacher. Or the local media, in this case. I'd say your friend feels pretty good about his showing, insulting a prominent local businessman and gubernatorial candidate in his own office building. A building not two weeks old. Yeah, that pissant will sleep fine tonight. Now, you know, you could have just ignored him and walked out of the elevator. That's what Montgomery would have done.

Oh goddam.

But we both know he's smarter than you anyway. Hell, we knew that yesterday.

Roland smiled.

That's a hell of a view you got.

With this Roland came around the table and past Teague to peer out at the city below him. His put his hands in the pockets of the sleek, almost shiny navy suit. Too sleek and shiny for the electorate of this state, thought Teague, and the hair too fastidiously cut. The irony of an election pitting the Princeton-educated son of a doctor in overalls against this country boy in a Fifth Avenue suit was not lost on Teague. Strange, our presentation of self in everyday life. And Roland was right, had he donned the overalls, or tooled around in a battered pickup, he'd not have confirmed his common-man status, but the more pernicious and unflattering one, of a hick come to the city. Screwed either way, thought Teague. A tough sell, tough to package.

As he pondered for the hundredth time why Roland would want to hold public office, giving, as he did, every appearance of having life by the tail, he noticed a fly skitter by a glittering and discreetly monogrammed gold cuff link. The fly zipped past that expensive haircut, buzzing from one picture window to the next, confused, one would surmise, by all that open air outside and no way to get to it. The Democratic candidate for governor seemed not to notice the fly, which buzzed here and yon about him, but never landed on suit or head, never alighted for more than a second on the window. Teague watched the man looking out the window, looking out much as he himself had just minutes before, wondering about the strange forlorn ways of men in their forties. Neither here nor there, thought Teague. A vague and indefinable state of existence.

It is a nice view, said Roland.

Best shot of the mountains I've ever seen in Glennville. And the river too.

Roland nodded but didn't turn.

I'll call the *Herald*, Teague said. Give them a heads up about today. I don't think they'd run with it even if the guy were to tell. They seem to be neutral at worst toward you. I think it's forty-sixty you get their endorsement.

I still wouldn't carry Glenn County.

This area's been Republican since before there was ever anything called Republican. Hell, FDR didn't carry Glenn County. These people want to keep their money. And keep you out of their business. And they like things fine they way they are, thank you, and progress is a fancy word for fixing things that ain't broke.

Roland looked to be following the slow progress of the barge down the river. He didn't speak for several seconds and Teague began to think the conversation was over. Then he suddenly laughed. With his back still to Teague, he said: So Daddy asked me to come up here for a bankers' meeting when I was just getting started in the business. Acting as Daddy's VP at the Henry City Citizens Bank. Spent a whole weekend up here at the Lewis House trying to make friends with these old Glennville farts, buying drinks and whatnot. I knew I was just a young pup from the outskirts and I didn't want anybody to think I was too big for my britches. So I was yes sir this and no sir that. And they still didn't want to have nothing to do with me. By Sunday, I didn't give a damn and had stopped saying yes sir every five minutes. When I got back home and told Daddy about it, he said, yep, they have two cocktails every day at five o'clock. Never one, and never three. And they don't like us and we don't like them.

Teague smiled, taking in the still man against the blue-skied window, the flickering, buzzing fly. I don't know that we're necessarily bad folks, said Teague. Just kind of tight-ass and provincial. My father, who's from Middle Tennessee, mind you, said it was because most of the people here were descended from mountain folks and that living down in hollers and up on hills, you just got a skewed perspective on things. Down in that holler you couldn't see your neighbor and it was damn hard to travel anywhere, damn hard to build roads up and down the mountain. His theory was the landscape just made you kind of naturally suspicious. You didn't know enough people to know that most of them were all right. And the landscape naturally made you independent too and self-reliant and like any government man in your neck of the woods couldn't be bringing good news. Glennvilleans just don't like much government. And they don't much like strangers either.

You could have just said they were assholes and got it over with a lot quicker, said Roland.

Teague laughed, wondering if he'd be talking to a man's back all day. He'd done it before. These politicos and bigwigs liked their semi-public brooding when the mood fit. Frankly, he'd just as soon look out the window as well.

It was then that the fly alighted on the window. It walked one way and then the other before stopping to commence a self-satisfied buzzing about three feet to the right of Roland's head. From the conference table Teague saw blue sky out the window and a wispy passing cloud and then the small buzzing fly, a tableau of large and small, interrupted by a sudden flash of gold cuff link and a resounding smacking hand.

Yet you worked for them, said Roland, turning now to face Teague. And you'll work for them again.

Who?

These damn East Tennessee Republicans.

I never said I was an ideologue.

No, you never did, said Roland, turning back to the kaleidoscope of life teeming out the window. Fish beneath the river. Snapping turtles sunning on logs then flopping overboard with each passing boat. Ants and trees and what mammals prefer life in the alley. Hot humans on foot or idling in traffic, cursing the humidity, the clatter and din of the city so soundlessly rendered from where they now stood.

What a load of shit, thought Teague. The earlier dialogue with brooding back was enough to try his patience. Now this random exchange of what sounded suspiciously like moralizing.

You reckon my ass is beat?

Teague laughed, then checked himself. The tone of the question was impossible to decipher. Then laughed again. We just got started on our Memphis plan, said Teague. We'll have a better feel after our meetings in Nashville.

Roland seemed to notice for the first time the splattered fly above his head and took a handkerchief from his pocket to wipe his hands.

Want to see where we'll put the Expo?

Teague rose stiffly and came over.

Bad back, said Roland. Or knees?

Huh?

You groaned when you got up.

Back, said Teague, standing now beside Roland. I groaned?

Like a bullfrog.

I'm falling apart. And my father played hard-pitch baseball till he was thirty-nine.

Too much sitting on our asses, said Roland, pointing toward the west.

Right there, he said. Right there, running along Rather Creek, is where we'll put the Federal Pavilion. Can you see it?

Teague squinted to find the creek. He'd forgotten there was one there. He'd forgotten anything was down in that gully other than a railroad trestle, several dilapidated warehouses, and the long-abandoned Glennville train depot.

Said Teague: Do you mean that runty brown sewage creek running between that old warehouse and the dead-looking willow?

No sewage runoff, said Roland. We had the water tested a year ago. Just muddy. And the warehouse will go, obviously. All of them. But yes, that's the spot.

If we get the Expo.

If? said Roland. How much is J.T. paying you?

It's a fine spot for a pavilion, said Teague. I can see the tourists milling about from here.

Girl on a Bike

FADE IN

INT: UPSCALE RESTAURANT—DAY

ROLAND, TEAGUE, and J.T. sit in the VIP Corner of Le Bistro. In their SUITS and TIES, they look a little out of place, and older, among this YOUNGER CROWD, off-duty bartenders and waitresses, and others who eat lunch at two, many in jeans and just-out-of-bed hair. See and be seen, yes. Glennville's TRENDY SET.

CRANE SHOT:

A WAITER approaching the Coles' table. A few patrons follow the waiter's progress toward the corner booth, but laissez-faire seems the order of the day, even with the Democratic nominee for governor in their midst. The waiter stops at the table and eyes the men sitting before him.

CLOSE ON:

THE WAITER. Who places two clear, neat COCKTAILS, olives bouncing plumply, and another drink the color of wheat in front of the waiting hands of the men. We cannot see their faces, but when the waiter departs, the hands of the men reach simultaneously for their drinks.

ZOOM TO:

SWEATING GLASSES, BOBBING OLIVES, CUBES OF ICE in the WHEAT-COLORED DRINK. BIG-KNUCKLED HANDS REACH for their GLASSES. We hear J.T. begin to speak.

>   J.T. (O.S.)
Corrine is wearing my ass out about this damn debu-
tante thing.

                              PULL BACK TO REVEAL:
The three men drinking cocktails.

>   TEAGUE
>   (with a wry smile)
You're going? I knew I'd get hoodwinked into it, but
I figured a man like you could come up with a decent
excuse.

>   J.T.
Didn't see it coming. Corrine got my daughter to ask
one night at supper after I'd been out of town for a
week. Now (pausing to sip) it's dress this, dress that.
I said, hell, if five hundred dollars won't buy a dress
that fits, there ain't a dress that fits.

>   TEAGUE
Teenage girls. That's where you earn your money as
a parent.

J.T. places his glass on the table and turns it slowly round his coaster.

>   J.T.
Corrine's as bad. Maybe worse. Gets so worked up
every time we have to do anything formal or fancy. I
said, hell let's just get out of that country club, then. I
never wanted to join in the first place. But she won't
hear of it. I'm starting to think she just likes being
miserable.

TEAGUE

Why don't you have Corrine give Jan a call? Maybe we
could all go together or something. Jan's been going to
Riverview since she was a little girl. She knows about
everybody there and would be glad to show Corrine
around.

J.T.
(TO ROLAND)
I believe Teague here married up.

ROLAND
So did you.

J.T.
(laughing, putting on for comedic effect)
Shit. I bought her daddy the first car he ever owned.
Corrine doesn't meet me, she's fixing hair down at the
Hair Shack and raising vegetables in the back yard.

TEAGUE

Have Corrine call. Jan's met her and liked her and the
four of us would have a good time.

J.T.
(turning serious)
Thank you. We may take you up on that. I'll run it by
Corrine tonight.

ROLAND

Tell him about the first time. The image. The image
that was the beginning of the end.

J.T.
(laughing)
Nah. No.

THE WAITER sets a basket of rolls down on the table. Roland takes one.

ROLAND
Come on, it's a good story. Teague will like it. He's got that artistic sensibility.

TEAGUE
Well you've got to tell me now.

J.T. picks up his whiskey glass then places it back down on the table in a hyperbolic summoning of recall and narrative verve.

J.T
So me and Daddy are riding to town in the old Ford. Get some feed or something. It's about three in the afternoon, so believe it or not, there's traffic in Henry City. First shift is just getting off at Tyco and those guys were just hell for leather to get out of there. Only time of day you might actually see a traffic accident. Okay, so we're riding along. I'm in the passenger seat, and we're in this long line of cars, going, say, twenty-five, thirty miles an hour.

TEAGUE leans back in his chair, settling in and smiling. The waiter approaches and points at his empty glass. Teague nods yes.

TEAGUE
What time of year?

                           J.T.

Fall. Early fall. School's started, but there's not yet a
nip in the air. Leaves just hinting at a turn. Yellow here
or there. Sunny day, pretty day. Guys just getting off
work probably heading down to the river to fish.

                        ROLAND

Tell him what Daddy's saying.

                          J.T.

Schoolwork. School comes first. I was out for football.
He said, Son, you're fourteen now. Life's about to get
complicated. But keep your eye on the bull's-eye when
it comes to the books and everything else will take
care of itself.

THE WAITER approaches and hands Teague a fresh drink. He grabs it
and takes a sip.

                        TEAGUE
                       (smiling)

Life's about to get complicated?

                          J.T.

Life's about to get complicated. Yes. Those are his exact
words.

                        ROLAND
                       (laughing)

This is the Corrine story, remember?

                          J.T.

Yes, Teague. Remember that. So it's a sunny beautiful
fall day and I'm kind of half listening to Daddy. I'd

about decided I didn't need school and I'd just work
at Tyco once I turned sixteen. Bunch of guys I knew
were working down there and they always had cash
in their pockets.

                    ROLAND
J.T. ran with the old crowd.

                    TEAGUE
                I bet he did.

                     J.T.
                  (smiling)
Hey man, I was ready to make me some money. Was
going to get me a 46 Plymouth Coupe like Randy Har-
lan and start in on the good life.

LAUGHING all round.

                     J.T.
Anyhow. We were just about to the square, just about
to town. And at the edge of town was Elkins Grocery
Store. Really more of a bait and snack place than a
grocery store. So we're just about to Elkins, when I
see these three gals on bicycles coming our way, riding against traffic. They're riding in order, shortest to
tallest, and right away you could see they were sisters.
All of em got Cokes in their hands.

                    TEAGUE
Little one's usually bringing up the rear.

                     J.T.
              (smiling broadly)

I know, I know. So not only is the little one leading the way, pedaling like hell, she's also drinking her Coke and steering one-handed. The older girls haven't opened their Cokes. They're kind of holding em up against the handlebars and still steering with both hands.

TEAGUE
How old?

J.T.
Twelve, fourteen, fifteen. And the twelve-year-old is just whizzing along, gulping her Coke, and hasn't looked the first time at the line of cars breezing by. I mean she's up on the road, maybe two feet from the cars. Just gulping that Coke, bike without the first wobble in it, drinking and steering one-handed and getting farther and farther from her sisters. I'm sitting there getting more and more nervous about this little gal who's not looking where she's going. Dad said something about it. Said, that little girl best look where she's going. Well, right about when he says that, she starts to come by our truck, and now I can see that the bike she's riding is all old and beat-up. Red, but more rust than anything. And she's wearing a matching yellow top and shorts. Drinking that Coke. Not looking where she's going.

ROLAND
You've got the window down.

J.T.
Yeah. If I stuck my arm out, I could have touched her. And right when she passes by, she puts her CoCola

down by her side and smiles the damnedest smile at me I've ever seen. And I mean to this day. Just cocky as hell. Like she knew all along she was playing the daredevil, but by God, she wanted to drink that CoCola and didn't want to wait to do it.

ROLAND pushes his chair back, smiles and loosens his tie.

                    ROLAND
Daddy always loved that story.

                    TEAGUE
              (a faint smile working)
So life was about to get complicated?

                    J.T.
        (looking off across the restaurant)
Yes. It was. A little more complicated.

                              FADE OUT

Dressing the Part

Corrine Cole stood in her enormous walk-in closet, riffling through dresses at a rate to send the hangers singing a lively and metallic tune along the rod. Her pretty auburn hair was pulled back with a plastic headband and she wore nothing but panties, for the dresses she was trying on were of the formal variety, backless, and thin if any straps along the shoulders. She was a broad-shouldered, full-hipped woman, one who was sometimes hard to fit. In jeans, sweaters, most any of the more casual clothes, she looked good and thought she looked good. Walking into a grocery store, she might not make the teenage bag boy take notice. But when she was in line to pay, he would, were he astute, were he interested in such matters, come to a small epiphany about the difference between girls and women, and begin to wonder, perhaps, about the difference between what men and boys know about them.

And standing in her underwear, a viewer of any age, any gender, would say, yes, yes, I see how it all fits together now. The parts that looked too big or too broad in certain clothes, on certain days in certain light, when viewed in sum, as an integrated whole unencumbered by a designer's limited imagination, were what anyone might desire of proportionality in the physical form.

For the record, Corrine was hell on the teenage bag boys. The quick, casual smile, the hips in front of the grocery cart a slowly paced metronome.

Formal wear, however, proved a different matter. All the strapless and backless dresses, so silky and feminine and pleasing to the eye and hand on the hanger, were lost, dominated, after she slipped them on. They all seemed to favor the thin of shoulder, the narrow of hip. She yanked a sheer, shiny pearl-colored dress from a hanger and flinging the hanger to the floor stepped into it in one simultaneous and awkward and angry motion. Almost as quickly, she found herself turning before the full-length mirror in the closet, kicking away the shoes discarded harum-scarum earlier in the hour. It only took two turns. She stopped, regarded herself without facial expression or intentional pose, and said aloud, I look like a goddam truck driver.

Without moving, she hollered for her daughter. Then remembered midshout that she had gone to the movies with a friend.

Look at me, she said, I look like a goddam truck driver.

She hollered this time for the maid, but was not answered.

She picked up the phone and tried to call a sister in Henry City. Again, no response.

She stomped barefoot to the top of the stairs and hollered again for the maid. She cursed briefly and comically at the echoing of her voice down the grand staircase and about the great foyer.

She thumped down the hall, past a number of bedrooms, then came to the upstairs den where the boys were sitting on the floor with the TV at sound-barrier-crashing volume and playing their new electronic football games with tense and manic determination.

Look at this boys, she said.

The boys did not look. The boys continued to push buttons and jerk their heads this way and that, willing the beeping dots on the handheld screen to do as they were bid and to do it quickly and with utmost sweaty vengeance.

She ripped first one then the other of the games out of the boys' hands before they knew what hit them, then slammed about the control panel of the TV with the palm of her hand until the offending noise was silenced. Turning back to the boys, her sons, it was all she could do not to crack the tiny plastic machines over their heads, so sullen were their looks, so wrongfully done their upturned lips.

Look at me, boys, she said again, in the same voice and with the same volume she'd used when trying to speak over the television's blare.

The boys looked up slowly and with a belabored turning up of heads.

I look like a goddam truck driver, don't I boys?

The boys laughed suddenly and without reservation.

Tell me the truth, kids, in this dress, does your mother, or does your mother not, look like she should be driving a goddam truck?

Aw Mom, they said.

A goddam eighteen-wheeler, she said, turning in front of the silent television and glancing scornfully at her reflection in the greenish tube.

Come on, Mom, they said. You look great.

I want you to say it, boys. I want you to say, Mom looks like a goddam truck driver in that dress.

The boys looked at each other and began to laugh.

She pulled an imaginary truck whistle in the downward motion that the kids used when passing big rigs on the highway and requesting a toot of the horn. Honk, honk, she said, pulling the horn. Breaker one-nine, good buddy, breaker one-nine.

Then, sidearming the boys' plastic gizmos onto the couch, she crashed out of the room, the boys a laughing puddle on the floor behind her.

Back in her own room, she took off the dress with surprising care and tossed it without heat on the four-poster bed. The fire was out. In under-garment only, she plopped down on the corner of the bed and sat there without expression or movement. Were one to see her from the doorway, across the great expanse of sand-colored carpet, sitting on the corner of the bed with the soft yellow light coming in from the open blinds and bathing one side of her face, she would have looked unusually small against the vastness of the bedroom, and too young to be the owner of such a room in such a house. The room was about the same square footage as the house Corrine and three siblings had grown up in. She'd decorated it herself, had picked out furniture, drapery, carpet and color schemes for every room. And she had a good eye for such things, mixing old with new, and trusting her innate sense of style over any of the predominant trends. The result was a kind of relaxed propriety. Elegance would be too grand a word and one that wasn't quite right. But you would not be far wrong to use such a word.

Now, however, that the decorating was complete and the house was as she'd first seen it in her mind's eye, she didn't quite know what to do with her time. Time she had. What she lacked were sisters and good friends, ones whom she needn't be careful with, ones who could take her down a peg or two when she needed it. She found more and more that her friends, the people she talked with most, and most easily, worked for her in some capacity.

She thought back to the neighborhood she and J.T. had left only a year before. Houses with back yards that ran into one another's, kids using all of the yards and neighborhood like one big park. She missed, especially, her girlfriends in the old neighborhood, getting together in the midafternoon for wine and conversations before the men were home from work or golf or wherever they were. And always in one kitchen or the other. Why always in the kitchen? Kids darting in and out to grab a drink from the refrigerator, having to stop a racy story midsentence until the youngster had cleared out, the muffled laughs while waiting for clear air space again, the child at the refrigerator pausing in the afterglow of curtailed laughter, intuiting that something is amiss, that something good has been interrupted or is about to begin, but that that something will not begin again until he has cleared the premises, and so he lingers in the refrigerated breeze, fingering one then the other of the colored sugar drinks in the door, thinking to render himself invisible until the story or joke or whatever it is commences again, and then his mother saying, Jeff, get your drink and get out of here. You're letting all of the cold air out of the refrigerator.

Thinks he's missing something.

I swear to god, if I want to find a kid, I've got to holler on the porch for an hour and a half. Don't want him around for five minutes, and can't get him out the door to save my life.

I'm topping you off, honey.

Just a little, then I've got to get these kids home and fed.

Make them a sandwich here if you want. No need to rush off. We're just getting warmed up here. And Jeff, I swear to god, I'm counting to three . . .

And the time poor Allen, Lucy's son, walked in to find his mother with a *Playgirl* centerfold stretched out on the kitchen table. Corrine and Bertie had bought it at the bookstore as a gag for Lucy's ten-year anniversary, flipping a coin in the car to see who had to take it to the cashier and pay. Corrine had lost the flip and had found herself, surprisingly, a little flummoxed at the counter with the man's face and naked torso smiling back up at her while the woman behind waited to pay for her *Redbook*. And then Allen, poor boy, coming in to find his mother and her friends gawking at a naked man, gawking and pointing at the very same table where he drank his juice in the morning and dug around in the cereal box for a baseball card. How they laughed. Till tears rolled down their cheeks. And Lucy didn't even bother to cover it up. He's always rooting around for his dad's magazines, she said. I'm just going to keep mine out in the open so anybody wants to find it, will know where it is.

They were spread all over Glennville now—only Bertie was still in the old neighborhood.

Corrine got off the bed, put on a robe, and went to the window.

They had made so much money so fast.

Outside, the yard and driveway ran a quarter mile down to the road. Her neighbors to the right, the only house she could see and a football field away, had not been sighted, not one of the family of four, in over a month, save the back of a head in a car moving smoothly down the drive. She'd called on them her second week in the new house when they'd not called on her, using the flimsy excuse of asking about neighborhood babysitters. The woman—Susan or Sharon she could never remember—had met her at the door, cordially, formally, but hadn't asked her in, had not asked the first question about her move to the house, her kids, or anything else to do with her existence on planet Earth. And walking back to her own house in the falling dusk, across the expanse of connected lawns, with the comingling floodlights shooting sharp beams across her feet in the rich grass, she'd felt the old flare, the still-fresh flare, of poverty like a red-hot iron in the back of her eyes, that rage her mother had warned her about so many years ago, and said she'd be damned before she called on the neighbors again.

That had been a year ago. Now, down the hall, the sound of high-pitched protestations and subsequent bully-in-training giggles. She turned from the window, grabbed a robe, and began a leisurely stroll to see what all the squawking was about. In the den, she found the older of the boys with a pillow over the younger one's head. All that could be seen of the younger were kicking feet and fly-on-its-back wings. She watched for a moment the writhing and taunting, the furious and ever louder muffled protests of the victim. At some point, the older turned to see his mother standing in the doorway.

I'm trying to cure him of claustrophobia, he said.

Corrine nodded and smiled. Okay. But I'm curing you next.

With this, a look of dawning recognition, to call the bluff or not to call the bluff, a lessening of pressure on the pillow, a cessation of squirming legs.

Oh.

Oh is right.

Then, no longer smiling, she made a quick motion with her finger. Up now. And walked back to her bedroom. Down the hall came the sudden roar of a vehicular chase of some kind on the television. In the foyer, the grandfather clock groaned the loud ticking seconds. She took off her robe again and looked in the mirror, turning to the side and observing her body, looking it over with dispassion and objectivity. She turned to the other side, then placed herself back to mirror, craning her head around to see. When she stood again looking at her reflected self head-on, she considered, briefly, how nice it would be to talk to one of her old friends. But the notion left as quickly as it came. On the few occasions when they'd gotten together at her house or one of the others'—even Bertie's—their attempts to recapture the ease of manner they'd known in the not-so-distant past had failed quietly and without fanfare. Something about those cramped kitchens, she thought, and the pipsqueaks interrupting us every two minutes.

She turned from the mirror and grabbed the discarded dress from the bed. Then she went to the closet and put it back on its hanger. She sorted and arranged the pile of shoes. When she was finished, she stood motionless in the closet, facing out toward the bedroom. The closet smelled still of new carpet and fresh paint. Without thinking, she began lightly touching J.T.'s clothes, which hung opposite her own, running her fingers along the rough tweeds, the cool silks and wool blends, the armaments, suits especially, that held such talismanic power to make money. In the eighteen years she'd lived in her father's house, she'd never known him to have but one suit, a mildewed brown and too long in the arms. Now she bent down to put her face in a stiff shirt—starch—that was the other smell in the closet. Then, slowly, methodically, she began going through each and every one of J.T.'s pockets, beginning with the suits: jacket, vest, pants. And then the sports coats, and ending, finally, some ten minutes later, at the far end of the closet with her hand in the last pair of folded jeans. Nothing. Not a scrap of paper, nor the first book of matches. She briefly considered the shoes at her feet—shoe polish—that was another smell, and the jewelry box where he kept his watches and cuff links, but each of those would have been too premeditated, both for J.T. and for herself. J.T. was careless but not sneaky. That was something, she supposed. Feeling oddly disappointed, or rather as if she'd just watched an anticlimactic movie, she exited the closet, lit a cigarette, and lying down on the bed, soda can for an ashtray, she flipped through the phone book till she found the number for Janet Teague.

The Other Sibling

Beatrice, called Sis, heard the steady thunk of shovels hitting soil in the distance, the occasional metallic clink of metal on rock, the higher-pitched glancing blows, the duller and muted direct hits that are felt all the way up the arms and into the shoulders. Quieter, nearly inaudible, the swishing of dirt on shovel just before it is tossed onto the pile. Sis stroked the head of Sassy Tex with one hand while the other moved the soft brush firmly down her back and over her feathers in swift, rhythmic motion. Every so often she would take her free hand and splash soapy water up from the big iron tub onto the red-and-orange-speckled feathers. The chicken sat silently in the tub, lifting one leg, setting it down, then lifting the other in a kind of jerky cha-cha. Around them in the dirt and behind the oversized and climate-controlled chicken coop, the other birds strutted and pecked at the ground and clucked fatly about their business.

The coop had begun as a girl's playhouse, a kind of tree house up on cinder blocks. In not much time, however, the quiet six-year-old had moved in several of the laying hens and with these hens and the other animals on the farm, domestic and otherwise, she'd spend her childhood days. Over time, she'd painted the coop pink and midnight blue, put up shutters, added a peaked roof and shingled it, and built an elaborate assortment of perches within, all painted a different bright hue.

Now she swabbed the back of Sassy Tex, putting on the final touches, murmuring a stream of sweet nothings to the ever-moving head, the jerking and bobbing neck. *Pretty Tex, pretty pretty Tex, oh you're so pretty Sassy Tex, so fancy and pretty, oh that red and orange looks so pretty, and your feathers are so clean, so clean and pretty, puffy feathers, oh pretty puffy feathers, that's right, puff em out, puff em Sassy Tex, pretty pretty Tex.*

When she was finished, she pulled a towel from around her neck and gave the chicken a good drying. Then tossing a few handfuls of feed from her overalls pocket into several loose groupings of clucking and pecking, she called them by name: *Button, Dora, Bluebell, Old Blue, Teensy, Ducky, Tom-Tom, Catfish, Patricia, Rhubarb, Egg-Girl, Ruth, Biscuit, Cricket, Lulu, Redbud, Rover, Bobcat, Lady-Bird, Crayola, Dizzy, Clucker, Honeycomb, Farmer Bill, Betty-Ford, Raspberry,* a melodic and wistful litany that hung in the thick and thickening morning air.

Afterward she left the coop and walked in the direction of the shoveling sounds. Past the family garden, the scarecrow she'd outfitted in J.T.'s old hunting gear, and then along the cornfield nearest the house. A month earlier, she'd have cut through, walking along the rows, enjoying the mini-maze of waist-high corn and watching the grasshoppers that sprang across her path, the occasional snake, king or black, sliding along the cool and shadowed soil. Enjoying as well the furtive hum and buzz of the dragonflies and honeybees about their business, the raspy, scratchy sound of stalk rubbing stalk in the breeze. But the corn had grown too tall and too closely together and she'd disturb its growth, break a few stalks, no matter how careful her walking, if she entered the field. And the wolf spiders were thick now, fattened up after the thin spring, and she hated to disturb their intricate and far-stretching webs. So she went around, walking in the dried ruts of the tractor road between the fields and the outlying woods, up the slight rise and past the equipment barn, modern and unsentimentalized save for a few crepe myrtles now in purple bloom, and an outdoor thermometer affixed to the side nearest the fields. Past a fallow field that was soybean last year, wheat the year before, and then stopping where the fields stopped, at a green and shady grove of sugar maples.

The men digging under the trees, standing now five feet deep in the ground, stopped to observe her for a moment until they realized that she was there to observe them and meant to do so intently and without cessation, seemingly without blinking, for as long, they feared, as it took to complete the job. In a quiet tone and shoulder-high in the hole, they said their hellos.

Sis nodded in response, did not shuffle her feet, did not waver in her gaze.

Perhaps it is common knowledge that gravediggers don't care to be observed while about their work. Of course, most people feel likewise when working or supposed to be at work. The feeling of unease, however, that pressure to maintain professional decorum, is nowhere as keen as in the readying of eternal resting spots. When alone, they act as anyone doing a physical job, talking in normal tones, joking, loafing as the mood or weather dictates, mopping a sweaty brow or eye with a dirty T-shirt and exposing the startling white swath of stomach underneath for a leisurely moment if the wind is right. The work is hard and monotonous and rarely do they know for whom the hole is dug.

In this case it was for James Cole, who died only two weeks after Roland and J.T.'s tardy arrival for dinner. And on the day that he passed from this realm into either: (A) another realm of existence, one that would seem to presume life eternal, or (B) the infinite and irrefutable nothingness of death, he'd been walking toward the garden with a straw basket in his hand. While he walked, he noticed the dim morning sunlight through the trees behind the old barn and wondered if the five or six cucumbers he'd eyed the day before had ripened in the night. He was thinking about two other things as well, the first being that his son Roland was sure as hell beat in the election for governor. The second was that he thought he'd have bacon for breakfast after all.

The young men digging the hole stopped for a moment to drink from a thermos of cold water. One man drank from the cap, then refilled it and passed it to the other. Neither spoke. Both cut swift, awkward glances at the woman in overalls and old-timey glasses staring at them. Their T-shirts were soaked through, as were their ball caps. Each of them had been digging long enough to forgo gloves, and after they drank, they searched about on their clothes for a clean and dry spot to wipe their hands before running the same hand over sweat-streaked and tearing eyes.

I'll get you a towel if you need one, said Sis.

The two men looked up as if a deer they'd gotten used to had suddenly spoken from the woods.

No ma'am, they said finally and in unison. No need to trouble yourself.

It's no trouble.

Thank you all the same. We'll be done here fore too long.

Hot day to be shoveling.

Yes ma'am.

Can I see your hole?

Though their feet could not be seen, the men seemed to shift about. Their heads rocked. They looked at one another. They weren't from this town and had been called by the mortician only because the regular crew was busy with two funerals on the cemetery grounds. The cemeteries in Henry City and Lynnchester did this, loaning out gravediggers as need arose. The pay on these jobs was time and a half plus travel and much appreciated by the diggers.

If you like, the younger one said.

If Sis had paid attention while approaching the men, she'd have noticed that the younger one's T-shirt, covered in the red clay of the area, was from a rock concert he'd attended in Glennville a few years back and that the elder was experimenting with his first scraggly sideburns. But she did not look at the men as she walked, only at the shadowy chasm in the ground. It took a moment before the men realized they ought to vacate the hole, but once the decision was intuited they sprang up quickly with one-handed leaps, holding their shovels decorously behind them. Then they drifted off to lean against a tree apiece, dirty T-shirts and jeans clinging, shovels still in hand.

Sis got to the hole and walked around it at an easy pace, no discernible look on her face. One of the men reached for a pack of Camels on the ground, took a cigarette, and was about to light it before he thought better of it, decorum and respect for the presently bereaved and all. He was in the process of placing the cigarette behind his ear when Sis leaped into the hole.

The diggers watched her slow pacing in the cramped quarters—shoulders and head inspecting the floor, hands running along the walls.

I never been in a hole this big before, she said.

The men nodded in response.

Not counting caves.

Again the men nodded.

I bury my little chickens when they die. But that don't take much of a hole. Did you see my chickens?

Yes, ma'am, said the one with the rock T-shirt. I saw a few of them.

She smiled. I washed ten of them today. Ten tomorrow. Ten Thursday. Ten Friday. Then they can all raise Cain over the weekend and get as dirty as they want. Won't bother me none.

The men laughed quietly at this, not sure exactly if she meant to be humorous.

But Sis laughed a little at this too and the men knew that it was all right.

It's cool down by my feet, she said. More worms or less worms this low?

The gravediggers looked at one another, but neither seemed to know. Bout the same up top as down low, I'd guess, said the man with the sideburns, once you take out the first shovelful.

Ooh there's a fat one, Sis said, disappearing into the hole.

Ooh there's another one, said the muffled voice in the ground. She stood up then and placed the worms in one of the long side pockets of her overalls. Can I borrow a shovel for a minute? she asked. I want to scrape around here and see how many I can round up.

The next ten minutes consisted of light scraping of the walls and floor, such that they were, and a running commentary to and about her bounty. *Oh you're a fatty aren't you now. Thought you'd done got away didn't you? Not so fast sunshine. Look at that un wiggle. Look here, boys, now that there's a nightcrawler.*

The gravediggers were sitting under a tree, smoking cigarettes, and talking in reverent tones about a fondly recalled combustion engine when they saw two cars pull into the driveway and men in suits, women in heels, get out. This got their attention and they began to wonder about the time. Neither wore a watch and the hearse was to arrive at eleven. The florist would be coming out before that with the arrangements. Down in the hole they heard, *I ain't gonna drop you twice, little fatty.*

What would they have done if it had come a big rain? asked the gravedigger with the sideburns. How could they have got the casket out through the mud?

The other shook his head. He didn't know. To worry about such things, bad things that had not happened after all, was not his way. This is all that we will know about the character of the gravedigger in the rock T-shirt. But isn't it enough to know that he is blessed with a restful mind? That his thinking mechanism separates the wheat from the chaff automatically and mercilessly?

There are worse brains to be had, that much seems sure.

Not long after came the flat distant call of a woman's voice. *Sis*, she called. *Sis-Ter.* Then the habitual and impatient ringing of the dinner bell.

I bet they'd have put the coffin on a flatbed and hooked it up to a tractor if it had rained, said the gravedigger with the sideburns. That'd do the trick.

And truth be known, his mind was not one to dwell on the negative either, this sideburned gravedigger. His mind was just active and needed to be working something over all the time. But he'd just as soon work over why something had happened as it ought to, finding a good lure hung up in a tree after he'd just lost one, as not.

Optimistic gravediggers. A tough one to pull off. But so be it. They are what they are.

Again the bell, again the call of *Sis-Ter.*

I hear you, I hear you, came the voice from the soon-to-be-grave. She scrambled out of the hole as effortlessly as she'd jumped in. Momma, she said, with a quick jerk of her head toward the house.

Looks like folks are starting to show up, said the gravedigger in the rock T-shirt.

Come for the burying, said Sis.

To this the men did not reply.

We're singing Amazing Grace, Bringing in the Sheaves, I Saw the Light, and something else, said Sis.

Those are good ones, said the sideburned gravedigger.

I hope they play the Hank Williams fast. I hope they got a fiddler and a banjo man. We're supposed to.

That would be nice, said the gravedigger in the rock T-shirt.

Sis smiled, pulled a handful of squirming worms from her pocket and held them up in the slanted sunlight through the trees. Half for the vegetable garden, she said. Half for the chickies.

Nashville

Teague had been coming to Rooney's, Nashville's historic steakhouse and legislative gathering place, since his earliest days as a lobbyist. His life as a high school history teacher had proven less and less satisfying. He'd enjoyed the classroom, the actual teaching, but the bureaucracy and behind-the-scenes politics proved beyond trifling, beyond exasperating. And the pay wasn't enough to raise a family. He'd just quit one day, in the middle of the year, decided enough was enough. Three months later when a college friend offered him an entry-level lobbying position with a big Nashville firm, he'd taken the job, moving from one form of political intrigue to another. His first account had been as a junior lobbyist for the liquor lobby, the biggest hitter in a town of big hitters and a plum assignment. The head of the firm thought Teague, still fresh from the classroom and earnest in appearance if not in heart, would be a great tagalong to the legendary lobbyist Price Daniels, a.k.a. King Tut, so named for an expense account that made his pockets seem perennially lined with gold. Renowned for picking up any and all legislative tabs, even from rival lobbyists opposing him on a bill, the King was a born headliner. Teague would serve as his low-key and sensible ballast.

The one big downside to the job was having to be away from home, away from Glennville, from Monday through Thursday when the legislature was in session, a session that traditionally ran from January through May. He'd weighed this absence from his family against the huge sums of money to be made, and with Jan's blessing, he'd accepted a job that meant spending three nights a week in a downtown hotel. The old Royal Court would be his home away from home and in the downtime of late afternoon, before hitting the restaurants and bars, he played tonk with legislators and lobbyists, listening in a smoke-filled hotel room to the wild and ribald stories of a cast of characters no novelist could invent.

Those first years on the Hill had been a lot of fun.

His last years on the Hill had nearly killed him. He'd come closer than he liked to admit to losing Jan and his daughter. Even now he couldn't explain his behavior of the later years, how being back home in Glennville left him with a crippling sense of boredom and lethargy. He simply couldn't muster the attention span to do much of anything but read the newspaper or spin a few hands of blackjack down at the American Legion. Julie was out of diapers and in school before his head cleared. It sickened him to think of the lost time. An ice-cream truck's music was nearly unbearable to him now, seemed cruel and haunting. But that was in the rearview. He'd quit the lobbying before it killed him, quit the life and the lifestyle, then gone almost exclusively to the consultant role nearly a decade ago. Then it was up and at em every Saturday morning to take Julie to ball games and recitals or wherever else she needed to go.

He pulled into Rooney's parking lot with the memories flooding his head, the good and the bad flashing by in one big jumble as they had during the whole of the three-hour drive from Glennville. And now the longtime valet, an off-duty cop, greeting him by name as he made way toward the door and the ghost of his past, who laughed one minute at the bar, stared sullenly into his drink the next.

He opened the door of the old restaurant, a Victorian mansion converted in the twenties to its present use, and stopped in front of the cigarette machine in the foyer. He pumped the quarters in and pulled the handle, marveling at the satisfying *thhnk* of the lever pulled and retracting, the instantaneous slippery sound of the cigarette pack sliding down the chute, the satisfying clunk of its landing in the tray. He unwrapped the pack, pulled out a cigarette, and lit it with practiced and rhythmic automation, a mechanized series of actions along the conveyor belt of nicotine inhalation. He checked his watch, twenty minutes early, and, knowing the Coles, more like an hour and twenty minutes early.

Nicotine-settled, he opened the door into the restaurant proper, caught Danny's eyes, and pointed toward the stairs that led to the bar. Danny nodded, got you covered, eating later and a good table when you're ready. The racket inside was considerable already, so Danny mouthed, *good to see you, Teague. Really good to see you.*

Then Teague was walking down the dark and narrow staircase and into the windowless basement bar, smoky and loud with chatter, the air conditioner cranked to the max. He found three empty seats at the corner of the L-shaped bar where he could watch the door and be left alone for a moment with a cocktail to settle into the present scene. Big Teddy, ironically dubbed how many years back, came over with the perfected slouching swagger of a tired jockey who just got beat at the wire. In the Derby no less. Big Teddy would hear none of it and hadn't for forty years. He placed the scotch on the rocks, tall glass, no garnish, in front of Teague and turned around without a word.

Thank you, sunshine, said Teague.

Big Teddy turned around, slowly, a waiter at the service end of the bar already flapping an order over his head. Now damn it, Teague.

Teague smiled but said no more and Big Teddy headed the other way to spread his Christmas cheer.

Teague was looking at the black and white pictures of dead Irishmen on the wall, including the original Daniel Rooney himself, Danny at the door's long-departed father and the founder of this establishment, and a variety of other scowling swells from the old speakeasy days. Back then they kept a man at the door to peer through a sliding peephole and decide if you were square or Fed. This was when they practically gave the steaks away to get you in for the good and pricey booze. Wait staff was all black then, as now, and then and now outfitted in the starched white and high-collared linen jackets. Every five minutes or so, one of the old waiters would holler from the server's well for Teague to sit in his section when it came time to eat.

All and all, the joint was hopping for a summer night, typically

Rooney's slow season. But the special legislative session, convened by the governor to ratify an increase in the sales tax, had quite a few of the regular crowd back in town. And from the looks of it, not a one of them was missing the home fires, the quiet charms of whatever broiling little country burg they called home.

The Coles and Senator Kirkwood, the state senator from Memphis, were now running about thirty minutes late, typical and expected, and Teague had just received a second silent, sullen drink from Big Teddy without ever asking for it when Ray Bennett headed his way.

He said: I'll bet my one good arm that's Mike Teague sitting right here in Rooney's.

That's a bet you'd win, said Teague. Pull up a stool and tell me what lies they're telling at the capitol these days.

Bennett was already halfway in his seat before being invited. He continued in the physical gyrations he'd begun upon first entering the bar, a kind of esoteric dance of his own creation meant to get the attention of the gruff Big Teddy, whose vision waxed and waned according to your status with him and within the whole of the Rooney's hierarchy. Bennett swung up under the bar and sat on the stool, the side with the missing arm next to Teague. Teague watched the bobbing head, the hand that would go up with every turn of Teddy's head in their direction before dying in vain again on the bar. Ten years coming to Rooney's and Teddy still treating him like a newcomer. Now Bennett looked ready to resort to verbal request, a desperate and dangerous measure, but thought better of it and cleared his throat in a beseeching way instead. Goddam Big Teddy, he said in a sideways whisper. Thinks he owns that liquor. Thinks he owns the restaurant.

With this he sang: *What do you call a mystery like Ted-dy?*

He sang it three times, with ever-increasing volume, until the gruff barkeep headed their way. He placed a napkin in front of Bennett and waited, red Irish eyes glaring, for him to spit out his drink order. Teague watched the exchange with unfettered bemusement. Two famous characters in the ongoing drama that was the Nashville political scene. Bennett had lost his arm at eighteen in Vietnam and had made a living off of it ever since. Worked as the assistant commissioner of regulatory boards up at the capitol now and always had the dope on the wonkish angle of government. Overseeing the Cosmetology Board, Board of Barber Examiners, Board for Licensing Contractors, Board of Funeral Directors and Embalmers, the Motor Vehicle Commission, the Private Investigators Commission, the Geology Registration Service, and twenty other such entities gave Bennett more information and avenues to gathering information than just about anyone else in the state. Such a position would tempt the most reluctant of political gossips, so a visit with Bennett was one-stop shopping for friends like Teague who'd been out of the loop for a spell and needed to get caught up on all things large and small up on the Hill.

Well, let me see, said Bennett. What am I in the mood for?

Big Teddy looked to the far end of the bar, feigned a move in that direction, swiped angrily at a wet spot to the left of Bennett instead.

Not beer.

Goddammit Bennett.

Teague, what are you having?

He's having scotch, damn it. Like he always does.

Teague swirled his glass to confirm Big Teddy's statement.

Bennett, I'm counting to three.

Maybe a frozen daiquiri.

Teague laughed.

Not at my bar.

What if I want a frozen daiquiri? It's hot as hell out there. I think a daiquiri would really hit the spot.

Gin and tonic it is, said Big Teddy, pushing off the bar with finality and walking without haste to commence mixology.

That's what I wanted anyway, said Bennett, reaching for a handful of mixed nuts and jamming them into his mouth.

Teague laughed.

It is.

I believe you.

I just got to mess with him a little bit.

Absolutely.

So you're working for the Coles now, is that what they tell me?

That's right.

Fast Freddy said you were going to show Montgomery a thing or two by putting Roland Cole in flannel pajamas and having him ride a unicycle up and down Franklin Street.

Teague laughed. You're about the fifth person to tell me that. Only I heard it was Larry Watson said it.

No, it was Fast Freddy. We were playing tonk up in Reynolds's hotel room.

You still the easy mark up there?

I'm getting better.

Teague laughed.

I am. Ask Reynolds and that bunch.

I don't believe I paid for a lunch for five years running thanks to that game.

Hell you were just lucky.

Probably so, said Teague. That seems as reasonable as any other explanation.

You weren't a bad card player.

Well thank you.

I wouldn't trust those Coles as far as I could throw em.

Luckily, I don't have to throw em.

Bennett smiled. That's good. I'm just warning you. Funny things going on with the Democrats these days. Our lame-duck governor is playing with fire, I'll tell you that much.

Teague smiled. It was good to see old Bennett.

Can you be a lame duck if you never was a healthy duck to begin with? said Bennett. That's just one man's opinion, of course. Tennessee's had good governors. Most of em in my lifetime were above average to very good. Would you agree with that?

I would.

This damn Hart, though. He's dumber than a bucket of hair.

Teague patted his old friend on the shoulder. So, he said, what's the real story? Are you privy?

Bennett glanced once behind him, a sure precursor to the dishing of dirt. Then he took a sip of his drink, made a face as if the drink had some bite to it. He said: Say what you will about Big Teddy, he don't pour a short drink.

Short man, tall drink, Teague agreed.

Said Bennett in a hoarse whisper: I'm not going to say much because none of this is confirmed, but from what I hear, it's a good time to have a relative in jail, a relative you'd like to get out a little prematurely, if you know what I mean.

Hell, even I heard that one. That's old news. You're losing a step, Bennett. You used to know the difference between fresh and stale news.

Okay, okay, said Bennett, straightening a bit and no longer whispering. The other thing I'm hearing is that the right price will get anyone who wants one a liquor license in West Tennessee.

Is that right?

Yep. And if you don't pay the price, you don't get your store.

Yeah, but that's gone on forever.

Not like this.

TBI on it yet?

Don't know. Wouldn't be surprised if they were, would you?

Not if he's as sloppy as you claim.

Well, said Bennett, for the record, from where I'm sitting, the Coles are painted with the same brush.

Teague smiled. He'd been waiting for something like this.

They're doing a lot for the city, he said. Hell, you couldn't get a business loan in Glennville before they came along unless your brother worked for the bank. And even then you'd better have damn good collateral. I'll tell you one thing, if you were a developer or any kind of entrepreneur, someone who needed some big money for a good idea, you'd be singing a different tune. I bet they're doing sixty percent of the business loans in Glennville right now.

Teague, said Bennett, I'm a philosopher, like yourself. Not an entrepreneur. But what I see is a one-building skyline and what else? A bunch of deer hunters waiting for football season. And that Expo? Who the hell is going to take a World's Fair in Glennville seriously? They might as well have it in Bucksnort.

We'll see, Teague said laughing. These guys are pretty sharp. And they're persistent as hell.

Governor Cole? And a Glennville World's Fair? With the odds you're playing, I'm ready to get you back in the tonk game.

You might be right.

Bennett rooted around in the bowl of nuts until he found the three remaining cashews. He popped these into his mouth then wiped his salty hand on the side of his polyester pants.

Said Bennett: I had a professor in junior college tell me that success consists of going from failure to failure without loss of enthusiasm. So you might be on to something.

Your man Churchill said that.

Really? Churchill? I thought I knew all his good quotes.

Apparently not.

Oh yes. Mr. Van-der-bilt. I get so used to talking to these legislative jarheads, I forget there are a few of us among the literati.

A few, said Teague.

Vanderbilt my ass. Teague, you should have gone to junior college. That's where the free thinkers are. That's where men like me get made. And the tail, my god, the tail. Twice the ass you'd ever see at Van-der-bilt and a tenth as expensive.

Teague laughed.

Did you learn anything in college but how to hold a cocktail glass?

I did learn that. Not too high, not too low. Casual but not sloshy. You middle-class hicks never get it right. Then again, that could have been my own natural talent in cocktail-holding. I might just as well have intuited that at UTC.

You didn't learn a damn thing. Spent your days toasting and saying ta-ta. What did you study anyway?

I studied the wealthy.

And?

They've got assholes and nice folks like everyone else.

That's it?

Big Teddy could just as easily be a tall Japanese woman.

That's perverse, Teague. And you're way off. There's a way higher percentage of assholes at Van-der-bilt. Hell, I've been around em now for twenty years.

Same percentage.

But your nice folk might be my asshole.

The true asshole and the true nice folk are indisputable. It's the in-between, the grey area between the sometime asshole, sometime nice folk, that makes life interesting.

But Big Teddy is an asshole, said Bennett as the barkeep picked up his empty glass and put down a fresh one.

Oh yeah, said Teague. He set the curve.

Bennett left after his second drink and Teague sat at the bar feeling cool and collected. Bennett felt sure that Teague was on a loser, but Teague was not so sure. Probably. But a lot could happen in a couple of months. The right advertisement, a blunder on the other side, anything could turn the tide. He checked his watch and waved Teddy off when he pointed to his half-empty glass. Two was about his number these days. Anything more and it cost him sleep. Then again, the drinks were going down well and he didn't have to do a thing in the morning but drive back to Glennville. He'd about decided to order a third after all when he saw Valerie and another woman making their way down the steps to the bar. Big Teddy saw the same pair, reached for the scotch, and poured Teague another. He placed the drink in front of Teague and shielded him as he did so from any curious eyes on the stairs.

Hhhm, said Big Teddy.

Teague stared into his drink and twirled the stirrer a few vigorous times.

Been two years since I've seen that number in here, said Big Teddy. You want me to phone Danny upstairs and tell him to get your table ready?

No, said Teague. I'll just play it as it lays.

Big Teddy nodded once, professionally, then headed back to the other end of the bar.

She was placing her drink order with Teddy, talking overhead to her companion in the process. The only empty chairs at the bar were the ones beside his own. He was dead in the water, and the wait to be spotted seemed interminable.

His shoes felt tight and he remembered, inexplicably, an old football coach telling him to always buy good shoes and a good mattress. Would be spending one hundred percent of your time in one or the other. But why think of that now? The shoes? The mattress? The brain worked oddly and there was no reckoning where in the memory bank it would next land. Only, in this case, it was memory in the flesh.

As she received the drinks, laughing with her friend and cutting up with one of the waiters, her glance found Teague for the first time. Her head jerked back almost imperceptibly, shot from a distance with the lightest bullet in the world, then almost as quickly a reformatting of the lighthearted façade. She smiled, tight-lipped and without showing teeth, then handed a drink over her shoulder to the mystery gal. When she looked again at Teague, waiting he supposed for a response, all he could offer was a mock-cheery wave. But as soon as his hand was in the air, he felt false and weak-willed. Why not a real wave, a real smile? Why not an unsmiling acknowledgment of the greeting and let that be it?

Alas, memories of the physical embodiment of his lost period had cut the wires from brain to body. He rattled the ice in his drink, a dinner bell for his missing composure. When he raised his head, he once again had possession of himself. He pointed at the empty stools next to him, the only unoccupied seats at the bar. I mean, what the hell? Why not? That water is long under the bridge, that bridge has been destroyed, and Teague is a grown man with his house in order.

Valerie conferred briefly with her friend, then turned to Teague, smiling, a near-apology, and pointed upstairs. Teague nodded. Gotcha. Smiled. Heading to dinner. Maybe dates waiting upstairs. Nods again. Is tired of nodding and smiling and nervous nonverbal communication. Is surprised that he is disappointed that she will not be sitting at the bar next to him. Perverse curiosity? What have you been doing these last few years? How are you getting on? The news I hear is filtered and uncorroborated. Snippets and apologies for bringing up the subject of you. And damned if I press for more details.

Then she waves once more and turns to walk up the stairs.

And Teague watches all the way. Figures she knows he's watching and might as well anyway. And finds, not at all to his surprise, that he still likes what he sees.

And wishes he hadn't had the third drink.

And nods, *Hell yes*, when Big Teddy starts his way with number four.

The Coles now sat at the bar with Teague, waiting for Senator Kirkwood. The Coles were often in Nashville and occasionally hired lobbyists for some banking bill or another, but the difference between a Rooney's outsider and Rooney's insider might as well have been stamped on everyone's head once they entered the door. The Coles were millionaires and well known throughout the state, and one of them was the Democratic candidate for governor, but they sat at the bar taking in the scene like kids at their first big-league baseball game. They smiled and looked over Teague's head and asked who was this and who was that again and again.

Then again, most of the insiders at Rooney's had once been small-town denizens themselves. It took a decade in and around the capitol and Nashville itself to knock off most of the bucolic dust, the too-ready smile, the big, open, earnest face that's just glad to be there, out of the sticks and into the action. And try as the Glennville resident might, he still felt the restrained yodel in his throat when feet first hit Nashville pavement. Teague sure had twenty-five years before when he'd first come to Nashville for school.

I don't know, said Roland. It just sounds like we're imitating Montgomery to me.

Teague waited a minute before responding. He felt about to tread on thin ice. The old man had not been dead two weeks. He'd attended the funeral and both sons had been dry-eyed and composed during its entirety. And not the first word since, other than a quick handshake and word of thanks for making the trip up to Henry City for the service. He felt certain, however, that emotions were right on the surface. His would be. Still, he'd have to say what he had to say.

Not really, said Teague. Shooting a commercial in the candidate's hometown is just standard fare. We would just go down and shoot it on the Fourth of July. Henry City's got a little parade, don't they?

Little, hell, said J.T. We had three fire trucks last year. And two Shriners in those funny cars to boot.

Roland smiled slightly, acknowledging an older lady across the bar who waved to him, the gubernatorial candidate here in the flesh.

It just seems hokey, Roland said. Especially with Montgomery marching around like the little engine that could and doing the whole back-to-the-roots campaign.

J.T. let fly with a mild profanity about the Republican railroad man, but the comment was perfunctory. Then he resumed scouting the room for people of interest, perhaps a conversation of interest. For this one, Teague could tell, was boring him to tears.

This will sound crass, Teague said. And opportunistic. But your father's death received a lot of press. Very good press. He did a lot for that town. It's not going to hurt us a bit to show you down at your father's old store or working on the same farm you worked on to pay your way through school. Show a picture of you in your old Army uniform or something. The people of the state just don't know enough about you yet. And no one ever lost an election in Tennessee by reminding folks where they were born and raised. Especially if they were born and raised on a farm.

Roland studied the dead angry Irishmen on the wall, nodded when Teddy pointed at his glass for a refill. I thought we were doing the Bright New Day campaign, he said. I was going to fly the Osmonds in.

Teague ignored the sarcasm. He said: You've been pushing your financial expertise from the beginning. I'm not second-guessing that. Your ability to handle a state budget is invaluable. But there's not a person I know who's going to vote for someone because they can crunch numbers.

Or balance a checkbook. The voter wants to relate, wants to feel like he could shake the governor's hand and not feel sheepish about his shoes or his wife's inexpensive dress. The voter, more than anything, more than anything else, wants to feel appreciated. And right now, I hate to say it, but people that don't know you might just see a slick banker. Somebody who drinks martinis and gets paid to sit in an air-conditioned office and decide whether or not to give them the money they need for a second mortgage on their home.

Wearing penny loafers without socks, said J.T. And starch in the shirt seven days a week.

Nobody but bankers like bankers, Teague said.

I don't like bankers, said J.T. And Daddy didn't like em. Only reason he started his own little bank is because none of the bastards at National would ever loan him the money he needed to buy the rest of the farm. Wanted to see him turn a profit one more year, one more year. Hell, Daddy was loaning more money out of the store than the banks were back then.

Okay, said Teague. That's what I'm saying. You've let Montgomery co-opt one of your strengths. The irony, as you well know, is that he was raised here in Nashville and his folks are well-to-do. He's third-generation Princeton. Now he's painted you as the city slicker out of touch with the rural folks and middle class in the state. I mean, if you put him in a room for an hour with any of the boys you grew up with in Henry City, he'd be a complete fish out of water. He wouldn't have the first thing to talk about. Never been on a tractor in his life. Never milked a cow.

Never drank moonshine, said J.T. Never fucked a girl till he got married.

Roland and Teague laughed.

Never fucked doggie-style yet. How many kids he got?

Three, said Teague.

Fucked three times his whole life. Oh man, that railroading outfit makes my ass want to jerk somebody up by the hair.

Roland and Teague laughed some more.

Teague, do you see what you've done? Do you see how your black magic has harmed the innocent people of this state?

I just thought the old boy needed to get the starch out of his image a bit, said Teague. Been up in Washington so long I thought he might have forgotten his constituency. He should have listened to me last time. We'd be running against an incumbent.

I'll challenge him to a wood-chopping contest, Roland said. First one to knock out a cord gets to wear the overalls and claim the hearts of our rural kinsmen.

Just think about the ad, Teague said.

Heavy on the banjos and the homespun homily?

Jug band, said Teague. Fried green tomatoes tossed to the crowd.

I still think it sounds hokey as hell, said Roland.

Hokey is as hokey does, said J.T. Where do you think you are, Roland? Paris, France?

Restaurant Vignettes

THE CUNNINGHAM ROOM

Named in honor of a storytelling rogue of an uncle to Daniel Rooney, the uncle who could never bear to leave the Emerald Isle and whose cheery countenance twinkles down on diners from the charcoal painting above the fireplace, never missing a ribald joke, always ready to catch a knowing wink or two. The room is dark, candlelit save for two small coal lamps done over to electricity sixty years prior, and even a novice to Rooney's, someone who's never eaten in a restaurant like this, would know this is the room to be in, the room for the heavy hitters and whatever celebrity might be passing through town. Tucked away on the top floor. Four small tables. The best waiter working the floor. Tonight only one other party shares the room, two near-deaf couples whose standing Wednesday night date is well into its third decade. No real big shots on the books tonight, so the room was open until Teague and his group came in. Now seating is closed in the Cunningham Room until further notice. Danny's orders. Danny's special seating policy for those in the know, those with the pull. He'd warned Teague about the other table before seating them, pointing out their hearing problems and likely disinterest in anything not related to dessert specials or who was on Carson later that night. Teague waved him off. No problem, full house tonight, seat us where you need to. This is a social visit more than anything. But Danny took the big red book of reservations, the same one his father used during the old gin and steak days, and put a big slash through the empty tables in the Cunningham Room.

ENOUGH WITH PRELIMINARIES

That's fine. No problem, said J. T. Cole. You need buses to get your people to the polling station, we can get you buses. And if a big picnic spread down at the community center and a few cases of half pints might help to get the voters out, that's no problem either. That's not too illegal, is it, Teague? There're still a few spots out in Berry County where the half pints are handed out on election day. I reckon that's true for other parts of the state. Would you agree with that, Teague?

J.T. and Senator Kirkwood looked to Teague, who was smiling and sipping on a glass of red wine.

Said Teague: Are you asking as a practical-minded friend or as make-do legal counsel?

Your call.

I'll say this. I wouldn't put the last name Cole on any checks.

We'll sign em Mike Teague, that'll do the trick.

The men laughed at this response and Teague took the last of the bottle of red wine and poured it into Senator Kirkwood's glass. A waiter came by and deposited a check at the table of the senior citizens, then stopped at the Cole table and began removing salad dishes and plates with half-eaten corn cakes, the house specialty. It was late, nearly ten, and all the men were hungry. The cakes and salad had helped, but each was now ready for the main course.

A SHORT MOVEMENT BACK IN TIME

The man in the olive-green pin-striped suit hit the service end of the bar where the waiters stood and immediately began shaking hands and joking with them as they waited for their drink orders to be filled. A few of the waiters looked his suit up and down or fingered a lapel and smiled approvingly. The senator received the compliments in good faith. He agreed with them, it was a damn sharp suit. Damn sharp. And what about this bullshit? I mean, seriously, tell me about this bullshit. All these half-dead white motherfuckers in here with more money than God and not one of them knows how to put on the threads. Am I lying? Am I making this shit up? Reggie there, busing tables, busting his ass for tips from you cheap-ass waiters, is there any doubt that Reggie is smooth as hell once he gets off and heads down to the Lamplight? Am I lying? Reggie, are you or are you not a smooth motherfucker?

I'm a smooth motherfucker.

Indeed. You are, you are. Hey, listen, I got nothing against my white brothers. I like my white brothers fine. Hell, I've loved some white brothers. But why, tell me why, not a one of those plaid motherfuckers can dress to save their flat white ass? And more money than they know what to do with? Am I lying?

Much laughter.

When those motherfuckers gonna learn?

Laughter, shaking of head.

Be bringing *us* some dinner. Bring me my dinner and I'll show your white ass how to dress.

One of the senior waiters orders the senator a drink, refuses any money from the senator for his gesture. Pay it out of his pocket or add it on to a running tab, no one the wiser, and Big Teddy's accounting gets a little lax this time of night anyway. Your money's no good here, Senator Kirkwood. No good at Rooney's. No. No sir. Wave that shit off. We're working day jobs nine to five and then humping it here till two. We're making the jack. Don't worry about our jack. Two kids at TSU. Hitting the books. Put that money in your wallet. Rooney's, baby, we run Rooney's. Let Danny and Big Teddy think they do. Let these rich country clubbers and these politico big shots think they do. But we're the show. We're the business. Two kids in college. They won't be humping no tables. Put your money in the pocket, Senator. Your money's no good here and we don't want it.

THE NIGHTLIFE, IT AIN'T NO GOOD LIFE

The steaks were polished off and wine glasses sat half to a third full. Any of the four who would presume to eat dessert would be crowned champion of the night. They had put it away, knocked back what had been set before them. Odd too, as none of the four were particularly big eaters. And Roland watching his telegenic waistline and Teague known to his loved ones as getting summer-skinny every year. Perhaps it was the late hour, the predinner cocktails, the surprising energy of the special summer session that had Rooney's twice as busy as normal during the slow season. It was now past eleven. The waiter came by and asked about coffee, but no one wanted any. One taking a moment to inventory their senses would notice that the din of the restaurant had faded. Individual sounds could be distinguished now: two waiters speaking in the back staircase that led to the kitchen. A woman laughing the next room over. But the men at the table likely did not hear these sounds, their heads filled still with the white noise of the evening, the murmur and roar of mingled sounds, the synesthesia of received sensory stimuli, a kind of interior clanging of the brain that does not quieten until one is back in a quiet bedroom. And it is then that the ears begin to reconnect with the brain. Ah, the faucet is dripping. Yes, and now the clicking of a minute on the digital clock. And thus begins the slow dissipation of the white noise, the disassembly of the concrete block of sensory overload that the night out has constructed, the reclaiming of the individual sense's dominion.

TEAGUE TAKES FIVE

Have you heard about our World's Fair? Teague asked.

A few whispered innuendos is all, said Senator Kirkwood. And a few chuckles, to be honest. Paris, Seattle, Glennville. You know what I'm talking about.

Teague smiled at this, the Coles less so.

So you're bringing the world to Glennville, said Senator Kirkwood.

We are, said J.T.

We hope to, said Roland.

Sure would be great for Glennville, Senator Kirkwood said. Don't think it'd help Memphis a damn bit. Except maybe cost us some tourist dollars.

What do you mean, cost you money? said J.T. Once they get in the state, they're liable to head your way. World's Fair and Graceland in the same trip.

The senator smiled. We're six hours away from Glennville. If you live on the East Coast that's adding twelve hours, a full day, to your trip away from home. The way I see it is there's a family in Lansing, Michigan, and they're going to take one vacation this summer. They were going to Memphis to see Beale Street and Graceland. Now, however, they're going to travel equidistance and go see a bunch of boring-ass exhibits. Then head on back to Michigan and get ready to start shoveling snow for the next nine months. No, as usual, what's good for Nashville and Glennville doesn't help us a damn bit.

The Coles laughed. As did Teague. Though from the look of things, his moon was on the wane. Past his bedtime. Out of practice and out of late-night shape. He sat uncomfortably, stiff back or pained liver or both, and tossed down half a glass of water.

Said Senator Kirkwood: Of course, I'm assuming there are some business opportunities if Glennville were to get a World's Fair. Some investment opportunities.

Yes, said Roland, absolutely. What they'll be is still up in the air. We'll know more when we get the okay from city council and the okay from the International Bureau of Fairs.

You don't have city council already in the bag? said the senator.

We haven't starting hitting it hard yet, said J.T. Once this campaign is over, we're going to get the iceman over there to cool their asses and make everything nice and smooth. Then we'll get going on the federal side. But we've already got an in on that side.

And who's that? said Senator Kirkwood. If you don't mind my asking.

Across the table, Teague was shaking his head no. Smiling, but giving the no-go.

I don't mind you asking, said J.T. But I'd just as soon not say. Not yet. You understand, I'm sure. It's still a ways off and no need to put the horse before the cart.

And loose lips sink ships, said the senator.

We know you're not one to gossip, said Roland.

Say no more, said the senator. Say no more. But I do have a few other questions. Feel free to answer or not to answer as you see fit. One, how do you see the World's Fair helping my constituency? Two, how could I personally help in your endeavors? Assuming, again, that I could help. I'm talking about with this election and helping Glennville to get the fair. And three, how does one go about buying bank stock from that big bank of yours?

Anyone can buy the bank stock, said J.T. As long as there's some for sale. So stock is bought all the time. Sometimes it's given away. A lot of people, consulting people and so on, prefer stock to cash. As long as it's not some kind of inducement, we can do with it whatever we please. I'm talking about the stock that Roland and I personally own, of course.

Of course, said Senator Kirkwood. I understand.

How many shares are you interested in?

Teague stayed at the table for just a while longer before excusing himself to go to the bathroom, kibitz for a while with Danny, and close out his bar tab from earlier.

A SERIOUS COMPLICATION OF AFFAIRS

Teague was back at the table and the men were talking football, high school football, and comparing notes on players they'd seen through the years. J.T. was not at the table, having gone to the restroom some fifteen minutes before. Someone watching from the waiter's stairway would have seen a table ready to wrap up the evening, waiting, leisurely, for the fourth in their party to show up so they could settle the tab and head their respective ways. However, when J.T. came back from the bathroom, he didn't come alone. On his arm, tipsy and a bit sheepish, was the woman who'd walked in earlier with Valerie.

This young lady got lost, said J.T., pulling up a chair from a nearby table. I told her there was some country boys in here from East Tennessee who got lost in the big city too.

This restaurant is so big, the woman said, looking at the other men at the table. I did get lost coming out of the bathroom. But I'm pretty sure I would have found my way back to my table sooner or later.

Said Roland: My brother can find em who aren't lost, get em lost, and claim to have saved the day when he brings em back to the spot where he first abducted them.

You sound like you speak from experience, said the senator.

His first victim. First one he led down the primrose path. It is my tender baby shoes that first trampled the briars, first knocked down the weeds, of his merry road to excess and waste.

And now you're running for governor, said the young lady.

My point exactly, said Roland. Were I an only child, I'd be leading an honest life.

During the whole of this, Teague said not a word. He watched Roland take a clean wine glass from a setting at the table behind him and fill a glass for the woman, thirtyish, thin and attractive, with eyes that were not quite so unfamiliar with this scene as one might first expect. Her name was Monique.

Now she looked at Teague and said: And you're Mike Teague. Valerie just told me that.

Teague said nothing but did manage to nod his head. Then the woman turned to Senator Kirkwood. And are you in politics too?

I am, said Senator Kirkwood. I am a lawyer by trade but a politician by perverse inclination. In my current capacity, I am the senior senator from the bluff city of Memphis, unrecognized capital of Mississippi and birthplace of the blues.

To this, Monique did not reply.

Said Senator Kirkwood: They keep trying to put me in a white jacket and have me fetch steaks, but I keep fending them off.

Oh, said Monique. Well, it's nice to meet you.

Can you join us for a nightcap? said Roland. We've been looking at ugly men all night. At least I have. You'd be a welcome addition.

Monique eyed the open chair, the glass of wine sitting before it. Let me get my friend, she said.

TEAGUE IS UNCOOL

Senator Kirkwood was long gone, had left for some ill-defined late-night meeting nearly an hour before. He had left with much shaking of hands and an understanding, Teague knew, that there was more to be discussed in regards to the Memphis electoral vote and the prospect of bringing a World's Fair to Glennville and how, again, it might benefit the good people of the Bluff City. And, as an afterthought, perhaps a little more on the buying of stock from the First Bank of Glennville.

Teague wondered why he didn't leave as well, why, in fact, he hadn't followed the senator out the door. He'd had the chance. Valerie had arrived, they'd exchanged pleasant-enough greetings, he'd stayed for a polite-enough time, and laughed at J.T.'s stories, Roland's addendums and corrections to same. Strange, strange, strange to so enjoy one's misery. Like working a loose tooth. He sat there with a sick feeling in his stomach, jealous, embarrassed, mortified, and reckless. He would sleep with Valerie tonight. He would whip Roland's ass. Because that's the way the pairings were going now. J.T. and Monique and Roland and Valerie. Predictable of Valerie, her choice of men. J.T. was not quite enough of a complication. But Roland. Roland, he might and he might not acquiesce. He probably would. He most probably would. But the chance that he would not. The bit withheld in the eyes, the part that spoke of loneliness. Valerie would fix him. Would fix herself. And Teague would whip Roland's ass.

And then he'd take Valerie for himself.

Oh what a fucking idiot he was.

Oh what a fucking high-schooler.

So leave. Get up and say goodbye and don't sit here with that obvious fake smile on your face. Go home. Go to your hotel room. You've had too much to drink. You're tired. Your back hurts. You're going to say something that will cost you a lot of money. You're going to make an ass of yourself.

Go home. Leave.

Your inertia is a thing to behold.

Your masochism is something for the ages.

AND SO GOODBYE

J.T. said: Teague, you coming with us?

Teague shook his head in the negative.

Now ladies, where are we going again?

The Zebra Room, said Monique. It's a private club, so they can serve after hours. Great piano player too. Don't they, Valerie?

Of the four, she seemed the least worse for wear, sitting erect at the table, her fine chin tipped a little upward as was her habit when listening, her profile a siren in the sea for Teague to look at without cessation as he sat like a wilted flower, like, yes, a brooding schoolboy to her side, slumped in his chair and needing to go home. Oh why doesn't he go home? thought Valerie. This is just bad form. Just not what you'd expect from Teague at all.

Yes, said Valerie. Yes, the piano player is very good. But you'll have to go on without me. I'm afraid I'm a little too tired to make the trek.

A discussion of automobiles, routes, riders, and destinations ensued. Valerie had ridden with Monique. Monique wanted to go to the Zebra Room. The Coles had ridden together.

I can give you a ride home, said Roland.

Teague moved in his chair. The chair squeaked and he said nothing and there was a moment of reflected silence at the table. But only a moment.

If you're sure it's no trouble.

It's no trouble, said Roland.

You're sure?

I'm sure.

You'll miss the piano player. He really is fabulous.

It's past my bedtime anyway. And it might ruin my reputation to be seen after hours when I'm up for election.

Nobody who'd see you at the Zebra Room would care, said Valerie laughing. And instinctively she looked at Teague. They'd spent many a night there, especially early on.

Might get you some votes even, said Teague.

Roland smiled, seemed to intuit Teague's unusual mood of this late portion of the evening.

No, said Teague. You're right. You best get on back. And give this young lady a lift home on your way.

Attaboy, thought Valerie. Now that's the Teague I know. Can't eat cake and have it too. Oh it was getting so awkward before. But that's a good rally for the old boy. Is he getting old? Old-seeming? Jumped the gun on the midlife crisis a few years back and doesn't know what to do now that the real one's knocking at the door. But. Eat your cake. Or have your cake. It was your call, big boy. Your call alone.

You're going to stick Monique with me? said J.T. Alone?

This isn't her first rodeo, said Valerie.

Second rodeo, said Monique. And the first one wasn't that good.

OH YES, ONE OTHER THING

Roland and Valerie in a hotel room. Drinks. Room service. Dialogue.

So you know Teague from before?

Yes. I was his mistress.

Ah. Well.

It was a long time ago.

It's none of my business.

But it was a long time ago. Like another life ago.

Roland nodded.

And you're married too.

Yes, Roland said. I am.

I seem to have a particular weakness.

Roland moved from the chair and joined her where she sat on the bed.

I don't plan it. I don't set out to like married men. It just seems to work out that way. It's complicated.

Roland put his hand on her hand.

It sounds complicated, he said.

Things progress as things do in the late hours of a hotel bedroom.

Knock on door.

Room service.

After a while, a muffled shout:

Leave it outside the door.

Debutantes

They were sitting at a patio table out by the Teagues' pool, drinking cocktails and listening to stories of J.T. and Corrine's early courting days. The women were drinking margaritas, the men gin and tonics. The night was breezy and surprisingly cool, one of those rare summer nights in Glennville before a storm that make the person sitting outside feel light and energetic and thin in the bones, as one feels when autumn gives its first hint of arrival. Clouds zipped overhead double speed as in a motion picture. Stars between the clouds brighter for the brevity of their appearance, peeking here and yon and seemingly in motion, the optical illusion of the racing clouds moving the star a fraction in the sky, joined now by another one, then covered again, until it is too dizzying to look at the sky. And the tree frogs in full chorus, steady and shrill, obstinate and obsessive. The cicadas scattered, electric, competing music then distracted or resting or satisfied and quiet for a time. Wind chimes whistling and clanging in the air and the women making jokes about havoc wreaked on hair. The smell of chlorine, faint and clean, honeysuckle on the breeze, the hint, just the faintest trace, of musky mold in the table umbrella above.

The doorbell rang, a delicate trilling of chimes. Well, here's our first victim, said Jan.

Corrine rose from the table and following Jan's lead headed for the sliding glass door and into the main foyer to greet whichever date had arrived first.

If he's good-looking, hollered J.T., you gals just keep him for your-selves. If he's a poor ugly bastard like me, send him on back for a snort.

The boy at the door was not a poor ugly bastard, the women soon dis-covered, but a tall and handsome young man who looked as if he should be swashbuckling across the silver screen or whatever it was that teen movie heroes did these days. Corrine found herself staring at the boy and blocking the door when Jan invited him in. She forced out a smile and threw back her arm in an awkward attempt at a welcoming gesture. This was the best antidote she could muster to the openmouthed nature of her gaze. Sarah didn't have boys like this by the house. Sarah had boys by the house rarely, in fact, usually friends of friends dropping by to sample the movie room J.T. had created in the basement.

Jan called upstairs for her daughter and was told in response that final preparations were under way and she'd be down in a minute.

Rather than subject the boy to the hazing ritual waiting out by the pool, the women took him into the kitchen for a soft drink and some chit-chat. In a few minutes, the doorbell rang again. Corrine left Jan Teague with the handsome young man in the kitchen and went to the door. Now, standing on the welcome mat, a boy similar in age to the one in the kitchen. There the likenesses ended. Awkward downward glancing smile, ill-fitting tuxedo, face without a feature of distinction, save, perhaps, the stunted chin awash in a patch of fresh pimples. The poor pitiful sad sack, riding his teenage misery like a horse that won't gallop.

Come in, Corrine said smiling.

The boy, Dean, was led into the kitchen where he shook hands with the teen hero and smiled with embarrassment at Jan who fussed over him and said how handsome he looked in his tuxedo. Corrine felt ashamed she hadn't done the same. It wasn't like her. She was usually on the lookout for those needing a compliment or a passing smile.

Yes, said Corrine, you look very handsome.

Then she said: Jan, let's leave the daughters with the old farts and take these young men to the dance instead.

And then a bit more of that kind of thing from Corrine, overdoing it for her earlier snub, her earlier disappointment. Had her disappointment shown to the boy? Had the look on her face made him drop his head and shuffle his feet? The thought made her head swim for a moment and she found that her drink glass was empty. It's not a competition, she thought, the manifest differences in their daughters' dates. She wasn't like that. She and her friends in the old subdivision had laughed at those types of women. Where was this coming from, this striving?

From upstairs came the call, *we're almost ready*. And the mothers and the boys walked out to the foyer to see the young ladies make their entrance. At first all Corrine saw was the gleaming white of formal dresses. And then she saw an abstract version of girls walking down a wide staircase. She was shocked by the image. Julie Teague looked like something from a fairy tale, a figure of feminine form out of an animator's imagination. The young woman smiled at Corrine. And then came the call, *hey Mom*, from Sarah, and Corrine realized she'd yet to look at her own daughter. She turned and found the other image just as enthralling, made so by its absolute unfamiliarity in form and presence with the image beside it. She looked at one and then at the other. And then the girls were at the bottom of the stairs. She felt the need to do something. She placed her fresh drink on a table and came over and began straightening a shoulder strap on Sarah's dress that hadn't before been out of place. Well, just look at you, she said to her daughter, caressing her hair, smiling, trying for some reason not to look again at Julie Teague. You look just beautiful, she said.

Oh Mom, said Sarah, approximating a blush, acting out some scene from a teenage movie with fluttering, overattentive mothers and their exasperated pubescent offspring.

The chinless boy came up and handed Sarah her corsage. Corrine took the corsage and began poking around with it, trying to find the best spot on the dress for its display. Nearby, the teen hero and the fairy princess were going through the same ritual, with Jan acting as attendant. The men came in and began fussing over their daughters, issuing hyperbolically early curfew times and so forth. It was comic fodder and there was much laughter and bustle. Corrine felt like crying. Her daughter looked huge, hulking. She called for more pictures. Her daughter didn't know how to stand or walk or how to smile at a boy. Three feet away Julie Teague was at ease as only beautiful women can be when dressed to the nines and cameras are about. Corrine felt something like hate for her. A feeling exacerbated perhaps by the girl's humility and lack of pretension. She either didn't know she was beautiful or didn't care. Through it all J.T. complimented their daughter and her date while snapping pictures at breakneck speed. The smile on his face was genuine and his delight in the proceedings complete.

Corrine excused herself to go to the bathroom.

Where she sat on the lid of the toilet and cried for only a minute or two. Everywhere she looked were little towels and fancy, colorful, scallop-shaped soap. The bathroom was the color of the ocean at dawn and someone's grandmother had embroidered the delicate curtains over the window. She daubed her eyes roughly with one of the small towels and laughed ruefully at herself, the ridiculousness of her parental vanity and shame.

Sun God

They sat out on the veranda of the country club, looking through the warm lamplight out over the bluff and the hazy image of the river below. The debutantes had been presented and the ballroom dance floor was now crowded with couples, the young ones having overcome shyness, their parents sobriety. Sarah had done well, looking sharp and alive when her name was called, meeting her escort at the foot of the dais with a well-timed and winning smile, then making the long walk through the tunnel of people on either side with a poise that Corrine didn't know she possessed. And her date had proven equally poised, knowing instinctively how to be present and attentive, but ceding the floor to the woman of the hour. Many of the boys had winked or waved at friends as they strolled past, or too quickly and cockily swaggered down the promenade, unmindful of their dates in high heels, their dates who'd been looking forward to this moment in the spotlight for many months now. Sarah's date had walked a casual quarter step behind, his presence probably unnoticed by most. His was a quieter kind of masculinity, humble but solid, one that could grow slowly on a woman, one that took a few years of seasoning to appreciate.

Corrine felt embarrassed by her reaction at the Teagues'. She'd missed the boat and mistaken shyness for lack of substance. What a bundle of nerves she was.

She forced the thought from her mind. The lovely night they'd first enjoyed on the Teagues' patio had followed them uptown. Sarah had been perfect, more polished in a crowd, especially a crowd such as this, than her parents would have even considered at sixteen.

Jan Teague was at another of the multitude of tables on the veranda, visiting with friends. Which left only Teague, J.T., and Corrine at their corner table nearest the bar. When no one else was waiting, J.T. could lean back, hand over a glass and denomination, and retrieve what drinks his crew needed from the amused bartender without ever having to leave his seat. Corrine tried to recall a bartender, secretary, anyone in the service industry that didn't warm to her husband immediately, but couldn't do so. Say what you would about him, he had a soft touch for the working people.

Teague said: Okay, so you need a symbol. Something that resonates with the proposed theme of the fair and something that will be used as a landmark for the city from here after.

J.T. turned to Corrine. See, I told you. The only way to free Teague's mind is to put him in his natural environment. I knew once we got him to the country club his faculties would improve.

Ignore him, Teague.

Oh, I do, said Teague. I do. But okay. The theme for the fair is energy. So you need something in that neck of the woods.

Right, said J.T. Exactly. What about hydroelectric power? Considering we're in the Tennessee Valley, that seems appropriate.

Too New Deal, said Teague. We need something more modern.

Atomic? Use a big explosion as our symbol. Or windmills? Get a bunch of Dutch tulips and a little boy sticking his finger in the dike.

Teague took a sip from his cocktail, then placed it on the table. He sat against the flowered landscape of the veranda and pushed his chair back till it was flush with the short wall behind him. Corrine noticed for the first time the distinct smell of mulch. And then, somewhere closer to the river, the smell of honeysuckle.

I've been thinking about it all week, said Teague. I even did a little research down at the library.

He said this with a smile and waited for J.T. to comment.

All right, said J.T. smiling, not taking the bait. What did you come up with?

Helios.

What?

Helios. The Greek god of the sun. He drove a chariot across the sky every morning and night. Solar energy would be our tie-in.

A Greek god? said J.T. I don't know. They might run us out of town as pagans.

Greek and Roman gods are defunct. We'd be okay.

Shew, said J.T. I like the tie-in with the sun. But Helios?

J.T. pronounced this word in his most exaggerated fashion, mirroring what he anticipated local reaction would be. *What the hell's a He-lee-oss?*

Corrine found J.T.'s hand across the table. She patted that hand. She said: I think it's a great idea. It's like Vulcan down in Birmingham.

Yeah, said J.T. And that always struck me as a little presumptuous for a city like Birmingham.

Do you remember taking the kids there when we went down for the ball game?

Yes.

Do you remember how much they liked it, how cool they thought it was?

I do.

If the kids like it, they're happy. If they're happy, the parents are happy. Isn't that what you're looking for when you're trying to entertain millions of people?

Yeah, okay. I see your point.

Trust me, said Corrine. Women will like it. A Greek god? What woman doesn't like a Greek god? Also this. Who picks our summer vacation every year?

You and the kids.

Okay, said Corrine, I rest my case. Actually, I rest Teague's case. It's a winner.

J.T. handed his empty glass back to the barman and in a moment got a fresh one in return. He said: What about the cost? Birmingham couldn't afford to build Vulcan today with the price of steel.

Make it an observation tower like the Space Needle, said Teague. So you just build the tower and put a statue of Helios and the horse and chariot on top of that.

J.T. nodded. He was coming around.

Call it the Sun Tower, said Teague. Observation deck, maybe a small restaurant, then the statue on top of that. That doesn't sound too expensive.

No, said J.T. We might be able to swing that.

Said Corrine: I got our slogan. *Glennville: your chariot to the world.*

J.T. looked over at her. Then he looked at Teague. What do you think?

It's good. Short and catchy. That one will be hard to beat.

J.T. said the phrase aloud. He nodded his head forcefully and handed a bill and an empty glass back to the bartender. Then he came around the table and hugged his wife about the shoulders. He leaned down and kissed her full on the mouth. He turned to Teague and said: Right here's the brains of the operation.

Said Teague: Tell me something I didn't know.

The Fourth of July

Already hot and the dogs in town are off the streets and under shade trees, front porches, the long beds of pickup trucks. The bunting, red, white, and blue, stretches taut across the street, affixed to ten or so light poles running up and down either side of the road. At this early hour only slow-moving pedestrians can be seen and the occasional child bicyclist lazily tracing the route the floats, fire engines, and Shriners figure-eighting in tiny cars will take here in a few hours. Some of the smarter children scout for the best posts from which to collect the candy and doo-dads tossed in great handfuls from the passing parade. Lawn chairs have claimed the shady spots on the route and folks busy about icing coolers and spreading blankets, the odd engineer among them rigging a canopy on poles, the quick and sure hammer on stake, the *little tighter, little tighter, almost there*, to the tallest in the group holding the frame until all the ropes are staked and pulled tight. The air is shimmering already over the street, molecules indolent with water, a trick on the eye, the wavy and hazy heat made visible. The town seems void of cats, seems also to have drugged the children, such is their early morning polite shuffle among the adults, instincts telling them to save energy. Long day ahead. Longest day of the year of unsupervised fun. Watermelon-eating contests, pie-eating contests, prizes, rides on the fire trucks, food and yet more food, and fireworks, yes yes yes fireworks, like sacks of favorite candy waiting in trunks of cars, garages, back pockets. And so the children sit now, mutely and at ease, on the spread blankets, waiting for an errand run, an unlamented errand run, to the car for the forgotten jug of lemonade. Savvy children. Wily beyond our knowing. Fireworks, yes, oh hell yes.

At the town square, where the parade will begin, is a plywood platform, ablaze in the colors of the day and more flags, limp and moist-looking, than could casually be tallied. Just this side of the platform is the city park, and then the highway heading west as far as you want to go, Pacific Ocean notwithstanding. In the park, several people move about an aluminum refreshment stand on wheels, readying soda tanks, attaching them to the plastic fountain dispensers, unsleeving plastic cups, emptying ice into large aluminum bins. Beside the stand, three long tables covered in red and white plastic checkerboard. On the table, buns and more buns, take your pick hot dog or hamburger, and jar upon jar of condiments: mustard, mayonnaise, ketchup. Those wanting pickles, relish, onions, or other will have to bring their own. In back of the tables are two of the largest charcoal grills to be found, briquettes already in place, waiting only for lighter fluid and match. In front of the refreshment area stand two women, attractive and in their twenties and not from around here, who are arranging buttons, bumper stickers, pencils, coin holders, key rings, and plastic envelope openers. All of these things will be given away free of charge. All of these things are emblazoned with the simple phrase: **Cole for Governor.** Indeed, that is the phrase of the day, and it is to be seen in huge bold letters—**Cole for Governor**—across the speaking platform, and on the hats and shirts of the people in the refreshment stand, the men readying the charcoal grills, and, of course, the attractive young women arranging the giveaways. Everything at this end of the street is free: CoCo-las, hot dogs, trinkets. And, yes, the speeches too. A county clerk, a school superintendent, a mayor not even up for reelection, a state representative, and, cause celebre, a hometown boy running for governor.

In The Pickle Jar

FADE IN

INT: PECK'S STORE AND BEER JOINT; FORMERLY THE COLE
FAMILY DRY GOODS STORE—DAY

Though the store is more a relic than anything, kept open for nostalgia
more than profit, and as a place for the casual drinking of beer by longtime residents of the town, there are still tins of CANNED ITEMS on the
dusty shelves, an assortment of DIME-STORE CANDY, long floor coolers that hum and rattle slightly when the cooling mechanism starts up
again, a mishmash of assorted tools and utensils on shelves, a glass case
filled with a hundred different kinds of POCKETKNIVES, a few sports
pennants from the high school team, and a thousand other odds and
ends that seem unlikely to be sold anytime soon. In the corner a WARM
MORNING STOVE sits like a bucolic Buddha. In the opposite corner, a
JUKEBOX. In between is a space large enough for dancing, should anyone care to. Overhead, three FANS turn in syncopated rhythm. Above
the booths on the back wall, a large banner: COLE FOR GOVERNOR.
Working the counter is PECK himself. Behind him is his back room where
he does his TAXIDERMY work. Several locals sit at the booths, rustic
OLD-TIMERS to a man, saying little, at ease and enjoying themselves.
J.T. plays CHECKERS with Earl, one of the old-timers at the booth farthest from the door. Earl works a large QUID of tobacco. TEAGUE and
ROLAND stand at the COUNTER talking to the TV MAN, who has just
driven up from Atlanta.

TV MAN

So, I was thinking we could start out getting some
footage of you at the old home place. Walking the
fields, surveying the barn, petting the dog, that sort
of thing. You do have a dog?

ROLAND

We have a dog.

TV MAN

A big one, right? Like a Lab or a golden retriever.
Something like that. A proper farm dog, you know.

ROLAND

(smiling over the man's shoulder at his brother and the old-timers
at the booth)

We have a proper farm dog. She's a setter. An English
setter. But she'll do, I reckon.

J.T. gets up from his checker game in an animated fashion and makes his
way over to the counter, the OLD-TIMERS behind him SMILING as he
goes.

J.T.

You reckon? You can't have a more Tennessee-looking
dog than Queen. She's pretty as hell, just like Tennesseans are.

Quiet LAUGHTER from the booth. The TV man smiles, though he's not
quite in on the joke.

ROLAND

Didn't her grandmother bite you one time?

More laughs all around, TV man included.

> J.T.
> (BEAT)
> And like Tennesseans, Queenie and her kin are as nice
> as can be. Until (raising a finger, setting his eyes in
> mock-sincerity) . . . until you do something to us that
> we don't think you ought to be doing.

> ROLAND
> You just petted her, didn't you?

> J.T.
> You never pet a sleeping dog. I knew that. Especially
> an old one. She was about twelve at the time. You can't
> pet an old dog when she's asleep.

> ROLAND
> Duchess just had a mean streak.

> J.T.
> Hell, so do I. So do Tennesseans.

> ROLAND
> I promise not to pet you when you're sleeping.

> J.T.
> That's a good decision. And (placing his hand on the
> TV man's shoulder) Queen has a mind of her own.
> She won't just do whatever it is you want her to do.
> She's got to want to do it too. She's got to think it's the
> right thing to do.

The TV man looks at Teague for a moment, Teague who set this whole thing up. To the producer's beseeching look, Teague offers a smile void of empathy or kinship, a smile void of everything but a creasing of lips, passing the buck on back from whence it came.

> J.T.
> Queen's not just going to jump in a cold river because you say the quail's in there. She likes her eyes better than yours. She's going to spot that bird first, then head in. If that doesn't work out, then in she'll go and stay in till the bird is found or you call her out. And even when you call her out, she might not come.
>
> (BEAT)
> She aims to finish what she starts.

> ROLAND
> (nodding in an insincere fashion)
> Big brother's right. She's a damn fine Tennessee dog.

> J.T.
> The perfect Tennessee dog. The epitome, the embodiment, of her two-legged friends in the state.

> ROLAND
> (BEAT)
> Sounds like the dog should be running for governor.

> J.T.
> That's what I'm implying.

J.T. walks back to the booth, to Earl and the waiting checkerboard.

TV MAN

Listen, if you all think this is a waste of time. If you
think it's just a bunch of, just a bunch of bullshit, then
I'll just pack up now and be on my way.

ROLAND

No, now, come on. My brother's giving me a hard time,
not you. We're glad you're here. We hired you to do a
job and we're going to let you do your job.

J.T.
(from the table, eyeing the checkerboard)
We hired Teague too. And I still don't know what
he does. Make him be the gaffer or something. Best
boy or what have you. Otherwise we're paying him to
drink iced tea and smoke cigarettes.

Teague laughs, as do Roland and the others. The TV MAN appears to be
smoothing his ruffled feathers.

ROLAND

Ignore the jackass in the corner. He's been against this
idea from the go. Thinks my opponent has already
aced us out on the good-old-boy routine and this
will look like we're copying him. He thinks it looks
desperate.

J.T.
Teague's got some extra overalls if yall need em.

TV MAN
(looking at Teague)
I thought this was all agreed-upon. We talked about
this several times over the phone. I'm just going with

what you all brought me. I could care less if he's in
overalls, a suit, or a leather corset.

TEAGUE
(laughing)
We're going with the agreed-upon plan. Roland here
okayed it, Roland is on board. I'm on board. Everyone
is on board but that fellow over there. It's very simple.
Just a slice of life. Show the roots, where Roland came
from. A look at the farm, a look at the town, some
shots of Roland talking to folks in and around the
Fourth of July celebration.

J.T.
Chewing tobacco, whittling, skinning a possum.

ROLAND
You all work it out. I'm game for whatever our man
from Atlanta suggests.

Roland walks outside as J.T. looks at the checkerboard with feigned Bobby
Fischer intensity. The man across from him, Earl, has spoken no word
since the game began, his only articulation a THHHHT of contemplative
TOBACCO JUICE into an empty bottle after each hurried and impatient
move by J.T.

TV MAN
(motioning toward J.T.)
What does he want us to do?

TEAGUE
He thinks, as Roland said, that it will look at this
late stage like we're copying our opponent. Since the

campaign began, every commercial he runs shows
him in railroading overalls visiting one rustic setting
after another. Via old-timey steam locomotive. This
is galling for two reasons: One, our opponent is about
as rural as you are. He's more the Izod and penny
loafer type. And two, the hokey railroad motif was
my idea four years ago when I was the consultant for
the opponent.

TV MAN
Aah.

J.T.
What did he pay you again, Teague? (He jumps a black
checker into the back row.) King me if you will, Earl.

TEAGUE
So he's liable to be a pain in the ass all day. Just ignore
him. That's what the rest of us do.

J.T.
At their peril, Earl. They ignore me at their peril. Why,
you sly fox. They get me distracted and you put me
in the pickle jar. I reckon if I did nothing but play
checkers ten, fifteen hours a day, I could learn a few
moves like that.

EARL SMILES, lets fly a sly jet of amber fluid.

J.T.
In the pickle jar, Earl. Sealed tight. Floating in a vat of
vinegar. How many hours a week you spend playing
checkers?

                         TV MAN
                         (to J.T.)
Excuse me, I hate to interrupt the game. But I'm curious, what would you have done for this spot? What
was your idea?

                          J.T.
I'm in the pickle jar here, can't you see? Ole Earl has
sealed it tight. You ever know a man to play checkers
for a living?

                         TV MAN
Seriously. I'd like to know. Maybe we can work it in.

                          J.T.
Pickles to the left of me, pickles to the right.

                         TV MAN
                        (to Teague)
                       Do you know?

                         TEAGUE
                          I do.

                         TV MAN
                          And?

                         TEAGUE
                         (BEAT)
Roland with the wife and kids coming out of church.
Then cut to a shot of the bank building, the camera
panning up, catching the sun off the windows, etc.
Then show Roland and family coming into the lobby,
Roland opening the front door with a key, kids spilling

into the lobby and racing to punch the elevator key. Then coming out of the elevator and racing to Dad's office window, Roland and Libby following behind, to look out over the river and all of downtown Glennville. Roland tousles a kid's hair, turns to Libby, and points out over the horizon. Then the voice-over: *A man of values, a man of vision, a man for Tennessee.*

TV MAN

It's not bad. Especially the kids racing for the elevator.

TEAGUE

No, not bad. Takes all the negative stuff they've been saying about Roland being a big moneyman, a slick businessman, and turns it all around. Instead of running from the charge, you take it straight on, and flip it to a positive. Progress and values in the same package.

TV MAN

That's really not bad. So why are you doing this downhome number instead?

TEAGUE

We're trying to reclaim Roland's natural constituency, the rural folks. If we don't make a dent there, we're dead. Roland will take Nashville and Memphis, no problem. Montgomery will take Glennville. And Chattanooga is up for grabs. But this state's still got more people outside of the cities than in. The other thing is that Roland and Libby didn't want to use the kids. They didn't want the kids under the microscope any more than they have to be.

TV MAN

We could do it without the kids.

TEAGUE

Then it's just a rich guy and his wife entering a huge building and looking out over the land. A bit world-by-the-tail, don't you think?

TV MAN

A bit. Maybe we could splice up some of the bank building stuff with the farm stuff and show the well-rounded modern southern man. Hasn't forgotten his roots, but has adapted to modern world and all that it entails.

TEAGUE

That might work. I'll run it by Roland. But no kids.

TV MAN

No kids, I got you. Just anything to take the shine off the country boy who's made himself a little money.

TEAGUE

You can have old money and you can have no money. But you damn sure can't have new money.

J.T.

(with his head frozen over the checkerboard)
In the pickle jar, Earl. Floating in a tart and briny sea.

FADE OUT

The Commercial

Libby Cole stared into the pantry, trying to find a snack to hold her over till the camera crew had come and gone and she could have a proper lunch. She'd slept late and now the plates were all put away and the coffeepot empty. Breakfast was always so heavy at the farm, and she was not much of a breakfast person. She came out of the pantry empty-handed and put on water to boil for tea, wondering where Mrs. Cole and Corrine were and when Roland would be back from town with the television people. They hadn't decided, Libby and Roland, whether she'd be in the commercial or not. She didn't care one way or another, but wanted to know what she was to wear, were she to be included, because each of the potential five outfits, from business-sophisticated all the way to picnic-at-the-farm, would likely be creased a bit from the trip down, and she wasn't going to iron five separate outfits.

It was rare for her to have the kitchen to herself and as she went about slicing lemons for the tea, she found its never-changing décor homey and relaxing. She decided to unload the dishwasher when the load was done. Then she decided that the lingering after-smell of country ham and redeye gravy was something she could do without for the rest of her life.

In the refrigerator she found cottage cheese and sat down at the table for a bite. Back when she was in the public eye, back before she met Roland and was something of an up-and-comer as a Broadway singer, she could go days on cottage cheese, cigarettes, chewing gum, and coffee. Her manager then had stressed the importance of a trim figure. Two girls with good voices, tie goes to the thin gal. What a talker he'd been. Leaving Broadway for some hick in the sticks? The next Dinah Shore? Right when we're making some progress? Well, sweetheart, that's true dumb love for you. The truest and dumbest kind of love there is. If you don't get pregnant in the first month or so and change your mind, you've got my number. I'll take you back. Otherwise, good luck and tell em hey on the farm for me.

Libby smiled at the memory. Emmanuel Hines was his name. The water came to a boil and she went again to the pantry for a tea pitcher. When she came back to the kitchen, Corrine stood at the dishwasher, pulling out steaming plates, drying them off with a towel, and placing them into the cabinet.

Let me do that, Libby said.

Corrine turned and said, oh hey, good morning. How'd you sleep?

Fine, said Libby, pouring the boiling water into the pitcher. But let me get those dishes.

It's no trouble.

I haven't done a thing since I got here.

I'm halfway home, said Corrine, turning back to the dishwasher. I'll give you dibs on the next load.

Libby dropped the tea bags into the pitcher and looked out the window where Sis and Mrs. Cole were corralling chickens, Mrs. Cole with much waving of hands, shooing forward, and stomping of foot, Sis calmly and steadily heading them off and tightening the circle like an Australian sheepdog. Mrs. Cole stopped once to smile at Sis without Sis seeing, appreciative it seemed of her calm, her ontological ease among the feathered chaos, and then Mrs. Cole, mother of the Democratic candidate for governor, was again whisking and shooing and caring not where her shoe might next step.

Emmanuel Hines had said she could be the next Dinah Shore.

What time are the TV people coming out? Corrine asked.

In an hour or so, if they're running on time, said Libby.

Do you need any help? Do you have your outfit picked out?

I'm not sure I'm even going to be in the commercial. But if I am, I want to see what Roland's wearing and what the director has in mind. I brought several things.

Well if you need any help, I'm free. Can iron a skirt or whatever you need. I'm so used to having the kids underfoot, I don't know what to do with myself when I get a free weekend. I'm thinking about a long bath and a cold bottle of champagne. From here on out, if anybody needs me, I'm upstairs in the tub.

We should all go out tonight, said Libby. Just the four of us. We haven't done that in so long. I can't remember the last time.

It has been a long time, said Corrine, drying a frying pan and placing it under the stove. But I'm betting they'll need to kiss babies up until the midnight hour. Or at least that's what they'll claim. And after that, they'll just want to go up to the store and listen to old football stories or play cards with Cut Worm and Duncan and the rest of that old crew.

Let's go with them then, Libby said.

Corrine turned and looked at her. From the look on her face, it was as if she'd suggested they go squirrel hunting first thing in the morning. Corrine smiled and then Libby found herself smiling too.

Said Corrine: You want to sit there and listen to the same stories we've heard fifty times before?

Not really, said Libby. But I think I would like to get out of the house.

I'd rather take a beating than stay in this house another night, said Corrine. Trust me, I've had enough of crickets chirping and WSM to last me a lifetime. So I'm in. Write it down and put it in your shoe, we're going out tonight one way or another.

As Corrine was saying this, the phone rang and it was Corrine who went to answer. Hello, she said. Hello. Who's there? Hello.

Corrine stood looking at the phone as if it might suddenly speak and say something worthy of a brisk slap across the face. Libby turned away. Behind her, the mumbling and muttering had commenced.

They didn't say anything, said Corrine.

Libby nodded and tried to think of something to say.

Do you know the number of the store? asked Corrine.

Libby said that she did not.

Did she know what time J.T. and Roland were supposed to be home?

Soon, said Libby, looking about the kitchen for some task, some distraction. Corrine's public boils were something she'd married into, but she'd risk no comment or gesture that might draw her into one of Corrine's dramas. Libby didn't know for sure what Roland did when he was away from home. She had a good idea, but knew nothing for sure. She might leave him one day. She might stick it out. The one thing she knew was that she'd never say a word about it, about Roland's actions, to another living person.

Unfortunately, there was no way, absolutely no way, to leave the room at the moment. But then Libby caught a break. The voice of Mrs. Cole talking to Sis could be heard just on the other side of the breezeway door.

They're coming in, Libby said, the words sounding desperate to her ears, obvious, the words saying, for all apparent purposes, please shut up, do please keep some things private.

Did the phone ring? asked Mrs. Cole.

It did, said Corrine. But they never said anything.

We had a couple of those last night, Mrs. Cole said, beginning now to wash her hands in the sink. Sis stood in the doorway listening for a moment to the conversation about prank phone calls. Then she turned and walked back out the door from whence she came. Libby watched her troop out toward the chicken house, then on toward the old, original, barn. Through the window, she noticed the corn for the first time of the summer. Odd, she thought, not to have noticed it sooner.

They didn't hang up right away, said Corrine, sitting down at the table and lighting a cigarette.

Mrs. Cole didn't like smoking in the house. Corrine didn't like going outside to smoke every time the urge hit. Libby decided to count to fifty then excuse herself to get ready for the television people.

Kids probably, said Mrs. Cole.

Uh-huh, said Corrine, watching the smoke spiral up from her long cigarette. Kids. That's probably it. Seems like they're calling and hanging up every time we come down.

Well, said Mrs. Cole.

We get quite a few hang-ups in Glennville too. Must be a fad these days, with kids. Used to be, back when we were kids, we'd ask if your refrigerator was running. Or if you had Prince Albert in a can. You remember those?

Mrs. Cole smiled.

Nowadays, the fun part is just hanging up I guess.

Mrs. Cole went to the dishwasher, opened it. Why someone put my dishes up, she said.

Corrine, said Libby.

Well thank you Corrine. It's so nice to have help in the kitchen.

Corrine waved a handful of red nails and looked out the kitchen window. My pleasure, she said.

Libby said, I believe I'll go upstairs and start getting ready for our guests.

Corrine said, let me know if you need something ironed or need me to run to the store for anything.

Thank you, said Libby, turning to leave. I'll call you if I need any help.

She'd almost made it to the steps when she heard a match lighting in the kitchen. Then Corrine hollered: We're still on for tonight, remember? It's girls' night out.

Libby checked her step. To her right was a photo of Mr. and Mrs. Cole with two chubby children in their arms. It was a studio photo, one of those old black and whites that had been tinted, the colors on baby Roland's jumper an unusual greenish hue, J.T.'s clip-on tie a red never before seen on the color spectrum. The Coles looked too young to be as serious as they were and too serious to be as young as they were. The colors of their clothes were muted, and it was impossible to tell if the drabness was the artist's rendition, a fading with time, or simply the colors the young Coles had chosen to wear for the first family portrait. Regardless, it was the boys who stood out, Roland's chubby smiling baby face, J.T. slightly sullen with the tie and the slicking of his hair.

Libby, can you hear me?

Yes, said Libby, without really enough volume. We're still on.

———

Teague stood in the shade at the backside of the carport. He was smoking a cigarette and thinking how thirsty it made him to smoke a cigarette. It was damn hot. How Roland was not sweating was something he'd been working his mind over for about an hour now. He checked his watch. The parade would be starting in three hours. So far they'd filmed Roland walking along the cornfields clad in new jeans, broken-in cowboy boots, and a golf shirt. Teague was not sure what look was intended here, for Roland looked ill-dressed to drive the tractor or to negotiate a dogleg left. And his hair bespoke less humble agricultural background than oysters Rockefeller at Tavern on the Green. The TV man now suggested that Roland take the wheel of the tractor.

In this getup? said Roland.

If he's supposed to be a farmer's son doing some actual work on the farm, get him some overalls and a John Deere cap, said Teague. Let him look the part. Right now he looks like a lost golfer or a bad farmer. I can't tell which.

I'm not wearing overalls, said Roland.

Sitting on the hood of his Cadillac, which he'd driven over the yard and into the field where the camera crew had set up, J.T. began to laugh.

Then Roland did too. I'll be damned, he said. I spend forty-two years trying to get out of a pair of dusty overalls and now that's all they want me to wear.

Which is it then? said the TV man. Once and for all. Farmer on the farm? Or businessman back home on a tourist excursion?

Teague, said Roland, this is what I'm paying you for. How do you beat a man in overalls in the great state of Tennessee? Where's my overalls? Metaphorically speaking, I mean.

Your opponent's wearing them, said Teague. But here's what I say. We start with Roland and Libby driving up the driveway. The family meets them in the driveway. Mother, sister, brother, and sister-in-law. Corrine's here, right?

You asking me? said J.T.

Yes, said Teague.

Well she drove down with me last night. Your guess is as good as mine whether she's still on the premises.

Car's still here, said Teague.

She's liable to have taken off afoot. Horseback. Stolen mule.

Let's assume she's here.

Fine, said J.T. But I'll go ahead and start looking for the lasso.

So, said Teague, the family comes out to greet Roland. Roland's wearing khakis and a short-sleeved shirt. But one without alligators.

That might be all I got, said Roland. Libby packed for me.

You can borrow one of mine then, said Teague.

Fine, said Roland. But keep rolling. And anybody writing this down? Creative juices are really flowing here.

I'm getting it down, said the TV man, looking as if he'd settled, finally, into the rhythm of things in Henry City and would be playing checkers, chewing tobacco, and discussing the high school team's prospects well before nightfall.

He's driving the Mercedes then? said J.T. When he comes up the driveway? That should help us out with the farmers and the factory workers.

We need to borrow a car, said Teague. None of the ones we got will work.

A Buick, said the TV man.

Cut Worm's got a Buick, said Roland. It's not brand-new, but it's a nice car.

Perfect, said Teague. Not brand-new is better. So the whole family meets Roland and Libby in the driveway. So that gives us four women total. That's good. Right now, if you ask me, we're hurting with the fairer sex.

Is that right, said Roland, smiling in mock chagrin.

That's got to sting a bit, said J.T., as the dog, the beautiful dog emblematic of the fine folks of Tennessee, came up to him for a sniff and a careless pat on the head.

My hunch, said Teague, is you look a little too much like the guy in high school who said he'd call and never did.

Said J.T.: payback is a bitch, little brother.

Okay, so we've got the women in Roland's life surrounding him as he gets out of the car. He's rendered harmless and domesticated and it's apparent now that he helps out with the dishes.

What if Libby's knocking him in the head with her purse? said J.T.

We're going to disarm all the women before the cameras start rolling. So it's a low-key greeting, a hug for mom, the sister by her side. Then J.T. and Corrine greeting Libby. J.T. opening the car door. Friendly family greeting like we've all done. Not conquering hero returning.

Got to get Queen in there too, said J.T.

Oh hell yes, said Teague. Queen is wagging the hell out of her tail. Then we pan out. That's the term?

That's the term, said the TV man.

And get the farmhouse and the mountains behind and the trees and all that bullshit. I mean, the setting here is pretty ideal, don't you think?

I do, said the TV man. Idyllic and quiet. Solid but unpretentious.

Solid, that's what we want, said Teague.

Teague walked over to J.T. and grabbed the offered cigarette. J.T. struck a match and lit first Teague's cigarette then his own. Queen sat in the shade of the car's hood with her head on her paws, mouth open, tongue out, but alert. Teague thought she would need a big drink of water before the cameras starting rolling.

That's a good dog, said Teague.

I told you, said J.T., reaching down to pet Queen in earnest.

Photogenic too, I bet.

Absolutely.

We may have found our overalls, said Teague. I could see this dog making a few stops on the campaign tour. So why don't we put her in a truck with Roland for the next scene? I'm thinking we see a shot of Roland reaching across the seat and opening the passenger door for the dog.

Shoot it from the driver's window, the TV man said.

Then use another camera to show Queen hopping on in, said Teague, and getting a damn nice pat from Roland for her trouble. Then we show

Roland driving off toward the fields. Will Queen hang her head out the window?

You know a dog that won't? said Roland.

We could have the truck stop at the chicken house for a look-see, the TV man said.

No, said Roland. And behind him J.T. was shaking his head as well.

Not even the hickest man in the state wants a chicken farmer for governor, said J.T.

Or a pig farmer, said Roland. Cows and crops, that's it.

And chicken is just one word away from chickenshit, said J.T. On a subconscious level, it's no good.

The TV man looked at Teague. Are they serious?

They are, said Teague. No chickens. By the way, do we even have a truck?

That old work truck that Daddy's had for years is out in the barn, said J.T. Looks like hell, but it'll drive us around the farm.

Sounds perfect, the TV man said. A real truck you'd use on a real farm.

It is hotter than hell, said J.T., looking up at the sunless sky.

It was. Teague had not thought of the weather for several minutes. It was always hot in Tennessee in the summer, but this was really something to talk about. Twenty years ago, the house in front of him would have had no air-conditioning. Probably ceiling fans, fans in the open windows. People twenty years ago were stronger, tougher. He walked around in the driveway for a moment, trying not to make a spectacle of stretching an aching back. I'm not sure about the old truck, he said. Might be pouring it on a little thick. How do folks around here react to a man with a new truck?

They like it, said Roland. Usually want to take a walk around it and ask about the engine and that sort of thing. A new truck's not something anyone would begrudge, not around here at least.

It is fundamentally impossible to put on airs while driving a pick-em-up-truck, said J.T. Any truck. That's just the rule of the road.

Can you get us one quickly?

One call down to the store, said J.T. Thirty minutes or so.

Baseball cap or no baseball cap? said Teague, smiling and affecting a down-home accent.

Cap, said the TV guy.

I don't own a baseball cap, said Roland.

Cap will arrive with the truck, said J.T.

The watch has got to go, said the TV man.

What's wrong with the watch? said Roland.

Too gold, too shiny, and too big, the TV man said. Why don't you and Mr. Teague switch around?

Teague unfastened the leather band of his watch and passed it over, modest, square, understated. When he took Roland's in exchange and affixed it to his own wrist, the whole of his arm changed, the tone and tenor of the arm. He noticed the arm and was distracted by it, the watch three times heavier than his own and catching the sun's light and reflecting it this way and that with each movement of his hand. Not many men in the eastern portion of Tennessee would wear such a watch even if they could afford it.

It's a nice watch, said Roland. Really light on the wrist.

Keep it, said Teague.

No, said Roland. Thanks, but I'm not taking your watch.

With what you're paying me I can get another. I insist.

Okay. If you insist. Thank you. You want mine?

Not really my style, said Teague.

I didn't know you had a style, said J.T., getting up and walking toward the house with Queen at his heels. He walked until he was standing at the back door of the house.

Said J.T.: So I'm getting a Buick, a new pickup, and a baseball cap. Is that all?

That's all, said Teague.

J.T. looked at Queen lying still in the shade of the driveway. Yall take care of the star, he said. And look after Roland too.

———

Teague had hoped he would not end up alone, somehow, with Corrine. Perhaps he'd felt her watching him, perhaps he just felt the most vulnerable to a flank attack, new as he was to their rituals of intrigue, the patterns and repetitions, the foretold rising action, climaxes, and denouements that everyone else who knew them seemed to take for granted, moving in and out of their drama like an irrelevant chorus, unaffected by the action, unmoved by it as well. Yet here they were, the two of them, standing in the large carport beside the borrowed vehicles for the commercial, smoking cigarettes and drinking Cokes. Everyone else was either changing clothes or visiting inside. The camera crew was out in the baked dirt road that ran along the fields. The road was a reddish brown, the corn crop behind a vivid green. A multitude of bugs flew over the crops and the whole tableau before him, busy TV crew, busy insects, looked hustling and industrious. It all made Teague feel sleepy and inert. He was attempting to keep the conversation away, at all costs, from J.T., J.T.'s recent movements, J.T.'s plans for tonight, tomorrow, next week, or next month. He felt the cross-examination had gone well so far, especially considering his fatigued condition, and even though he'd nothing to tell, no beans to spill, about future actions, events, or characters to be named later, he felt always on the verge of a slip of the tongue. What he wanted was to shoot this last scene, the one with Roland and the dog in the truck, head to town for the parade footage with Roland and the home folks, then get the hell out of Dodge.

Corrine asked about the shooting schedule for the rest of the day and whether her services would be needed further. Teague gave the basic outline, said her debt to society was paid, and that were he her, he'd be kicking back in the air-conditioning with some cool drink or another.

Corrine rolled her eyes. It's duller than dirt in there.

Cooler though, said Teague.

This heat doesn't bother me. I never lived in a house with air-conditioning until I was twenty-five or so. Ah, I'm just an old poor white trash girl J.T. took pity on. Don't you know that? J.T. took me to town, shod me, and commenced to knocking me up. All in the name of air-conditioning.

Teague laughed.

Then Corrine did too. She took out a cigarette and offered it to Teague. It was menthol but he took it just the same. His return to smoking was really going quite well. He lit the cigarette off of Corrine's lighter and breathed in deeply. Hot menthol smoke on a ninety-five-degree day. This was living.

What's Jan up to today? said Corrine, sitting down on the tailgate of the borrowed truck, swinging her good legs and looking down at her bare feet.

She and the kids are at her folks's house. Her side of the family gets together every Fourth of July.

So you're missing out on the in-laws?

Teague laughed. Yeah. But they're not too bad.

Neither are Mother Superior and the Fairy Princess, she said, motioning with her head toward the house. Just dull dull dull.

Saying this, Corrine flopped dramatically backward into the bed of the truck and now lay looking up at the garage ceiling, stretching one tan leg and then the other. Teague looked once at the leg stretching, once at the other leg, then moved his eyes to the discarded shoes on the floor. The image of tanned and painted toenails danced around in his head and he decided to look around the corners of the garage for wasp nests or spiderwebs or any such thing besides shoes, feet, and legs. He did not know if the Fairy Princess was meant to be Sis or Libby, but he thought he had a pretty good guess. It was just these kinds of casual admissions, casual and humorous insights into the Cole clan, that could lead to admissions, avowals, and ultimately interrogatories that Teague was on the lookout for. What he really wanted to do, he realized suddenly, was to stretch Corrine out in the bed of the truck and roll around a bit. He wouldn't, of course, even had she been willing. He'd sworn that sort of thing off after the Valerie epoch. Nonetheless, it's what he would have liked to have done. He thought perhaps that monogamy was overrated.

I believe Sis has flown the coop, said Corrine.

Are you surprised?

No. I knew once those camera trucks showed up, she'd be heading for the hills.

What do you think of the commercial so far? Teague asked. You think we're on the right track?

Sure. Seems good to me. Can't believe Queen hopped in the truck right on cue.

Teague smiled. It had been a nice stroke, the family, other than Sis, coming out to meet Roland and Libby, then Teague letting the dog go on the director's cue and the dog heading straight for Roland, tail wagging, head lolling in earnest. Nothing fake about that dog. Then Roland's impromptu taking of a knee for a friendly and sincere and masculine roughhouse petting of the dog's neck and head. A good scene and Roland with the casual look of a winner.

Corrine sat up and watched a June bug crash recklessly around the carport before landing like an early model alien spacecraft on the rail of the truck. She watched the bug wheeling slowly, flying in a circle about the truck, then landing again, in search, it seemed, of nothing but movement of the most inconsequential kind, movement without plan or volition, as if any motion made in earnest were its own reward and needed no further explanation.

It seemed that a long time had passed without anyone speaking. Teague didn't mind. It was just noticeable. He stood watching the June bug, wondering how long until it miscalculated speed and angle of approach and landed unceremoniously on its back, legs spinning in futility, hard green thorax rocking this way and that trying to get righted. He'd held many a June bug as a boy and remembered how sticky the legs were on your hand, how hard they were to disengage once affixed to a shirt. A harmless, flighty, inconsequential creature, but interesting in its fashion, a month-long free spirit during the dog days of summer, a cosmic signal to be sure, indecipherable, perhaps inane, but a signal nonetheless.

What are you doing messing around with these boys anyway, Teague? said Corrine. They don't seem quite your style.

I'm not sure I know what you mean.

You just don't seem like the fast and easy kind. That's what I mean.

Teague smiled. I could ask you the same question, he said.

I was young and dumb. What's your excuse?

I don't have one.

Corrine lay down in the bed of the truck and lit another cigarette. She said: I just figured that you could make out fine with the folks at the country club and down at the university and what have you. You know, the more *established* folks. I'm starting to think you might be in it just for the adventure.

Maybe so, said Teague. I've never given it much thought.

Corrine sat up and hopped down from the truck, then started walking toward the house, flipping her cigarette into the yard on the way. Well, said Corrine, I'll see you tonight. Me and Libby are going out with the boys. You might want to spread the word.

The Henry City Crew

A small but raucous affair. To say it more precisely, the crowd, such that it was, was not yet raucous, but raucous was on the bill, raucous was in the air. For tonight the Henry City locals were out on the town, out when normally they'd be cleaning up the grill or talking to relatives or watching television themselves, because their old friends the Coles were back and they didn't get back often. For the locals, it was a chance to rub shoulders with old friends they saw on the news and read about in the newspaper, and whatever plans they might have made, whatever family traditions they normally had for the holiday, were cast aside. A visit from the Coles was like a visit from the city, all cities, and for that day your quiet life was a little different, a little more energized, the mountain come to Muhammad, and afterward what you said, what you said every time, was this: the Coles hadn't changed. Not a lick. And Corrine was still ten kinds of hell in a handbasket.

They were spread out in three loose groups in Peck's beer-joint/gro-cery/taxidermy, a building known for forty years as Cole's Dry Goods. Glancing about the place, one could almost pinpoint the moment in transition from dry goods to beer joint, the moment when Peck had decided to hell with it, to hell with making it this or that. Why not this and that and a little of that too? So what was here before stayed, and what was added stayed too. Now the place had something of a frozen look about it, as if the adding was all done, the museum of mismatched artifacts complete and let the dust cover what of it it will. Ode on a Grecian Urn. Static motion. In perpetuity neither here nor there.

To wit: country hams spread out on a dusty table next to a scale and index cards with Magic Marker weights and prices in front of each. Twenty or so pairs of Red Wing work boots for sale. The Warm Morning stove, relic of local jawers and pundits spitting and philosophizing over the current events on frosty winter afternoons. An L-shaped counter made of good oak locally grown back when hardwoods were still plentiful. A banjo with no remembered history or origin. Jars of marbles, gumballs, and candies, a bobtail quail thermometer, the largest hornet's nest anyone in the county had ever seen, and twenty or so black and white photos of Main Street and its quaint and aimless-looking sedans as it looked at particular moments in the mid-1930s. Photographer unknown but not unappreciated. Clean shots and precise composition. No tipping to the sentimental, no hard-boiled realism. The scene rendered, unmolested. A lost art, some would say. All of these were remnants from James Cole's Dry Goods, gifted to Peck or abandoned to him or loaned and now forgotten. Peck's nods to modernity and to his own vision for the space included the jukebox, plastic tablecloths for the four booths running along the far side of the room, his collection of antiquated and archaic beer cans, a few seashells from a long-ago trip to Daytona when Peck was first married, a framed display of arrowheads, Peck's hobby as a boy, and a framed map of the United States, turn of the century or so, listing the Tribes of the Indian Nation and the territories they once called home.

The taxidermy work was done in the back room, where Mr. Cole had kept his surplus and his hot peanut machine. Peck was proud of his handiwork with what the hunters brought in, but had tired of the jokes from some of the regulars and the complaints of what few women came in about socializing amid so many lifeless animals. Now the only nod to his current passion that could be seen in the main room was a largemouth bass, mouth agape, and the unimpressed head of a twelve-point buck. The rest of the menagerie was kept back with his tools and dyes and plastic eyeballs, away from the jokesters and the womenfolk and most especially Mrs. Peck, who cared not for the unprofitable business and tended to think Peck just liked jacking around with his playthings more than he liked making money.

Teague sat in a booth with Libby and the TV man, talking about nothing of importance and glancing every so often at the muted black and white television in the corner.

Libby was talking about the commercial, how well it seemed to go, and laughing with considerable charm at the performance of the old bird dog, Queen. Said Libby: She hit every cue. That is the term for it, isn't it?

Yes, said the TV man, that's the term. And you're right, that dog was unbelievable.

Teague glanced at the half-finished longneck in front of the TV man and the two empties beside it. The TV man was now smoking one after the other and had made inquiries about the local hotel. Earlier in the day, he'd been calculating the miles to Glennville and inquiring about nice restaurants, nice hotels, en route to Atlanta. The Coles had snared another one without even trying.

Would you mind if I smoked one of your cigarettes? said Libby to the TV man, and without missing a beat he procured and handed over and lit the cigarette.

I didn't figure you for a smoker, said Teague.

A passing fancy, said Libby, with a really quite charming smile. I heard it's what all the cool kids are doing.

She was wearing jeans and a summer top. She could not hide the fashionable haircut or the face that looked keen and unfathomable, the kind that left small towns never to return. But overall, she projected a much more human persona than Teague had thought possible. It was nice to be surprised by people, surprised on the plus side of the ledger, and Teague considered how he really didn't know a damn thing. Then he considered how he'd spent a large portion of the day admiring other men's wives and wondered without really wanting to about Jan. Perhaps some stranger had come to the Carothers family outing and was now admiring his wife.

Said Libby: What do you think this commercial can do for us?

The TV man took a long pull of his beer. We've found your answer to the railroad man, he said.

Libby smiled.

I'm serious, said the TV man. I think we did. The dog and Roland project a real image. Roland looks like a man comfortable in his own skin. That bit in the truck where he opens the door for the dog and the dog just jumps right in with that happy, nice look on her face, well, that's just doing a lot of work. Roland doesn't look like some financier. I'm not from the South, but that just seems, that guy on the farm today, just seems like what a Tennessean should look like. On a subconscious level, it's just doing all kinds of things.

Libby and Teague didn't say anything. The man seemed not quite finished.

I mean on a subconscious level that dog and that farm are doing a lot of work. A hell of a lot of work. Am I drunk?

I don't know, said Libby laughing. Are you?

It is a good commercial, said Teague.

Damn good, said the TV man.

Then Libby was asking the TV man how he got his start in the business and so on, making the newcomer feel comfortable as only a certain style of woman can. Behind him, Roland and J.T. had pushed three tables together and were catching up on all the latest town news. Always the way. A man from a town such as this could travel the world, spend a year in Istanbul, and when he returned the only thing on his mind is who bought Tucker's Feed Store. And was it true that Jim Turner's mother has cancer? They won't talk a bit, Teague thought, or only briefly under direct questioning, about politics, banking, the prospects for the Expo, or anything else in Glennville. For home, the right kind of home, is where they can't make you talk about the present.

Teague turned to the TV man. Did you know, he said, that Libby spent a lot of time in front of a camera?

Is that right?

Oh hush, Teague.

She did, said Teague. She was an up-and-coming singer. Big news in our part of the world. I saw you several times in college when you were on that show out of Louisville. Used to come on Saturday nights. What was it called again?

Libby shook her head no, smiling, and trying to wave off the whole conversation.

A singer, said the TV man. What kind? Country?

Libby made a face and Teague said: No, no, no. Nightclubby stuff. Siren songs. Peggy Lee.

A far cry from that, said Libby.

Weren't you on *The Lawrence Welk Show* too?

Libby laughed but wouldn't confirm.

That is really interesting, said the TV man. What made you give it up?

Lack of talent.

Not that, said Teague. I won't let you get away with that.

Libby raised a charming finger and asked for one more cigarette. She said: The name of the show in Louisville was *A Night on the Town*. Now please let's talk about something else. I was having such a good time.

Directly behind him, an old raconteur closer in age to Esther Cole was telling, retelling, no doubt, some story about a barnstorming ballplayer of a bygone era. Teague thought he ought to join the large gathering, but saw no way of making the move. To stay meant being further charmed by Libby Cole, and that promised to do him no real good.

It was then that he glanced to the front of the bar where a boy had just placed his hand on the volume knob of the television. It was Peck's son, a strapping young man of twenty or so. The boy glanced briefly about, a cursory look to see if anyone was watching him, then turned the volume up loud enough for Teague to hear it from where he sat.

Leave it be, Peck said from the opposite side of the bar.

The boy turned to regard Peck, his hand still on the knob, a look of amused insolence about his face. I want to hear this, he said, nodding toward the screen where a minor network drama played. Then the boy turned the knob an infinitesimal turn, the decrease in volume barely noticeable. By now the storytelling had stopped behind Teague and several people were looking toward the television and the boy.

You heard me, Peck said. Turn it down or go home.

Why do you have it on, if nobody can hear it? the boy said.

Turn it down or leave, said Peck.

With a dramatic and jerky movement of his hand, the television was again muted. Then languid as a scolded cat he walked to the jukebox. Once there, he placed his hands on the glass casing, blue-jeaned legs spread far apart, beating time on the machine, lost now in the music, giving not a whit, he seemed to say, about his father or the television or if anyone in the bar was presently regarding him. When he turned once to feign a look at a beer clock above Teague's head, Teague saw that he was a nice-looking kid with a mop of sandy hair. The hair seemed undecided about a country-boy or post-hippie look. Smiling at nothing, he turned back to tapping on the jukebox and bobbing his head in time to the song. Teague was willing to bet a lot of money that sometime within the year that sardonic smile would be knocked sideways.

Or else he'd just be shot dead.

The TV man excused himself to go to the bathroom and while he was gone Libby said, I guess I better join the crowd behind you.

Teague smiled. It looks like they're having a good time.

So am I, she said. But I'd hate to seem rude.

I understand, said Teague. Sometimes you've just got to mind the account.

I've never heard that phrase before.

Well it's not particularly gracious.

But it fits the job description.

Yes, said Teague, it does do that.

Won't you join me? I'm sure you'll want to hear all about Roland's high school exploits and the time they beat Hunter County on the fake punt.

Teague smiled. Men are boring, aren't they?

Libby said: Not at all, not at all.

Said Cut Worm: Tell the one about J.T. pitching that time. Against Laneville.

The old-timer, whose name was Duncan, adjusted the bill of his cap. J.T.?

I don't care, said J.T. Corrine, do you care?

Why no, J.T., said Corrine. That hussy's waiting tables at the truck stop and I'm married to you.

Much laughter around the table. Ah, thought Teague, this is an old gag.

Course, said Corrine, exhaling cigarette smoke with demonstrable flair, I bet you meet some good men down at the truck stop.

More laughter, J.T. leading the way.

Said Corrine: I'm holding the short straw, now that I think of it. But go ahead, Duncan, tell the story about J.T. and the hussy and the baseball game.

J.T. was pitching, said Duncan as the laughing continued around the table. And he was just wallering around out there. Laneville wasn't much good that year and we had a pretty good summer squad. So he's walking a guy here, letting a guy steal a base there, and just throwing it around the fat of the plate. He just didn't have his head anywhere in the game.

He balked once, said Cut Worm. Didn't he, Roland?

Balked in a run, said Roland.

You were catching, said Duncan. And Cut Worm, you were in left field.

That's a good memory, said Cut Worm.

I remember a little, said Duncan. So anyway, we're about in the third inning and they're winning three-two or something like that. Was it three-two, J.T.?

Hell if I know. I was just out there wallering on the mound.

Three-two, said Roland. And big brother had just let a guy go from second to third when he was tossing the ball up and down on the mound and dropped it.

Again, laughter. J.T. looked away as if not paying attention. Corrine talked with her friend at the far end of the table. Libby sat next to Roland, her hand casually on his shoulder.

Anyhow, said Duncan, this young lady walks in wearing the shortest shorts anyone had ever seen around here.

Denise Bollenger is the young lady's name, said Corrine. She used to wear those shorts to church.

The friend sitting beside Corrine shook her head and said, you are so bad. So bad.

Yeah, I'm going straight to hell, said Corrine.

Anyway, said Duncan. These were short shorts. And this is way before that was the fashion. So she's standing behind the backstop and cheering and clapping for one of the guys on the Laneville team.

Hank Lang, said Roland.

A tough customer, said Cut Worm, looking at Teague. Damn good linebacker.

You tell it now, Roland, said Duncan. You know it better than I do.

No, said Roland, go ahead.

Tell it, said Libby. I haven't heard this one in forever. I forget how it goes.

As she said this, she rubbed the back of Roland's neck and asked with a smile and a gesture for another of the TV man's cigarettes. Roland has a gamer in his corner, thought Teague. And only this afternoon he'd have bet a good deal of money on the opposite. He thought that perhaps J.T.'s whiskey was going to his head. Whiskey often gave him the illusion of epiphany. But how could he have so misjudged Libby, when his job, his reputation, was made on knowing people, great bodies of them, as well as the wide spectrum of individuals. Perhaps, thought Teague, it was really only men he knew.

The big fellow's up on deck, said Roland. Taking some mighty practice cuts. And his gal is clapping and jumping up and down and hollering for him. Duncan didn't mention it, but for those of you who have never heard the story, we were playing in Laneville.

My mistake, said Duncan. That does add a little spice to the story.

It's three-two, one out, and damned if J.T. doesn't walk the guy at the plate on four pitches.

By this time I was distracted, said J.T.

I bet you were, said Corrine.

When she said this, Teague heard for the first time what might have been a slight slurring of words. His antennae went up a bit. A scene was something he could do without. But then her friend whispered something in her ear and Corrine laughed and nodded her head and mouthed the words, *you're right*, and looked directly at him. Corrine waved at him across the table. Teague smiled and waved back, feeling as if he'd been caught spying.

Big brother *was* distracted, Roland said. And they've got Hank Lang, their cleanup hitter, coming up. So I decide I best go out to the mound for a quick conference. Just to make sure we had our signals straight.

Roland paused here and took a sip of his drink. Then Corrine and her hometown friend got up and went to the bar.

More drinks, thought Teague. Or just tired of high school stories. And then he saw the boy at the far end of the bar watching the muted television. And then that same boy snap out of his TV reverie and turn to look at the women at the bar with a kind of whimsical frankness, as if to say, *oh, now the night will get interesting.*

Conference, said J.T. Right. First and only conference of the year. Go ahead, tell him how we got our signals straight.

Well, said Roland. After all that wallering and the balk and now the young lady with the shorts, I thought I needed to get J.T.'s attention back on the batter in the box. I mean, even as I'm walking out to the mound, he's looking over my head at that gal and smiling. So I get out to the mound and J.T. says, did you see that gal? What gal? I said. Are you blind? The one in the shorts.

Much laughter around the table.

Well, I had seen her. I saw her walk in and I could hear her behind me cheering for Hank Lang. But I said, hell no, I haven't seen any gal. I want to win this ball game. And J.T. says, just turn around and look. No, I said. J.T. says, act like you're asking the ump for more time. You're not going to believe this gal in the shorts.

Hell, even Duncan noticed her and he was eighty years old back then, said J.T. Isn't that right, Duncan?

Duncan smiled but made no plea. Across the bar, Corrine and her pal, fresh drinks in hand, were making their way toward the jukebox. The confident young fellow had turned back to his television show.

So I said, listen, J.T. We got guys on first and third and one out. We need to walk this guy, he's their best hitter. I ain't walking nobody on purpose, J.T. said. So I said, do it on accident then. Like you have everybody else. No, hell no, said J.T. And behind us that girl hadn't stopped yelling, c'mon, Hank, knock it out of the park. So I said, why don't you just hit him then? Just knock the hell out of him.

Roland was looking at the TV man now as he told the story, the only stranger at the table, and smiling a kind of professionally embarrassed smile, recklessness of youth, etc.

And what did J.T. say? said the TV man.

Before he answered, Roland looked at J.T. and laughed. Then J.T. laughed in return. And for a moment it seemed as if they were telling a story just the two of them could understand. A hundred times. A hundred times they've told this story and every time it's just as good. J.T. being J.T. and Roland being Roland. And more than that, much more than that— the thing itself. It was them being Roland and J.T., the brothers Cole from Henry City.

For the record, this guy was a yow-yower, said J.T. I want that known on the front end. Duncan? Cut Worm?

They concurred that Hank Lang was a yow-yower. A tough guy and not averse to the occasional unsportsmanlike gesture or vocalization while on the playing field.

What did J.T. say? asked the TV man, well in the cups and smiling.

He said: Oh hell yes, I'm going to hit him. I decided that as soon as his girlfriend walked in.

Long laughter around the table and again that quick cutting of eyes, brother to brother. Then Roland put his arm around Libby's shoulders and they too shared a look. *You understand this now*, the look seemed to say, *after all these years*. And Teague could tell that she did. And tell, as well, that she hadn't always.

Duncan, why don't you finish up? You gave me all the good lines and the rest of the story gets boring.

Boring? said J.T.

A third-rate squad. Cut Worm, am I right?

Yeah, they weren't any good. Otherwise we'd have been using one of our good pitchers.

Oh hell, said J.T. Now Cut Worm's jumping in.

J.T. hits the big man, said Duncan. He starts to charge the mound but the ump grabs him. The crowd's going crazy wanting the ump to throw J.T. out. I mean that pitch was nowhere near home plate. It was blatant. Anyhow, order is restored. Bases loaded. One out. And J.T. strikes out the next two batters on six pitches. Rest of the game he's giving em nothing but little pills to hit. Ends up striking out about fourteen and not giving up another hit and we won something like nine-three. Was it nine-three, Cut Worm?

That's right, said Cut Worm.

That's as good as I ever saw anyone pitch in that league, said Duncan.

Well, I thank you, said J.T.

Said the TV man, well whatever happened with the girl in the short shorts?

Nothing, said J.T., drawing on his cigarette, then taking a sip of the highball.

Nothing? said the TV man. Nothing, Roland?

Not that I know of, said Roland. Not that I ever heard.

And Teague found that he was smiling to himself, smiling without meaning to. And then he found that Libby was looking at him and he nodded and smiled at her, a different smile. He hoped that she wouldn't notice the difference, but knew that she had.

———

Corrine and her friend had selected a series of fast songs with a western swing feel and were now recruiting members of the table to join them in front of the jukebox. Several of the couples did, and Duncan as well, dragged nearly from his seat and placed hand in hand with Corrine's pal, and then the TV man and Libby. Roland and J.T. pleaded fatigue. Then Corrine grabbed Teague's arm with a firm suggestion that he get the lead out.

No thank you, said Teague.

Come on, Mr. Teague, I won't bite.

Maybe later, Teague said.

J.T., do I bite?

Yes.

Oh go to hell. Roland? Last chance.

Roland shook his hand.

Honey darling? Sugar dumpling? Apple of my eye?

J.T. smiled but didn't get up.

All right then, said Corrine, you had your chance.

They watched her from the table make a sharp diagonal cut through the dancers and toward Peck's son at the bar. The boy had his back to her, nonchalantly sipping a beer, but when she tapped him on the shoulder, he turned slowly and without surprise. There followed a quick exchange, something funny said by Corrine, and then perhaps the cockiest grin Teague had ever seen on a living human being.

The boy took one last sip on his beer as Corrine went to the dance floor and started without him. Then he rose from his stool, looked once at the table where Teague and the Coles sat, and joined Corrine on the dance floor.

Well, said J.T., Corrine looks well taken care of.

That fellow can really move, said Roland, smiling and looking at Teague. Teague, can that young fellow move or can't he?

Teague laughed and took a sip of his drink. He'd begun to notice that Corrine's friend was actually quite nice-looking. Here soon, thought Teague, I will have to act. I will have to do something, anything, to see if I still can. Kill a man. Become an evangelist. Run off with a fifteen-year-old girl. Join the Peace Corps.

He wondered if the Valerie/Roland connection was in the back of his mind. Then decided such a notion was much nicer when sublimated, regardless of what subconscious motivation it might provide for a reckless act.

Then J.T. was pushing away from the table with nary a second look toward the dancers. If you fellows will excuse me, he said, I'm going outside for a breath of fresh air.

Ah, thought Teague. Minding the account. A phone booth to be found somewhere in the near vicinity.

I thought it went well today, said Roland. Your TV guy was sharp.

Yes, he's good. And I agree, I think we made out okay.

The stuff downtown might not be as good, Roland said. It was kind of chaotic with the parade and all.

No, it'll turn out. I mean the dog is the topper. But the Fourth of July stuff is still pretty sharp. I've never seen a political commercial that was filmed without being totally choreographed. We got some good, spontaneous footage. It'll look like a mess in the editing room but when we're done, it should have a natural feel.

That was a good idea.

Thank you. That old lady bringing up the pie, we couldn't have written that in.

Miss Nancy Murdock. She's got to be pushing ninety. Used to do Daddy's books. But, yeah, that was good.

So I think we'll end up with two commercials. One on the farm, and then the Fourth of July one. I'm with you. I like em. They're sharp. Now who's that friend of Corrine's?

Emily, said Roland. Corrine's old running buddy. Peas in pod. But I'm not sure you're ready for one of these Berry County gals.

No, no, no, said Teague. Just asking. I'm no longer a threat to society. I've seen the circus before and have no need to see it again.

Hell I never get tired of the circus.

Teague laughed.

You think I got a chance in this election? Honestly.

I do. You're still in it. A lot can happen between now and November. A hell of a lot. They might catch Montgomery in a tryst with a preacher and a little albino boy.

A man can't drive a train all the time.

Teague smiled. Knew, almost for sure, that after this drink he was going for a few twirls around the old dance floor.

Said Roland: You want to come work with me full-time?

Doing what?

If I win, I'll get you some kind of post in Nashville.

I'm not going back to Nashville full-time. That's definite.

Well win or lose, I'm going to need a point man on the Expo.

I've never been one for the point, said Teague.

My point man. We'll get Johnny Boy to deal with the press and all that jazz. I'll give you a title with the bank, executive vice president or some bullshit like that. And you can operate from there. And we'll call you vice president of the Expo Commission. That will be your actual position.

I thought that was J.T.'s job.

J.T. doesn't want a title. He just did it while we got the ball rolling till we could find someone to fill the position full-time. That was the plan all along.

I don't know the first thing about banking.

What's to know? You give money to people and they give more of it back to you. It's simple. Plus you won't be doing any banking. We'll put you on the board and give you a title. Then we can pay you through the bank.

Teague looked for a moment at the dance floor. Emily, dancing now with Cut Worm, caught his eye and smiled. Then Corrine saw him and began waving him up to the floor. It was a midtempo song and the young cowpoke had his arm, casually, on Corrine's hip. They were doing a slow kind of swinging number that matched the tempo of the song. Everyone else seemed to be dancing too fast.

I just assumed I'd move on once the election was over, said Teague.

Listen, said Roland. We get through these last few hurdles with city council and the state and we're ready to break ground a year from now. Spring of 80 at the latest. And the state won't be a problem. And we've got the White House in our corner. The main problem is those Glennville stubborn jackasses. And that's where you can help me. Admit it or not, you're on the inside with those fuckers.

Teague shook his head to disagree.

Hell, your father-in-law is one of them.

That much is true.

But I'm going to beat their asses. Wait and see if I don't.

Hey, I'd like to see it. Working for you or not, I'm all for shaking up the old boy network. But let's back up a minute. Did you say you've got the White House in your corner?

Roland smiled, took a sip of his drink. You remember our friend in the Department of Commerce?

Teague nodded.

Anyway, it's a long story. I'll tell you later. Actually, I'm not sure that I will. Only permanent employees get all the news. So you might end up high and dry.

Right, said Teague smiling. I understand.

But the Expo is going to happen. And it's going to be a good deal for us. And a good deal for Glennville and the state.

There'll be lots of construction, said Teague. That much I can figure out. Hotels, pavilions, parking decks, what have you. And builders need loans, don't they?

See, you're a banker at heart. And we've got all kinds of things going on. All kinds of things. When we first met down in Clearwater, you said the Expo was what you were interested in. Well, here's your chance.

Yes, I said that. But it's looking more and more like a three- or four-year job, the way you're talking about it. I was thinking about just helping out in the initial phase, if at all.

You've already helped out with the Sun Tower idea.

That was nothing.

Well, it's what we're going with. We've already ordered lapel pins with Helios on a chariot riding over a globe.

I've never been a company man, he said.

What company? It's me and J.T.

I'll think about it. It's a long commitment.

We'll go year to year. Hell, I'll give you a six-month contract. Renewable for as long as you want. Then you can bail out whenever the mood hits, no hard feelings.

Teague nodded but said no more.

This is your chance to do something for the city. I know that's got to have some pull for you. We're going to put Glennville on the map. You'd hate to miss out on that.

Teague was back at the booth after a few quick turns on the dance floor and was now sitting next to Emily, his dance partner of record. Libby and Roland were at the other end of the table, talking casually with Cut Worm and Duncan and the rest of the Henry City crew. The impression given was that Teague and Emily were held within the bounds of this conversation, but in reality theirs was an exclusive matter, the quiet tones and sly jokes of the proverbial slippery slope. The others in their party had filed out, babysitters to relieve and so on. Peck sat on the customer side of the bar with a beer, watching the muted nightly news. His son moved slowly, languidly, about the dance floor, more rhythmic embrace than anything, with Corrine Cole, her head resting on his shoulder, one hand in a back pocket of his jeans, his hands occasionally rubbing the small of her back. J.T. had been gone for nearly an hour.

But now he returned. Tired-eyed and sunburned from the long day outside, he entered his father's old general store and observed his wife slow-dancing with Peck's son. He did not look at his brother or friends at the table, but simply walked in a normal stride toward the couple dancing. When he got to them, he tapped the shoulder of the young man as if to break in. This gesture received an insolent, dismissive look in return, but no break in the slow rhythm of the dance. Corrine's only reaction was to raise her head from the boy's shoulder, look at her husband as if he were some stranger, and then place the head back snugly on the same shoulder where it had been before. After this, with a kind of mechanized motion, perfunctory and precise, J.T. grabbed the boy by his free shoulder and spun him around till they were face to face, separating the dancers in the process. Teague found the movement so smooth as to be surprised at its force, the boy jerked full around, Corrine spun off toward the jukebox. The totality of effect was that of a choreographed dance, unhurried and pre-ordained. Then, without a word, without a scowl or threat or preliminary push, J.T. knocked the boy to the floor with a deft and decisive blow. In the same motion, he was stepping over the prone body and taking his wife in his arms. They now assumed the same pose as the earlier dancing couple, Corrine with her head on J.T.'s shoulder, his arms around her waist.

Teague was not sure what he'd just seen. Where there was a boy, there was no boy. Where there was no J.T. now was J.T.

Uh-oh, said Roland, smiling and rising from his chair. Peck had done the same from behind the bar and each approached the area of confrontation with a brisk but measured step.

Roland grabbed the boy under one shoulder and Peck the other, and they hoisted him with a jerk to an upright position between them. His nose was a mess. As they tried to steady the boy, Teague debated whether to keep his seat or head up and see what he could do. Cut Worm and the others at the table hadn't moved, and after only a few glancing looks toward the scene of the drama had returned to their conversation.

Thought Teague: Aaahhh. The folks at this table have seen this sort of thing before.

So had Teague, in other fashions, in other settings. Though never quite like this. It was usually much more drawn out, with lots of posturing and yakking back and forth. What ensued more often than not consisted of a few wild punches, someone tackling the other, then enough sweaty wallering on the floor to embarrass even the most hearty eggers-on. But this now, this had some form to it, a clean narrative arc, a firm and sensible resolution.

No one was looking at the dance floor but Libby. She looked ready to get up and lend a hand, see what she could do to make things somehow better. Teague thought that wouldn't do. Depending on Peck's frame of mind, this thing might just be getting started.

I'm going to freshen my drink, Teague said. Would you like anything?

I'm fine, said Emily. Just don't punch anybody.

Teague smiled. Not me, he said. You don't have to worry about that.

He had to pass by the others on his way to the bar and as he did, he inquired about drink orders. They all shook their heads. Libby was still looking up toward the dance floor where Roland and Peck were limp-walking the boy toward the bar. Though doing her best to treat this as a minor situation, Libby's smile betrayed her. This is the last time, thought Teague, that she will ever hit the roadhouse circuit, husband or no husband, old buddies or no old buddies.

Are you going up there? she said.

I'm getting a drink, said Teague. I believe the fireworks are over.

That boy needs to go to the hospital.

We'll get it all taken care of.

Teague came around the table and Libby grabbed him firmly by the sleeve. Get them out of here, she whispered.

Teague nodded his head. He knew who *them* was.

They had the young man stretched out on a cot in Peck's taxidermy room under a menagerie of deer heads and arching dead fish. There were raccoons on file cabinets, a possum hanging by a plastic tail from a light fixture. Weird shimmering plastic eyes, deader-looking than those seen upside down on the side of a country road.

Teague stood in the door watching, then went out to the bar, scooped ice into the cleanest bar rag he could find, and returned to the back room. This might help, he said.

Peck took the packed rag without a word and swapped it for the clot of paper towels he'd been holding to the boy's nose. His movements, even the way he held the rag, were professional, clinical. Teague looked for a spot on the wall where Peck's son might fit once mounted. The boy murmured and tossed about but didn't open his eyes. Whether incapable of doing so or milking the crowd for what little sympathy was coming, Teague didn't know.

I guess we'll be heading off, said Roland. I'm sorry about this.

No need, said Peck. Stay as long as you like.

Well I hate that it happened.

Bound to happen sooner or later, said Peck. Might as well happen now. Raised five kids without a one of em saying boo. But this one. They said I was spoiling him and I guess I did. Well he's either going to get better or he's going to get worse. I've known that for a couple of years now. Ain't nobody stays the same.

He's still young, Peck, said Roland.

He's old enough to know if you're slow-dancing with another man's wife, you damn well better be able to whip the other man's ass when he walks in the door. That's being dumb twice. Dumb two ways. First off, by not doing what's right. You don't dance with another man's wife like that. And secondly, not knowing when you best step down. Not knowing that some men you just don't bluff. Hell, he ain't never had a lick of sense.

Well, again, I'm sorry it had to happen, said Roland, motioning with his head for Teague to lead the way out.

When they were both on the customer side of the bar, Teague looked once more to the father bent over his son. And then Peck shut the door, closing out Teague's view of the shimmering eyes of his animals and the private moments between a father and his son.

Roland shook his head. Son of a bitch.

Teague agreed.

Well welcome to Henry City, Teague. I'm glad you were able to take in some of the local color and see big brother in his native habitat.

Teague smiled.

They were standing in the no-man's-land between the bar and the zombie dancing couple on the floor, disconnected from the couple and the family Peck and the Henry City crew at the table.

I'm glad Peck took it like he did, said Roland. It could have got ugly otherwise. He's got a jackclub behind the bar that would bust big brother's head like a melon.

Teague smiled. The view from here, under the fan, with the smoke wafting off in all directions, was quite nice, away from family matters, comatose dancers, the thought that he'd likely offer to drive Emily home. Standing thus, content and past the halfway point toward drunk, he happened to look at the television set in the corner, long forgotten these last two hours.

Now let's get that jackass out of here, said Roland.

But Teague was on the move, pointing toward the silent, flickering television, and walking toward it as he did.

On the screen above him, there was a reporter standing outside the iron gates of the governor's mansion. A photo of Governor Hart, smiling slickly, was pasted in one corner of the screen. The phrase *Breaking News* flashed at the bottom. Teague turned up the volume and heard the phrase *cash for pardons*.

Behind him Roland said, well I'll be damned.

Very quickly, everyone from the back table moved up toward the television. They stood at the bar, the whole of them, watching a series of field reporters and local anchormen weighing in on the night's proceedings. The gist was that after a year-long investigation by the TBI, Governor Hart had been indicted for taking cash payments, some up to twenty thousand dollars, for the early release of state prisoners. In the last month alone, he'd given clemency to twenty-four inmates, some with multiple years left on their sentence. Tape recordings and secretly filmed footage implicating the governor had yet to be released. But from all accounts, Teague's friends in Nashville had been right all along about Hart.

Teague felt a constant fluttering in the pit of his stomach. That he'd been warned about this Hart situation a year before made it no less surreal. No one with any sense, not even in a place like Louisiana, would have tried to pull off this many pardons on his way out of office. It seemed, at that moment at least, as if Hart's primary goal could only have been the sinking of Roland's run for office, a murder-suicide in the Democratic

Party. He'd known Hart was dumb and arrogant, but this, this was well beyond the pale. It made him want a drink and not want a drink. He looked at the man beside him, the TV man. How long ago had it been that Queen jumped into the truck on cue? What day had it been that the old lady approached Roland with the homemade pie?

Libby sat at one of the stools at the bar next to Roland. Her hand was on his knee and her eyes blinked faster than they ought. Behind them all, oblivious it seemed to the breaking news, Corrine teetered against J.T.'s chest, the unsinkable Molly Brown, a testament to strong legs and damned insistence. J.T., meanwhile, was a hazy statuary, drunk or not drunk impossible to tell. Strangely silent. Fixed stare. Sometimes looking at the television, sometimes out across the bar. A rush of complicated thoughts rushing through his head or not the first one. Spent and insensate after application of fist to nose. Or biding his time till friends left for a private discussion with Roland.

Teague had long since quit watching, essentially from the moment his eyes first saw the screen, and now sat at the bar with his knees touching Emily's beside him. Accidental or no, who was to say, this brushing of knees, so like a high school soda shop, so like a picture of first love done up in middle age in a run-down excuse for a tavern. He wondered when would be the time to break up this morbid little gathering and see what course of action would be his upon arrival at Emily's house. But this was not his call to make. Tomorrow was church and the family for Cut Worm, for the Coles, for everyone still at the bar save him.

He looked now at Roland. It was time to close up shop and move on. To watch further was simple masochism. On TV, they'd come up with a catchphrase: *Pardons for Pay*. And the newspeople seemed to be dropping the phrase every chance they got. Roland, a historical footnote at the bar, his shot at the governor's mansion now floating out there in the land of Never-Was, smiled once, not too ruefully, Teague thought, and then turned his back to the television.

He said: We're still going to run the commercials.

The others said nothing but nodded their heads to agree.

———

Teague pulled into Emily's neighborhood and made ready to take the next right. All the way home, he'd been looking for wayward fireworks, but had seen nary a one. He tried to think of another Fourth without bright lights across the sky, but couldn't do it. Surely it'd rained one Fourth in his life. If so, the skies had been lighted the night after or the night after that and the memory had mixed with all the other Fourths in a barrage of pops and bangs and the image of Julie running across the yard with her first sparkler. He'd managed to think very little of his wife and daughter today and now, as he pulled into the driveway of the woman he'd just met, he decided to keep his streak intact.

Emily's house was a rancher, dark against the dark sky and the dark woods running behind it. One light was on in the kitchen and another on the front porch. Emily had mentioned that her children were with their father and Teague looked around the driveway and yard for a symbol of their existence. The only sign: a bike leaning against the house, its reflector blinking red once in the headlights of his car and then gone again in the night.

They sat for a moment in the car with the engine idling and the faint, staticky music of a radio they'd not known was on. Teague bounced around several things to say but none seemed right.

Would you like to come in? said the perfumed voice beside him. I have a bottle of wine.

He turned to see the woman beside him and felt a strange and sudden empathy with her. Her voice: not expectant. Her eyes: unblinking and unapologetic above a wan smile. She knew the answer already.

I can't.

She looked to the bike leaning against the house and then Teague did too. Had the bike been the difference? Teague thought not. Then again, his morality was unpredictable, fleeting, never quite fully this or that. He wondered what kind of men a woman with kids met in a town like this. And what there was to do besides raise kids.

It was nice to meet you, she said.

I enjoyed meeting you as well.

He thought to say something about how things might be different if he were single but that seemed neither their styles. I'll walk you to the door, he said.

There's no need, she said. I'm not afraid of the dark.

On the way out of the subdivision, Teague kept his eyes peeled to the sky, but there was no flash to be seen, no streaking light up and then gone before it seemed possible. And the stars were an unblinking still shot in the vast expanse of space. What moon there was stayed sheepish behind a cloud, the dull and inconsequential glow unworthy of observation. As he drove down the dark county highway toward the motor lodge where were his bags and a stiff mattress and three channels likely gone off the air, he felt like the only moving thing on the planet. But by the time the door slammed hollow in the parking lot and the key clicked one final time in the door, he knew he'd throw in with the Coles for the long haul. And that night he slept like a dead man, never dreaming, never stirring.

Six miles away, Roland walked down the creaking wooden steps of his childhood home and into the kitchen. He stood gazing into the refrigerator. He stood there like that for he knew not how long, in the cool air, the bright light, with the smell of produce and eggs and a multitude of colors and shapes and packages before him. When he shut the door he was empty-handed and heading out the back door. Before he could remember, the screen door banged with a clack, and the echo of the clack bounced around in his head for a while, bounced around against the sounds of night on the farm, until the other sounds stopped and there was only silence and the memory of an echo.

He walked out along the fields, past the barns, the sleeping chicken coop. One by one, as if waiting in line, the sounds of night returned. First a lonesome and sonorous frog, deep-throated by the creek. Then the tree frogs, shrill and staccato, the start and stop of crickets in the field. Finally, the cicadas, the thrumming monotonous overdub that is the essential noise of nights in the South, a sound infinite and omnipresent, unnoticed until the rare moment of cessation. And then the night is complete again, the constant oceanic hum, less electric by the moment, the steady hum and black sky indistinguishable, a synesthesia of impressions—sky, cicadas, humidity, pungent soil—all one thing, womblike and inexplicable, until the nightwalker knows not whether to be comforted by this womb or terrified by the sleight of hand, the impossibility of parceling out the particular. And then the wonder: Am I a part of this or separate? Until the sound of your own shoes along the old path traveled so many times becomes the only sound you hear, a sound disparate and intrusive, the self-consciousness of being, and you must stop walking to stop the sensation of being not quite real, a ghost alongside the fields occupying no real time or space.

And then you remember what to do and you turn sharply into the stretching field of corn beside you. You walk until you find a spot that seems dead center in the field and that is where you stop. You look all around you, life at your feet, at your head, life at either side. You stand there, barely moving, for as long as it takes to vanquish the earlier sound of yourself, until you are no thing at all but eyes and ears and sense, a cricket, a star, the breeze just now rolling through the breathing corn.

Roland stood thus, his back to the house, looking out over the farm and into the sky. He could not recall the last time he was outside, really outside, not simply rushing down a street to a parked car or riding in a golf cart or hosting an outdoor barbecue. He thought it something he should do more of, but knew that he would not. Not for a while at least, with everything still to do. When he retired, he'd buy a piece of land and play the gentleman farmer. Putter around with the tomato plants as the grandkids ran free in the yard.

He began walking, down the other side of the row he'd entered from the path, toward the new stand of sugar maples. The new stand was now thirty-some-odd years old. The old stand, the cool and shady boundary of his youth, the entryway to the wild proper, a youth's wild, a boy's wild, had met the big saw in his ninth year, victims of the blight that wiped out nearly all of the maples in the region. He walked on, sounds of the night, his own steps, unheeded. What a day that had been when the men with the big circular saw came to the farm. It was the tradition then for neighbors, kids especially, to come and bear witness as the timber was fed into the growling, spitting metallic beast. The sheer danger of it, how close the lumbermen got to the blades, their hands and meaty fingers mere inches from the spinning jagged blade. And bango-presto, amid the sailing sawdust, log after uniform log plopping without fanfare to the ground, a kind of mechanized anticlimax after the danger and chaos of its genesis. Then the kids scrabbling in to move the logs so that more could fall, so that the succession of chaos and order could go on unabated, a loud and impressive logic at work here, and never the first thought of the hours of splitting and stacking that the next few weeks would bring.

Heading to the back of the property, with the mountains to the east a brooding and darker backdrop under the cloak of sky, he recalled the great fire of his childhood. One of his earliest vivid memories. Awakened in the night and cradled by his mother down the stairs, groggy and still warm from the bed. And then the sudden cold of outside, a frosted and piercing November night, and all around, a horseshoe, a broken halo, of yellow light, eerie and awesome. His father placing J.T. narrow-eyed in the backseat next to him, Sis still a toddler and sound asleep on the floor wrapped in a blanket as his father cranked and cranked the car, the dry wheezing, the catching sound, a scrape in the ears, and then finally turning over. And the fire on the mountain like the carnival at night, day and night simultaneously, strangely logical. He saw the hazy smoke snaking in the headlights and turned to speak to J.T., the light through the window illuminating his brother as if by gigantic flashlight, his brother's shadow stiff and formal against the front seat. Before he could say anything, J.T. lifted a finger to his mouth and shook his head no. But the way he looked at him let him know it was all right, that he needn't worry. So all the way to his grandmother's house, he watched the glowing mountains in the distance, a glow some two miles away that would get no closer, unable to leap over Louder's Creek and onto the land that was their farm.

Now he arrived at the back acre and turned to face the house. A dull light flickered in the room where J.T. and Corrine were sleeping. It had been their thumping around in bed that had finally driven him from the house, insomnia compounded by banging-bouncing physical exertion one room over, Libby staring at the ceiling from the coverless bed, a rueful smile on her lips, another poor hot night of sleep at the farm.

He sat down on the rough-hewn wooden bench that Sis or one of the men who worked on the farm had moved out. He was sitting under a pecan tree, whose fruit had been one of his father's great pleasures, great luxuries. Beside him the grave of that same father. The woods behind him seemed quietly electric, the scurry and leaf-sweep of a small creature, the cacophony of buzz and chirp, the loony lonely call of a whippoorwill. He looked toward the house, a forgotten glow in the distance.

He thought: I am not ready to have no father.

Then faint steps coming down the same darkened path he'd just gone down. He'd heard no door knocking from the house and no flashlight pointed the way for this fellow nightwalker. He strained his eyes and saw a hand brush away and part several stalks of corn in rounding the corner of the field toward him. He made out a dim silhouette, a darker shadow against the dark background, straw-hatted and walking surely, without haste. Something carried in one hand, a basket perhaps, a small bag.

I reckoned it was you when I heard the door slam, Sis said.

She stood there looking at him, then looked at the spot where their father was buried. Roland scooted over on the bench, trying to summon the actual memory, not the learned one, of the night when Sis came to live with them for good. But he could not. The actuality of recollection no match for the oft-heard tale: the ladies from the church, his parents' nearly instantaneous decision, the strange silence of the baby, he and J.T. as dutiful brothers. These were the facts such that they were, such that he'd been told from his third year forward.

Sit down, he said. I got room on the bench.

Been tossing and turning all night, she said. Momma keeps it too hot in there. Let me stand here a minute and feel the breeze.

Roland nodded, regarded the sister before him. A wicker basket. That's what it was.

You want a sandwich? said Sis. Meatloaf sandwich.

Roland said that he would. He'd forgotten he was hungry and quickly recalled his aborted attempt for food while standing in front of the refrigerator. It seemed a long time ago and as if that were some other person, a distant memory, a dream.

He took the sandwich out of the aluminum foil and began to eat in earnest. He'd not eaten supper, moving as he had from filming the commercial to shaking hands in town.

This hits the spot, he said.

Sis did not reply but gave an affirmative shake of the head. The basket was on the ground and she reached down and pulled out an apple. She handed it toward Roland.

Yes, he said. Thank you. He threw the crumpled foil in the open basket and took the apple. Sis was again reaching in the basket, this time pulling out a thermos. She unscrewed the cap and poured, then handed the full cup to Roland. Springwater, she said. Cold.

He drank the first long sip while still chewing a bite of apple. The cold water and sweet apple together were better than he might have thought possible.

Headstone's supposed to be ready next month, said Sis, pointing at the dirt, discolored and reddish but swept clean at their feet. Fresh flowers had been placed on the spot where the headstone would lie and they gave off an aroma that was too sweet, an aroma Roland had registered but somehow not yet accounted for.

What kind of flowers are those?

Hyacinth, Sis said. They're pretty, but I don't like the way they smell. Do you?

No, said Roland.

She pointed at several plastic wreaths, glowing dully on their stands, a few artificial arrangements on the periphery of the grave. Momma says we can move those when the headstone gets here, she said. I don't like em.

No, said Roland. I don't either.

Plastic, said Sis. Fake-looking. Momma thinks it'd be too bare looking out here if we were to move em and the fresh flowers don't last in this hot weather.

Roland nodded and took the last bite of the apple. He tossed the core in the woods behind him.

That dirt looks better than plastic flowers, said Sis. You can tell they're not real from fifty yards away. Church sent em though. That big purple one with the fake laurel wreath. And the bank sent the other big one. The rest are just from friends and such. I put real flowers on when I find em. Purple clover and jimson. I put some dandelions on there one time, some yellow ones. Momma said, what are you doing putting those old weeds on there?

Roland smiled in the darkness. Sis was smiling.

She was just joking.

Roland nodded. His sister had an ear cocked to the woods.

Whippoorwill, she said.

I heard it, said Roland. It's a lonely sound, isn't it?

Sometimes. Other times it's like they know you're out there and just want to say hello.

Trains do me that way, Roland said. Sometimes it's a lonely sound. But mostly it's just a sound to remind me that someone else is out there, someone else is awake out in the world.

That engineer's awake.

He is.

That'd be fun.

I suppose it would.

See all kinds of places.

Yes.

Well I'm going back inside now. Good night.

Good night, said Roland. Thank you for the picnic.

You're welcome, said Sis, picking up the basket and turning to go. Over her shoulder she said, set out here as long as you like. Daddy'll like that.

And then she was gone. Roland watched her bend around the corner from which she came, the stalks fluttering briefly in her passing then still again. The cicadas had settled into a low and perfunctory hum. The stars above flickered faintly like dolls' eyes through the cracked door of a child's room. He listened for the whippoorwill but that seemed finished for the night. An interlude of leaves rustling: lizard, field mouse, wood thrush. Then nothing. He seems now a small figure on the bench, a man carved from wood by a giant's hand, a part of the unblemished night tableau. The recently turned ground at his feet might not be noticed by a stranger walking these grounds, hardened as it is, dry as it is. Only the faint blink of starlight off the plastic flowers might catch the stranger's eyes.

The Long Sell

1979

Fall came, and J.T. felt a remarkable spring in his step. To be in good health during this season of change emphasized what you were not: old, enfeebled, dying. He felt wonderfully undead. And this knowledge of his own vitality lingered poignantly around him, would sneak in for minutes at a time, sometimes an entire day, and he would find himself wired and optimistic, his blood coursing against the tide of the world's mortality. Such was his kinship with the crisp day, the clean city street, that he entered the First Bank of Glennville with more than a little hesitancy.

Good morning there, Mr. Cole, said the security man at his desk.

J.T. veered away from his path to the elevator and came to lean at the check-in point. Good morning, Ralph, he said. How's the world treating you this fine day?

Just sitting here getting rich. Not doing a thing.

J.T. smiled. This was an old routine.

Said Ralph: Wish somebody'd told me about CDs a long time ago. I'd be retired by now.

Thirteen, fourteen percent interest is about as good as you're ever going to get, said J.T. May not always be like this.

Well I'm riding this horse till it drops. I'm ready to see if those fish bite during the week too.

Do they bite Saturday and Sunday? said J.T., walking toward the elevator.

Why sure they do.

You keep telling me that. But nobody's bringing me any catfish.

Monday, said Ralph. Guaranteed on Monday.

J.T. waved a hand over his head then rounded the corner to the elevators. Ten seconds later came the dinging announcement of his arrival on the executive floor. Immediately he was set upon by Roland's secretary, Mrs. Barnes, who came rushing at him with a sheaf of papers and an accordion folder packed to the brim. Roland wanted you briefed, said Mrs. Barnes.

And then she was fairly goose-stepping him down the hall to the conference room.

Good morning to you too, said J.T.

Roland wanted you briefed, said Mrs. Barnes.

J.T. turned about in the hall, looking for his own secretary. He thought he'd made it clear that Sally was to run interference on these type of things, keep him out of harm's way and the earnest and excitable Mrs. Barnes. But Sally's desk in the foyer across the way was empty and his own office, a mirror image of Roland's, sat woefully unprotected. Where's Sally? he asked.

Her son's sick today, said Mrs. Barnes. She couldn't find a sitter. You've got a few minutes to look over the loan agreement before Mr. Knight arrives. Coffee?

She swept off toward the office kitchenette and J.T. entered the conference room alone, weighted down with documents, face set in a mock scowl. His brother sat at the long table, flipping through pages of his own.

You got to get her off me first thing in the morning, said J.T.

Roland smiled. It's good for you.

That's just a little too efficient, don't you think? said J.T., flopping his papers on the table and sending them sliding across it in a disheveled heap.

She is efficient.

She's a right pain in the ass is what she is.

Speaking of secretaries, said Roland. Do you know anybody who needs one? Or a receptionist or anything else? Becky Randoph called this morning and she's looking for work. She started crying about halfway through the conversation, so I'm not sure what she's looking for or what she's qualified to do. I couldn't make out half of what she was saying.

Becky who?

Randoph. Jim Randoph's wife.

Oh yeah. Sure. Jim leave her or something?

A few months back, said Roland. Met some young thing and just took off for Florida. Becky says she's about to lose the house and Jim hasn't sent the first child support.

He always was a sorry piece of shit.

He helped us on that Parnum deal though.

Yeah, and made about fifty grand to do it. So his wife wants to work?

I don't know that she wants to. But she's got a couple of teenage kids.

I'll make some calls, said J.T., pulling out a chair but not sitting down. They might need somebody down at the new Craigsville branch. I'll call Steve today and find out. Could she sell CDs?

Roland again took his seat, glancing at a loan application in the process. I think so, he said. She's smart. Personable. Looks good. Good dresser and all that.

Call her today, said J.T. Tell her we'll get her a job. I don't know what or where, but if she's ready, we can put her to work on Monday. I'll sort it out. She need any money to get by?

I asked her that, said Roland, and that's when she broke down. I asked her to call back tomorrow. But I'm betting she could use some cash.

All right. I'll front her.

Roland nodded and set the loan form once and for all on the table. These bankers are hell on their women, aren't they?

Not just bankers, said J.T. How many people do you know who are getting divorced?

They're dropping like flies.

J.T. nodded but said no more.

Well, let's get down to business, said Roland. Jerry Knight wants two million for that shopping center out in West Glennville.

J.T. now took his seat opposite Roland. He got any collateral?

He's got twenty houses under construction in a subdivision down in West Branch. A few of them are near finished.

Half-finished houses. Yeah, everybody needs half-finished houses. Isn't that the subdivision he used on the marina deal? Hell, that was over a year ago.

You got a problem with that?

I don't, said J.T. pointing at himself for emphasis. But the FDIC might.

We'll run it through Citizens Bank in Quincy.

J.T. opened and then closed the folder in front of him. Stenciled on the tab was *Jerry Knight/Shopping Center*. The handwriting was tight and precise, legally impressive, as if decorum were the rule of the day. J.T. looked out the window where the river ran below toward smaller towns and farms, perhaps a few areas not yet developed. It's nice to have options, he said.

It certainly is, Roland agreed.

Then Mrs. Barnes was entering the room with a steaming cup of coffee. She placed a napkin squarely in front of J.T., then the mug of coffee squarely upon it. Neatly to the side, she lay sugar packets, a plastic stirrer, setting them there as if with golden tongs, necessary instruments all in the urgent world of finance. Finishing the preparations, she nodded once at her handiwork then left with a brusque flurry of heels. Across from him, Roland was grinning.

She's overqualified, said J.T.

Roland nodded.

J.T. picked up the coffee and blew upon it with delicate angel wisps of breath, lips pursed, eyes rounded in cherubic innocence. This was performed for the viewing pleasure of his younger brother, a gag perfected over the better part of forty years.

That never gets old, said Roland, but he was smiling despite himself.

Pfff, pfff, pfff, said J.T.

Hot, said J.T.

I have sensitive lips, said J.T. You know that, brother.

Said Roland: You know Teague's going to the city council meeting tonight.

J.T. poured exactly one and a half packets of sugar into his mug, then began to swirl the stirrer in his coffee with utmost vigor and concentration. And how's old Teague looking forward to that?

The new Expo vice president, said Roland, is looking forward to his first council meeting much the same way the shoat looks forward to the farmer's blade.

J.T. took a protracted and satisfying gulp from his mug and said: Did you tell him the mayor's got things under control? That they're jumping through whatever hoops he holds up like the trained poodles that they are?

I did. He seemed unpersuaded.

J.T. smiled. I'd say our man in the shadows doesn't care for the bright lights.

Would you want to mess with that gaggle of half-ass businessmen and old-money druggists?

Not with a gun to my head, said J.T. What's that citizen's group again? KGB or something?

GCG. Glennville Citizens' Group. Small but vocal.

Groups like that, said J.T. They're like a bunch of kids. Just got to let them cry it out. They'll fuss and holler and raise all kinds of hell. But if you wait them out, just stonewall the hell out of em, they'll peter out eventually. Only family things and your own pocketbook can keep you pissed off for long, pissed off till you're going to take it all the way. Five percent property tax increase? We're talking thirty, forty dollars for most folks. That's not enough to stay huffy about.

That's what we're counting on, said Roland. How long can they sustain.

Said J.T.: And the thing is, they wouldn't like anything that might be good for the city, might get this city in the national discussion, if it means somebody in town making a little cash on it. Some folks would rather live

in the shithouse than see their neighbor move up in the world. They don't
care what they got or don't got. All they care about is what *you* got. Even
if what you got might help them out sometime down the road.

A lot of them already have money, said Roland. Had it from the day
they were born. They just don't want you to join the club.

That's why you start your own club, little brother.

That's exactly why.

We going to make some money today?

We are.

That's good, said J.T. And if you don't mind, I'll leave this Jerry Knight
business to you. I've got a few things I'm working on myself. But tell
Knight I said hello. Tell him I'm still interested in those Derby tickets if
his man can still get them.

Back in his own office, J.T. left a message at the Craigsville branch regarding a job for Becky Randoph. When that call was through, he considered
dialing Corrine at home. The interior decorator was coming today and
she'd been in a frenzy to straighten the house. The maid looked on the
verge of hara-kari, such was the bustle and boss around the house, and
he'd narrowly made it out the door before he'd been put to the mop himself. He thought that at a hundred dollars an hour Daniel the designer
could have cleaned the house himself. Already he could picture a house
of blushing pastel and big cushions and furniture no one was allowed to
sit on. He couldn't figure out why the house needed decorating. It looked
fine to him. He'd have paid her a hundred dollars an hour to leave the
house as it was. But Daniel, who apparently had no last name, had done
Libby and Roland's house and half the houses in Thousand Pines where
the muckety-mucks lived, so now he was doing theirs, fixing what wasn't
broken.

J.T. picked up the phone and dialed. He could see her rushing around,
barking orders, moving a coaster here, a framed photo there, cursing
the ringing phone over the roar of the vacuum cleaner, the humming
dishwasher, every television in the house turned to a different channel

and blasting at full volume. A calm and relaxing house, his. Placid as a mountain lake. He let the phone ring and ring, perverse to do so, mean. He could see her stomping back and forth across the kitchen, the bedroom, the den, a ringing phone in every room, whichever way she turned, thinking, who in the goddam hell can't figure out that I'm not home?

Finally, a rushed and harried and aggressive HELLO!

May I speak to the man of the house? said J.T., disguising his voice in a weak attempt at smooth and earnest elocution, the voice of the phone solicitor.

He's not here, said Corrine.

In the background, J.T. could hear the roar of assorted electrical cleaning machines. Otherwise she'd have recognized the voice. May I ask if you are the lady of the house?

Yes, said Corrine, I am. But I'm very busy right now.

I ask just a moment of your time.

Fine, yes, go.

Is your refrigerator running, ma'am?

What?

Your refrigerator, ma'am. Is it running?

Oh goddammit.

J.T. was laughing.

J.T.?

This is Daniel, ma'am. Ma'am, if your refrigerator is not running, I can bring over a lovely lavender one. If it is, well, then . . .

Corrine let go with several seconds of rollicking and rhythmic oaths.

This set J.T. to laughing harder.

I got no time for you right now, J.T., she said, ending the call with a jarring click.

He hung up the phone, picturing his frazzled wife, the incipient meeting with the hoity-toity decorator. He'd love to be a fly on the wall for that rendezvous. He swiveled in his chair and looked out the great and seamless panes of glass. His view of the river was farther upstream and he could trace it, a sodden brown worm, bending listlessly up around

Moore's Landing and then straightening out, the straight section of a fishhook, before it would turn sharply at Creech Bend, where Roland's view commenced and his own came to a close. The city beneath him was the backside of downtown, factories and old plants, rusted-looking railroad tracks and abandoned grey buildings, all of the industrial side of the river. Also William Glenn Fort, the first white settlement in the area and the founder of Glennville's home. A two-story log cabin surrounded by twelve-foot timber walls, a raised sentry post at every corner. Standing now as an isolated antiquity, an island of wood surrounded by steel and concrete and the highways that looped in all directions around it. Strange to look at. What here doesn't fit? Behind the fort, the black pocket of town, housing developments and small houses huddled closely together, fading greens and yellows and blues, and everywhere you looked, clothes on lines hung out to dry. He and Roland had flipped a silver dollar to determine offices and his call of tails had proven the loser. But after a few weeks, he'd decided his was the view he preferred. The greys and browns of the underside of industry, the wrong sides of tracks, he found oddly compelling, plaintive and intractable, a slice of Glennville completely lacking in the promise of money. Looking out over it now he wondered if this was the reason he found it so calming and serene.

He felt serene. Though they'd lost the election the year before by a sizable margin, they now had larger quarry in their sights. He couldn't now say how the Hart pardon fiasco played into Montgomery's victory. Sometimes you just got beat. Sometimes luck just wasn't with you. Running a Back to Basics campaign in the midst of scandal in the governor's office, well, that was smart or lucky or both. So they got beat. Time to lick wounds or holler, next!

To choose the latter was an easy choice. To win the fray, one had to stay in the fray. That there'd be some knocks on the head and some bloody lips along the way, well no shit. Only kids and silver spooners thought otherwise.

He pushed back in his chair and stood up. Paced around the office a bit. Any moment now the decorator would be arriving for tea and crumpets. How far she had come, he thought. So much farther than even himself.

And had not changed a lick. The battle between wanting to be herself and wanting to be one of *them* ongoing, ceaseless. It was easier for a man to be himself, more socially acceptable. He had known for a long time that the one thing that drew them together, that kept them together, was this idea of making it, of doing what the hell you're going to do without changing who you were. Corrine would only dish out the tea and crumpets for so long, would only come to you on your terms if you were hospitable to her efforts. But the first sign of the high hat and she was just like he was. All bets were off. An injuring kind of pride, yes, and one his younger brother seemed not to possess.

That wasn't true. They were raised in the same house by the same parents. What Roland could do was keep his pride in check better, smile at the high hat and never act insulted. But he'd file it away, it would register. And when the time came, when the moment proved opportune, the high hat would find his lid upended and being tossed by the wind, flipping end over end down a busy city sidewalk.

At any rate, he'd not have made it this far were he married to another. Too few people, man and woman alike, could stand the risks he'd had to take, the boom-or-bust mentality. But Corrine had. Being bust a whole life makes boom or bust an all-upside scenario.

He loved his wife and had since the day he first saw her on the bike. More than that, he liked and respected her. Respected her toughness and innate sense of pride. Her indomitability. So it was with some chagrin, some misunderstanding of self, that he picked up the phone to call the lake house, where April, the waitress he first met at the country club poker game, would still be lounging in bed, the bed he planned to be in sometime after lunch.

She answered, sounding fresh but sleepy.

Sleeping the day away, said J.T.

I work nights, she said. Or did you forget?

You need to quit that job anyhow.

A girl needs her independence, you know. It's a big scary world out there for a little old country gal like me.

Oh hell, he said.

A little ole country gal all alone in the big mean world.

You're laying it on thick now.

She laughed, a quick mischievous laugh, like tiny foreign currency spilling on a marble floor. All alone, she said. In this big warm bed.

Not for long, said J.T.

Bring cigarettes, she said.

And then, yawning leisurely, she hung up the phone.

J.T. looked once more out the window, at the still-shaded side of the riverfront, the factories spiderwebbed with dim light flicking through the alleys that intersected the tall buildings on Franklin Street, a dingy brown barge pushing against the brown river.

Then he swept out of the room without once glancing at his desk.

A Doorbell Rings

And it sounds too cheery. Corrine notes this as she fluffs one last pillow on the living room couch. The couch itself too brown, stodgy, earthy, boring, country, what-have-you. She walks over white carpet, plush and too predictable. The carpet says *established*. Says it too hard. Does not say modern savoir faire. It is time, she knows, to move past the Southern Living experience. Though she subscribes, though she reads through the articles with a sighing breakneck speed, she has not ever borrowed an idea. What has happened is subconscious. The stately, stale composure of the magazine features has seeped into her consciousness unawares and she has, without knowing it, become her poor departed mother. Her mother, who never had a nickel to her name. And in subconscious homage, she has been decorating the house in honor of her dear departed mother. Her poor mother. She'd have walked in this living room and never left. It must go, though. It must and it would. She hurried toward the front door, passing antiques of every shape and woody utilitarianism. Her mother's ghost followed in her wake, pleading for restraint, for the status quo. God love her, thought Corrine, but home decoration did not begin and end with Dr. and Mrs. Wallace of Henry City, Tennessee, whose living room you chanced to spy when your car ran out of gas in front of their house lo those many years ago.

Well hello, she said, en route. Her voice sounded country. By god, it was country. Elocution lessons next, she thought quickly, and spat out a brittle laugh, quick and ironic and self-aware. Glancing at herself in the mirror, she had to admit the hair looked good. And though she was loath to admit, so did the slacks and top. Casual-dress. See how Mrs. Dr. Wallace looked in these pants. HA!

She went to the door and opened. Well hello, she said.

JACKET, HAIR, FINGERNAILS

They'd been at it only a short time when she noticed the fingernails. The jacket, flamboyantly madras, a sneering wink at the sorts of jackets old men wear, had been the first thing to catch the eye. And then the hair: what there was of it. A silky egg-yolk color, slick against the narrow skull, so fine that it was all she could do not to touch it. Such was her fascination with the head of hair that the mustache of similar color, texture, and sleekness passed by her consciousness with little if any impact. It was when he ran his hand across the glass-cased whatnot that held her mother's spoon collection that she came across the fingernails. To wit: manicured, sleek, a pearly polish that caught the glow of the Tiffany lamp on the side table and sent it shimmering around his tanned wrist and madras sleeve and all about the room. On the pinky finger of the left hand the nail had been allowed to grow well past societal norms for either gender. It too was manicured, pearly, etc. But where the other nails were merely precise and decorative, this one seemed functional as well, such was the crisply round edge. It looked like a tiny, beautiful, pearl-colored shovel. And as the eyes above the hand looked once around the room as if suddenly saddened, the bearer of the gaze lessened and irreversibly so, Corrine had a sudden thrill of epiphany. *Cocaine.*

PERHAPS THIS WOULD GO BETTER IN THE DEN

Or your personal office. Someplace more casual, you know.

Corrine agreed quickly, barely restraining herself from making a mad dash for the whatnot and moving it bodily into the hall, garage, wherever, the antique spoons, the spoons she'd brought back to her mother from whichever trip she'd been on, clanking against one another in a mad tumble of sound. J.T. had given the whatnot to her mother one Christmas, picked it out himself in an antique mall downtown, then had it refinished and the glass replaced. Her mother loved it, had hugged J.T. and daubed at her eyes when he'd brought it in from the garage. Inside had been a beautifully wrapped box of tiny silver teaspoons from London.

But it must go. It would go. Was gone.

This, said the decorator, pointing at a spot on the wall to stand for all the wall and all the walls in the room, should be different.

Yes, said Corrine.

What do you see?

She did not know. Lighter? she said.

He made a head motion not completely dissimilar from a nod of assent then turned his back to her to face the windows.

The curtains, she thought. Those curtains cannot do.

These curtains, he said, won't do.

TEA?

Said Corrine when she heard the maid ask the same question faintly from the kitchen, against the dull rattle of pot, cup, and saucers being readied on a tray.

No, said the decorator.

Corrine nodded. She'd have liked some, but didn't want to sit down alone. No thank you, Alice, said Corrine over the decorator's shoulder.

THE QUESTION OF BIOGRAPHY, BEING TWO ALTERNATIVES:
  1. HE AIN'T HEAVY . . .
  2. OH FUCKING GET OVER YOURSELF

As Daniel walked around the room, silently, running a finger along an upholstered couch, the drapes, eyeing with unequivocal distaste all that passed before his disbelieving eyes, Corrine tried for the life of her to imagine where he came from. Who was he? What did his parents do? Which private school did he attend? Had he made his money doing this or was he staked at some point? How long did he live in New York? How long in Paris? Where did he eat supper when he went out to eat? Where did he buy his clothes? Had he a lover? Who were his friends and did they have long pinky nails too? Had he friends as a child? As a child what had he wanted to be? Was he born with nose in air or had it been a thing learned at school? Had he been mistreated by boys in the neighborhood and affected this air as a method of self-preservation?

She remembered the dress her mother made for her first year of school, the taunting of the kids, the week-long refusal to return to school, her father laying down the law: there would be no new dress. There was no money for a new dress. She would wear the dress her mother made or it would be the belt. The homemade dress was pink-figured and cotton, with white rickrack on the hem and collar. A lovely, lovely dress. And it had caused her only shame. How high she'd kept her head that first day back, in the homemade dress, with the boys hollering out, HOWWWWW-DEEEE, like Minnie Pearl on the Grand Ole Opry as she walked down the hall.

Where do you like to go out to eat?

Excuse me?

In Glennville. Where do you like to go out to eat?

Nowhere in Glennville, he said with a throaty, halting laugh.

You must cook.

No, I don't cook.

Corrine glanced at the oval wooden frame he held in his hand. It contained a small painting her mother had done late in life, after her father had died, when she was looking for ways to pass the time.

You must have someone to cook for you then, said Corrine, smiling, looking still at the small painting of her mother's.

I do, said the decorator.

And you never take your special cook out to eat in Glennville?

When we go out, we go to Fratelli's or the Brass Lantern. But I hardly call that going out.

We eat there, said Corrine. Both those places.

THERE'S JUST NO ACCOUNTING FOR TASTE

That they frequented the same restaurants had little apparent effect on the decorator. He glanced once at the painting in his hand then set it down on the coffee table. Corrine could see the mountains in the background, the sugar maples just about to turn, the small frame house set up hard against a sunny cove. Her grandparents' house. She knew nothing about composition or brushstrokes, dimension, the use of light. All she knew was that the small painting looked as the house had when she was a girl, down to the chrysanthemums running in big-headed bunches along the front porch. The decorator eyed an antique secretary in the corner, seemed to measure it against the angle of the couch, the light slanting in from the bay window.

What do you think of it?

The secretary?

No. The painting.

The decorator turned fully toward her and made direct eye contact for the first time. In the lazy lemony light separating the two of them, he looked vaguely angelic, mustachioed and beautiful and ridiculous. His beautiful nails flickered this way and that like forgotten bits of glass in a mall parking lot. Dust, faint like tiny flakes of snow, was wafting in the air all around his head. You were never rid of all the dust, no matter how many maids a-vacuuming. She wondered if the tea was still hot.

The painting, he said, should probably go wherever you decide to put the spoon collection.

I agree, said Corrine.

The decorator nodded. The look he gave now said, *go on, out with it, you are not finished yet.*

My mother painted that picture, Corrine said, going to the coffee table and picking it up. She was looking at it, looking through it, actually, talisman to her barefoot girlhood.

Yes, said the decorator. It has that homey feel.

I think I'll keep it where it is.

The decorator smiled, not unkindly.

And the spoon collection too.

AND HERE IS THE CHECK

They had come to the same conclusion simultaneously, painlessly. The check would be for two hours at a hundred per hour, a price that allowed for the drive out and back and the fact that there would be no future hours. Corrine had gone to the den for her checkbook and returned with it and with two of the pastries that were to have been served with tea. She handed the decorator the check and offered him a pastry.

None for me, thanks, he said.

Corrine smiled, glanced once at the spoon collection beside them in the whatnot. We're never quite rid of our families, are we? she said. Or our childhoods either, I guess.

I am, the decorator said, a smile sure and fleeting across his lips.

Corrine smiled at this bluff but did not call him on it. And when the memory of his footsteps going down the steps was but just gone, she was lying on the couch in her living room, her mother's painting where it had been, the spoon collection as it was, a feeling of uncertain ease coming with the light through the windows, a moment of almost certain peace.

Teague Under Fire

Teague sat in the auditorium of old Glennville High, converted some years back for purposes of city administration. He was on the stage, sitting at a long folding table with the mayor and eight members of city council. People were still filing in, shaking out umbrellas and removing wet hats. The storm had started just as Teague parked the car and he'd had to dash several hundred yards to the building. Now he sat, still a little wet, and listened to the rain falling on the roof of the auditorium. He found the storm prophetic, ominous. The people filing in did not smile and did not mind staring at the occupants of the long folding table. Their stares were unchecked and unapologetic and the people behind the clinical eyes seemed willing to have come a great distance in much worse weather, perhaps on horseback, camel, mule, to have a frank look at Teague and others on the city council.

Schools had long depressed him, especially on rainy days when everything smelled moldy and old, and he couldn't help thinking of faculty meetings and the smell of mildewed teachers in a room. Had there ever been a faculty meeting when it wasn't raining? He couldn't recall one. But now the chairman was calling the meeting to order with confident bangs of the gavel upon the cafeteria table. Then the chairman called on Jeff Thurman from the south side of town, an old baseball foe of Teague's from American Legion ball, to say an opening prayer. Teague was asked to bow his head. He'd never been to a city council meeting and found this ritual quaint and unnerving at the same time. He'd discussed the First Amendment in his high school classes, how different groups interpreted the argument about the separation of church and state. With his head bowed, he thought: (1) It will be a nondenominational prayer, and (2) there are no members of the Jewish faith on the stage.

He was wrong on both counts. They did pray in Jesus Christ's name. And it was David Abrams's face he saw first when he thought it safe to unbow his head. He wanted to exchange an ironic look with Abrams, a first-time councilman and owner of a chain of dry-cleaning establishments in the area, but Abrams only looked out at the audience with an implacable expression, benumbed it seemed by a lifetime spent in this land of Wesleys and Calvins.

Then he remembered that the state legislature still regularly prayed on special occasions, with the death of a member or a particularly troublesome event that taxed the limits of human understanding. How odd, he thought, public prayer at this late date in the twentieth century. How very fucking odd.

Then he was asked to stand and face the flag, limp and dusty-looking in the corner, and make his pledge to it. Everyone around him placed hand over heart and began to recite. They were all just a syllable behind the chairman, who intoned his pledge with ardor and a kind of stern determination. Teague, hand on heart but not saying the words, wondered why he so disliked the Pledge of Allegiance. It wasn't just the perfunctory nature of it, though that was some of it, the rote recitation of that daily boyhood desk shuffle and squeak before one teacher and then another. When he was young, he'd taken the pledge seriously and had not appreciated his classmates jacking around and manipulating the words to comic effect. But as he grew older, the forced nature of it, always in public, always with some pallid-looking politicos, had planted the seed of a minor personal rebellion. Saying the Pledge as part of becoming an American citizen? Yes, that would be moving and good. Saying the pledge in front of enemies of the state or with a group of fellow outcast Americans in a hostile environment? Yes, that might mean something. But this, this rote and sloppy and unfeeling ritual, it was below nothing and lessened him in a small but real way.

Quaker at heart?

Or is it that Teague has no allegiance?

Or is it that Teague does not like to commit himself?

Teague knew not. He had his inclinations, but even these he couldn't, or wouldn't, have sworn on.

Now it is that he stands at the podium, looking out at a small grey sea of faces, below and beyond him. The small affairs of city council have been attended to: the reading of last month's minutes, a tabling of a discussion on extending the hours of the city dump, a unanimous vote of aye to forming a committee to investigate the feasibility of adding five new railway crossing guards on the south side of town, a recitation of beer board violations. The chairman had then passed the podium to the mayor, who had said a few general words about his support for the Expo and what the Expo could do for the community. And then he'd given the floor to Teague, vice president of the Expo Commission, who would be glad to answer any questions you good folks might have.

The first of which had come from Andrew Timber, a plant by the mayor, Teague assumed, working as he did in the mayor's office. What, he asked, could the Expo Commission promise the Glennville community in both the short and long term?

Teague picked up the legal pad in front of him, then set it down again without looking at it. He listed jobs, short- and long-term, a state and federal pavilion to be turned over to the city after the Expo's close, a revitalized downtown, four new state-of-the-art hotels, the cleanup of the long-neglected Rather Creek area, a raised national and international profile for the city, a state highway project to correct the downtown log-jam long known as Mixed-up Merge, a signature landmark on par with Seattle's Space Needle, and tourists, millions of them, coming and then going, but leaving their millions of dollars behind to swirl up and down and sideways among all the denizens of the greater Glennville area.

And what is the proposed theme of the Expo? Timber, the mayor's man, shot out before any hand could be raised or any question fired.

Energy, said Teague, with what sounded to him like professional confidence. And he did, somehow, feel confident now, he who so loathed a public persona. The listing of community benefits had sounded tangible to his ears, had sounded imminent and lasting. He had a wild thought: We're going to do this. We're going to put Glennville on the map.

A middle-aged black woman now stood up. What would the Expo do for Glennville's black community? What specifically?

Teague again mentioned jobs: construction, restaurants, vendors, positions in hotels.

Maids, then? said the woman, looking directly at Teague. And a few laughs bounced around the auditorium.

There will be jobs for maids, Teague said. And desk clerks. And managerial positions. We're talking a wide spectrum of job opportunities. Anything that has to do with building, entertainment, or the service industry should see a boom. The Expo, in my opinion, will help the economic climate of Glennville for everyone, black and white.

Said the woman: The mayor said some of the off-site exhibits might be held in East Glennville. The mayor said we could expect to see some new construction in the Green Hill Avenue area and around the Municipal Auditorium. Looks to me like the money is going to come downtown and stay downtown. That might suit you and the mayor and the Cole brothers, but it doesn't do us folks in East Glennville any good.

Teague held up a finger to ask for time. Then he left the podium and walked over to where the mayor was sitting. He leaned down and whispered in the mayor's ear: What in the hell did you tell these people?

I said there was a chance of some off-site exhibits in East Glennville, came the reply.

Teague had his back to the murmuring audience, and was now focusing on the professional smile of the mayor, who sat facing the audience head-on.

From now on, said Teague, leaning in as close as he could to the seated mayor, you don't say a damn thing unless we tell you to.

Said the mayor through tight smiling lips like a ventriloquist: I'm the goddam mayor of this city. There won't be an Expo without me.

What there won't be is a third term for you the next time you put me in a position like this.

To this the mayor gave a warm nod of the head, a gesture telling the audience that all was simpatico on Team Expo and that Teague and whatever he might say had the good mayor's blessing. Then Teague walked back to the podium, his shoes sounding heavy and hollow on the wood floor, the smell of wet clothes and residual mold in the air.

Ma'am, he said. We're still ironing out all of the details of what will go where. I'm speaking only for myself here, because there's a team of architects and engineers who are handling the specific planning, but I think the ideal situation for the Expo visitor would be to have all of the events and pavilions on-site. If that's not feasible, everything, ideally, would be a short walk or commute away. But that may not be feasible. If it's not, I'm all in favor of moving some parts of the Expo to East Glennville.

The woman looked at Teague for a moment without speaking. She seemed to be assessing him and he felt dull and shifty under the harsh glow of the lights.

Same old bullshit, said the woman. Then she turned and walked without fanfare up the aisle and out the door.

Yes, thought Teague, the same old bullshit, and me the one up here shoveling it out for consumption. As the crowd shifted in their seats, Teague thought back to the day he'd walked out of a faculty meeting and out of academia for good. The meeting was well into its second hour by that point. He made no comment on the meeting or his departure from it, but simply picked up his coat from the seat beside him, excused himself to get past Nancy Beale, and walked out the door for good. But what he was thinking was, *same old bullshit.*

He knew that the question-and-answer session wasn't over. In fact, it likely would grow worse, much worse, from here. Anyone in favor of the Expo, and that number was sizable, or anyone who didn't care much one way or the other would be sitting at home right now, reading the paper, readying for supper, helping a child with homework.

Not a face in the crowd before him wanted to be won over.

He wondered if he should speak. To let the *bullshit* comment hang in the air seemed a bad omen. But to comment on it, especially when considering the forthrightness and believability of its speaker, would be insensitive at best. At worst, he might incite a riot.

A man with a sheaf of shuffling papers and a flannel shirt was brusquely knocking against knees in his row to get down to the aisle. When he got to the aisle, he stopped a moment to straighten his papers. He reordered them, even licking a finger for traction and more dexterous flipping. He seemed unaware that everyone in the audience and onstage was looking at him. Then running a quick hand through his bushy and uncombed mane of black hair, he bounded down to the edge of the stage. Ah, thought Teague, so here is Lionel Ginkowski.

The citizen activist walked toward the stage and stopped just short of the steps leading up to it. He stood at the foot of the stairs and looked at the mayor and the other members of council before turning his gaze, his magnificent myopic gaze, on Teague.

I'd like to speak from the podium, he said. From the microphone.

Teague met the eyes of the citizen zealot, the wild card in a stacked deck. It was all he could do not to smile. He turned then and caught David Abrams's eye, grinning and looking down at the table. The other councilmen looked, stony faces of Rushmore, toward the chairman and mayor. Where, thought Teague, was a nice, sturdy sergeant at arms when you needed one?

Said Teague: It's not my microphone to give.

As a United States citizen and a legal resident of this city, said Ginkowski, I'd like to address my fellow citizens from the dais.

The chairman and the mayor simultaneously began to rise from their chairs then stopped halfway upon receipt of the knowledge of their synchronized movement. Each waved to each to handle the matter with quick and proper nods of the head, indeterminate hand gestures in lieu of sketchy parliamentary procedure. Watching this Skip and Fetch routine, Teague felt strangely light and absolved, no longer the circus master, but a roadie, a ticket taker, a harmless guesser of weight. Like most events and happenings, like most everything at all, this was beyond his control. Things accumulated a weight and then they began to roll and then there was no stopping them, be it a smooth journey to success or careening bowling ball of destruction. The chairman deferred to the mayor, who now came to the lectern. Teague stepped back to give up the microphone, but didn't sit down, standing in no-man's-land between lectern and the seated council.

You are free, Mr. Ginkowski, said the mayor, to ask a question or several questions from where you're standing. You may also read a short statement that pertains to the Expo if you like.

I would like to stand on the dais and use the microphone, said Ginkowski.

Said the mayor: What difference does it make where you ask your question? We can all hear you. The acoustics in the auditorium are fine.

The microphone and dais give your position undue weight, said Ginkowski. We are, I think, meant to be having a discussion of civic matters. As such, we should be on equal footing. Equal visibility, equal volume. The back of my head is not where I prefer to have people look when I make a point about how taxpayer money is being spent.

The mayor turned to look at Teague behind him. In the audience came bouts of hand-clapping. Many in the audience were smiling, as if watching a play that was turning out much better than they'd hoped.

Teague gave what he hoped was an official nod in the direction of the mayor, he was never quite sure about the silent gestures of club members, then began walking across the stage toward the steps where the man was standing. Again he noticed his shoes echoing off the wood, the audience before him going quiet, and all the while his eyes were on the man standing like the last of the Mohicans at the bottom of the stairs. He walked down to the final step and stopped. Ginkowski seemed unsure whether to hold his position or let Teague pass. Finally he shuffled back a fraction and shifted his shoulders sideways and Teague joined him on the auditorium floor.

I'll speak from here now, said Teague. He turned to the audience and in a near-shout said, can you all hear me all right?

There was no reply. Ginkowski stood looking at Teague and rummaging through the notes in his hand. He glanced once toward the stage, seeking the comfort of familiar foes, the traditional higher ground to which he slung his scattershot arrows, but the councilmen were an army at rest, bivouacked and sipping water, looking with a mixture of trepidation and ease at the scene below them. Can you hear me? said Teague again.

Murmuring. Blank stares. Eventually some woman from the back shouted, we can hear you.

Good, said Teague. Then he said in a near-whisper: What do you want to do, Mr. Ginkowski?

The man looked at the audience, at Teague. I'd like to read from my report, said Ginkowski. I think the audience deserves to hear how much Expo is going to cost them.

Teague turned ever so slightly so his back was almost completely to the audience. He said in that same near-whisper: We're not giving speeches today, Mr. Ginkowski. I'm not, the mayor's not, and you're not. We're here to answer questions. It's an open forum. You may ask me whatever question you like about Expo and I'll do my best to answer it.

I want to read this, said Ginkowski in his normal speaking voice. You're not going to censor me.

Teague looked at the man before him. Let him talk, someone in the crowd yelled behind him.

Good idea, said Teague, turning to face the audience. Mr. Ginkowski, let's hear what you have to say.

Ginkowski turned around and took a step toward the audience. Several people in the front row unconsciously leaned backward as if to give him room. Pulling a bent and dusty pair of reading glasses from the front pocket of his flannel shirt and shuffling once more the assembled papers, Ginkowski began his speech.

Teague forced a smile. Without looking he knew more eyes were on him than on the speaker. Ginkowski was speaking in a serious and unanimated manner. He was walking the audience through the history of the Expo proposal and the genesis of his and the Glennville Citizens' Group's opposition to it. If the first paragraph was any indication, it was to be a long speech. Behind him the mayor seemed to be easing toward the podium, the phrase *parliamentary procedure* already forming on his lips. Teague caught his attention and shook his head. The mayor paused a few steps from the table, then with heavy reservations again took his seat. Teague walked to the edge of the stage and sat down upon it.

Teague's attention to the speech was rapt and insistent for one full minute. During that minute, Ginkowski never once looked up from his manuscript or varied his pitch or intonation. His body wavered not an inch and the only physical gesture made to indicate that this was not some sort of robotron orator was the systematic licking of fingers to indicate the pending progression of pages. Teague looked now to the audience, squeaking slightly about their seats, their eyes slowly being glazed over with statistics and legalese. It was in Teague's second year as a teacher that he learned the best way to combat the class clown was to give him the floor, unopposed, to simply stop talking, smile at the jester, and let him have the fullness of the audience's attention. For the class clown works the back of the room, the shadows, and is at his best in reaction mode, counterpunching, making his deft maneuvers with only a small cavalry of followers to lead. To have the attention of the entire class, and to script from thin air to keep the attention of that audience, an audience of mixed aims and desires on how that hour of the day should be spent, well, that was a tall order for most of the boys of Parker High.

Teague wasn't thinking about the lessons learned at Parker High when he gave the floor to his opponent. It'd been merely instinct, some snap decision made with perhaps the stirrings of experience at the core, but without premeditation. He did, however, feel the heat of the fray. His mind seemed to be going very fast. The belated and much-padded point of Ginkowski's filibuster was that the Expo Commission was refusing to allow a referendum on the issue. What Ginkowski wanted at the end of the day was a vote of the people of Glennville on whether or not they, the citizens, wanted the Expo to come to their city. Tied up in that referendum and the reason for the GCG's opposition to the Expo was, as could be expected, the proposed financing. To wit, how much would the city of Glennville be in for? What would the city's short-term and long-term debt obligation be? And what were the ultimate parameters of the Expo Committee's proposed bond issuance?

Our polls, GCG's polls, said Ginkowski, show that the lion's share of Glennvilleans feel that a civic undertaking of this magnitude must be voted on. A referendum, council. That is what the people want. And that is what the people deserve to have.

Ginkowski glanced once more at the councilmen onstage then walked back to the same seat he'd occupied before. Teague knew now what he should have known before: his own presence tonight was irrelevant. This was a drama well into its second act and no one in the dramatis personae or in the audience expected or wanted some deus ex machina at this late date in the action.

Mayor, he said in his normal speaking voice. Perhaps you'd like to respond?

And then Teague took his seat in the audience like any other Glennvillean to hear what the mayor had to say.

Which, it turned out, was a lot.

Halfway to the microphone and already speaking into it, the mayor said, thank you, Mr. Teague. I think I will.

Though he was progressing slowly toward the paunchy side, the mayor still moved with the subtle grace of the barber he'd been many years before when he'd worked his way through college at his father's downtown shop. The smooth spin of the chair, the effortless brushing of the neck, the silky smooth olé moment of the customer's apron removal. It touched Teague's sense of nostalgia and decorum that thirty years in the furniture business hadn't dimmed Mayor Bing's appreciation of a crowd.

Now he settled into the podium, made his elbows quite at home on either side of the extended microphone, loosened his tie, looked at Teague, and smiled, veteran to greenhorn: And thank you also, Mr. Ginkowski. If all citizens of Glennville were as persistently interested in the welfare of the city as you are, we could get a lot of things done. A whole heck of a lot of things. And if you all in the audience don't mind, I'll speak from here. I am not in good voice tonight and believe you would have a hard time hearing me without the microphone.

A person behind Teague made a joke regarding the mayor's voice, its capacity for endurance if not amplification, and the woman beside the jokester laughed loudly enough for Mayor Bing to glance briefly in her direction. Now hush, the old woman said. He looked right at me. And to this the old wisecracker chuckled low in his throat.

No one, thought Teague, gives much of a damn one way or the other. Just play it safe. Stall. Drag feet. Boosterism. Go Glennville. And we'll be all right. Maybe one juicy public plum. Fixing Mixed-up Merge might be enough. Just don't be arrogant. Can't look like we're shoving it down anybody's throat. Find three main things and repeat them until they're stone, until they're already done. Jobs and tourists and Mixed-up Merge.

The mayor quoted an independent research firm's statistics on the number of jobs the Expo would bring to Glennville, roughly ten thousand. He gave an impassioned vision of a vibrant downtown with a cleaned-up Rather Creek area and the permanent city park to be left there after the close of the fair. He went swiftly through the possibilities of a city monorail to connect the university and downtown, the research to be done for the good of the country and the world at large in the field of energy and energy conservation, more grant money for the university in science and technology, the federal pavilion, the state pavilion, the amphitheater, the permanent landmark that was to be the symbol of the fair and an eternal icon of the city, the untold and immeasurable and once-in-a-lifetime publicity that the Expo would bring to the city, the estimated, a conservative estimate, *fifteen million visitors* to the Expo. At a hundred dollars a person, again an estimate, again conservative, well, you do the math. In short, it was *a brand-new city in the blink of an eye.*

Said the mayor with a short laugh, a wondrous shake of his incredulous and numbers-boggled head: I ask you all, what, exactly, is there not to like?

Teague had his hand up immediately. A few others in the audience had theirs up as well, including Ginkowski, but for the most part they sat there benumbed, catatonic.

Mr. Mayor, Teague said. Mr. Mayor, I have a question.

Yes, said the mayor, suppressing the grin of a well-liked author answering a question from his next-door neighbor. What is your question, Mr. Teague?

Why can't we have a referendum? If the Expo is all that you say it is, all that I and the rest of the Expo Commission say it is, why can't we put it to a vote of the people? Frankly, if the numbers check, I like our chances.

The near-smile slid off the mayor's face. Well, he said, that's not something I can just say yes or no to right now.

I'm just asking, said Teague. Is it feasible? Is it a possibility? Can you tell us that you and the city council will look into it?

Well, said the mayor.

And how much will a referendum cost the city? What would it entail logistically and financially?

They've been stalling for the last six months, shouted Ginkowski, standing now and looking across the auditorium at Teague.

Said the mayor: It would take a vote of the city council, Mr. Ginkowski, Mr. Teague. And at present, individual council members have been going over the literature, what the Expo Commission is promising the city. This is a huge logistical operation. There are literally thousands of details to be worked out.

The mayor paused for a moment to see how his filibuster was being received. When no shouts came from the audience, he seemed to regain his footing, his voice rising with indignation, believing his words now like a great actor, actually and suddenly indignant that he should have to speak thus: I can assure you that I and the council members are spending every free moment we can spare on learning the ins and outs of the Expo. We are spending every free and waking moment wondering how on God's green earth we are going to pull off this Exposition. If, and it's a big if, folks, we are in fact granted a charter by the International Bureau of Fairs.

Stalling, said Ginkowski with a quick violent wave of his arm. More stalling.

How much for a referendum? said Teague. How soon can we get the answer to that?

We're putting the horse before the cart, said the mayor. We don't yet have the go-ahead for the Expo.

Said Teague: If a referendum is what the people want, let's give them a referendum. As I said earlier, the Expo Commission likes our chances. Especially when the public is fully informed of what they stand to gain.

The mayor nodded before shooting Teague one last accusing look. Then he said it really was time to get to other council matters.

Shouted Ginkowski: And who pays, Mayor? In your next report, can you be so kind as to tell us who will be paying for this brand-new city? I'm betting it won't be the Cole brothers. And I'll give you ten-to-one odds it will come down to a city bond in the end.

And though these last comments were directed at the mayor, it was at Teague that the angry man was looking.

With the wrapping-up of the night's agenda and the meeting's adjournment, Teague was hustling out of the building as many steps ahead of Mayor Bing as he could manage. The mayor had left him hanging and then he'd repaid the favor. Before he talked to Mayor Bing again, he'd like to know a few firm things from the Coles. He'd made it to the lobby, shuffling past staring and elbow-nudging Glennvilleans who seemed to want a closer, prolonged, and frank gander at the new head of the Expo Commission, when he was tapped briskly on the shoulder by a young man with sandy hair and a corduroy coat. In the young man's hand, a small notepad. In his shirt pocket, a well-chewed ballpoint pen.

Mr. Teague, said the young man, I'm Sam Tarvin with the *Daily Herald*. Do you have a minute?

Teague smiled, though he felt less than amicable. Now was the time for unapologetic retreat. It hadn't been an all-out rout in there, but close enough.

Got to run, said Teague. Trying to get home for dinner with the family.

The reporter started to grin, then thought better of it. The pen was in his hand now and his pad was flipped open to a chicken-scratched page.

Call our headquarters, Teague said. One of the secretaries will set up an appointment and I can answer any question you have.

The reporter turned then to see the mayor hustling in their direction. So, said the reporter, turning back to Teague, is that the way you guys are going to do it? Let the mayor be the heavy while you play beacon of light for the people?

Teague took in the young man before him, their eyes meeting in the uneasy land of open hostility and wry just-doing-my-job.

No, said the reporter. It was good. I was impressed. No one in the audience saw that coming. I didn't. The vice president of Expo quizzing the mayor, the head of Expo hand in hand with GCG when it comes to the referendum and looking out for the citizens' best interests? Seriously, it was good stuff. My hat's off to you.

Teague laughed. What did you say your name was?

Sam Tarvin.

And where are you from?

Glennville.

Yeah, but where did you go to school?

Harvard, said the young man, appropriately sheepish.

Ah, said Teague. That's where you learned your manners. And who are your folks?

Jack and Karen Tarvin.

That sounds familiar.

So I'm a local boy just like you, said the reporter. But can we expect more of this?

The reporter had now slipped into more of the dialect of the region. And later, on the ride home, Teague would realize that his own avuncular line of questioning about family and personal history had been delivered in a patronizing good old boy intonation, the traditional southern way of putting an upstart in his place.

All I can tell you, said Teague, is that I wasn't prepared for some of the questions. The meeting seemed less about the general overview of Expo and its benefits and more about city policy. So anything you saw in there was off the cuff and was a product of me not knowing the ins and outs of city government.

I have a hard time believing that a man of your experience is very often caught off guard.

By this time the mayor had managed to shrug off the citizens who'd corralled him and was heading at breakneck speed for Teague. I've got to run, said Teague. But one thing I can tell you, Sam, is that politics always catches you off guard. That's what makes it interesting.

Then he was out the door, saying over his shoulder, call the office. We'll talk next week.

Outside, the rain had slackened but was still cold on his hatless head. The cars heading in front of the school sent the water splashing up in a clean, systematic rhythm, and their headlights in the gloomy night looked spectral and warm. He heard the sloshy pounding of hard shoes behind him, running to catch up, then an umbrella was over his head and the breathless mayor was saying, let's talk for a minute.

Fine, said Teague, not slowing his stride. Have at it.

The mayor stopped and the sheltering umbrella stopped with him. Teague kept walking. Again, he heard the mayor's quick splashing steps hurrying to catch up.

Damn it, Mike, I said let's talk. And not while we're running a marathon in the rain.

The umbrella again was over his head. Cars were passing, their lights as they rounded the corner flashing across the pale and angry face of the mayor. Teague stopped. All right, he said. Talk.

The mayor's face was very close to his own and Teague wondered how he'd manage to gesticulate in such close proximity. The mayor was a known and inveterate gesticulator.

What exactly were you up to back there? What was that all about?

You mean my questions?

Yes, damn it, your questions. You made me look like a jackass up there.

I just asked what Ginkowski and several others were going to ask. You had to anticipate questions about the referendum.

I did. Of course I did. But not from the VP of the Expo Commission.

You made us look like some dog-and-pony show that didn't know which way was up.

You didn't need my help for that, said Teague grinning.

The mayor started to rebuke him, made a motion with his umbrella hand that took the umbrella off both their heads, then decided against it.

Teague said: And how about next time I come to address city council in an open meeting, you let me know what you have and haven't promised to the poor folks in this city? Pull what you want on the bigwigs, promise em the moon, I could care less. But don't promise poor folks something we're not going to deliver. Just don't promise em a damn thing. They won't come out to vote much anyway. Why tease them?

I didn't promise them a damn thing, said the mayor, his jutted jaw closing in on Teague's face, breath coming out hot and sour. I just mentioned a few things that had been discussed, that may or may not be on the table once the final plans are done.

No more inner-city promises, said Teague. Like always, they're going to eat shit. Let's not try to tell them it tastes good.

Fine, said the mayor. Fine. The information I'm getting from the Coles and Expo is sketchy at best, so I've been winging it, me and a few of our friends on the council, for about six months now. They're running my ass ragged with this referendum and with the bond issue. And now, tonight, you team up with them and make me look the fool.

Teague placed his hand on the mayor's round shoulder. Just keep holding the fort, he said. The publicity folks are about to turn it up a notch. The newspapers are about to come around to our way of thinking. When I ask a question that GCG wants to ask, it shows that Expo isn't trying to pull the wool over anyone's eyes. That we're not dodging a referendum. That we're not dodging questions about the bond or anything else to do with financing.

What about the bond? said the mayor. We've been telling people the Coles and Expo are handling the financing, that the city won't be on the hook for the first red cent.

As he said this, he fished around in his coat pocket for his cigarettes, more relaxed now, the dawning recognition that tonight served as the introduction of a new and improved strategy. Strategic retreat before unleashing the full arsenal. He pulled two cigarettes from the pack and Teague, lighter in hand, took one the mayor was offering. They might have been spies in the rain, hooded and private under the enveloping umbrella. They might have been lovers, Mafiosos, old friends chancing upon each other in a city other than their own.

The Coles, said Teague, are in the process of securing loans from banks all over the state and the Southeast. The state is going to be involved on a really big level. And so will the federal government, we think.

That all sounds good, said the mayor, his cigarette glowing dully in the gloom.

But, said Teague, walking out from under the umbrella, my bet is the city has to pony up too.

And the referendum? shouted the mayor.

Not if I can help it, said Teague, with a wave of his hand. Then the rain picked up and Teague was sprinting headlong toward his car.

The Mistress Alone

From the lake, one sees lights glowing like the eyes of a jack-o'-lantern. In the distance, the low bellow of a barge just through the lock of the dam, heading toward the city and parts north, a lonely sound. And the house itself looks lonely and forlorn in the wet night, small despite its size, its wrought-iron fence stretching down both sides of the property to the lake, the points of the fence like the teeth of a sharp comb.

All up and down the lake is darkness and the blocky and brooding outlines of empty summer homes.

A silhouette passes in front of the lighted window, stops for a moment to observe the lake below, the grey dock, the shore across the water visible in memory only. She is looking perhaps to conjure a summer that seems too distantly past, though it has only been a month or so since the boat was put up, the last of the summer regulars carrying the skis and life jackets from boat to garage, a wave of farewell to the young woman and her summer friend as they return from lunch or dinner at the Blue Gill Tavern, the restaurant at the marina where on summer weekend nights a slick country band plays.

She turns from the window and walks to the kitchen, isn't hungry, isn't thirsty. She goes into the bedroom and turns on the television, flops on the bed. It is still quite a luxury to her, a television in the bedroom. She thinks of her parents sitting in front of the square and implacable box in their small den, the largest thing in the room, a monument, a raison d'être.

This house has five televisions: a small nifty one in the kitchen, a sleek and expensive one hung from the ceiling in the den, and one each in the three bedrooms upstairs. It is odd, she thinks, to be alone in such a big house at such a young age. It is odd to be a mistress. Since quitting her job as a waitress at the country club, her days run more and more into one another: shopping with friends, lunch with friends, whatever small errands need to be done for the lake house. Two to three times a week, J.T. will meet her for lunch out this way in a small local burger joint where the clientele is not likely to mix with those who know him in Glennville. Sometimes he'll pick up lunch and bring it here, other times she will. Their afternoons are spent, like this one has been, in the bedroom, in the predictable ways. Lying on the comforter of the bed, she glances about the room at the artwork hung on the high walls, the photos of smiling children she may never meet, children who look so unlike their father: scrubbed, suburban, less. And the portrait, above the vanity in the corner, of the woman whose name she never speaks and the grey and knowing eyes of the portrait that look out over the bed and out the window to the lake, the city, and the house where J.T. lives.

Urban Cowboys

Roland's polished wingtips dodged the puddle at his feet as he got out of the car. He tipped the valet, ducked under the dripping awning, and walked past the doorman with a smile and a nod. Inside, he was met with a blast of swinging country music, the uptown variety, for the era of the urban cowpoke was at hand and clean steel guitars and too-polished fiddles were inescapable in the city. Had he thought about it, he surely would have found some irony in the music of the era. For it represented that from which he had fled, that from which so many in the city had fled. Fifteen years ago, it would have been jazz clubs and loungy crooners for the fast set. Now it was country music. Urban country. Whether it was this irony or anticipation of the night before him, he was smiling as he entered the bar area of Rodeo West, a new and flashy place in a new and shining strip mall, the strip malls and stoplights running one into the other. But where had the farmers gone? Where had they taken their old-timey music?

Several people at the bar, younger than Roland by a decade, turned to look at him as he passed, again a nod and a smile for bartender, wait staff, gawking patrons. His suit was not the least wilted, his tie not a fraction askew. At the bar sat men in similar suits, similar but not quite, not quite the cut, not quite the cloth. Many of these had discarded their jackets or loosened a tie after a long day at the office, car lot, or running up and down the Boulevard in one manner of sales call or another. Mixed in the

urban country business crowd were some of the local workers in the construction business, the service industry, a college student or two feeling
adventurous. Bourbon and Coke, longneck beers, scotch highballs.

The women here, in general, were younger than the men and less married, more likely to be of a slightly lower socioeconomic group. Almost all
were working women. Almost all were young and unmarried or recently
divorced and now back in the game, the kids at Grandmom's house or the
babysitter's or spending the night with a friend. It was, to be sure, Friday
night, and the place had that midevening pulse to it where early suppers
are about digested and the first few tie-looseners have been imbibed, and
the music that seemed so loud when you first walked in is now just a
backdropped cacophony, a muffled ocean of conversation and music and
waitresses shouting out drink orders. And the men had begun to notice
the particulars of the opposite sex, some seated at the bar, but most in the
lounge section of high-legged tables and chairs that ran along the plate-
glass window at the front of the restaurant, smoking cigarettes, exchang-
ing boss-boyfriend-ex-husband tales with equal parts humor and ire. The
construction workers, all the workers who had actually *worked* all week,
on their feet, lifting things, hammering things, muscling this into that,
they would be the first to begin the rounds of asking for dances. And they
were the ones who knew the proper Texas two-step. Later on they would
head a mile down the road to the Sombrero, where the crowd was younger
and the business element nonexistent. At the Sombrero their odds were
better. For though the women at Rodeo West preferred to dance with the
men actually in cowboy boots, the men actually in cowboy boots being
younger, stronger, more athletic, when the night got late, it was with the
men in the suits and the thick gold watches, the coiffed heads of hair, that
those of the opposite sex most often gathered.

It was known in some circles that the Coles were silent partners and
majority owners of Rodeo West, but they didn't advertise the point. Just
now, Dennis Langley, the owner of record, was coming through the
swinging doors of the kitchen, shaking Roland's hand and leading him
toward the Blue Room, an intimate enclave of four tables discreetly cur-
tained and partitioned from the rest of the restaurant, where J.T., Johnny

Boy, and Cut Worm were waiting. They gave his arrival nominal notice, laughing and lifting drinks under the faint blue lights that glowed softly above them.

Also at the table, glowing softly blue with her tired-looking eyes, was Valerie. She looked once at Roland, but smiled only after she turned back to the conversation at the table. Dennis busied himself adding a table to the party at hand. With the tables arranged, Roland sat down, away from Valerie. His brother was on one side, Cut Worm on the other.

Scotch and soda? said Dennis.

Yes, thanks, Roland said. He was looking across the table at Valerie, who nodded in a somewhat committed matter to whatever Johnny Boy said to her. One hour, he thought. We're walking out of here in one hour. Don't get caught up in one of those long nights. Two drinks, a quick bite, then out the door.

Cut Worm turned to ask Dennis about dinner specials and J.T. tapped Roland on the arm. He said no words and made no gestures, but Roland got the point.

Yeah, said Roland, speaking in a regular tone but quickly, a mono-toned flurry of fused words, shorthanded and acoustically coded. You're all set up.

Corrine's name, right? said J.T.

Yep.

Did Leary have any problem with it?

Not at all. He seems eager to keep doing business with us. What's the Smithville bank's assets anyway?

Around forty million, said J.T.

Then eight percent seems a little steep.

Price of doing business, little brother. We're not going penny wise, pound foolish at this late date, are we?

Roland smiled. You're assuming we still got the pennies.

Roland watched Dennis part the curtains and hold them for Teague's entrance. Teague thanked Dennis in that cool and understated way of his, sincere and impersonal at the same time. He seemed a man born to the life of valets and tables in cloistered back rooms. That said, his self-possession was now being tested as he made his way to the table and realized a surprise guest had joined them. Roland watched them catch eyes, an imperceptible nod from Teague, a passing smile from Valerie. And then a moment of hesitancy. At which end of the table to sit?

Thought Roland: Perhaps I should have told the old boy about bringing his former mistress to this gathering. But just as awkward over the phone as now. To hell with it. Not one kid at this table.

Then Cut Worm got up from the table and motioned for Teague to take his seat. Teague, composure restored, did so, handing Cut Worm his drink over his shoulder in the process.

Said Roland: Well how did you enjoy your first city council meeting?

Interesting, said Teague. We're damn popular.

That bad? What did they throw at you?

No, said Teague, it wasn't that bad. I had to set the mayor straight on a couple of things. Minor stuff. Then I let him carry the ball most of the way. For the record, none of the plans right now call for any projects or events in East Glennville? Nothing to get that side of town on our side?

No, said Roland. We did look into it. I made a special request that we check the feasibility. But transportation would have been a headache and no real bargains ever surfaced. What it comes down to is we want all the events and pavilions in a centralized spot. Doesn't have anything to do with concern about the other side of the tracks. It's simple logistics.

Teague nodded and glanced down at Valerie without meaning to. Well, he said, the mayor has been putting the carrot in front of the donkey a bit. Seems the folks on the east side thought they'd be an integral part of the Expo. Now they want to know what's in it for them.

Is that what you set the mayor straight on?

It is.

Mayor Bing's a bit excitable, said Roland. He gets a little ahead of himself sometimes. He's already sitting in the governor's office and thinking reelection. Pulling off this Expo will show he's a big player in the state.

No harm done, said Teague. Just caught me off guard a bit. Not used to being on the main stage.

I'm like you. I'm still not sure why in the hell I ran for governor.

Teague laughed.

Here's what we'll do. Tomorrow you give Tyson Taft a call, he's the councilman for that district. See what we can do to shore up support out there. I'd already planned on supplying free one-day tickets for all the kids in the city school system. Maybe we can get some more out through the Boys' Club and old folks home and that sort of thing. We'll see how feasible it is to have some sort of bus that runs a few times a day directly from the Expo site to East High School. So if nothing else, those folks will be able to visit the Expo.

What you do, said Teague, is tie in the bus line with all the jobs we're going to have. So then we could promise jobs as well as a way to get to them. Folks won't have to worry about transportation that way.

Yeah, that's good. We'll try to come up with some more stuff like that and see what Tyson suggests also. It if comes to a referendum, we'll need all the help we can get.

If your man Ginkowski has his way, we're going to have a referendum. And by the way, I played a little devil's advocate with the mayor tonight about the referendum. I think he knows what I was doing, but he might give you a call.

Roland smiled.

I basically just asked some questions that I knew some folks in the audience would ask anyway. And gave the impression that not only is the Expo commission not afraid of a referendum, but that we like our chances if one comes about.

And do you like our chances?

The waitress came by then, delivering drinks and taking orders. Roland wouldn't have minded another drink, but decided against it. Teague ordered vodka on the rocks.

Said Teague: It's a tough call. We East Tennesseans are a skeptical lot. The idea of someone else taking us seriously is just damn hard to digest. The main thing is, the only thing is, is the money. You've heard the term tighter than a Scotch purse? Well, this is the land of the Scotch-Irish. Basically, it comes down to what, exactly, is the source of the funding? Where is the money going to come from?

Roland nodded and took the last watery sip of his scotch and soda.

Teague swirled his straw around and then took a healthy swig. He said: I'm not going back out in public until I have the answer to that question.

Roland looked around for the waitress. If he had to talk business, he'd need another drink after all. He craned his head around, trying to spot her out in the hall. This room, he thought, really is blue. He couldn't decide what mood all of this blue was setting. He felt relaxed and impatient at the same time. At the other end of the table, Valerie was stuck between Cut Worm and Johnny Boy and a couple of younger women they'd invited to join the party. He'd hear about that later. Across from him, Teague's neck was likely stiff, stuck as it was looking straight ahead or left, any which way but where Valerie sat. Just then, the waitress poked her head in the room, and Roland pointed to his empty glass and held up one finger. She nodded and went back out again.

Said Roland: Well, as I said the other day, we hope federal grants will be the lion's share.

Teague said: I'm looking for specifics. If you want to trot me back out there in front of the public, I'm going to have figures for them and a game plan.

Our friend with the Department of Commerce should be coming through with the numbers any day now. Once we have those numbers, which are still estimates, mind you, we should have a better idea where we stand. Then we can start looking at what we'll need from the state. And from private investors.

Teague took a sip from his drink, his glass passing through the blue light en route to his mouth, blue on its descent back to the table. On the other end, Valerie had pulled her chair back from the table, out of the blue light, and sat there smoking a cigarette, its smoke blending with the fumes of the others', swirling in the hazy blue above the table. She looked not long for Rodeo West.

You're putting a lot of stock in the Commerce Department, said Teague.

And with good reason, I think. You wouldn't believe all the grants out there for cities interested in urban renewal.

Teague smiled.

Transforming downtown Glennville is urban renewal.

I didn't say a word, said Teague.

We're the Expo Commission, not the Expo Charity.

I haven't said the first word, Teague said. But someone, somewhere down the line, is going to want names and numbers. I guarantee that young reporter from the *Herald* isn't going to stop till he gets some particulars.

We're still firming things up, said Roland. I can tell you that I'm not an investor. Nor is my brother.

Teague nodded.

Said Roland: Okay, so J.T. and I aren't investors. But if some of the investors we line up end up needing a loan, then we'll attempt to accommodate them, assuming they qualify. And some of these hotel builders and on-site construction companies might need loans as well. We're hoping to use as many homegrown builders as we can.

Teague smiled.

There's any number of bankers in this city who builders can go to for loans.

But only one with an Expo he's bringing to town.

I never said I wasn't trying to make money. Does anyone assume that I wasn't?

I thought you were an altruistic banker, nothing more, nothing less. A civic-minded altruistic banker.

Roland laughed. I am civic-minded.

You are.

Sincerely.

I believe you.

Altruistic might be a stretch though.

A small one perhaps, said Teague. But the idea of you making money off of this fair will sink the ship for sure. You're already a little big for your britches for almost all of old Glennville. You start advertising or even acknowledging that you might make some money off of this deal, a deal that will change the landscape, literally and figuratively, of their beloved and begrimed stagnant city, and we're done for.

I'm with you all the way. I agree completely. So when the question is asked, you say the majority of funding will be at the federal level, with some assistance from the state. I'll leave it up to you whether the term private investor ever makes its way out of your mouth. And at this point, I really don't know who will invest or how much. That's the god-honest truth.

Forgive my East Tennessee roots if I say I'm skeptical that no city funds will be used.

I'm telling you that we are moving forward with Expo financing and that current projections show that the city of Glennville will not have to put up the first cent. Land? Yes. Manpower? Yes. Time and energy? Yes. But no dipping into city coffers.

That's what you're telling me?

Yes.

That's what you expect me to say?

Yes.

Okay. That's what I'll say.

You know I'm meeting with the president next month.

President of what?

President of the United States of America.

Are you kidding me?

Nope. Our friend from Charlotte set it up.

Ah, Mr. Graves from the Commerce Department.

That's the one. The president appreciated our help in the last election.

Well hell's bells, said Teague. If we've got the president behind us, that's clear sailing.

I thought you'd like that.

I do. I like it a hell of a lot.

You want to come along?

Well yeah if I'm invited.

Said Roland: You're invited.

In the smoky blue light, Roland watched the indecipherable smile playing on Teague's lips. He returned the smile, then got up from his chair to join Valerie at the other end of the table.

The Mistress Contemplates Her Role

She sat wondering just what percentage of her adult life had been spent with men in bars. Roland had stopped by for a bit, promising they'd be leaving soon, then J.T. had called him over to a side table for a conference with Teague. More women were gathered at the main table now, girls in their twenties out for the evening and having drinks with the older men as kind of a lark. She lit a cigarette she didn't particularly want and took a sip of wine growing warm in the glass.

Thirty-eight years on the planet. Sixteen years post-college. Twelve years after the divorce. Twelve out of thirty-eight, then. About a third. At the small table, Teague, Roland, and J.T. talked with serious faces and seemed like a disparate entity next to the boisterous large table. She'd been left with the B-team of the entourage and a group of giggling girls who excused themselves every so often to go to the restroom in pairs. She'd heard her father joke enough times about the social boutique of the women's room to rebel at that particular stereotype. She always went to the restroom alone and wondered if her father had been training her from the beginning. He, the former state senator from Nashville, had been dead nearly a decade now. A flamboyant, philandering yellow-dog Democrat of the old school. He'd have been right at home in this present scene, very forcibly at the small table during the present interlude, very successfully with the Powder Room Girls afterward.

She checked her watch: nearly midnight. She wondered if the floating party would close down Rodeo West or take its show on the road. But this was her last stop. If Roland wanted to keep going, he was on his own.

Cut Worm and Johnny Boy and the other B-teamers talked among themselves of local politics and football when the younger women were away. They didn't expect her to join in. They thought her snobbish, she knew, but she could live with that. If they'd just be more interesting. If they just knew how to talk to a woman who knew about politics and football and any other thing you wanted to discuss of the ways of the world, it'd be a different story. How many times had her father said in front of his cronies: This here's the one who should be in politics. Tough and smart and can't bluff her with a stick in your hand.

Alas, alas.

She checked her watch again. Five more minutes with the B-team and she was calling a cab. As if Roland couldn't talk business in front of her. As if she'd ever have a slip of the tongue or betray a confidence. But she knew it was the Teague factor. Roland saving Teague the embarrassment, nothing more.

Tough and smart and incapable of being bluffed. And malleable, Father, malleable. The greatest trait a politician can have. It was what a woman in the political arena had to have, a chameleon-like ability to transform to the man she was with. With Roland she was hard as a diamond, sharp and precise. She was the Urbane Woman to Roland's faux-country-boy charm, his winking and unapologetic flash of new money. As the Urbane Woman, the seductions of the city and old money and political power had been demystified. Such things could not impress her.

Such a role had its merits, but playing it in this cow town was like shooting fish in a barrel.

She'd taken up with Teague nearly a decade before, very soon after her divorce from the Older Gentleman, who turned out to be, if still a gentleman, really quite old. She'd been with the Department of State for a couple of years by then and Teague, fresh from the classroom, fresh to Nashville and politics, had arrived like a smart, well-scrubbed novice. Their courtship around the legislative plaza, in large groups at Rooney's, at barbecue fundraisers and passing each other in the legislative cafeteria, had been a long and drawn-out flirtation. She knew from the first time she saw him at Rooney's how the game would end up. Teague, the novice, thought the contest was in doubt until the very moment he fell into her bed.

The brunette with the perm waved to her now from the other end of the table. In the bathroom she'd offered cocaine and called her Miss. She seemed to think they were in on some prank together. Hijinks and derring-do. Miss? Valerie didn't know whether to laugh or slap her impertinent young face. Miss? Really? Miss?

She swept the notion from her head. Her mind and body were as sharp as ever. At the small table, Teague talked with his hands, paused, listened to Roland's reply. That might have worked, she thought, the Teague situation. But she'd played the role of Fallen Woman too well, and Teague, in his first incarnation as Fallen Man, had been frightened. He needed Fallen Woman to explain his own state of mind, the state of a soul in decline. She'd been masterful, mournful, unapologetic. She never called him, never contacted him in any way. She asked for nothing, nothing of his time, his self. And what he gave her, of course, was everything.

J.T. got up to go to the bar or to buy cigarettes from the machine up front and gave her a small smile as he passed. Their mutual lack of attraction for the other seemed to mystify them both. Pheromones, she thought. Something elemental beyond conscious knowing. To think too much of it destroyed its allure. And it was useless. It was sex. It was nothing.

The irony of Roland and Teague alone at the small table, observed without their knowing by their shared mistress, nearly forced a smile to her lips. Miss? she thought. An Over-the-Hill to that vacuous tart? She thought of her father's longtime concubine and the first time she ever saw that whispered ghost from her childhood, the unspoken and disembodied third member of her parents' marriage. She was twenty-four at the time and engaged to the Older Gentleman when that concubine, that mistress of her father's, came up to her fiancé in the lounge of the Oak Lawn Country Club. Her father had been dead three years. The Older Gentleman introduced her to his old friend, Irene Ray. When he said the name, it struck her like a thunderclap. Her knees felt shaky. This was the woman who tormented her mother's life, who made their household such a glassy and fragile place for all those many years. And here now in the flesh. The woman smiled and offered a graceful hand and why were all the things she'd rehearsed saying in her youthful ardor and anger now stuck in the back of her throat?

The concubine said, oh yes. So this is your fiancée, Edgar. She is as lovely as I've heard.

Then she smiled again and nodded in a way that seemed to indicate something in the face before her was pleasing, familiar. And then she'd made her way across the room, gracefully, a woman at ease in her own skin, leaving Valerie standing there with an empty bag of anger.

She wondered where Irene Ray was now. She wondered if she herself would ride off into the sunset. She knew she cohabitated in a world full of hangers-on, tanned and lined women, pickled, former concubines to a long-dead politico, sponging drinks and dinners now off lobbyists and former colleagues still repaying political favors to the ghost of the politico's libido. Late at night, when her date for the evening had left the table for a moment, these former concubines whispered to her: *Get the cash. Take all the cash they offer. And don't spend the first penny on yourself. There is no will for you, no gold watch for the years of service. You live by the code. You don't call him at home. You don't ask him to leave his family. And you live, as is preferable, in another town. So get the cash. Get what you can and don't think twice.*

But she didn't. Not even once. And the idea of being one of these late-night women, too drunk to drive home, waiting for a proffered ride, the proffered cash for cab fare, was more than she was willing to consider. She'd take up with Teague right now. She'd marry him and have children. She'd ask of him what he needed to be asked. And make such demands as were necessary. They would not be craven. They would not be fallen.

All this?

All this morbid introspection because some tart in the bathroom called you Miss?

No more, she thought. This is quite enough. This is simply beneath you. Of course you won't turn out like that. You'd fall on your sword first.

But one more. One more, insisted the long-neglected sentimental part of her brain. While we are playing the fading, masochistic, former slayer of men, one more and then we'll finish up this Teague business for good:

The truth of the matter is she misplayed the hand.

Yes, she'd been down with the flu for a couple of days. And yes, it was February with a disinterested rain falling from a dishrag sky. Out her apartment window, the quaint apartment on Music Row, she'd watched the drops fall on the landlord's concrete birdbath. Not a bird in days. The man who'd just moved in below, the man who played Mozart, had left his cardboard boxes on the curb for pick-up and they sat there like mushrooms, wilting and sinking. There'd been fog that morning and would be again that night and the occasional car swooshing by was worse than no cars passing at all. She was running a slight fever. It was the first time she'd called in sick to work. When Teague called, asking if he could stop by and bring her anything on his way out of town, on his way back to Glennville, she should have said no. Normally she did say no. The quick awkward guilty farewell after their three or four nights together left her feeling school-girly, moony and dumb, and Teague's manner, his ill-at-ease nonchalance, showed a man already halfway home and thinking about his daughter. Always the kids. No way around the kids.

Was it fair to say she was not in her right mind when she said yes, would he mind bringing her some juice, some magazines? Could she tell herself that now, blame it on the fever?

Or was it the idea of family? The sturdiness of hearth and home and Teague in a role she'd never seen him play?

Or was it the wife? Of whom she knew little, other than she came from money and birthed a beautiful child if the pictures in Teague's wallet could be trusted.

And also that Teague still loved her.

Credit the decision how you will, it was made. Teague came over, bearing juice and snacks and reading material. She'd met him in a negligee at the door. She felt feverish, chilled and hot and light-headed. He'd taken to calling her Cool Customer and laughed, a little nervously, at this change in her demeanor.

Afterward, after the negligee and the ardor, what she'd done was ask him to stay. She asked him once, quickly and still under the feverish guise, then gone to the kitchen for a cigarette. She'd not claimed to need nursing, she'd not claimed anything. All she'd said was, I want you to stay.

When she'd returned to the bedroom, dressed now in a robe, smoking a cigarette, her hair pulled back in a ponytail, she felt halved. Already the strange woman who'd asked Teague to stay, the feverish and needy one, the lonely and rain-benumbed one, was fading away. The smoke from the tip of the cigarette was forming her again into Teague's Cool Customer. She saw him reach for the bedside phone. He sat on the edge of the bed, back to her. He'd put on his pants to make the call, but not his shirt. He'd never stayed an extra night before. His back looked shamed, his posture reluctant and shamed. The Cool Customer thought: *Never mind. I'm feeling better. Just go on home.* But she'd said not a word. And when she heard the first clicking dial of the phone, she knew, without the first doubt, that this was the beginning of the end.

The very end, the ugly, nasty thing that was done just to put the stake in Teague's heart once and for good because he was already gone from her and would not just go ahead and go, well that was something she'd not think about. Time and perspective had rendered it anticlimactic. Sordid, yes. Premeditated, yes. The one thing she'd done in her life that could unequivocally be called *bad*. But anticlimactic nonetheless. The bell had rung, the decision rendered.

And now J.T. was at the table, joking with the B-teamers, the Powder Room Girls, and then they were up in a bustling flourish, gathering up things, stubbing cigarettes, taking last swallows of drinks. The ensemble was en route, the floating party on the move.

At the small table, Roland said one more thing to Teague. Teague nodded, smiled, then he was up and heading out without a word of goodbye to anyone. Roland came over and said: They're all going to the Sombrero. What do you say?

I'm going to the room. You do what you want. I'm fine to get a taxi.

No, said Roland, I'll come with you. I'm all done here.

The Big Game

To stand at the top of the hill looking down at the stadium on game day, to see the throngs of people like a constantly moving and shifting organism, a walking lava lamp, blobbed up here, a pocket of space there, the school colors on shirts and hats, fluttering on pennants and banners, is to witness something writ large. Even better if the game is in October. The alternately raucous and old-fashioned sounds of the band marching down University Boulevard toward the stadium hit the ear that much cleaner, that much more crisp, on a day such as this. The crowd moves leisurely, time yet before kickoff, and the outside ambience is clean and redemptive, the whirling synesthesia of movement-sound-color. Inside the stadium, the stimulation is more crowded, a broad sword of sensations: cigar smoke, popcorn, the cool swig of an iced Coke, batons tossed on high, the audible crunch—POP—of a firm tackle.

There is no need to hurry yet. Youngsters shoot off quickly and without warning from their parents to eye the jerseys and room adornments of the souvenir stand, or suddenly break into dance as the band plays a current hit from the radio. Those of the older generation walk with an easy stride, calling out to old friends only seen on these days, a quick hello or *gonna get em* over the heads of a hundred people, the band launching into the alma mater and the ritual flood of memories—other games, school days, former lovers—that the song provokes.

It should not be underestimated, game day in October.

With the mountains in the distance as clearly seen as they ever will be from town. And those who come by boat, unloading down by the river, honking their humorous boat horns, grilling their burgers. And the scalpers calling, *who needs two?* And those without waving two or three or four fingers as is their desire and then the swift and awkward haggle: *I'll take em* or *believe I'll keep looking.* And those with tickets passing the scalpers, passing those with fingers raised, subconsciously touching a jacket pocket as insurance, yes, still there, and the private good feeling afterward because this is a big game and tickets are scarce and you'll be there. You *are* there. And everywhere boys are tossing small plastic footballs, catching one in three, the errant throws skittering under feet, clonking cars, and each successful catch accompanied with a mad dash for an imaginary end zone, the boy hero zigzagging here and there among the opposite moving crowd, and how far will he run? How long will he milk the moment of his glory? How long can he suspend his disbelief?

Until a parent calls, come on back, son.

The little girls are all dressed like Shirley Temple. They are too cute to look at long, carried on their father's shoulders, clapping to the passing band.

The women wear their nicest nonchurch clothes and their hair under their fancy hats is just the way they like to wear it.

The men feel a kind of happy longing, loose-limbed and prodigal, hand to wallet more readily than usual, memory and moment merged as nearly to perfection as this life allows.

The stadium behind dwarfs the moving, flowing organism, all huge girders and ramparts and concrete stairs, the shadowed bowels into which the crowd will enter proving a brief introspective interlude, a necessary interlude that makes one feel briefly alone and small and circumspect in the cool shadows under the stands, a moment after the bright and cloudless walk and before your entrance into the encompassing and embracing stadium proper, where you are once again a part of the organism, a part of the ritual of fall.

And the team is good. And the team might take home the crown.

And it is an odd thing how the eye works. Or rather it is an odd thing who and what is the target of the eye. Why, when looking at this amorphous thing, this throng of people flowing toward the stadium, does the eye go to the man in the Harris Tweed sports jacket and blue tie? He is somewhat larger than most in the crowd, but fifteen men of greater stature walk within thirty feet of him. Watch him move though. He and his wife are holding hands and they walk in unison, a gliding, powerful stride like that of large cats, cats on familiar territory forgoing all need to slink. He smiles and says quick hellos to many of the people he passes and though the crowd is thick, his path is never blocked. Ah, it is a subtle weave he does. Never breaking stride, but always finding the open lane, the gap wide enough for two to pass, quickly but unhurried. Occasionally, a passerby will stop to look at the man and woman. They might double-take, for he is bigger than he looks in the newspaper, or nudge a friend and point with a slight nod of the head. His pace is just this much quicker than that of the crowd. Walking with him, among the throng, it would be imperceptible. He seems not to hurry. The stride is relaxed, natural, his everyday stride. And only from this vantage point, only with a studied calculation, would the observer notice the matter of pace. So who can explain this thing called *it*, why the eye, any eye, standing on top of this hill, would go to the man in the Harris Tweed and blue tie among all the unusually shaped humans below, those brightly and ridiculously dressed, those with ambling, awkward gaits, those bustling to get inside, those as tall as the man in the English-style derby cap or as small as the little girl holding the souvenir program and dressed as a miniature university cheerleader? Do some just put off more energy, like a magnetic field? An energy not necessarily equated with looks or talent or intellect or creativity? But often so. Quite often so.

Interior or exterior?

A sense of self that propels and shapes the future?

Or an external magnetism, placed from beyond?

Doesn't the person know? Know before they even have words for it, the way strangers regard them, the way the world presents its multifaceted stimuli?

Roland Cole has it. As did his father. But J.T. has it more than either.

This J.T. knows but keeps tucked away in his own breast pocket.

Stand here a moment and watch him enter the stadium. Nod to the usher and smile. Hand a ticket stub back to Corrine. And then he's gone into the shadowed iron depths of the stadium. Now glance back to the throng. Where does the eye rest? Where does it linger? Or does it, as is most often the case, move from subject to subject, sampling an unusual chapeau here, someone waving a pom-pom there. The utter and comforting sameness of those with whom we share the name *Homo sapiens*, vaguely interesting, worth a moment's voyeurism before we too descend the hill to see the game.

Damn it, J.T., slow down.

He smiled but did not break stride, heading up the series of ramps that led to the press box.

I can see you smiling from the back of your head, said Corrine.

No response.

I don't know why we couldn't take the elevator. You try walking in these heels.

Another smile.

I swear to god, if you don't slow down I'm going to smack you in the head with my shoe.

He moved near the rail and stopped. They were two ramps up, with four to go. Shake a leg, he said.

I'm going to kill you.

We're late. Little brother's going to give me a lecture as it is. You're not supposed to keep the Secretary of Commerce waiting. Or the president of the university.

I'm sweating like a pig, said Corrine. Look at me. You've wrecked my hair, I've got blisters on both feet.

She wasn't sweating and her hair was an immovable object under a wide-brimmed stylish hat. The blisters he didn't doubt. We should have taken the elevator, he said. I'm a little winded.

Oh damn you J.T., she said laughing.

How you feeling about the game?

I could care less about the game.

You could care less?

You heard me. Football is BOR-ING.

Boy you're a sassy one.

You got that right, buster.

You trying to get me to spank that butt?

I'd like to see you try, she said, turning slightly and making a sass-sass-sassy wiggle of the intended target. She stopped and lit a cigarette and looked out over the railing at the crowd below, the river in the distance, the fans still unloading from their boats. Then, taking her first leisurely drag on the cigarette, she offered another sideways and defiant va-voom of the hip.

J.T.'s hand met target with a brisk and satisfying frankness. Of this caboose, he did not tire. A caboose for grown men. A caboose to write home about.

A well-to-do-looking couple was passing as hand met rump, as Corrine spun, cursing and laughing and grabbed J.T.'s index finger with all intention of bending it till it snapped.

J.T. wrenched his hand away and smiled at the couple as they passed. Both averted their heads as if yanked by a puppet master in the opposite direction. Corrine nodded fiercely toward J.T. at the passing couple, the universal not-in-public gesture. When they were still not fully out of earshot, Corrine said in a harsh whisper: Have you lost your mind?

J.T. smiled.

I can't take you anywhere.

You better watch where you shake that thing.

She looked him in the eye and shook it again.

Then they wrestled about, J.T. trying to reach around for another swat, Corrine pinching his biceps and shouting about her hair and the dangers of lighted cigarettes, trying to keep the hat on her head with the same hand holding the cigarette. Neither seemed concerned with those passing on the ramp, old people and young kids, perhaps someone from the country club or city council, a parent of one of their children's friends.

They paid one and all no heed, jostling about, laughing. When they had finished, J.T., tie askew, a small red mark on his face where he'd been accidentally backhanded in the melee, said: We're going straight home after the game.

Corrine shook her head no.

Straight home and straight to bed. I believe you got a little energy you need to work off.

Said Corrine: I don't think so, big boy. A gal like me likes to be wined and dined a bit. We'll see how you act. But I wouldn't hold my breath if I were you.

Then she was walking up the ramp in front of him. Sass-sass-sassy.

Three Monologues Heard Just Before Kickoff

ONE

He's a cocky son of a bitch, I'll tell you that much. You ever met somebody and you just didn't like the way their face looked? Their face just kind of set you off and made you want to slap it silly.

No, he's never done anything to me. We just played fast-pitch together when he first moved to town. Used to kind of smile when you got a strike by him. Say something out of the side of his mouth to the catcher. A joke or something, then make a big show of digging in. He smiled at me one time when I was pitching and it's all I could do not to fire one at his head.

I'm not saying he's a bad guy or mean or anything like that. We played cards down at the back room at Tubby's a couple of years back and he lost a bunch. Never cried about it like some guys do. So he's all right. I just don't like him. I don't like the way his face looks. It's funny, I know. But you're lying if you say nobody's ever struck you that way. Like you just wanted to jerk em up by the hair and whip their ass and let that be the end of it.

I didn't say I could do it. Just that I'd like to. Hell, I wish I hadn't even brought it up. Warm up this here Coke for me and let's watch a little football.

TWO

You ever hear of Roland or J. T. Cole before six, seven years ago? I hadn't.
So they're just going to move to town and bring Glennville a World Expo?
Glennville, Tennessee?

I know the Secretary of Commerce is here. I read the same article you
did. Maybe he needs a loan. Maybe he likes football. He's just some hick
banker from Charlotte himself. One smart enough to make some nice
loans a while back to our current president. Maybe we'll get the federal
money. Lord knows the Democrats like to keep piling it in each other's
pockets.

I was down at Riverside the other day for lunch. Last Saturday. And
Fred Rinkshaw told me J.T. gave his caddy a hundred-dollar tip. A hundred dollars. That's not being charitable. That's not being nice. That's
having too damn much money and not knowing what to do with it. Or
it's hot money. Money you got to keep moving.

Only about ten people down at Riverside will even play golf with
him.

Glennville? Glennville, Tennessee? With a World Expo? I'll have to see
it. I might eat my words, but I'm going to have to see it to believe it.

Who are they? Where did they come from? You can't tell me and neither can anyone else. They're just here all of a sudden and tipping caddies
a hundred dollars for a round of golf.

I say we lose by a touchdown or more. I'll take the Tide and spot you
the seven.

Tell you what. I'll give you eight. The jig's about up on this outfit.

THREE

I was down at practice one day, leaning on the fence with Sloane and
Russell and Jarvis and that bunch. First week of practice. Well, this rangy-
looking fellow was just knocking the hell out of people. I guess really
he was thinner than he was rangy. On first look you'd have thought he
would have been more of a finesse type, more like a pass-catching end.

But he was just laying the wood to some boys. Some folks hit with their shoulders and some use more of their legs. Let me tell you, he was using all of it, head too.

We were looking at each other wondering where this boy could've come from. Hadn't heard of any new families in town and he sure wasn't somebody from the year before. By the end of practice we figured he must be one of those last-minute transfers. You get those sometimes. Families moving at the last minute so they don't have to pay two rents if they signed on for a certain time.

So Coach Roberts is walking off the field after practice and he'd usually stop over at the fence for a minute before heading on in. I say, Coach, who's that rangy boy ringing them bells out there?

He says, that boy is a Bankwalker.

You ever heard that term? I hadn't either.

So I guess I had a quizzical look on my face. I didn't know if he was saying that was the boy's last name or what.

Coach says, you remember when you all were boys and used to go skinny-dipping down at the swimming hole? Every time some girls would happen by all the fellows would hightail into the water. Modest, don't you know. A little shy and flustered. But usually, if you'll recall, there was one fellow who stayed on the bank. Strutting his stuff and just taking his sweet time getting back in the water.

Well, that there's a Bankwalker. When everyone else is heading for cover, he's the one who just ain't scared.

Well, we were all laughing. None of us had ever heard that. Coach Roberts was over from Middle Tennessee near the Alabama border, so maybe that's one of those local sayings. He had a bunch of em. Best coach Henry City ever had. Those boys would just play for him.

He's kind of got that smile going as he walks away. You never really saw him laugh. He wasn't that kind. Then over his shoulder he says, that's James Cole's boy. The Bankwalker. He's an eighth-grader.

Eighth grade. Yes sir. You never heard Bankwalker? I didn't reckon you had. That twenty-one down there's a Bankwalker. The Crimson Tide's about to find that out if they didn't already know.

The Ivory Tower

The private suite of the university was awash in cocktails and finger foods and no one would shut up quite long enough to watch the game. Peering intently through the Plexiglas window that faced out toward the field and shielded the box patrons from the elements and the rabble below, J.T. sat wishing he was down in the stadium in his regular seats. He disliked the press box, the disconnected and sterile bird's-eye view, the players below like multicolored ants, the roar from the crowd muffled and spectral, a faraway crowd in a dream. He felt only partly engaged. He'd come in and got the glad-handing out of the way, then taken his seat to watch the last bit of pregame warm-ups. He sat in the first row of two, nearest the wall, his sole intention to watch the game that he and those in the press box and the eighty thousand others sitting in the sun, in the brisk and clean sun below, had presumably come to see.

Alas, it was not to be.

Seated in the two long rows around him and standing behind, spilling into the hallway that connected all the booths of the press box, were the noteworthy players: Garrett Graves, the U.S. Secretary of Commerce. Mayor Bing. The president of the university. The contractor Jerry Knight. City councilmen Tyson Taft and David Abrams. Monte Shiloh, the publisher of the *Daily Herald*. Teague and the Coles and all their respective spouses. This booth belonged to the university and was used for the purposes of entertaining special dignitaries, often dignitaries who might in some way benefit the university as a whole, often by bequeathing large amounts of money, land, or infrastructure.

J.T. glanced out over the stadium to look at the bank building that rose up behind it from a mile away, sleek and gleaming in the October sun. Not just dominating the Glennville skyline, but consisting of it in its entirety. Moments before, he'd heard the university president refer to it as *Roland's building* when speaking with the Secretary of Commerce. He'd not flinched at that moniker, had heard it too often in the past to be surprised. But it registered. It always registered. He'd known from early on that his lot was in the background, especially when it came to the politics, the public politics, of which he had no interest. But the perception of him as coattails-rider, if that was the perception, well that wouldn't do. Roland didn't see him as second banana. He didn't see himself as second banana.

Watch the game, he thought. Every time you're with these muckety-mucks, your brain goes foreign on you. He took a swig of his soft drink, put his arm around Corrine, and said, how're you feeling about it?

About what?

The game, honey, the game.

I got my fill of football-watching in high school. Back when there wasn't anything else to do.

He reached for her hand across the armrest, clasped it, then let it rest in her lap. She leaned over and whispered in his ear: It drives me crazy when they call it Roland's building.

J.T. smiled but looked straight ahead, saying nothing.

Corrine leaned and whispered again: Was that the university president? I didn't want to turn and look.

J.T. nodded, smiled.

Whispering again: I know you don't care. But I do. Nothing against Roland. I know it's not Roland's fault. But that's your building too. You did every bit as much as Roland.

J.T. gripped his wife's hand, felt a heavy sudden weight, a kind of passing cloud on a sunny day, as he thought of his dalliances during the week, his dalliances over the years, the woman beside him who was as tough and good as they came.

He said: Maybe we'll build our own building one of these days.

Halftime, and Roland had him talking to the university president at the top of the booth. The first half had not gone well. The opposition was simply better. They had bigger, faster players. Frankly, J.T. was ready for a team with such players. At the moment, however, he wanted nothing more than to mix himself a drink from the flask in his sports jacket pocket then hit the buffet line out in the lobby. But here he was, dry-mouthed and hungry, listening to Teague list the innumerable benefits of the Expo: the proposed site adjacent to university property, a conjoining of downtown and the university. More money for the university in the field of energy research. The federal pavilion to be converted to a basketball arena for the school team after the Expo.

How many seats again? the university president said with a laugh.

One more than Kentucky, said Roland.

The president tilted back his head and laughed. His laugh was meant to be of the hearty variety, the jolly good man among jolly good men, but it didn't quite pass the test. J.T. shuffled in his snakeskin boots. The president was not from the area. From the east somewhere. Boston? He'd been at the university four years, but J.T. was still not acclimated to his colorful bow ties. He tried to estimate how many soft academic and museum fundraiser hands he'd shaken since this Expo business first got under way. How many patricians he'd met. Too goddam many.

We think, said Teague, that there will be a lot of opportunities for grant money. The university will be able to tie in with some of the science and technology things we hope to do with the energy theme. If the cards fall right, East Tennessee could end up the energy capital of the nation.

Thought J.T.: Teague is really and completely full of shit. I didn't know that about him. He might be worth what we're paying him after all.

I like the sound of that, the university president said.

Here he paused and struck an intentionally faraway pose, saying, *energy capital of the nation.*

J.T. thought: I wonder if he's ever thrown a football. I wonder if he uses a long filter on his cigarette like F.D.R.

Said Teague: If we get all the money we hope to get, we're going to propose a monorail from Franklin Street to University Boulevard.

Now that, said the president, gently poking Teague in the chest, sounds like a winner.

J.T. could see the steam coming off the trays in the buffet line, smell the gravy and roast beef, the potatoes. His flask, he noticed, was poking him in the rib.

A whole new city in the blink of an eye, said Roland with a smile.

It all sounds wonderful, said the president with a patrician smile, neat white teeth all in a row. But right now I'm afraid it's a bit of a political football.

J.T. watched the university president smile at the pun, which has surprised and delighted him.

Then the president recovered from his wordplay reverie: Some people might think it inappropriate for the university, for a state-funded public university, to get involved, publicly, with such a hot-button issue.

We can wait for a public statement of support from the university, said Teague. At least for a while. What about behind the scenes? Putting in a word here and there with a few of the influential boosters?

The president smiled. A patient, winning smile. Practiced first on students in his political science classroom. Then on faculty members when he was their department head. Then on the heads of departments when he was their dean. Then on administrators when he was their vice provost. Now, however, it was reserved almost exclusively for the well-heeled booster, the important dignitary on a campus visit.

He said: I am a man who likes to ponder a matter a bit before I fully commit.

J.T.'s stomach growled. The man's bow tie seemed rakishly askance, a propeller in midquarter turn.

If I do commit, I'll be behind you a hundred percent. And depending on how things go with city council and the state legislature these next few months, the university may be able to throw our weight behind you, publicly, and again, one hundred percent.

When he'd finished talking, he turned for some reason and put his hand gently on J.T.'s shoulder. The president was a perceptive man. And J.T. was not a man especially good at hiding his emotions. The gesture was a patented one, one used to good and practical effect all the years of the president's tenure in academia. A placating, kid-gloved hand to shoulder. Meant to soothe. Meant with warmest regards and utmost sincerity.

J.T. took the president's hand from his shoulder in a slow, deliberate way. He was looking the president in the eye as he did so.

He said: Listen here, pussy. We'll do the goddam Expo with or without you and the university. But when it comes—and it will come, you can bet your sweet ass on that—no goodies for you. No goodies for the school. You got me? You understand that?

I only said I wanted to think about it for a while, said the president, looking with shocked and injured eyes at first Roland and then Teague.

Right now I couldn't give a rat's ass what you want, said J.T. I'm going to get something to eat.

What in the hell are you doing?

J.T. stood at the sink washing his hands. Washing my hands, he said. How bout handing me a towel?

Roland grabbed a paper towel and flung it in his brother's face. A man just exiting one of the stalls saw the towel being flung and thought better of washing his hands.

J.T. thought: So little brother is pissed. This should be interesting.

Then he thought: Goddam motherfucker, I'll kill him.

At this point, thinking stopped. What took its place were low blood sugar, birth-order hierarchy, and a coursing of adrenaline through his veins. The walls of the bathroom narrowed swiftly out of focus and all that remained were the hostile eyes and pose of his younger brother. He grabbed this brother by the knot of the tie and rammed him into a stall with some force.

You're a fucking idiot, said Roland, pinned against the wall but not immobilized. He grabbed J.T. just under the tie. A button popped loose as he did.

I'll beat your ass, said J.T., hot but coming to his senses. The notion was dawning on him that he had his little brother around the neck.

You might do it, but I swear to god I'll make you bleed before we're through.

Thought J.T.: What am I doing? My god, he's mad as hell. He really would hit me.

He loosened the grip on his brother's tie and looked down for a moment. He was trying to shake the image of an irate eight-year-old just whipped and crying over a game of soldier. But still defiant, still not capitulating. He felt suddenly tired and oafish. The young years of physical dominance, dominance of presence and posture, came to him like an unwanted dream. Roland's shirtfront was wet from his undried hands. He let go of his brother and walked back to the sink. He grabbed a paper towel and in doing caught a glimpse of himself in the mirror. The bully.

Roland came up behind and spun him around, eyes narrowed, teeth gritted. As were the boys, so too the men: J.T. quick to anger, quick to defuse, Roland slow to anger but volcanic and implacable when he did.

I'm not through with you, he said.

J.T. turned to face his brother who was now jabbing a finger mere inches from his nose.

What in the hell, what in the fuck, are you thinking, talking to the president of the university like that? Are you fucking crazy? Are you insane?

J.T. said nothing. He could not stop seeing the angry eight-year-old. Roland had once chased him around the barn with a ball-peen hammer. Had J.T. stumbled, he would have been brained.

He thought: What a truly magnificent temper.

He thought: People are the same from the day they are born.

Roland jabbed once more with his finger toward J.T.'s nose then turned and kicked with the heel of his Italian loafer the bathroom stall. The creak and ping of a screw loosened and falling to the floor ensued. He said: What in the fuck!

And for the first time J.T. wondered what could and could not be heard outside the bathroom door. They stood now less than thirty feet from the buffet line where all the assorted dignitaries were loading up plates of food and chatting aimlessly in the tones of ladies and gentlemen.

We're right rednecks, thought J.T. And nearly smiled despite himself.

You're crazy, said Roland. You really are. Self-destructive too.

J.T. smiled. Roland's feathers were puffing down. The kick to the stall had been the last needed blow of steam.

You want me to apologize?

I'm sorry, Dr. Turner, for calling you a pussy? You're really not a pussy? What the hell could you say?

I guess you're right. He is a complete pussy though.

Well of course he is, said Roland, taking a towel and daubing at the wet spot on his shirt. That's immaterial.

Graves hear?

I don't know. If he did, he wouldn't care. He's more rye whiskey than martini anyway.

Do me a favor, said J.T. Next time we're up in the ivory tower, how bout leaving me home?

Oh trust me on that one. You've met your last academic.

J.T. went to his brother and straightened the tie knot he'd grabbed three minutes before. Patted his jacket down, smoothed his shirt. When he was done, he stuck out his hand. I'm sorry, brother, he said.

I know, said Roland. Forget it. And you're right. We'll get the Expo with or without these university fucks. At the end of the day, they can still kiss my ass.

Then they were walking out of the bathroom together and greeting the many eyes that turned to watch them enter the hall and head to the buffet table. They walked with confident smiles, joined at the hip.

A Private Talk

FADE IN

INT: PRESS BOX HALLWAY

WIDE ON:
The ENTRANCES leading into the various PRIVATE SUITES of press box row, no longer packed to the brim, no longer electric and anticipatory. Just visible are the PLEXIGLAS WINDOWS, the field down below, the opposite side of the STADIUM now only HALF FULL, the top of the FBG BUILDING in the distance. The hall is empty, but for the occasional stadium worker carting off trays from the dismantled buffet line or someone walking leisurely to or from the restroom. Everywhere the eye can see are DISCARDED plastic CUPS. The HALLWAY is dank, GREY, and the lighting in the various press boxes is dim and insignificant. Outside the windows, the LIGHTS of the STADIUM make for an ARTIFICIAL NOON. Above the stadium, dusk is descending. The buzz and cheering of earlier has subsided, only a ghostly and muted MURMUR remains. One senses the game is in its late stages, the outcome long since decided. THREE MEN stand talking against the far wall, nearest the elevator. They are smoking CIGARS, the SMOKE of which rises in steady plumes and lingers in the short ceiling above their heads. One of them is smiling.

CLOSE ON:

The smiling man: Secretary of Commerce, GARRETT GRAVES. He has enjoyed his day and his role as guest of honor. The outcome of the game is insignificant to him. The CIGAR, a gift from the university president. The whiskey in the plastic cup, his third, is straight from J. T. Cole's flask. Secretary Graves waves his cigar as he speaks, savoring the smoke that wafts around his head in the low-ceilinged light.

> SECRETARY GRAVES
> When you come to Washington, I'll have to take you
> to Pokey's. Best cigars on the East Coast.

> ROLAND
> Sounds good. I'm looking forward to our visit.

> J.T.
> (taking a sip from his cup)
> I'm thinking about buying a plane for the trip up.
> Don't want to be mistaken for some hicks from Henry
> City just fell off the turnip truck.

> GRAVES
> (bemused)
> Write it off as an Expo expense?

ROLAND histrionically grabs his brother's arm as if to keep him out of the company till.

> ROLAND
> We knew better than to give big brother an expense
> account. (turning to J.T.) A plane?

J.T. takes a long drag from his CIGAR, exhales.

                    J.T.

A business jet, actually. I'm looking at a Dassault
Falcon 20.

                    ROLAND

That's news to me.

                    GRAVES

Big brother gave himself a raise.

                    J.T.
                  (deadpan)

Somebody had to. If I waited on the bank board to
appreciate what I'm worth, I'd be heading to D.C. via
pack mule.

                    GRAVES

Back in my banking days, we were doing good to get a
new Cadillac every five, six years. And even then the
neighbors would talk about you putting on airs.

As the men LAUGH rotely, a pall settles visibly over the party, as if cued
by some kind of decorum known only to men of large enterprises. To
wit: preliminary pleasantries have been exchanged. We are now free of
social considerations and any moment now someone will intrude upon
our privacy. Brass tacks, men. Brass tacks.

The COLES puff CIGARS, wait for Secretary Graves to bridge chitchat to
business. The secretary is for all practical purposes of their kind: southern,
a former banker, urbanized when in mixed company, urbanized only to
a certain degree among men like the Coles. Rounder, older, softer now
than the still-youthful and clear-eyed Coles, SECRETARY GRAVES is
a man easily underestimated. Last word to the wise: Gentlemen such as

these will leave you feeling like the smartest person in the room. Be sure that you are.

> GRAVES
> (in a different tone)
> In case you fellows are wondering, I think you're looking pretty good in Washington. The Commerce Department has got the proposal. The president is about to come on board too, I think. Someone down here has been squawking that the locals aren't all the way behind you. The only qualms the president has is he doesn't want to look like he's interfering in city government. Especially if that interference happens to help the pet project of some of his supporters. No matter how up and up it is, some folks will claim pork belly. These East Tennessee Republicans don't much care for our man in the Oval Office.

> ROLAND
> The city's behind the Expo. It's just a vocal minority that's not.

> GRAVES
> But you haven't rammed it through city council yet, that's what the university president was telling me. Is that right?

> J.T.
> We will. It's in the works. We just need a couple of undecideds to swing our way. It'll happen. We're not sweating that.

> GRAVES
> How about the state? Have they committed yet?

It's going to take tri-level funding, according to my math.

J.T.

State should be our easiest sale. We've got one first-term representative from up in Ridemore trying to make a name for himself by cockblocking us every step of the way. But our folks are just letting him blow hard for now. Once the vote comes up, that deal will close. No one who cares anything about East Tennessee is going to vote against fixing our highway up here.

ROLAND

We're losing for the time being in the paper. But we're winning in the back rooms.

GRAVES

Can't see the duck's legs paddling.

J.T.

And we haven't really started hitting our infrastructure angle. Once highway improvements and new basketball arenas start getting tossed around, we'll win the newspaper side too.

GRAVES

Here's my suggestion. Make nice with your U.S. senator from Chattanooga. I know you two have had your differences, Roland, but that stuff happens in politics. When the president puts forward his energy bill, he's going to need every vote he can get. Up to this point, your senator's been on the fence. If you quote me on this, I'll say you're lying, but if it were me, I'd ask Bill Smiley to let it be known that his vote on the energy bill is more or less tied to the president putting his weight behind the Glennville Expo. The Expo's theme is energy, after all. Seems like an easy couple of things to tie together. I think that should counter any qualms the president has about interfering in local business.

J.T.
You'd think.

(smiling at his brother)
Roland, I'll let you make the call to Smiley. I know you're anxious to be reacquainted with the boy wonder.

ROLAND
(with a grudging smile)
Thank you, brother. I'll look forward to doing that.

(turning to Graves)
I'd have thought our help in the last election would be enough to seal this deal. But if you think we need this angle too, I'm all for it. I've got no problem making a call to mend some fences. He's a horse's ass, but like you said, it's just politics.

GRAVES
Just makes it easier on the big man. He's putting out fires all over the place. Makes it an easy call for him if it's tied in with his big bill. He won't be penny wise and pound foolish, I'll tell you that much.

ROLAND
Done then.

SECRETARY GRAVES glances toward the row of suites and the field of play, a willful and DISTRACTED look, practiced and noncommittal.

> GRAVES
>
> Once we're all systems go, my contractor friend from Charlotte that I mentioned will likely be putting in a bid.

> ROLAND
>
> We expected that. Good. I'm glad to hear it.

> J.T.
>
> His proposal will get a good look, I promise you that.

> GRAVES
> (still looking off in the distance)
> That's fine. I'll pass along the word. Now what say we get back to the suite? That university president of yours was just about to tell me about his ornamental garden.

FADE OUT

The End of the Day

He has stayed long after the game has ended, letting the traffic clear, playing the social man, the civic-minded man. He has nodded genial assent as his wife promised to attend the opening of a local gallery and to donate to the Glennville Arts Festival. He has added two cents here and there as Teague pitched, always pitching, ever pitching, pitching without seeming to pitch, yet another feature of the Expo to one influential Glennvillean after another. He has cornered the publisher of the *Daily Herald*, Monte Shiloh, as they simultaneously came to the hallway for a smoke, the *Herald* whose one hard-ass reporter, the one hard-ass on the whole staff, has been riding the Expo up one side and down another since the beginning.

Said J.T.: So you're a member of the Glennville Citizens' Group too?

Monte Shiloh smiled at this.

If I'd have known that reporter of yours was going to be on us like this, I never would have slept with his wife.

The publisher laughed.

What is he, eighteen years old?

He's thirty. And he's single.

So who's riding your ass to ride ours?

I don't have a dog in the fight, J.T. I assigned a man to the Expo. And he's writing what he knows and thinks. Sam Tarvin is a damn good reporter.

He's something all right. So the old guard hasn't put the word out? I

240

thought you might be feeling a little heat from some of our Republican friends. Some of your old golfing buddies down at Riverside?

Number one, I don't get pressured. Number two, I haven't heard the first word from anybody. Far as I can tell, no one who matters gives a rat's ass one way or another. Except a few folks who might get a little smile out of seeing the Coles take a bath.

J.T. dropped his cigarette on the concrete floor and stubbed it with the heel of his boot. You're not one of those, are you?

What would I have against you, J.T.? I'm just a newspaperman. We didn't endorse Roland, but that can't surprise you. The *Herald* hasn't endorsed a Democrat for governor in a hundred years.

That's water under the bridge. Maybe I'm just paranoid, but it seems to me like some folks around here don't like a fellow who's putting a little money in his pocket. Especially if he's new to town. And a Democrat to boot.

You're not new to town.

I'll always be new to town. My grandkids will be new to town. I got this joint pretty well figured out.

We haven't weighed in one way or the other, officially, on the Expo.

Oh, you're weighing, all right, official or not.

I'm not going to censor any reporter of mine. Never have, never will.

I'm not asking you to. I'm just asking for a fair hearing.

In my opinion, you're getting one.

Two words: Bull. Shit.

What do you want me to do?

Why don't you come walk the site with us? We'll walk you through everything we have in mind. I think if you could see the physical reality of it, or the physical possibility of it, you might be a little more willing to get on board. Right now it's abstract. It's all theoretical. Once we can show you what can go where, and how it will affect the city for the next hundred years, I think you might be impressed.

Okay. You're on. When?

How's next Tuesday?

Tuesday it is. And after my tour, no more bellyaching, right?

Absolutely.

And if my reporter keeps writing things you don't like, you won't think it's personal, you won't think it's at my behest?

Fair enough. But if your reporter keeps doing like he's doing, I don't want to run into him walking down a dark alley late one night.

That sounds like a threat.

A joke, Monte. Only a joke.

But, when it comes down to it, J.T. has spent the majority of the second half contemplating the altercation with his brother. He can't stop seeing his hands on his brother's tie, the fantastic anger in his brother's eye. He can't stop the echoic adrenaline sensation, the vivid brief moment of intuitively wanting to harm his brother, and his brother wanting even more, yes more, to harm him. How do men do this? He has considered this for nearly two hours. What creative madman gave such powerful anger to such ill-equipped creatures? Do other brothers do this sort of thing? Or do they choose a more subterranean warfare, unannounced and lifelong in nature, with hazily recognized skirmishes, and rules known only to the warring participants?

He would not hurt his brother for all the world, would rather kill himself than harm his brother, and yet, for a moment, for a moment.

He has left the press box after the game with the self-imposed mark of Cain. Throw in the residual guilt of his ongoing affair and the high cost of business, the high cost of politics and ambition, and he is in an unusual and indefinable mood. He would like to be at the farm with his mother and sister, would like to wake up early and split some wood, walk along the creek with the dog. He wishes suddenly for a young child, a toddling bundle of uncomplicated energy and animation who will receive without complaint all of the affection he has to offer. He kissed his small children, boys and girl alike, incessantly on the round cheek, the back of the head with its soft, sweet-smelling hair. When the children were small, he'd been a very good father. A baby in the house, a toddler, keeps a man focused on life. Life itself. The breathing, the beating of the heart, the excellence of sleep. Now he feels Corrine grip his hand as they enter the elevator. To be married as long as they is to remove the hidden mood. The source of the mood may remain a mystery, but not the mood itself. He pushes the button and offers her a smile of understanding about the mystery that he isn't. As the door is about to close, a large hand reaches in from the side and halts its progress. A tall man in his early sixties, bulkier than he is strong, enters with his wife. They are overtly well-to-do and the woman wears a wide-brimmed fancy hat and is faintly tan in a way that speaks of a recent trip to the winter home in Hilton Head.

Just the notion of Hilton Head makes J.T. smile.

Well hello, J.T., the man says with boisterous rough-hewn volume. It's been too damn long.

J.T. shakes the offered hand, the elevator door closes with a brisk ring, the ladies exchange greetings. Within seconds the phrase Hilton Head comes out of Mrs. Palmer's mouth.

Hilton Head. Golf and men on bicycles. The safest place in the world.

Colonel, how are you? asks J.T. It's been a long time.

I'm right as rain, says the colonel. But I'm afraid our team has a drug problem.

J.T. smiles. He's heard this one several times before. He plays along. A drug problem?

Yeah, they keep getting drug up and down the field.

Corrine hasn't heard the joke before and laughs with gusto. Mrs. Palmer smiles upon Corrine in a becoming manner then is back on the weather in Hilton Head.

Says the colonel: I don't believe our coach is cutting the mustard. What do you think?

J.T. smiles. The fickle nature of all things Glennvillean has about lost its novelty value to him.

Too early to tell, he says. Once he's playing with all of his own recruits, then we'll know what kind of coach we got.

That was an ugly display I just witnessed, says the colonel.

Warn't pretty, I'll grant you that.

The elevator opens and the men pause to let the women exit. The colonel puts a fatherly arm on J.T.'s shoulder as they walk out into the bowels of the stadium, dank and gloomy, dusk stealing away like a thief, the skittering rattle of a plastic cup thrown from on high. The women walk side by side and the colonel leads J.T. by a shoulder behind them. A World's Fair in Glennville, huh? Is that the story, young man?

This is said with a short, snorting laugh, amiable on the surface.

We'll see, says J.T.

Paris, Seattle, St. Louis. And Glennville.

That's right.

The Cole brothers are storming the Bastille, aren't they?

As they walk, a father and his son pass them in the opposite direction. They're dressed in the school colors, the boy wearing a popular running back's jersey. The father points to the river and J.T. turns reflexively to see a large passing boat, a party boat. On cue, the boat lets loose with an electronic and out-of-rhythm and abbreviated version of the school fight song. The father smiles wanly and pokes his son in the side playfully. The boy is taking the loss hard and the father pokes again. The boy smiles reluctantly at first and then breaks into a wide grin.

Just seeing what we can do, says J.T.

The colonel removes his hand from J.T.'s shoulder and slows his pace. Just trying to shake things up a bit in dusty old Glennville?

J.T. feels very close to saying something he shouldn't, something about the colonel and his group and all the tight-ass, tightwad things they hold so dear. The hand on shoulder, the amiable and inappropriate familiarity, evidences a man who sincerely thinks he's talking to an upstart, a fly-by-night.

I like Glennville, says J.T. Ever since I was a kid I liked Glennville.

You just like it better with a few skyscrapers and a World's Fair, the colonel says with a laugh.

Well goddam, thinks J.T. How much more of this shit am I supposed to listen to?

But his impolitic words to the university president and his bathroom confrontation with his brother weigh upon him still. Up in front, a man staggers into a car, curses the coach, reaches into his pockets for the keys.

Between me and you, says the colonel, just us boys. Is this thing going to fly?

We'll have to see. Still have to get all our ducks in a row.

Paper's been whipping you boys pretty hard. Keep saying the common man like me is going to end up footing the bill.

I think you can afford it, says J.T. smiling.

Cora here might have to sell some of her fancy hats.

Mrs. Palmer histrionically grabs her hat at this. Oh no I won't, she says. She stops, turns to face the men. *Why* will I have to sell my fancy hats?

Corrine is smiling. J.T. knows her fondness for women of this generation. They are kinder to those women more recently moneyed. Some remnant of the Depression. J.T. knows that when they are alone again, the word stylish will be one of the first out of Corrine's mouth. Now, in on the joke, Corrine proprietarily grabs her hat as well.

This Expo the Coles are bringing to our scruffy little town, says the colonel with a wink. Newspaper keeps telling me that the taxpayer's going to end up footing the bill. Retired man like me might have to hold an auction. The figure I read for the city's end of it was thirteen million. That right, J.T.? Thirteen million?

Corrine stands now with her face in a state of flux. J.T. watches that expressive face as it tries to simultaneously weigh the grace of Mrs. Palmer with the winking, premeditated horseshit of her husband. These old assholes, thinks J.T. These old busybody assholes. And if I want it to happen, I just have to let them carp. Oh, if the colonel were younger, what a thrashing he'd be talking himself into. To tag that bulbous nose just one time.

As if reading his mind, Corrine moves imperceptibly closer to him. She lets go of her hat. She looks first to the colonel and then to Mrs. Palmer: It won't cost the city taxpayer anything.

J.T. smiles.

The colonel smiles.

Mrs. Palmer waves her hand dismissively, business, politics, she's too old for it, then begins walking again on up the road.

It won't, says Corrine. Between the federal grants and the help from the state, all Glennville has to do is sit back and enjoy a once-in-a-lifetime event. I for one can't see how anyone, anyone who claims to care for this city, can be against it.

She stands looking at the colonel, sizing him up. Behind her, Mrs. Palmer has stopped to inspect a batch of zinnias still in bloom at this late date. Stadium Drive is about empty now, save the occasional player walking slowly, sorely, with his family up toward the athletic dorm. They have been not just beaten but beaten up today. And now an assistant coach, hair wet still from the shower, laundered shirt crisp and juxtapositional to the grim smile offered to a well-wisher. At the south end of the stadium, out of sight, a sudden cheer goes up and the traveling, skeleton pep band of the opposition begins a jaunty version of their own school fight song as the victors empty from the visitors' locker room and board the waiting Greyhound. The images of loss, the humming Greyhound of victory, circle slowly in J.T.'s head.

He thinks: Corrine will bring it all day long.

Says the colonel: Well Mrs. Cole, I'm glad to hear it. I'm going to take your word for it.

With this he has offered a slight and formal bow.

Says the colonel: Will there be need of any more private investors?

You'll have to ask J.T. about that, says Corrine. Then she turns and walks to where Mrs. Palmer is standing.

Well, says the colonel with a smile.

Yes, says J.T. We're still gathering investors.

And Mike Teague is still on board.

Mike Teague is one hundred percent on board.

You'll call me next week?

Yes sir I will.

And Cora will keep her fancy hats?

I think so.

And then the men catch up with their wives and head their separate ways.

Says Corrine: Have you ever seen anyone so stylish?

Polls and Referendums

FADE IN

INT: THE OFFICE OF ROLAND COLE

WIDE ON:

The immense plate-glass WINDOW, a dark and rainy day, a gloomy DOWNTOWN below, the RIVER bending like a muddy sock in the distance.

CLOSE ON:

ROLAND COLE sitting behind his DESK. He wears an immaculate three-piece suit and reclines as far back as he can in his chair without resorting to placing shoes on desk. The LIGHTING on him is a little HARSH in comparison to the scene outside the window.

PAN OUT TO:

J.T. PACING the leathery and carpeted and wood-plush room, a caged look on his face, looking as he often does, out of place in an indoor setting. TEAGUE is sitting in a leather chair facing Roland, taking no notice of the elder brother's swift movements around the room. From here, it seems apparent that the opening shot of the GLOOMY day outside was Teague's view out the window. Like Roland, he and J.T. are dressed for business.

J.T.
(in midsentence)
. . . the polls. That's what I'm talking about. Everyday
Joe loves himself a goddam poll. Other men on the
street thinking like him, talking like him. Well if fifty-
seven other Joe Schmoes think it, I guess I think it too.
We need some damn polls of our own.

ROLAND
(smiling)
They just aren't polling the right people.

J.T.
(taking the bait)
Who are they polling? Who are these four hundred
and thirty-two Glennvilleans? My bet is they're hanging out somewhere between Reddick Hills and Riverside Country Club. Hitting Drake's Drug Store. The
Brass Lantern. Shit, they hadn't sent the first person
over to north Glennville.

ROLAND
North Glennville? They might catch something over
there.

TEAGUE
(unamused, looking out the window at the rain)
We're meeting Monte Shiloh in thirty minutes. Anything you guys want to talk about, specifically, before
we head over?

J.T.
(catching the brusqueness of tone)
What would you like to talk about, Teague? If polls
aren't interesting to you, what is?

TEAGUE
(looking out the window)
It might be interesting if you bent over and kissed my
ass.

J.T. LAUGHS. Teague turns to see Roland smiling at him from his desk.
Teague acts unaware of comedy or insult or any attempt at either.

TEAGUE
You're not getting around this referendum issue.

ROLAND
You don't think?

TEAGUE
Those polls don't lie. And actually, I haven't heard
anybody but us who gives two shits about this city
getting the Expo. We're getting killed in the paper.
It's not so much GCG, though they're the ones doing
the hollering. But we don't have the first old fart on
board with us. That's fine. I think we can do it without old Glennville. But their objection to the fair has
nothing to do with city bonds. It's the small-potatoes
folks who are worrying about that, the ones who feel
it when their property tax goes up. So the old guard
just lays back and lets the GCG folks do their dirty
work. They're afraid that if they ever have to come
out and say that they're against the Expo, then the cat
will be out of the bag, that what people have said about
them for fifty years is true. Namely that they're against
progress. Right now they can play man of the people.
They can say the people don't want it, so why shove
it down their throats. So what we've got to do is face
the referendum head-on and get that argument off the
table. Then we'll be able to define the battle lines. It's

like the old saying: If you're explaining, you're losing. I say we stop explaining, win the referendum issue, and just start kicking some ass.

J.T.

If there's a referendum on Expo, we lose.

TEAGUE

Fifty-fifty, I'd say. But this popped into my head this morning. What we need is a vote on a referendum, a vote of the people to decide if we need a referendum. A vote to see if we vote. That will give us two shots. If people vote and say no, we don't need a referendum, we win. If they vote in favor of having a referendum, we still have a shot.

ROLAND

A slim one. Fifty-fifty is optimistic. We don't want to go to referendum.

TEAGUE

Agreed. But we can't dodge the subject anymore. We're looking sketchy, shady if we do. So here's what we do. We propose a referendum. It's a yes-or-no vote, right? Yes means we have a referendum. No means we don't.

ROLAND

Right. Okay.

TEAGUE

Don't you see? If you vote yes for the referendum, that means you're really voting no on having the Expo come to Glennville. The whole yes/no question becomes

counterintuitive. Voting no on the referendum question means you don't think we need a referendum.
Which means, essentially, that you do want Expo.

J.T.
You lost me there.

TEAGUE
Exactly. Basically, we'd be flip-flopping the yes/no
issue. A yes vote becomes a no vote and vice versa.
My bet is a lot of voters will get confused about what
they're voting yes or no to. Especially if we spend some
money on signs and get a little help with the newspapers. We'll splatter the town with VOTE NO signs.
Which means that they'll be voting no on the issue
of whether or not we need a referendum. The whole
semantics thing will make the opposition start doing
the explaining. And then we've got the whole thing
flipped.

ROLAND
(standing up)
That's not bad. Of course, we'd have to worry about
our Expo people voting yes to the referendum. That's
just the converse.

TEAGUE
The history of the South shows us that the empowered
minority can always get the disenfranchised majority
to do their bidding, to absolutely vote against their
best interests. States' rights, states' rights. Now go get
your ass shot off for some slaves you don't own and
never will own. The old guard has got the down-and-
outs against us without really knowing why they are.

The folks who are for us are most of the Democrats, some recent outsiders moved to the area, and just anyone who would like to shake up the status quo. And our folks read the paper and our folks, most of them, will be able to parse the semantics. They'll know what the hell is going on with the reversal of no and yes. The folks who want to vote against us have heard bad things about Expo by word of mouth. But those word-of-mouth campaigns take awhile to get round town. At the end of the day, the people against us have two words firmly in their heads: *No Expo.* There won't be time to educate them by word of mouth that no means yes and yes means no.

J.T.

That's damn diabolical, Teague. I'm impressed.

TEAGUE

Nothing diabolical about it.
                    (smiling now)
It's a simple yes-or-no question.

ROLAND

You fellows ready to go woo a newspaper publisher?

J.T.
            (waving at the weather outside)
Hell of a day to do it. But my god, my head's still spinning. Yes means no and no means yes.

TEAGUE

If it makes you feel better, we're at least tricking people into voting for their best interests.

> J.T.
>
> You seem to think I give a shit how we beat those
> fuckers.

J.T. leaves and Roland follows behind him, looking once over his shoulder
to see if Teague is behind them. Teague looks absently around the office
then walks to the great glass window.

WIDE ON:

The great expanse of CITY and HIGHWAYS, the great river, the BRIDGES
and zigzagging ROADS, the scurrying CARS like multicolored bugs on
so many intertwining twigs.

CRANE SHOT:

WILLIAM GLENN FORT, wooden and empty, dwarfed and insignificant
in the concrete city, encircled by slick, sleek highways, swift and efficient
automation.

FADE OUT

Fair Site

The rain came down in constant, discouraging drops. It fell along the forgotten road the men walked down. Abandoned warehouses. Ramshackle hovels with smoke from coal fireplaces rising thinly in the wet, grey air. A remnant of chain-link fence climbing a steep weed-slick hill. Why? What to lock in or lock out? A broken parking lot. Scattered piles of dull glass. Warehouse windows splintered in spiderweb patterns. Rocks. And the neat conical indentations of gunfire. The road they walked down was cracked and weed-strewn and rushing water swept against the high curb. Beside the road was Rather Creek, little more now than a muddy ditch. Rusted cans and dead tires and a hobo's convention of cardboard piecemeal against the embankment. Random paper whipping limply in the lower limbs of trees like chickens with no roost to call home. The creek ran through a scruffy lowland and into an indeterminate tunnel overgrown with grass and where it came out next was impossible to tell. The men, in suits and dress shoes, jumped the larger pools of water, hopscotched the medium-sized ones, and plowed through ones that came nearly to their socks. They were drenched from the knees down and their fine shoes were mud-flecked and shiny. Behind them, their brightly colored cars looked lonely and immature against the dull brick, the industrial grey, the endless grey rain, like boys lost at the fair as the greater darkness of night encroaches.

We're down in a big ditch, thought Teague, looking up the hill at the city overhead. The tectonic shifting of plates that had produced the Appalachians thirty miles to the east had done its work here too. Teague recalled his morning drive to work, downshifting the car into low gear as it whined its way up Jackson Drive. He wondered how many times a week he was made aware of hills and valleys and how he might feel in a flat city.

A valley, yes. They were sunk in a thin valley. A scorned and half-civilized one. Teague had lived in the city all of his life and never once ventured into this parcel of land half a mile from the heart of the city. He'd walked the viaduct ahead of them as a boy with his father and stood there as the train came huffing down the line below, the thrilling and surreal sensation beneath his feet as it passed, the vibration and the whooshing, rambling echo. But he'd never once walked down Front Street to this no-name road.

What road is this? he asked.

Kessler's Lane, said Roland.

Who the hell is Kessler?

I have no idea, said Roland. You're the Glennville boy. Monte, do you know?

The publisher stopped under his umbrella. All of the men had umbrellas and all but the publisher sported the official chariot lapel pin on their suit jackets: Helios slashing across the globe, the epicenter of which was Glennville, Tennessee. None wore hats. The era of wearing hats was over and Teague found this unfortunate. His father's generation had looked like men in hats. The hat made the man or the man made the hat? Hard to tell. A different generation any way you sliced it.

The publisher said: I was just wondering the same thing. I'll get one of the reporters on it when I get back. Fact is, I've only been down here one other time. And I can't remember what for. Maybe some parking lot plan that fell through. Shame about the old station, he said, pointing toward the hulking abandoned depot that abutted the viaduct.

Daddy let us ride the train up to town ever so often once we got to be old enough, said J.T. I remember all the cigar smoke and the brass spittoons.

Chicken salad sandwiches in wax paper, said Roland. And that good lemonade.

The publisher smiled. They were standing five feet from the viaduct and could have been out of the rain for a moment, but they were transfixed by the dead building, the railroad yard below, the rusted and implacable tracks of a long-abandoned Tinkertoy set, leftover boxcars unnerving and inert, ancient toys strewn by a bored giant and left to rust where they fell.

You fellows are probably too young to remember, said the publisher, but there was this old-timer used to work the cigar stand.

Played Dixie on the harmonica to drum up business, said J.T.

I remember a man with a monkey, Teague said.

Same fellow, said the publisher. Monkey would go around with the end of an umbrella and pick up cigar stubs people had dropped then throw them away.

Teague laughed. It sounded far-fetched.

He did, said the publisher. I swear on it. Cigar man would shout: We sell em, you smoke em, we clean up the mess.

I don't remember the monkey, said J.T.

Monkey might have been before you started heading up here on your own. But the cigar man played the harmonica until the end.

I remember the harmonica, said Roland. He play anything but Dixie? That's all I can remember.

Seems like he played Battle Hymn of the Republic ever so often, said the publisher. Working both sides, you know.

They laughed and paused for a moment, the four men looking up the hill at the old train station, looking backward in time to their boy selves, the clack and rattle, the quaint bustle of another era.

It was Teague who made the first move toward the shelter of the viaduct and the other men followed quickly behind him. It was here, with the rain pouring over the scarred and beleaguered landscape, that the Coles began their pitch: private investors plus federal grants plus state funding. No city money. The city getting a free ride. Permanent amphitheater for the city. Permanent basketball arena for the university. A monorail connecting downtown and the university. Four top-of-the-line hotels. Dozens of new restaurants and retail stores. Thousands of jobs during the fair. Highway construction to fix, once and for all, that interstate abortion known as Mixed-up Merge. Environmental cleanup of this Rather Creek area you see before your eyes, a city park afterward built in and around the new infrastructure. A whole new vision of downtown. The Sun Tower, a symbolic building on scale with Seattle's Space Needle or the St. Louis Arch, permanently associated with the city in the national consciousness. Can't put a price tag on that. Incalculable national publicity equals incalculable long-term boon to the tourist business. Fifteen million. Count them. Fifteen million visitors.

A brand-new city in the blink of an eye, said Roland, pointing out past the proposed site and into the vast and sunshiny future. It's a once-in-a-lifetime opportunity, Monte.

You're going to fix Mixed-up Merge? said the publisher.

The state is.

That's not due to come around for another decade.

We aim to speed that timetable, Roland said. The state doesn't want to be embarrassed if we throw a party for the world and they have to sit in traffic all day every day. They'll fix it. We're talking fifteen million visitors to our city, visitors who may decide to head on to Nashville or Memphis afterwards. Trust me, it'll get fixed.

We got to hit that, said J.T. If we could find a friendly publisher who would headline the morning paper with *Fair to fix Mixed-up Merge*, I think it would help our cause immeasurably.

Teague smiled. The plan had been for him to make the pitch, the Coles to be the demure professionals, disinterested businessmen and civic leaders. The publisher looked at him now. You know any newspapermen can help these boys out?

If I find one, said Teague, I feel confident the Coles will know how to wine and dine him. You ever been pitched to while standing under a viaduct with your socks soaking wet?

The publisher agreed that this was a first. Then he waved his hand out over the proposed site, a wave grandiose and ironic. Well, he said, you've certainly picked an idyllic spot to begin building your brand-new city.

Roland smiled quickly then let it fade away. He began talking. His preference usually was to fill in gaps, to stay in the background when in intimate settings such as this. But now he talked, walking the publisher through the architectural plans. Here will go the state pavilion. Here is where we'd like to place the Chinese pavilion. This is where we see the amphitheater. This creek, yes, this creek, will feed the International Lake, vendors selling food from forty nations along its banks. He pointed out the Fun Fair, the rides for the kids, across the railroad trestle and adjacent to the river down the hill and out of their field of vision. He named the countries that had been contacted, including Russia, whom they thought they had a good chance of landing. He mentioned the entertainment. European ballets troupes, Hungarian folksingers, the Chinese gymnastics team. He walked the publisher through the opening day ceremonies with the president of the United States acting as master of ceremonies. He ended with a vision of the fair at night, the softly glowing lights, the smells of food emporiums, the nightly fireworks and laser show, the myriad foreign accents punctuating the night air.

It sounds almost too good to be true, said the publisher. This is Glennville we're talking about, you know.

Said Roland: If the fair happens, *when* the fair happens, that old Glennville will be long gone. We'll be passing Nashville and Memphis in thirty years' time.

The publisher turned and looked at Teague and then at J.T. He seemed to be weighing his words. For reasons known only to him, he stuck an arm out from under the viaduct and let the rain strike his open palm. Mike, he said finally, you're an old Glennville boy. This thing really going to happen?

Yes, said Teague, looking out at the urban wasteland before him, the leaden sky. I'd be willing to bet on it.

You don't back many losers.

Not many, said Teague.

Just the odd gubernatorial candidate here and there, said J.T.

Well, you got one ally in Colonel Palmer, said the publisher. He's an old friend and he's on the board of the paper. Not sure how much sway he holds with the old guard though. He's always been kind of *with em but not of.* Like old Teague here.

Roland and J.T. laughed at this and exchanged glances as if they'd said something similar on more than one occasion.

Said Teague: The old colonel married up too, as I recall. But Colonel Palmer or no Colonel Palmer, old Glennville or no old Glennville, this thing can happen. Old Glennville will soon be irrelevant, a quaint vestige of the gin-and-tonic-bridge-club era.

He stopped talking then. What he'd said was hyperbole. Something J.T. would say. The old farts of old Glennville and their old fart sons and daughters would be going nowhere soon. They were entrenched, electing ambitious bumpkins and those from the lesser families to do their bidding. Just as they'd done for all of Teague's life. To root them out, now that he thought about it, would be a dangerous business.

To be honest, fellas, said the publisher, I think you're putting a little too much stock in what the newspaper can do for you. I think people have made up their minds, those who gave enough of a damn one way or another to have an opinion in the first place.

We're just getting started, said J.T. Just getting really geared up. You start saying it loud enough and often enough, and it becomes reality. You of all people should know that.

Said the publisher: Sam Tarvin says there's no way you do this without city bonds. He crunched the numbers, and your best-case scenarios with the state and federal grants still leaves a shortfall of fifteen to twenty million. Sam sees the city picking up the lion's share of that.

Sam Tarvin is a right pain in my ass, said J.T.

He's thorough, the publisher said laughing. We won't be able to keep him long. He'll be in New York or D.C. soon enough.

How soon? asked J.T. As far as I can tell, his main interest is stifling local business.

Newspaper reports the news. We're not owned and operated by the Chamber of Commerce.

I thought part of your duty was to serve the public good, said J.T.

We report the news.

Some folks say you make it.

City bonds or no?

On or off the record, said Roland.

Off.

Okay, we think we can get the money through private investors. We've already secured eight million in loans from a wide assortment of banks in the region. There's going to be a neat mix of private and public funding. There may be a little of what used to be called land speculating. All up front. Those who believe in the fair may put their money where their mouth is. Those that don't can sit on the sidelines and say I told you so if it doesn't happen. It's gambling, Monte. The whole thing. But what the hell isn't?

The publisher looked his way and Teague had the feeling his presence at this conversation wasn't particularly desired. The money stuff. Yes, tricky tricky. But it always was. Corners rounded here, a backroom handshake there. He had money. He didn't worry about it. The need to have ever more money was an instinct he never quite understood. But the game, the competition, the strategizing, well that was something. Can we get this newspaperman to go against his better judgment, against his years of playing it close to the vest as his readership would have it? Yes, that was something else, something that kept a man interested.

The publisher said: Let's say the private investors don't come through. What's the fallback?

Roland looked at Teague and then at his brother to see if they expected him to speak. He smiled as one about to point out the rather large pink elephant in the room. He asked Teague for a smoke. He struck the match and held it to the cigarette, then threw the match onto a puddle just in front of them. The match went out with a quick, harsh hiss and Teague found himself staring at it without really knowing why as it floated in the puddle, bounced and buoyed by the steady popping drops of rain.

Let's say we did have to ask the city for a small loan, said Roland. In the form of a long-term bond. What the city will get is all of this land, usable land, that will be worth ten to fifty times what they paid for it. And they'd be able to spread the payments over a twenty-, thirty-year period.

The publisher smiled. So Sam Tarvin was right?

I thought we'd established that Sam Tarvin was a pain in the ass, Roland said smiling. But yes, there's a chance. If we don't round up all of the private funding we'd like. Fifty-fifty, I'd say.

Then you're going to have to have a referendum, said the publisher. You've finessed it long enough. If it's fifty-fifty city money is at stake, then the people have a right to vote.

Let's have the referendum then, said Roland. We were just saying the same thing this morning. We haven't been dodging it. Just didn't want to put the cart before the horse, especially before the public was fully informed. Can I trust that the public is going to hear the other side of the story?

The publisher looked once again at Teague then back to Roland. You'll let me know when you start looking for private investors for specific projects?

Absolutely, said Roland.

We're not choosy, said J.T. smiling.

Why don't you have your PR man send something over? Just the general overview.

Mixed-up Merge, said J.T. Let's lead with that. We'll send over the plans for that and what the state department of transportation had to say about our time frame.

All right, said the publisher. That's the way to go. We'll lead with Mixed-up Merge.

The Coles shook hands formally with the publisher and then, almost as an afterthought, Shiloh reached for Teague's hand as well. They looked at each other for a moment, Glennville boys both, each knowing the lay of the land. The publisher seemed to be seeking out confirmation that he was throwing in on the winning side.

Life's a gamble, said Teague with a smile. They might run us out on a rail.

To this the publisher laughed. And then it was he who first put up his umbrella and began walking back to his car in the rain.

Said J.T., hollering at his back: Am I safe in assuming that Sam Tarvin may not be the right man to cover the fair for the *Herald*?

The publisher said nothing in response, but the nearly imperceptible nodding of his head under the umbrella seemed to indicate that he'd heard what J.T. said.

Our man Sam will be covering the local bingo game this time next week, said J.T.

Roland smiled, but his eyes were sweeping the proposed fair site in a look Teague found hard to analyze. Optimistically fatalistic, perhaps. And then he was out in the rain bareheaded and striding hard, keys jangling in his hands, water splashing up all around his feet.

J.T. looked at Teague, madman country-boy charm playing on his lips. I ever mention I don't like getting fucked with?

No, said Teague, opening his umbrella. But I always kind of assumed it.

A Phone Conversation: Lake House Bedroom: Limited Perspective

April: *I know, but that's not what you said.*

She lies sideways on the bed in sweatpants and a man's button-down shirt. She wears no makeup and her hair is pulled back in a ponytail that stretches across a satiny white pillow. The cord is twirled around her finger, and her bare feet, still faintly tan, toes polished and glimmering in the overhead light from the vaulted ceiling, beat time, too quickly, to the rock music banging off the wide walls of the empty den and through the open bedroom door.

A: *You said, I remember exactly what you said, that when you try out the new jet, I was going to be the first passenger. You made a little joke about the Mile-High Club. Ha ha ha. Do you deny saying that?*

The song ends and the DJ comes on. He's telling about a live remote from the new dance club in town. He'll be there and you should too.

A: *I've never even been to Washington, D.C. I've never been anywhere. You've never* taken *me anywhere.*

Ladies free. And dollar mixed drinks until nine.

A: *I don't care who Roland's taking. I could care less who Roland's taking. All I know is what you promised me,* promised *me, you were going to do.*

Valet parking. Dress code will be enforced. A rocking good time. Bet on it.

A: *I understand about business. It's always your goddam business.*

She sits bolt upright in bed, eyes blazing.

A: *I'll cuss if I* goddam *want to. You're not my* god-damn *father.*

She stands up, paces around the bed a bit, pulls the phone away from her ear and looks at it with uncensored rage, the voice on the other end faintly monotone, calm. She eyes her cigarettes and matches on top of the television. The cord will only stretch so far. To hell with it. She hangs up. Walks across the room and fires up. Counts two. The phone rings. She walks to the bar in the den and pulls out a bottle. Takes out a bar glass and carries both to the kitchen. The phone rings, shrill and ridiculous, urgent and teenagey, throughout the house, the sound in between rings another rock song, fast and testosterone-fueled. She runs her glass through the ice bin in the freezer, pours freely from the bottle, but doesn't take a sip. Goes to the stereo and increases the volume, simulates for a moment a head-banging guitarist, this song an obvious favorite of bygone high school days, boys in souped-up cars and drinking tallboy beers.

The phone stops ringing. And in that lessening of sound, the amplified stereo seems less defiant, less righteous rage. It is simply loud. The house filled with sound is that much more empty, emptier still when she turns down the volume, turns off the stereo completely. She bangs the ice around in her drink, takes a sip, walks to the bedroom and stares at the phone: black, plastic, mute. It rings. She lets it ring three times then picks up. Holds the receiver limply to her ear and listens.

The Free Agent

Out the kitchen window of his parents' house, in a neighborhood not so slowly going to rot: a deer pelt freshly skinned and stretched and tautly crucified on four nails hammered crookedly above the front porch steps. No way up or down the steps but by ducking under the blood-spotted hide. Head hanging limply, grotesquely, nearly backward, dead eyes staring across the road at Teague. A front porch swing in the background, broken loose on one end and dragging the ground, lilting, a ship about to sink in a mummified and decadent manner.

Who in the hell has moved in across the street? said Teague, voice raised to carry from the kitchen to the den where his father watched football at a high volume.

His mother, from the den: I know. Can you believe it?

Are they keeping chickens in the back too? And where's the outhouse? I can't see the outhouse from here.

Jan pinched him on the arm and laughed. Hush, she said. And don't start in on them again.

Oh, I'm starting in, said Teague, leaving his glass in the sink and heading for the den.

Said Teague senior: That, son, is a redneck. His father was a redneck. His granddaddy was a redneck. As long as there has been rednecks, that fellow has been one. His children are rednecks. His grandchildren and heirs from here till Doomsday will be rednecks. Some things just are.

Sugarcoat them all you want. Make what excuses you will. But what it boils down to is piss-poor protoplasm.

Teague sat down in the matching recliner next to his father, laughing and looking again at the flayed carcass across the way. His father has not looked up from the ballgame, has not cracked a smile. Piss-poor protoplasm? Is that what it is?

His father: When Fortune was lining em up for the first time to dollop out the genetic material, his folks were out back aggravating some dog on a rope.

Our ancestors were up front, of course?

The Teagues were, yes. Now your mother's folks, the Wrigleys, they were in church and never got the word, God bless em.

So I've got the Teague morality and the Wrigley brain?

It's time you knew, son. You're old enough to know the truth.

Teague's mother hollered from the kitchen: Ask your daddy who helped him with all his homework in high school.

His father shook his head to the negative but made no reply.

Don't deny it, came the call from the kitchen. Ask your father who was valedictorian of Burton High, class of 1931.

Was it Barbara Nash?

Barbara Nash? Psshhh. Barbara Nash wasn't in the top five and she took half her courses in home ec.

A truck with a sawed-off muffler and raised mag wheels rumbled down the street, spewing smoke and shaking the windows of the house. Teague looked out the window at his parents' small but neatly raked and landscaped front yard, the sealed and power-washed driveway, the mailbox now entombed in brick so often has it been mangled or decapitated by roadway vandals. His father watched the game on TV, peacefully reclined, unbothered by deer carcass or 160-decibel trucks. How had he gotten crotchety and his father had not? Or was it softness, ease? The distance from day-to-day brushing of elbow with John Q. Public. His own house sat nearly a football field from the road. His own backyard was like a small park, with pool and patio and absolute privacy. His parents shared a fence and a row of boxwoods with the neighbor twenty yards back. In the summer they talked over the shrubs and compared tomatoes and azalea blooms.

So you still don't want to move, said Teague.

No, said his father. I don't.

My offer stands. There's always houses in our neighborhood.

They're just tired of making the drive out east, said his mother from the kitchen.

No, we'd just love to have you nearer, said Jan, sitting on the arm of his chair and loosely draping an arm around Teague's shoulder.

Mary Kay can move when I'm dead, said Mr. Teague. She's going to outlive me by fifteen, twenty years. You can talk her into it then.

They talked on, Teague and Jan, about the pros of moving out west, delicately navigating around the declining neighborhood or the fact that all of their old friends were either dead or moved on. Moved west. But there was no convincing to be done. Too set in their ways. The smooth, seamless beauty of routine. Knowing where the light switches are, how long to run the water before the shower was hot. It would take a broken hip. Or one of them to die, like his father said. They could move a methadone clinic across the street and his mother would take over a pie the day they moved in and welcome them to the neighborhood.

To be honest, now that he was reclined and watching the game and no longer looking at the fading, rusting world, Teague had to admit he felt comfortable in this den. They'd moved in when it was brand-new his sophomore year of high school. Before that, they'd lived in the large, rambling house of his maternal grandmother. The wonders and treasures of her attic. The smooth hollow feel of bare feet on a hard-swept wood porch. This house pure modernity in comparison. Three, yes three, bathrooms.

His father's shined shoes had been resting atop the Sunday paper, which was neatly stacked on the footrest. Now he reached for the paper. Picked up the front page. Showed it to Teague. Teague smiled.

The *Herald* seems to have had a change of heart about your World's Fair, he said.

It looks that way, said Teague. The headline read: *Bye-Bye Mixed-up Merge?*

Beneath the headline was a rendering of the revised highway zipping through a modernistic-looking Glennville, cars evenly spaced and uncrowded on the byway, the downtown shiny and futuristic and dotted with high-rise hotels, a monorail zipping soundlessly through the university, past the new basketball arena, a tree-filled city park and a spiffy-looking guy on a chariot. Destination? The FBG building majestically on the hill. The byline read Phillip Evers, but it was nearly a verbatim rehashing of the generic Expo Commission press release, the same one that had been sent to the *Herald* and ignored months before.

If this comes off, it will be the best thing to ever happen to Glennville, his father said.

It was halftime, so he walked over and turned off the television.

I think so, said Teague.

I still can't figure out which way I'm supposed to vote if I'm for the fair. It's confusing.

It is, said Teague smiling. Vote no if you're for the fair.

That makes no sense.

You're voting no against the referendum. We're afraid if it goes to referendum we'll either lose or it will put us too far behind schedule. We couldn't do a referendum until August.

Vote no for the fair?

That's right.

People are going to be confused as hell.

We hope so.

His father glanced at Teague from the corner of his eye, started to delve further, but couldn't quite garner the energy. Lately, he was choosier about what he expended his mental energy on. Perhaps at that age you just intuited better. Or the accumulations of experience as they related to gut reactions were enough to give you the gist of most things. The gist was enough. If it was truly important, it would come up again at a later date. At a later date, there would be time to learn what needed to be learned. If it was the typical passing nuance, the slimmest of curiosities, why worry about it now?

And now you're going to meet the president of the United States?

Yes, said Teague smiling. His father was not one to brag, but this would be hard to keep under his hat down at the clubhouse of Sandy Hill, the public course where the East Glennville locals came to knock it through the crabgrass and clover.

It's just so exciting, his mother said, coming into the den. What are you going to wear, Janet?

I haven't decided yet, said Jan, turning to Teague to smile. Probably just throw on a sweat suit or something. The first lady claims to love casual clothes.

Pssshh, said Mrs. Teague. Famous people always say that. But every time you see them, they're dressed to the nines. Oh, I'd love to see what you wear. You all be sure and take lots of pictures. I'm going to need physical evidence to show all my friends. Not a one of them, by the way, thinks we need a World's Fair. And not a one of them thinks it will ever happen. I may frame today's paper and take it to bridge club on Tuesday. I've never known a city to run itself down like Glennville.

Mountain folks are skeptical by nature, his father said, sitting down again in the recliner. They don't like the government or big projects. They really don't like any kind of large gathering of people. Just give em ten acres of rocky land to farm and leave em alone. They won't be happy with just that, but they won't be agitated either. They can stand misery, but not agitation. The devil you know versus the devil you don't.

Teague looked at his wife. She'd heard his imitation of his father's musings on the native stock of the city for the twenty-one years of their marriage. The Teagues, as his father was always proud to point out, originated from Middle Tennessee, the cradle of cultivation and right, i.e., Democratic, thinking.

Those Coles are something else, his mother said, coming over to pat him on the shoulder. They're movers and shakers.

Teague agreed that they were.

Do you like them Janet?

They're interesting, she said with a laugh.

A little rough around the edges for Jan, said Teague.

I didn't say that, she said. You make me sound like such a snob.

They're interesting?

There's nothing wrong with *interesting*. I like them fine. I really like Libby Cole. She's harder to get to know, but I like her.

Your mother wants to move our savings to Valley Industrial, his father said.

They're paying almost thirteen percent interest, said his mother. That adds up fast.

It's a good interest rate, said Teague. But you do know Valley is uninsured? It's a state thrift. It's not like a bank backed by the FDIC where you're basically safe no matter what. If something happens to the institution, you're flat out of luck.

You think their bank is going to fail? his mother said. They've got banks and S&Ls popping up like mushrooms all over the place.

No, I don't think it's going to fail, said Teague. I'm just telling you there's some risk involved. A very small risk. But in a one-in-a-thousand chance it happens, you're bust.

Do you mind if I ask who you bank with? his mother asked.

First Union, where I always have.

I never knew you to be so conservative, said Mrs. Teague.

You marry old money, you take on old money ways, said Teague as Jan rolled her eyes skyward. But you all do what you want with your money. If you need to hit a lick so you can get out of this neighborhood, then I'm all for it.

His father got up and walked over to the television, turned it on. The players were lined up for the kickoff of the second half. The announcer was outlining what adjustments the losing team needed to make.

So you work for them, his mother said, walking toward the small secretary in the corner with the crossword. You're trying to bring a World's Fair to Glennville with them. But you don't bank with them.

No, I don't, said Teague. And I'm sure they could care less. They hired me to do a job. Listen, I'm a free agent.

Yes, said his father, and you always have been.

Teague paused for a moment and wondered what his father meant. And then they were watching the game and the ladies were talking about sightseeing in D.C. And to dwell on the metaphorical implications of being referred to as a lifelong free agent seemed imprudent and perhaps a little irrelevant, a nuance of the eternal mystery of father and son that might or might not be explored another day.

A Conversation, the Tone of Which Is Made Possible by the Confluence of:

1. The afterward of Sunday dinner with the folks
2. A fall day, moody and swirling-leafed
3. The excitement of an impending trip
4. The close confines and intimacy of a car heading for home on nearly empty city streets

The question comes from nowhere, from the smooth hum of tire on road, the unlistened-to song on the radio:

I heard that Roland Cole is seeing Valerie.

Teague does not reply.

Is that true?

Again Teague says nothing.

He is then.

Listen, that question is walking the border between social gossip and what I do for a living.

This is different or I wouldn't have asked. And you know it.

Do you think your source is reliable?

Yes.

Okay, then trust your source.

Do you see her?

I'm not going to answer that.

Yes you are. You're answering the question or you're stopping the car.

I've seen her twice.

With Roland?

Yes, with Roland. Once in Nashville and once here in town.

In Nashville?

When we went down to meet with Senator Kirkwood. Listen, that's over. We say hello and that's it. There's usually about twenty people around and we're sitting on opposite ends of the table.

I thought I was done with her.

You are. So am I.

Poor Libby.

Yes, thought Teague, poor Libby. But he said no more. And when he reached over to rest his hand on hers, she let it lie there, and when they were home again and the house was bright with televisions and the comings and goings of their daughter, the matter seemed dropped, the conversation shut up for good with the slamming of car doors in the driveway.

Is There Coffee?

It was four in the afternoon and she was still in her housecoat and slippers. She sat at the kitchen table reading the Sunday paper and drinking a second round of coffee. The first round, this morning at eleven, seemed not to have taken. It had led to a light breakfast, eggs and toast, a shower, and then, without really a lot of prompting, the bed. They'd snoozed a bit afterward, watched, piecemeal, an old movie on the television, and talked and laughed in the indolent way of adults stealing the day away, wasting it, using up a perfectly reasonable day for errands, or museum visits, or exercise in the park or some other form of self-edification. Four in the afternoon and they still weren't dressed. She couldn't stop yawning. Too much sleep made you tired. And she was hungrier by the minute. Where should they go out to eat? Nothing better than going to eat on a Sunday, off hours. Three to five in the afternoon or nine to ten o'clock at night. So private, those times, so intimate, the restaurants virtually empty, the staff languorous and good-humored. She went back and forth about taking another shower then decided against it. Better right before bed. She was yawning through the newspaper, glancing over the arts section, the book page. Maybe a jazz bar would be nice. She thought of the few Sundays she'd spent in New York and was envious of that sophisticated self. Perhaps a band worth hearing would be playing. And a martini was beginning to sound like a good idea.

He came from the bedroom in his boxer shorts and nothing else, looking youngish and trim in the legs. He sat down opposite her and grabbed a section of paper, glancing around the table and the room as men do when they pretend to be looking for something but really want you to get it for them. You need something? she asked.

Is there coffee?

She smiled. In the kitchen there is.

He nodded, began reading the paper. She considered going to get him a cup, but decided against it. After a few minutes he rose and went to the kitchen. Fumbled around for much longer than it should have taken to locate the sugar on the counter, the cream in the fridge, and a spoon from the drawer. When he returned, blowing on his mug and looking pleased with his efforts, she said, you really don't know your way around here very well, do you?

I'm not often in the kitchen, he said smiling. Did you decide where we should go to eat? Are you hungry? We're kind of in between lunch and supper.

No, I'm hungry. Let's read the paper and get dressed and go out.

Okay. Wherever you want to go is fine with me.

He sat reading the sports page. After a few minutes, he held up the paper and pointed out a photo of a young man, a fraternity type, dressed in a coat and tie, walking into Vanderbilt stadium hand in hand with his well-heeled date. The couple was oblivious to having their picture taken and looked impossibly young and self-possessed, as if the world would have pretty fall days and pretty partners to hold hands with for all of their days to come.

My college experience was not like that, said Roland smiling.

Valerie smiled back.

I bet yours was.

You mean going to football games or cute boys or what?

I mean going to football games with cute boys and all dressed up and looking like you know what the hell you're doing when you're twenty years old.

I studied most Saturdays, she said. And my only dates were to church.

Uh-huh, said Roland.

She smiled again. He looked like a man with more to say.

Me and J.T. used to sit around and imagine what was going on up at Glennville, up at the university. Everybody going to movies and dances. All the pretty girls. A campus with a big tower on it and those old buildings with ivy climbing up the walls. I went to one football game up there when I was in college. My dad took me. We went by the Pogo Room on the strip before the game. All these fellows with their dates and me with my dad.

Were you miserable?

No. Not at all. I was glad to be there. Not many people in Henry City had season tickets. It was Dr. Wade gave them to Daddy. Somebody in his family was getting married, I think. Anyway, I thought Daddy would take Mother or one of his friends. He asked Mother first but she said she'd rather I went. So, no, I was just glad to be there. I was just glad to see it with my own eyes, that what we'd been imagining wasn't that far off.

She started to say something, but couldn't tell if he was finished. He sipped from his coffee in a contemplative manner, set the cup down, and looked her in the eye.

I bet it was a lot of fun, he said. It sure looked like fun.

It was, she said, going to the kitchen to refill her coffee. She came back with the pot and topped Roland's mug as well. Why didn't you go?

I don't know. Scared, I guess. J.T. was already engaged. So I just went on up to Eastern like most of the kids who went to college in the area did. But we always dreamed of going to the university.

She smiled. You make it sound like Harvard or UCLA or some really exotic place.

Roland placed the cup down quickly, smiling and animated. A bit of the coffee spilled out of the cup onto the paper. Hell, it was Harvard to us. We all knew we were at some cow college, we didn't have the first illusion about where we were. The locals would razz you a bit about being a college boy, but they knew you'd end up back in Henry City. They knew that you would be, essentially, what you always were, what your folks were. But

every year one or two from the high school would go off to school, go up
to the university. And you'd see them at Christmas and over the summer,
and they were just different. Not putting on airs or anything. You could
just see they'd been shined up some, had learned a bit about the world and
weren't ever going to be exactly what they were before they left.

She smiled. She could tell he was thinking of a particular boy or girl
from home, his idea of what college should look like, dress like.

He suddenly laughed out loud, animated again. He began walking
around the room, trying to recollect the thought. We had this one teacher
up at Eastern, he said, facing her and smiling, barefoot and shirtless in
his boxers. His name was Dr. Pelphrey. I don't know if he was British or
not. I'm pretty sure he'd been over to Oxford or Cambridge at some point.
Always wore a tweed jacket with patches in the elbow.

You had a teacher from Britain at Eastern in 1955?

Hell, he might have been from Boston. Or New York. To us, anybody
north of Virginia all sounded so slick and different it might as well have
been the same thing. He taught British Literature. But one day out of
the blue, he said, my British accent is horrible, so bear with me. He said:
Mr. Cole, I don't believe you're long for this little burg. I didn't know what
he was talking about. He just said it out of the blue in front of the whole
class. *Mr. Cole, I don't believe you're long for this little burg.* And then he
said, *some of us, however, will spend our last dying days in this fair burg,
teaching Shakespeare to the sons and daughters of yeoman farmers.*

He said that in front of the whole class?

Oh hell yes. He didn't care. And we didn't either. There was this one
boy, he had the worst accent you ever heard. Dr. Pelphrey would make
him read Hamlet out loud and just sit there and laugh until the tears were
rolling down his cheeks.

That sounds really mean.

Nah, this old boy didn't care. He was one of those guys who's the same
at two as he is at ninety-two. He was in on the joke. Dr. Pelphrey wasn't
a bully. Hell, he'd make the guys in the class read the girls' parts. Made
me read Ophelia one day in class.

You did it?

Sure. Read it like I felt it. But my god, my accent. You could blackmail me good if anyone had a tape recording of my Ophelia.

Your accent's not that thick.

Listen, for back home, maybe it's not. But drop me anywhere else in America and I'm hick on a stick.

She laughed. Why do you think he said that to you? About getting out of your little burg?

Roland stopped. He'd been heading to the bathroom, presumably to shower before dinner. He paused in front of a picture of her father on the mantel above the gas fireplace. Picked up the picture and looked at it. She could see her father in profile, the tuxedo, the sly, proud smile. She didn't tell Roland that the picture was taken on her wedding day, not that he'd have minded.

I think I would have liked him, said Roland, placing the picture back on the mantel.

I think you would have too.

He paused for a moment, looking at the picture, or the mantel, or off somewhere else. I've often wondered about that, he said. I don't know why a man like Dr. Pelphrey would have said what he said. I hadn't spoken a word in class that day. Afterwards, a lot of my friends were razzing me about it. And I laughed it off. But when he said that, it made me wonder. I kind of took it to heart. Of course I didn't tell anybody that. I was a little superstitious about it. Or at least private about it. But for the first time ever I considered that I might not live my whole life in Henry City. Strange, isn't it? How a passing comment like that can set you to thinking.

She allowed that it was strange.

I guess you've had enough of strolling down memory lane, he said, turning quickly. I'll just take a quick shower and then we can get on our way when you're ready.

She said nothing to this. When she heard the shower running, she stacked the newspapers on the kitchen counter and placed her mug in the dishwasher. It was strange, she thought. Most all of it. Ask a man what he was thinking, and get a grunt or a lie in response. Make a man fresh from your bed get his own coffee and learn the genesis of his ambition. She wondered for a moment how she knew these things intuitively, things women seemed often to struggle with if you could believe what you read in the magazines. She moved from the kitchen to the bedroom, her father's smile catching her out of the corner of an eye. You too, she thought. In time, I'd have found you not so opaque. Then she was picking out her clothes for the evening, thinking again that a martini was the way to go.

A Parting Shot

He read the article again. Checked the byline. Again. Sam Tarvin. Glanced, furiously, again at the headline: *Expo Credit Inflated?*

According to the article, the Coles had not actually signed on the dotted line for the eight million in loans from area banks that they claimed. According to Tarvin, he'd called every bank listed with the Expo Commission. His calls revealed a figure closer to three million than eight. From here, Tarvin hypothesized that the Coles and the Expo Commission would almost assuredly have to tap into city funds to make up for this shortfall, especially with time being of the essence. The Expo group would have to show they had their money in line before the state and federal agencies would commit theirs. And the International Bureau of Fairs would want their paperwork from the Glennville group sooner rather than later with the fair proposed for four years in the very near future. He speculated that the Coles would float the idea of long-term, thirty-year bonds, a plan that would saddle future Glennvilleans, Glennvilleans now in elementary school, with the task of paying for their elders' folly. He closed by saying the whole deal would come down to a write-down from the city, explaining that a write-down is bureaucratic shorthand for an unbelievable deal given to a private enterprise by a municipality.

He stopped short of calling the Coles liars for the eight-million-dollar claim, but just barely, allowing that entrepreneurs sometimes, necessarily, have to inflate numbers to get the ball rolling on a project and that by nature entrepreneurs were an optimistic lot. The idea that the World's Fair was a civic-focused enterprise, one that would benefit the city, one prompted by civic and altruistic motivation, was never broached in the article. No, the article all but said, the World's Fair was an entrepreneurial enterprise, first and foremost, whose prime aim was to make money for its investors, i.e., the Cole Brothers and their cronies.

Roland buzzed Mrs. Barnes, his secretary, and asked her to get Monte Shiloh on the phone. He stood up and paced around the office. He thought he would like to break something. Then he thought that that was what J.T. would do right now. Then he did it anyway, swatting a lamp from his desk with a sudden, satisfying backhand. The lamp landed five feet away with a muffled thud on the plush carpet and then Mrs. Barnes was saying over the intercom: Mr. Cole, I have Monte Shiloh on the line.

Put him through, said Roland. He went around the desk and switched the phone to speaker mode and paced behind his desk, looking furiously out on the city and river below. Hello, Monte, said Roland.

How are you, Roland? said the publisher.

How are you, my ass, said Roland. How do you think I am?

Not too happy would be my guess, said the publisher, and something in his tone—too light, too distant, too goddam professional—didn't sit well with Roland.

That's right, Monte. That's goddam right.

Roland had turned to face the speaker and looked furiously upon it.

If you'll calm down a bit, said the publisher, I'll try to explain what happened.

And now the publisher's tone had changed. His intonation less even, less professional. Less the man of stature confronting a hotheaded upstart. A bit rattled, a bit angry. Back on his heels but trying to get level again. This tone Roland found preferable, but not yet quite right.

Monte, said Roland, voice modulated but keen. I am calm. Trust me, when I'm not you'll know it. But the next patronizing phrase that comes out of your mouth, the next time your *tone* sounds patronizing to me, then you might well have reason to tell me to calm down.

The publisher paused for a good long while. Roland stared at the black speaker on his desk. He was leaning over it, his hands on the edge of the desk.

Roland, said the publisher, sounding tired and patient and careful. I'm sorry about the article.

You see, said Roland. That's the way this conversation should have started. Not with *how are you, Roland*. Much better, Monte. Much much better. Now we're making some progress.

Roland, said the publisher, I am sorry. I was going to call you. I had a meeting first thing this morning and I'm just now back at my desk.

Roland said nothing, but stood up straight and turned his back to the speaker.

Said the publisher: Our regular editor was out sick this week. Tarvin has been writing that city column for a year now, every Wednesday. My editor had told him that we wanted him to move off the fair stuff for a spell. He pitched a fuss about it, but, according to my editor, he was going to play ball. Then when the editor was out of town this week, he slipped in the article. The assistant editor didn't know anything about it.

Why would he? It'd just be par for the course for the *Herald*.

Here the publisher paused and Roland debated whether to be gracious and accept the apology or not. He said: All I want to know is if you're with us or not. I want you to declare. Because if you're with us, that's fine. This is just one of those slipups that happen sometimes. But if you're not, if you're trying to play both sides, or you're a bit indecisive because some of your cronies gave you grief about the article last Sunday, or you just don't know what the hell you think, then just say that too. But at this point, if you're not with us, you're against us. It's too late in the game to be dicking around with people who still don't know what they want for the city. And we're pretty close to getting this fair without you. Very close, in fact. And when we get it, we're going to have the president here for opening ceremonies. We're going to have entertainers and exhibits from all over the world. And you can bet your ass you won't be sitting at the head table for any of it. You can bet your ass you'll be paying full price like everyone else. And you can bet your ass that everyone in this town will know that you and your paper bet on the wrong side of this deal. I'll personally make sure of that.

Roland, began the publisher.

You let me finish. Tarvin is right about some private investors making some money. He's damn right about that. A whole bunch of regular, honest Glennvilleans who know a good opportunity when they see one. If they do something that's a once-in-a-lifetime for their city and make a little change in the process, then what the hell's the matter with that? I'm asking you. What's the matter with that?

Nothing, Roland. Not a thing.

I want that situation taken care of.

Tarvin?

Hell yes Tarvin.

You want me to fire him?

Roland sat down in his chair and absentmindedly opened a piece of mail. Monte, I want you to handle the situation. I thought we'd established that during our visit.

I can't fire him unless he fabricated his story. If he did, I'll fire him and print a retraction tomorrow.

Listen, Monte, if some jackleg little reporter calls me up today and starts asking me about loans I'm securing, I'm not going to tell him shit. Those banks he called, they don't want their business out there for public consumption. Their investors read your paper. And your paper makes this whole thing seem like some kind of scam. And the last thing they want to hear is that the place they bank is loaning money to a bunch of sharks. So the banks deny it or beat around the bush a bit. I mean, come on. What kind of business tells their business to the paper?

At the risk of pissing you off, said the publisher, some could argue that public money is at stake, that public money is tied up in a private venture, so that everyone has a right to know. Federal money. State money. Possibly city money.

And I'm telling you that bankers don't give a shit. They're not going to tell you on the record every little loan they make for a project that they think may or may not come off. It's not yet a matter of public interest. No public money has yet been committed. If it flies, then yes, certainly the public has a right to know where all the money comes from. I'm just telling you how a banker is going to react when a hard-ass reporter calls from the local paper and wants to know if his bank is involved with the Expo project. I'm asking you, if you were a local banker and you've read the *Herald*'s articles on the Expo, would you admit over the phone that you'd invested in the Expo? What's the upside?

Do you want a retraction? If so, it will take an investigation.

No, I don't want a retraction. Listen, not only do I not cry over spilled milk, I very rarely stop to clean it up. I want the situation handled.

I'll have to think about it, Roland. See what the best way to handle this will be.

You do that, Monte, said Roland reaching for the speaker button on the phone. You do a little thinking about it.

And then the button was pushed and the speaker went silent. Roland leaned back in his chair. He noticed for the first time, noticed in absentia, that Monte Shiloh had been breathing loudly into the phone during the whole of their conversation, a kind of continual, wheezy, fitful background noise. Did he have a cold? Emphysema? How old was he anyway? Nearly as old as his father? He was not used to talking to his elders like that. He didn't like talking to anyone like that. When he glanced around the room, he saw the broken lamp on the floor. He recalled J.T.'s conversation with the university president. How was this conversation different? And why was he so irritated by his brother's temper and so oblivious, so *nurturing*, of his own? When it came down to it, why did he, why did most people, consider him the even-tempered of the two? How else to handle it though? It was one of the hard lessons of life, that to get people to do things, you had to give it to them hard. Hard, fast, and to the quick. His own father had not operated that way, at least that he knew of. But he had, if you looked at it with hard, cold eyes, never been this high up on the flagpole. No one in Henry City was trying to knock him on his ass. Everyone in Henry City knew him and knew he meant well.

He rose from the desk and walked down the hall toward his brother's office. As he passed Mrs. Barnes, he said, I'm going to need a new lamp. She nodded and made a notation on a pad. When he got to his brother's office, J.T. was just finishing up a phone call and motioned for him to take a seat. The *Herald* was on his desk and J.T. pointed at it and smiled a *can you believe this shit?* smile. When he got off the phone, he said, good article, don't you think?

Roland picked up the paper, glanced at it, tossed it again on the desk. I just got off the phone with Monte Shiloh.

Did you have a firm word?

Yes.

J.T. smiled, slyly, with just the corners of his mouth. He said: Little brother's got himself a temper sometimes.

To this Roland smiled.

You remember chasing me around the yard with that hammer?

Roland shook his head, disbelieving of his young angry self. He said: Daddy wouldn't like me talking to Monte Shiloh like I did. How old do you reckon he is?

I don't know how old he is, said J.T. But a certain kind of old fart just asks for it. I saw Daddy throw old Mutt Please out of the store one day when he came in drunk and wouldn't stop badgering one of the counter girls about cheating him out of a nickel's-worth of hoop cheese.

Really? I don't remember that.

Rode him out on his knee like you would a hog you're trying to jam in the chute, said J.T., rising and grabbing his suit jacket from the brass coat rack in the corner. And hell, he was near twenty years older than Daddy.

We going to lunch? said Roland.

Yeah, let's go, said J.T. And let's walk down Franklin Street like two brothers who are fixing to meet the president of the United States. That one-horse paper can kiss my ass.

Vignettes on a Plane

TEAGUE REGISTERS SURPRISE

The plane had just leveled off after takeoff, still in that in-between-rattling-and-smooth state, when J.T. popped the first bottle of champagne. A day before, Corrine had cracked a similar bottle across the nose of this plane. They were on their way back from Washington after a whirlwind visit: land, hotel check-in, night at the symphony, late dinner. Today they'd met with the president, Treasury Secretary Graves, and U.S. Senator Smiley. The meeting was short and perfunctory, a formality really. Senator Smiley had set up a tour of the White House for the three couples and then the men had peeled off for a twenty-minute meeting with the president while the women met with the first lady in the Rose Garden. The president had decided to put his weight behind the fair and would write what letters needed to be written to the International Bureau of Fairs and the Commerce Department.

Garret Graves's influence had helped. And of course Smiley all but claimed that his threat to withhold support of the president's energy bill had turned the tide. But what it all came down to, thought Teague, was a president taking care of a fellow party member, one who'd supported him with donations and public campaigning in historically hostile territory. He'd carried the state, but been romped handily in East Tennessee, one of the few regions in the South not to vote his way. As they were leaving, the president said, *I guess we're sticking it to those hill country Republicans with this one, don't you think?* with a surprising and disarming gleam in his eye. He looked so frail on television, so meek and humble and like the dutiful altar boy, that to see him up close and on his own turf had been a little discombobulating. More forceful, more savvy than he'd have ever guessed. Sitting on the plane now, Teague wondered how he'd let himself be fooled by portraits in the media. You did not, you simply and absolutely did not, get to be a major player in the public arena without being rough and ready.

What's so funny? said Jan.

Nothing, said Teague, sipping on the cold and refreshing champagne.

She looked at him in a queer manner and smiled.

The president, he said. He wasn't like I expected. He's a killer. Not ruthless. He's honest, I don't mean that. He's just like one of those old-good-guy sheriffs in the movies. He doesn't *want* to kill you, but he sure as hell will.

Jan smiled. You sound like you find that appealing.

I do. Before today, I thought he went against everything I thought I knew about politics. What it took to make it in politics. I thought he was just a fluke. A post-Watergate fluke. But he's not. He's one of us too.

And that's good? she said playfully.

Not good or bad. It just is.

She touched her glass to his. Sometimes, she said, I think you're a bit of a cynic.

And you're toasting me for that?

I'm toasting because I love you anyway.

THE FIRST LADY

Corrine didn't like to fly and avoided it when she could. It bedeviled her that her husband had bought a plane and she'd felt queasy and superstitious in the week leading up to this trip. When she expressed her concerns to J.T., he had, purely to agitate her, hinted at taking flying lessons himself. This she claimed would lead to long-overdue divorce proceedings. Let someone else play widow lady. She was too young to wear black and was afraid her mourning period would be swift, her widow's bed filled with handsome gardeners and pool boys. He'd laughed and threatened nightly visitations, coitus interruptus from the spectral region:

Booooo, Boooooo, geeetttt yooouurrr scraaaawwnnnnyyy aaasssss oooooofff myyyyyy wiiiiiiife.

Crazy thing.

She'd had nightmares about the plane wrecking. It seemed once a year a small plane went down somewhere in Glennville. Always front-page news. And with their luck going so well the last few years, and their luck with the fair looking as if it were about to turn around, it seemed only right for fate to rear up now and remind her of the proper cosmic order. All the stories in the news about quick, sudden family tragedies seemed to happen right when the family was at its zenith, right when things were happiest. And despite the ups and downs of her marriage, despite what she knew about J.T. and his wanderings, she had to admit she was happy.

But happiness never lasted long. How often in her hardscrabble youth had she been reminded what a fragile and wanton creature it was. It was enough to drive you insane, happiness was. The other shoe forever about to drop. She'd long stopped confiding her fatalistic vision of the world to J.T., her husband not one to dwell on the negative, trusting his luck, his fate. Both brothers were this way and she wondered if that was an inborn trait or the product of rearing.

She knew for certain it was easier for a man to trust his fate.

Her foreboding about the trip to Washington rose to such a point that J.T. said to either stay home or get a prescription from the doctor for anxiety. Either way, he was going and so was everyone else. After some deliberation, she'd chosen the prescription route. And now, having taken a little pill with a screwdriver in the airport cocktail lounge, holding a second glass of champagne and sitting in the plane she'd christened the day before, she decided to trust her fate. At least for a little while. At least for the rest of the day. Let come what will. Her husband sat beside her, nearer the window, the Teagues in the two seats beside them. But when she spoke, she addressed no one specifically, was looking toward the front of the plane, at the memory of a young girl riding a secondhand bike down a dirt road with her barefoot sisters.

I never thought I'd see the inside of the White House.

Then:

And wasn't the first lady gracious?

WHO ACTS LIKE THIS?

Refill? said J.T., standing above her, bottle tilted in her direction.

Sure, she said, offering her half-filled glass.

Attagirl, he said. I can't hardly get Corrine to touch the stuff.

Oh go to hell, said Corrine. I only had one drink in the airport.

J.T. blew a sarcastic kiss in the direction of his wife. In reply, she pretended to scratch her head with middle finger extended.

Jan laughed.

Teague, said J.T., pointing across the aisle and out the window. Below us now are the Blue Ridge Mountains. If you'll just look out that opposite window you can get an excellent view of them.

J.T. pointed with his middle finger, waving the finger up and down. With every waggle, the digit inched closer and closer to Corrine's face.

Corrine grabbed the finger and began twisting it back with all of her might. J.T., laughing and trying to wrench it away, reached down and began roughly tickling his wife under the arms. They were both laughing and sloshing their drinks and cursing at the other.

I'll tell you where you can stick that finger, said Corrine, still yanking the finger this way and that as she thrashed around half out of her seat.

And J.T. laughing and laughing.

Teague looked at her and smiled and she realized that she was smiling too. What else could you do? Who acts like this? Who, exactly, are these people? *What*, exactly, are these people?

THE SYMPHONY AND OTHER THINGS

She and Roland sat in the row behind the others. She was reading a novel when Roland gently picked up her leg, removed the high-heeled shoe, and began rubbing her foot through the hose. When she looked up, he gave her a quick smile but said nothing. Last night he'd surprised her with tickets to the symphony and then a late dinner in the Georgetown area. Somehow he'd roped J.T. into going along as well and the brothers sat through the performance with steely and predetermined diligence, J.T. especially looking like a boy scrubbed and dragged by an ear to his own piano recital, Roland affecting the quiet diffidence of one not quite in his element, unawed but respectful. Once when the drums had blasted suddenly and her glance had moved to the opposite side of the stage, her eyes had met Teague's. And, as one can do, he'd held her glance while simultaneously giving the once-over to Roland and J.T., whose rapt attention, the dutiful redirecting of attention to the drum section, was a study in sincere effort. Teague had smiled at her then, sharing the joke. You could take the boy out of the country . . .

Would you like another glass of champagne? asked Roland.

I don't think so, she said. I think I'm a little tipsy.

Let me take your glass then.

She handed him the flute and he took it toward the rear of the plane where they kept the food and drink. Across the aisle, Jan Teague leaned against her husband's shoulder, eyes closed, relaxing. Some couples just seemed to fit together. Some men could make a woman rest easy.

Roland came from the back with his own glass filled and sat down across from her. He reached for the other leg, removed the shoe, and began again to massage her foot.

THE BALANCING ACT

I was sitting in the Oval Office with the president of the United States three hours ago.

Yes you were, said Libby.

That's pretty good.

She smiled.

When he spoke, he stopped rubbing her foot for a moment. But now he went back to the task in earnest. She continued to read her book, the only sound coming from her seat a crisp and efficient turning of page. One glass of champagne. One. After the two days they'd just had. Corrine had her faults. And rough as a cob, yes. But she knew when and how to have fun. What it was, was this: he felt euphoric. And as usual when he did, Libby thought it best to remain irritatingly restrained. Did she predetermine this? To encourage such a mood might lead to an increase in the volume of Roland's speech, animated storytelling, raucous laughter. What some people liked to consider having fun. Shouldn't they be celebrating? This thing was going to happen. He was going to bring a World's Fair to Glennville. He could feel it in his bones. A done deal, state politics and referendum be damned. He rubbed her feet like an artist, hitting the pressure points, the lovely arch, the balanced and delicate toes. Lovely, lovely feet. A highlight of summer was Libby in open-toed sandals. But to encourage his euphoria was to encourage the parts of him that reminded her of J.T.: loud, uninhibited, unpolished. In short, a redneck. Indisputably she thought his brother one. And in her heart of hearts, she probably felt the same about him. The champagne had done about all it could do. A man could only drink so much of it. He wanted a scotch, a big one, and to talk loud and brag and be just generally as brash as he wanted with whomever else on the plane cared to join him. Let Libby read her book and have her one glass of champagne. Her palpable restraint, keeping the lid on the pot, was about to make his ass want to walk a barbed-wire fence.

Unexpectedly she smiled at him. Then she put her book down, got comfortable, and closed her eyes. His hands glided along the thin fabric of the hose. That feels good, she said.

With eyes closed she said: I had a great time in Washington.

And then: The symphony was lovely. So so lovely.

And: I think I'll have another glass of champagne after all.

CELEBRATION

The pilot says over the intercom: Folks, we'll be landing in Glennville in about fifteen minutes. And there's a nice sunset over the mountains if you'll look off to your right.

They do look, a glancing, perfunctory look. For what is one sunset among so many in the course of a life? And sunsets, really, are for those quiet moments, those moments of introspection and finding one's small place in the vast universe. To hell with that. This is Roland and J.T. Cole. Hands still warm from shaking the president's hand, they are laughing about the VOTE NO signs and giving Teague his humorous and sly due for the plan. Teague is the quiet one in this group, relatively speaking, but he has fallen under the sway of the moment, smiling without reservation, offering the half-filled cup when the bottle of single-malt scotch comes round.

It should be mentioned that all the shades are up and the light in the plane is odd and fantastic.

WHAT J.T. SAYS

Okay, when we get back to Glennville, here's what we gotta do.

Chariot to
the World

1983 World's Fair, Opening Day

They'd arrived at the office at six, the Teagues and the Coles and the rest of the Expo brass, to watch the opening of the fair from leather chairs pushed up against the plate-glass window of Roland's office. The official ceremonies at the U.S. Amphitheater, with a speech by the new president, the Republican president and not the one who'd help make the fair possible, had been the night before. Their meeting with him had been quick and businesslike, a couple of standard jokes and niceties, then the president had read a short, prepared speech to the Expo Commission, assorted dignitaries from the represented countries, forty-six all told, and anyone else willing to fork over fifty dollars for a ticket. Thirty minutes later he was en route to the airport. Roland had spoken later and so had Teague, the mayor, and a few city councilmen. Then the feast, a sampler buffet from the exotic cuisines of the participating countries. The night concluded with fireworks and a laser show, the laser acting as virtual tour guide, illuminating first this pavilion and then the next. *And here is the Fun Fair*. Roland acting as tour emcee. The laser's last lingering look had been upon the four-hundred-foot Sun Tower, shiny and futuristic and imposing against the night sky, Helios an antiquity with an eye to the future.

It was hard to believe you were in Glennville.

They'd stayed late at the fair, for the taverns were up and running: a German Strohaus, an Australian pub, a Western-style roadhouse saloon, a Japanese karaoke bar. And now, bleary-eyed after getting perhaps two hours of sleep, they waited with their coffee to see how the fair worked with the rank and file. Below them was John Q. Public at large, whom they hoped would be turning the tills for the next six months. At eight o'clock, when gates were to open, an already sizable crowd milled about the ticket windows, peering through the fence and gawking back behind them at the FBG building and the nearly completed Valley Industrial Savings and Loan tower next door. Below them: traffic bumper to bumper, the parking garage next to the World's Fair Inn filling up, people streaming from the lobby of the hotel, bus shuttles blowing black smoke as they huffed up Brewer Avenue to the south gate where all mass transit passengers would disembark.

The day had come up warm and breezy, the sky a sparkling blue gem in the sky. To look to the river or the mountains or the university bell tower a mile away was to see just another spring day in Glennville, a lovely one, but like a million others before it. And then to look down at the fair site, with the buildings and the people and the colorful flags of forty-six nations, well it was disorienting, and the people sitting by the huge window found themselves checking again for the river, the mountains, the bell tower, to make sure the scene below them was actually happening and not some wondrous mirage.

What time is it? said J.T.

Roland looked at his watch. It's ten after eight.

Why the hell is everyone still standing outside?

When J.T. spoke, his voice was harsh and loud, and those in the room became aware of how quiet it had been before, how relaxed and intimate the gathering had been, with an easy kind of anticipation: the work was done. Now let's have some fun and enjoy what we did, what we built.

Roland said nothing as he reached for the phone. He had to leaf through several pages of phone numbers until he found the one he was looking for, a number for the kind of low-level functionary he never would have imagined needing to call. He ignored the faces who looked at him as he dialed, glancing instead to the crowd at the fair, which seemed more packed together now, pushed up toward the ticket booth and the gate where before it had been a loose and shapeless gathering. Roland asked for the ticket manager in a hesitant manner as if not sure exactly who he should be asking for. They spoke for a moment then Roland said, okay, I see, well we need to get on it quick, you understand.

When he hung up, he said to the group at large: Everything's locked up down there. Some kind of electrical problem. So neither the ticket-printing machine nor the cash registers are working.

Are they letting people in with season passes? said J.T.

No, Roland said. There aren't that many down there right now anyway. Probably staying away from the first-day crush. And the ticket booth manager thought it would be too confusing to let some in and not others.

That's probably a good decision, J.T. said, standing up and looking once more out the window.

I think so, said Roland. The manager, Jim something, seems like he's staying calm. They're trying to track down the on-site electrician. Hopefully, we'll have it straightened out here in a few minutes.

With that, J.T. nodded and walked out.

Forty-five minutes later and the crowd still stood outside the main gate waiting to buy tickets, waiting to enter. The people in Roland's office had scattered, and now they paced the halls, talking to secretaries, getting drinks of water they didn't want. Only Roland and Teague remained in the office, Roland's silence and intermittent glances from phone to crowd below too hard for the others to witness. Then someone called. Roland listened for a moment and said, I'll call you back in a minute. Just keep calm. We'll figure something out. When he hung up, he said, well damn it to hell.

Sitting in the big leather chair on the far side of the office reading a magazine, Teague said nothing. He waited for Roland to give the update, but Roland simply stood and went to the window. He was standing there when J.T. burst into the office.

Those fuckers are getting pissed off down there, he said.

Teague smiled. Roland kept his back to his brother.

I'm serious, said J.T. They're waving money around asking what the holdup is. Some of em are trying to make everybody line up. Others are saying to hell with that. Kids are fussing, people are bitching to go to the bathroom. And your ticket man is just about to lose his shit. That electrician ever figure it out?

No, said Roland.

He looked dumb as a stump, said J.T. . He's sweating all to hell and talking to himself. So what's the story?

They're going to have to find the company that installed everything, all the equipment.

Hell it was working yesterday.

That was yesterday.

How long? said J.T., walking over and standing next to his brother at the window.

No idea.

Today though?

One would hope.

Well I'll be damned.

Yes. First day. Had to figure.

So what do you think?

I think, said Roland, that we open the gates and let all those people in for free.

Shew, said J.T. There might be fifty, sixty thousand show up today. That's a lot of jack.

Yep.

J.T. turned from the window and walked a few steps. Then retraced his steps and stood again beside his brother. They looked like boys on top of the Empire State building, gaping at the massive mystery beneath them.

Said J.T.: We sure as hell can't have bad publicity on the first day.

That's right.

Man, that's a lot of cash going up the chimney.

There's no other way. Maybe they'll get it fixed by lunchtime. We could salvage some of the gate then.

J.T. clapped his brother on the back. Well that's the call, brother. I'm with you. That's the way to do it.

From the leather chair, Teague said: If you're taking a bath, you might as well take it all the way and keep free entry all day. Even after they get the problem fixed. Better publicity that way. And folks who stayed away because of the crush can kick themselves a little. Might get em down here in more of a hurry.

Yeah, that's what I was thinking too, said Roland.

I'll tell Johnny Boy to call the radio stations and let em know what's up. And then the newspaper. *Free Admission at Fair* would be a good headline.

Roland nodded but didn't look Teague's way. He picked up the phone and dialed. Open the gates, he said into the receiver. Let em all in. Free. Gates are free today. All day. Call your friends and cousins and tell em to come on down. It's on-the-house day.

When he hung up, he said to his brother, you reckon this is an omen?

Said J.T.: Aw to hell with omens. Let's walk down there and watch the freeloaders have their fun.

Teague Tallies It Up, a Surprise Visitor, and Then a Request

The city teemed with people. All that summer Teague watched them stream into the city, efficiently and without much delay. The monorail had proved too expensive in the end, but Mixed-up Merge was a thing of the past. He'd taken an office one floor down from Roland's, right beneath, in fact, the first office he'd ever called his own. He liked having a routine, liked coming into the excited and buzzing city every morning, watching the early-arriving tourists pulling into the parking lots and garages, all the different license plates from across the nation. And the shuttles from outlying areas, the emptying shuttles at the south gate and kids running ahead of their parents, folks gazing up at the Sun Tower, the Federal Pavilion, the flags of the represented nations flapping with the morning breeze.

Teague now spent his days in minor consultation about publicity and public relations, his nights entertaining dignitaries. It would all be over in a few months and he'd be looking for other work, but for now he enjoyed the easy routine his position afforded. So nearly every morning he stood in his office, as he did now late in the month of July, looking out over the fairgrounds, already dotted with people, lines forming in front of the more popular pavilions: the Chinese, the Australian, the Peruvian. Alas, the Russians hadn't come after all, the presidential election two years before not going the way they'd hoped. Or, for that matter, the way the Coles had hoped. But Teague didn't dwell on regime change this morning, or potential roadblocks that might come along from the party spoils system, the same system that had helped pave the way for the miracle before him. He could no longer remember what the Rather Creek area looked like before, the day of the walk in the rain with Monte Shiloh a distant and shadowed memory. He could summon the rain and standing under the viaduct, but nothing else. That memory, that area, had vanished. The viaduct, painted the golden hue of the sun, served now as a pedestrian walkway from the World's Fair Inn to the shops and restaurants of the renovated train station. Where there had once been a muddy creek now stood the International Lake, two feet deep and two thousand in circumference, where people took off their shoes and cooled their feet as they ate their strudels and kabobs from the adjacent food emporium.

The whole referendum debate seemed a lifetime ago as well. The signs, the innumerable, ubiquitous signs that they'd planted like wildflowers in yards and vacant lots and every weedy corner in town, saying only VOTE NO, had indeed carried the day.

After the initial frenetic days of the World's Fair, the city had settled into a comfortable rhythm. A sizable number of Glennvilleans had season passes and came two or three times a week, often just to people-watch and sample the food. Other locals had come in the early days of the fair, when lines were longest and kinks were being ironed out, and the information about where to park and where not to park had not made its way through the city via word of mouth. These locals never came back. There were plentiful free one-day tickets for Boys' Clubs and senior citizens' groups and others in the community otherwise unable to attend. Some, as hard as it was to fathom, had the means and never came at all.

By this midsummer juncture, a number of independent entrepreneurs had long since gone bust. Those who'd invested in campgrounds and privately run shuttles and parking lots located out in the county had bet on infrastructural hassles—parking, traffic, etc.—that had never materialized. And those who'd price-gouged their small hotels or built flimsy condos downtown, hoping to capitalize on room shortages that never occurred, had also folded up their tents and gone home. The planning, swift and chaotic as it had been, had managed to handle the traffic, parking, and room situation to a surprisingly high degree. So it was those dice-rollers who'd bet *No Pass* on the fair's organizational ability who were the first to limp away from the table.

Those on the inside, officially sanctioned contractors and hoteliers and retailers and parking lot owners, had come out all right, had come out really quite nicely.

And subsidiary businesses—convenience stores, taxi services, restaurants, legitimate Mom and Pop hotels, caterers, and the like—had done nicely as well. Those who came, and they came from all over, spent an average of eighty dollars per day per person. And bartenders, waitresses, valets, and everyone else in the city who lived by the gratuity went round town heavy on the hip, smiling and eager to buy a round. Many, it was rumored, found the tourists eager to sample all that the natives had to offer, and talk of fly-by-night romps in the hay was in all the taverns and watering holes. And so it was a happy, if briefly more libidinous, city that summer, the smell of youthful optimism thin and effervescent in the air.

Today, the inventor of the Rubik's Cube would be in town, special guest of the Hungarian Pavilion. Teague smiled at this bit of pop culture schmaltz. In front of the Hungarian Pavilion was a replica cube, fifty feet high by fifty feet wide, constantly shifting and changing and solving itself every twenty-four minutes. A huge favorite of fairgoers. So too the moonshine man, an old-timer from up at Newcastle who set up a running still at the Pavilion of Appalachia and told visitors from up north the proper way to make white lightning. And the bricks of Peruvian gold, the replica of the Great Wall of China, the spooky and awe-inspiring mummies from the Egyptian Pavilion. More dusty antiquities than could be taken in in a single day. And such a mix of high and low culture: priceless artifacts in the morning, laser shows and fireworks at night.

The national reviews had proved a mixed bag, the earliest ones turning out to be the harshest. The negative reviews tended to focus on the architecture, the Erector Set look of the fair and its overdependence on elaborate tents. In the end, they'd had to opt for more temporary than permanent fixtures and so what one got did tend to look a little prefab.

Even the permanent fixtures, the Federal Pavilion and Tennessee State Pavilion, looked stark and impractical, modern but not particularly stylish, likely to be outdated within the decade. Only the Sun Tower and amphitheater looked built to last as landmarks the city could be proud of for the next fifty years. Some reviewers knocked the dated topic of energy, the fuel crisis of the seventies a thing of the past. Very rarely did one hear the phrase *solar heating* anymore. Others didn't like the overly scientific bent of the Expo. Fair enough, all of those. But what set the locals off, what the locals read in the negative national reviews, was the same old Yankee condescension. One review spent half its words mocking the moonshine man with the still, unaware, seemingly, that the locals were in on the joke, a reviewer tone deaf to irony or the southern mode of self-deprecation. The straw that broke the community's back, that brought former fence-riders, even the odd opponent of the fair, into a united front was the article in *Newsweek* that called Glennville *a bleak little town hosting an overgrown state fair*. This engendered a barrage of letters to the magazine, a communal outroar that was beautiful and too long in coming. From then on it was *our fair* and if you didn't like it, Glennvilleans didn't need you anyway.

Down at the site, the multicolored cars of the sky lift moved the tourists in a steady, easy circle in the mile-long loop of the fair, the cars swaying gently and strangely, like some toy ski lift above a model-train-replica town, so steady was the pace, the stops and starting of the lift, the cars paused halfway, rocking slower and slower, and then jerking forward again as the circuit continued. The positive reviews came later and praised the fair for being family-oriented and having something for all ages, all tastes. They praised the more historic and sweeping exhibits, the general ease of getting to and navigating the site. Most of all, the positive reviews focused on the friendliness of the city, the friendliness of all the fair workers, the earnest, oh so earnest desire that the visitor *like* the city, *like* the fair, *like* the person the travel reporter was talking to. Even the *New York Times* man had been worn down by politeness and friendliness and sincerity and managed to enjoy himself despite the architecture that reminded him of a low-budget sci-fi movie.

At any rate, polls of exiting tourists, neutral polls, showed positive reactions running 75–25. Teague thought Roland's call to open the gates that first day had set the tone. Friendly and practical. And fun. The Coles—hell, the whole city—wanted you to have fun. If you learned something along the way, so much the better.

And one heard very little criticism of the Coles these days, the Lionel Ginkowskis and Sam Tarvins of the world having either moved on or receded into the woodwork. One block down, the Valley Industrial Savings and Loan building, J.T.'s flagship, was nearing completion. Once finished, it would stand four stories higher than the FBG tower and double the Glennville skyline. Already the two buildings were referred to as *The Roland* and *The J.T.* and it varied speaker to speaker whether these monikers were said ironically or with smiling fondness.

Teague was standing at the window when a woman came bustling into the room, breathless and calling his name.

He turned to find a disheveled Corrine Cole in the middle of his office, red-eyed and wild, her pretty auburn hair unbrushed and tangled, her pantsuit slept in the night before, the blouse of which was one quick movement away from dissociation with the pants.

Calmly: Have you seen J.T.?

Teague didn't reply, having just noticed the slip-on beach sandals.

Do you think it's funny that I'm looking for my husband?

No, said Teague. I don't.

Then why are you smiling?

I wasn't aware that I was.

You were goddammit.

But she said this without heat, without really looking at him. He wondered if he should offer her a seat or just slip out the door unnoticed, such was her distracted manner. She looked badly in need of composure. Would you like to sit down?

She came to and looked directly into his eyes. Her own sat above black and yellow circles, red and watering. No, she said. I want to find my goddam husband.

I haven't seen him.

She looked so deeply into his eyes that it was all he could do not to turn away. Her eyes made his hurt. I promise, he said, I haven't seen J.T. all morning. And if I do see him, I'll have him call you.

I'm not a child, Teague. Why do you talk to me like I am?

I haven't seen J.T.

Well he's a son of a bitch is what he is.

She looked at Teague as if expecting confirmation or opposition to this opinion.

He said: Well hell, everybody knows that.

When she laughed, Teague felt profound relief. By now she had him completely blocked from the door, so escape was impossible without some kind of martial arts or improbable gymnastics. And his relief proved illusory. For after the initial hearty laugh came the tears, tears that poured from the red eyes, shameless and unwiped, tears upon tears. He went to the desk for a tissue, but with the squeak of the desk drawer opening, she was gone. He came to the door of his office as she pushed the elevator button, paused for a moment, and then headed for the stairs, the secretary in the main foyer with her head down, busy with nothing but avoidance, then the heavy stairwell door slamming shut with a neat loud precision. And nothing then but echo of the slam and silence, and where only a moment before had been an unavoidable presence, now was nothing, an empty office, an empty foyer, a potted plant. And then the cheery *ding* of the elevator and the crisp opening of doors to no one. End of scene. Fade out.

Thought Teague: That was pretty bad.

He went out of the office and to the stairwell, up one flight of stairs. When he got to the top floor, the receptionist and two of the secretaries were talking, shaking their heads. They seemed to be in conference about something. Teague had a good guess what the roundtable was about.

Roland in? he asked the receptionist.

Yes, Mr. Teague, just go in.

He entered Roland's open office door just as Roland hung up the phone. What do you say, Teague? Grab a seat.

Teague remained standing. Corrine just came to see me.

You must have been the second stop, said Roland. Or the third, actu-ally. The ladies out front got first honors. She's a worm in hot ashes.

I'd say so, said Teague. Well, I just came up in case I was the only one who saw her. I didn't know if she should be driving. Or if someone should help with the kids or something. I could ask Jan to help, get the kids from school or whatever.

Oh hell no, said Roland. Jan doesn't want to get involved with this shit. I'll run by and check on the kids after school. They're driving now anyhow.

Teague took a seat opposite Roland. He said: This is none of my busi-ness, but I thought J.T. was done with that gal.

Roland stood and walked over to the door. Shutting it, he said, I don't know why I bother. Nothing goes on up here the secretaries don't know about. But no, he's not done with that crazy thing. About every six months, Corrine will give an ultimatum, act like she's going to leave him and take the kids. So J.T. will break it off. And that'll last about three months. Then they're back together again and the cycle starts all over. Hell, J.T. and Cor-rine are still in high school, haven't you figured that out yet?

Teague laughed.

Now the poor bastard is getting ultimatums from both sides. I mean, what kind of pleasure can he be getting out of this? He's got somebody fussing at him twenty-four hours a day. If a man's going to have an affair, it's got to be with somebody who can keep herself together. Somebody that knows the deal and knows the deal is not ever going to change. I'm not talking about a fling, a fly-by-night deal, though god knows they can be dangerous enough as well. What I'm talking about is that if you're going to keep going with some gal who's not your wife, she damn well better have some sense. Or you're going to lose your wife, your family, and your mind. Am I right?

You're right.

When J.T. was doing the hit-and-run routine, I think she could live with it. But he's been with this gal on and off for going on five years now. Corrine's worried he's actually going to leave her, I think. You haven't noticed how she's been acting the last six months or so? Corrine's falling to pieces.

Yes, said Teague, I've noticed.

That Valium will screw up more people than it helps.

You might be right.

Anyhow, I'm keeping an eye on the kids. But J.T. and Corrine? They're on their own. I love em both, but thirty years of the same old shit is enough. It's worse now, but it's really just the same old song and dance. It's not going to change.

Teague nodded. He wondered what it'd be like to have a brother. He felt pretty sure he'd like it, having someone who knew you better than maybe you knew yourself but liked you anyway. He thought that spouses might never quite know one another as siblings do, coming as they do to an almost fully formed creature, one, perhaps, who's been playing an assumed role from the beginning.

I'm just asking for the hell of it, Teague said, but do you know where he is?

Oh sure. He called this morning. He's shacked up down at the lake house.

Teague nodded.

Roland leaned across the desk and pointed at him in an exaggerated fashion. Don't kid yourself. Corrine knows exactly where he is too. She just wanted to cause a scene. Prolong the drama a bit. She'll raise hell when he finally drags his ass home, and he'll stand there and take it, and next morning things will all be back to normal. Or normal as they get over there.

Teague nodded. He thought back to his own days of running the road and felt a sense of profound guilt. That guilt never left. He and Jan were fine now. Things were good. But they would never be exactly whole again. Never exactly as they were before.

He was walking to the door when Roland said: Hey, listen, now that you're here, let me ask you if you can do me a favor.

Sure, said Teague. What do you have in mind?

Roland leaned back in his chair. He looked glad to be off the subject of J.T. and Corrine and infidelity altogether. He said: This is bush league stuff, but I need you to go down to our little bank in Lofton tomorrow. The bank examiner is coming for their annual report and my manager's in the hospital with an appendectomy. I just need somebody down there with a decent suit on, so it looks official. These bank examiners want to be taken seriously, by god. They want you down there quaking in your boots and chop-chopping and all that business. And if you're down there the tellers and everybody won't go apeshit with worry because the manager's out. You'll just let him in the vault, show him the books. Routine stuff. The assistant manager will be down there, I think she's all of twenty-four, but she'll know what to do and where everything is. Everybody up here is tied up or I wouldn't ask.

Can I even do that? Won't the bank examiner wonder who the hell I am?

You're a bank board member. You're allowed to act in an official capacity.

Will I have to sign anything?

Probably just sign off that you were present when the examiner did the research for his report. As a bank board member, you've got signatory's privileges. It's a formality. They may have the assistant manager sign. I just need somebody down there to babysit. They're a new bank with us and absolutely just walking around on pins and needles. I could send a janitor down there, and they'd be pacified just because he was from Glennville.

Is the janitor busy? Teague said smiling.

No, but his suits aren't as nice as yours. Can you do it? If you're busy, no problem. The Lofton folks will just have to handle it themselves.

No, it's no problem. I can stand there in a suit and look official. I've got to earn my paycheck somehow.

I appreciate it.

Teague stood up. I'll see you tomorrow night at your house. Jan and I are looking forward to it.

Yes, said Roland, standing up and extending his hand. So are we.

Teague shook the offered hand, odd as it was to have such a formal handshake after an impromptu meeting like this.

It's a shame about Corrine, said Roland, sitting down again.

Teague nodded but said nothing and when Roland turned his chair to face the window, he headed for the door.

Said Roland behind him: Sometimes I don't envy the women.

Teague turned and Roland offered him a rueful smile.

It isn't a fair life, is it, Teague?

Teague offered that some days he thought so and others he didn't. And then he was out the door and down the stairs, thinking he'd see if Jan might want to meet him for lunch.

Teague in the Country

Considers the crimson clover, beautiful weed. He finds it too much:
the overalls flapping like the ghost of a farmer on a clothesline,
the silkworm sacks in the redbuds. Take a pointed stick and poke:
see the multitude squirm, dangle by a thread, fall. So many.
A boyhood of visiting country cousins.
An abandoned flour mill. A daytime moon.
That stream dried to a trickle, stones on the bank bleached
and shiny as long-dead coinage: Buffalo nickels,
Mercury dimes, Liberty dollars, the Flying Eagle half dollar.
An uncle? A mother's cousin? Proprietor of Ruby Red Flour.
Long defunct, confined to mercantile memory. His father
toting the gifted flour sacks to the trunk after a visit.
Homemade biscuits, piecrusts at Granny Wrigley's.
How they ate in the country. His young belly taut as a drum,
the busy, steady aunt assembly line, the buffet table in the shade.
A lone farmer on a cultivator among the neat and windblown wheat,
fine yellow dust kicking behind. In the distance, the limbs
of pecan trees like the gnarled fingers of witches
How Grandfather loved his pecans. Pecan rolls.
Roadside southern confection of his youth, young adulthood.
A horseshoe pit, a girl on a trampoline in front of a mobile home.

A pair of shoes tied together and flung over a telephone wire,
comical and forlorn. Earth dark and abundant.
A leaf butterflying on the wind. And then the town.
Goodbye to grandparents and the casseroles of dead aunts.

The Lofton Bank

He arrived at the bank a few minutes after they'd opened. It was located on the corner just before one entered the town square proper, a new reddish brick building, shiny and forgettable, a modern wart sitting on the edge of the anachronistic charm of downtown Lofton with B&T Hardware and The Scoop Ice Cream and the awnings of geriatric lawyers. In Glennville, it would have passed for a minor bank branch. Teague parked and looked up the way he'd come, where the newer part of town was: two small strip malls, two convenience stores, a car lot radiating in the distance. He got out of the car and looked toward the square and then back to the concrete sprawl, minor as it was. He looked at the Lofton City Bank, located halfway in between. What thoughts he had seemed a mishmash of metaphor and symbol that didn't add up. The sun above him was already hot and the asphalt around his feet seemed reptilian and ancient, a new unnatural order that would survive when trees and grass and dirt were no more. His suit felt stiff and sticky as he walked toward the bank and before he'd even made it a few steps in, the assistant manager was rushing up to him and saying, Mr. Teague, I'm Joyce, we're so glad you could make it down.

He wondered how she knew it was he who walked in the door. Did he look like a banker? Like the face of officialdom? Then he remembered Roland's rejoinder about needing a man with a decent suit and thought about books and covers. He looked, he realized with some irony, like the proverbial big shot come down from the city. God almighty, he was in for a day of yes sir this and no sir that. Already the tellers were eyeing him, making eyes at one another, putting on their own faces of corporate propriety. He gave a general smile and wave in the direction of the tellers and received shy smiles above busy fingers, the two customers at the counter turning to see what the fuss was about. As he followed Joyce toward the break room and the coffee machine, one of the customers at the window turned to head out the door. They passed one another in the carpeted foyer, the customer an older man in work khakis and short-sleeve shirt with his name in an oval on the breast, face brown and creased as it moved toward a friendly smile. Nice bank you got here, said the man.

Teague, in his suit, silly in his suit, envoy from the world of air-conditioning and the bistro lunch, said thank you. And then the man was gone and the second customer was filing past, younger and baseball-capped with a curt nod of the head and no smile, Teague's smile unreturned, Teague's smile under analysis and probably not passing the condescension test. And why is it so difficult for a man in a suit and a man who works for a living to carry on a conversation? And why is it that both Roland and J. T. Cole can pull it off? Is it their face or their carriage that renders the three-piece armor irrelevant? Joyce waited at the door of the break room and Teague followed her on in. My face, he thought, has lost its rural roots. My face is that of the city.

Joyce moved around the break room at great speed, preparing the coffee, arranging the fruit and breakfast sweets that were placed on a plastic tray above the minifridge. She was dressed smartly in a grey skirt and matching jacket, black hose, black heels. Not a day over twenty-four, he thought. She looked surprised when she turned and saw Teague standing by the door. Oh, she said, please sit down. I don't know where my manners are.

Teague smiled and took a seat.

I'm a little nervous, she said.

You are? said Teague. What's there to be nervous about?

I've just never been on the management side for one of these things. I was a teller, she said, pausing to add up the years, for six years before I got bumped up to management. So I've been here lots of times when the examiner came.

But never when you were in charge?

Right. Great time for Walter to get appendicitis. Just my luck.

But she was smiling as she said this. The talking seemed to have taken the nervous energy. You'll do fine, said Teague. Roland told me there's nothing to it.

You mean you've never done one of these things either?

Nope. Your luck again.

At this she smiled. Blind leading the blind, she said.

Roland said to just show them the books, open the vault, and let them see whatever there is to see.

Joyce swapped an apple for a Danish, so now each row had an equal number of fruit and pastry. When she'd started it'd been fruit in one lane, sweets in the other. Better this way, thought Teague. Organized but not fanatical.

Been a whole lot of action this week, said Joyce. But there always seems to be when the examiner comes.

She said this in a way that Teague could not quite figure. She'd positioned herself again so that her back was to him, reaching for napkins in a cabinet on the other side of the room. The posture of someone dangling a hook, seeing what bites.

Is that right? said Teague.

We don't get eleven million in deposits in a three-day period every week.

She spoke in that breezy conversational manner that folks in small towns use as they circle around an enticing topic, deciding whether to go in full force or leave things in a state of conversational flux. Ball back in Teague's court.

Hhhmm is what he said, reaching for a Danish.

Then again, said Joyce, before the Coles bought us, we were just a little podunky bank getting by on hundred-thousand-dollar farm loans. We're in the big leagues now.

She said this last part with a smile and whatever conversation she'd been trying to have or that Teague imagined she'd been trying to have was no longer on the table.

So you like working here, said Teague.

Oh goodness yes, she said pulling up a chair. Mr. Cole pays a lot better than the old group. And we get more vacation days. Did you know he gave every one of us, even Carol, the teller with the blond hair who'd only been working here a couple of weeks, free passes to the World's Fair? Season passes.

That sounds pretty good.

My mother loves that falafel. We go up there about every Saturday and all she wants to do is eat falafel and go up to the top of the Sun Tower. She doesn't care the first thing about the exhibits.

Teague smiled. Well, at least she's having fun. What do you like doing up there?

I like the Strohaus.

You go with your mother?

Joyce laughed, and when she did, you could see the woman she would be on the weekend, out with friends, hitting up the big city. The smile was wide and uninhibited and Teague had a hard time matching it up with the earlier small-town gossipy manner. Much preferable, though, the Strohaus smile.

No, she said. Definitely not with Mother.

They sat in silence for a moment. Joyce glanced at the Lofton City Bank clock mounted on the wall, looked back at Teague, and smiled. Something, he thought, something fun and exciting has happened at the Strohaus recently. Something that would make Mother's hair stand on end. He felt a sudden pang, like a dart to his brain, of longing for youth and indiscretions that could be tossed like sand in the wind.

So do you like it? she asked.

Working for the Coles?

Yes.

It's exciting.

It is, she said. It is exciting. You feel like you're a part of something big.

Yes, said Teague. You do.

And getting that bank stock isn't bad either.

Teague smiled but said no more. He thought of his daughter away at college, what kind of weekend fun she might be having, what kind of not-so-secret smiles she might offer on occasion at a newly minted memory. And then one of the tellers was at the door saying the bank examiner had arrived and Teague stood and straightened his tie as Joyce went and rearranged a piece of fruit on a tray and then they walked out, officials of the bank, to meet the man who would conduct the annual audit of the Lofton City Bank.

Said the bank examiner, early thirties and Kafkaesque in his off-the-rack brown suit: I guess that wraps it up.

He stuck out a hand, which Teague shook, a smooth and hairless hand, ink-stained around the cuticles.

Teague said: Thanks for making my job easy. I didn't know what to expect.

The examiner removed his hand and stuck it into a coat pocket to retrieve a pen, made a note on the file he'd placed on the table in the break room. On second thought, he said, eyeing the goodies atop the minifridge, I think I will take a couple of those. Long way back to Chattanooga.

Sure, said Teague, absolutely. He brought the tray over to the bank examiner, who eyed a raspberry Danish and then a chocolate éclair. Take them both, said Teague.

Which the examiner did. He smiled abashedly as he slid an apple into the outer pocket of his suit jacket. Apple a day, he said.

Teague nodded and grinned, about to wrap this up and head on home. A boring, boring day. He brought the coffeepot over and filled the examiner's Styrofoam cup. For the road, he said.

The examiner nodded, took the cup, put it down after testing its temperature with a delicate sip. He took his pen from his pocket and wrote again in the file. The thoughts just kept coming or else a compulsive note-taker. He jotted for a moment. Teague checked his watch. Would have an hour once he got home before he had to head to the big party at Roland's. Needed to call Jan on his way out the door and say later than expected. But he'd already decided to enjoy the ride home, with the windows down and the smell of honeysuckle and freshly cut wheat filling the car.

Sure is a lot of big loans for a little ole country bank, said the examiner.

Teague looked up. He didn't know where he'd been looking before, somewhere in the middle distance of memory and foresight: rolling down a two-lane highway, country music on the radio.

Is that right? he managed.

You're darn tooting it's right. And so many of em out of state, out of the area. You wonder why they don't just do the deal from the big bank in Glennville.

The examiner nodded at his own statement and took a bite of the chocolate éclair. The filling popped out of an unexpected hole and he grasped around for a napkin, looking at his feet and around the floor and wildly without seeing around the room, the gesture indicating: (1) I am aware that I have made a mess and (2) would you, who should know where one is, please get me a napkin?

Teague guessed cabinet above minifridge and guessed correctly. He handed the napkin to the examiner, who stood holding the éclair upright to prevent further spillage. He wiped the custard from his mouth, wrapped the napkin around the éclair and set it on the table. Thank you, he said.

Teague waved him off, nothing, nothing.

Of course, said the examiner, the money's all here. It's all covered and the books add up.

Teague nodded.

You just don't see these big loans at small banks every day. And they got these banks just popping up everywhere. Never seen anything like it.

That seems to be the general impression, said Teague. I'm not sure there is a precedent for the Coles.

But their paychecks don't bounce, do they? said the examiner with a small smile.

Not so far, said Teague.

The examiner shook his head and started to reach again for the pen, a physical tic by this point, else it was a note to avoid chocolate éclairs in the future while on the clock. But then he decided against it. He wiped his hand with the napkin then offered it again to Teague. Well, I guess I'll see you sometime down the road.

Maybe so, said Teague.

Not too exciting, is it?

Not too, said Teague with a smile.

Better than the dentist, but not much.

And then Teague watched the examiner say quick formal goodbyes to Joyce and the tellers and walk out the door to his small, plain economy car, where he opened the passenger door and guided the accordion folder to a gentle resting spot on the seat.

Skyland

The great house glows like a tiara to greet the guests who ride up the long and curving drive in FBG limousines, escorted as all the guests are from the lower lawn, dotted here and there with delicate red cones, that serves as parking lot. Behind you, even now, the valets greet car after car as they enter the wrought-iron automated gates, fifteen feet high and topped with the estate's moniker in a stately cursive script. On one flung-open gate: SKY. And the other: LAND.

The drive up feels too short. Your preference would be to savor the lighting against the black night a bit longer, the warm fire glow of the tiki lamps that line the drive, the gold and silver shimmer, a school of fish catching the sun, from the windows of the house, the lighting flickering and changing with every second, every changing vantage point, until the whole of the picture seems a thing both solid and elusive, and you feel both happy and overwhelmed at the absurdity of the tableau.

When disembarking from the limo, door opened by chauffeur, helping hand extended, it is to the sound of music from the backyard, a ten-piece orchestra lightly touching on Arty Shaw's Any Old Time, the music flitting through the artificially lighted trees and around the bend of the massive house. Standing here, in front of the five-car garage, it is impossible to take in the immensity of the home, overwhelmed as you are by brick upon brick upon brick and the chauffeur with arm extended pointing you to the landscaped walkway that will lead to the back.

You walk in a crowd of near-strangers, groups of seven and eight who are dressed as you are in evening wear and suits and tuxedos, who have just shared a brief, intimate limousine ride, and whatever conversations were started in the drive come to a quiet, abrupt end as the guests make the trek among the lighted flower beds, the tiger lilies and tulips unnaturally colored and beautiful, the pansies planted this morning, purple and delicate along the walk, the lighted fountain and fish pond, glowing fish circling beneath a small statue of Venus, and then you are in the back and where do you look first? You would not have thought it possible for so much lawn to be in back, knowing as you do that on the other side of the darkened trees and down the sheer limestone cliff lies the river, night-colored and quiet. But there it is, the lawn, and you find yourself understanding, truly, what the word estate means, a word you formerly thought applicable only to houses one hundred years old and attached to the dusty names of Eastern Seaboard society pages. And you would think: Five years ago, this was just a hill leading up to a cliff that looked over the river.

And now. Now the eye did not know where to go. Perhaps to the pool, subtly spaced from the house, a separate entity, the cool blue of the water like an exotic drink one would try on a cruise. The urge to jump in bordered on the vertiginous, to disrupt and then become a part of the placid sheen, to see if that is water in there after all, so clearly it reflected the lights and the people moving about it that it seemed a kind of trick mirror. And to the right of the pool, and back, the tent half as large as a football field, the wooden dance floor underneath it polished to a fine sheen, the few faces under the tent unnaturally vivid in the brightness, the orchestra members crisp-looking and loose in tuxedos.

Tables were set up at the back of the tent, all empty for the time being, and also on the wide swath of lawn between pool and tent. On top of each chair was a program printed on World's Fair letterhead listing the rest of the night's entertainment. At nine-thirty would be local favorite Josh Connor, longtime piano-bar star of the Bijou Lounge whose crossover song, This State of Mind Ain't Worth Living In, has recently gone Billboard Top Ten, country and pop, and will prove inescapable for the rest of the summer and into the early fall. After Josh Connor, a jazz quartet, listed to play from *11:00 until ?* In-between musical acts would be the touring troupe of Polish acrobats, and later the Grin Brothers, sibling local comedians who dressed in high-water overalls and chewed corncob pipes and were a kind of guilty pleasure à la Jerry Clower to the local citizenry. Finally, throughout the night, three magicians would wander table to table doing card tricks and sleight of hand.

Flitting about, here and yon, Cole kids and their friends, running from spot to spot, shadows and then the corporeal version under a light and then shadows again, filching desserts from the buffet table along the back patio, the older kids filching stronger medicine when a bartender left his post for more ice or fresh limes. To be a child, even a middling teen, at an event such as this is to know true freedom. You are living in the kid world but moving about the adults like a spy. You can now observe them as they prefer not to be observed. Now the genie is out of the lamp and you see what you've always intuited about how things are after you've been tucked in and kissed on the forehead and the adults have tiptoed away to begin their surreptitious lives. At a large party such as this, you are invisible to adults who have the night off from parenting, who will imbibe and dance and flirt with those who are not their spouse and never know or care about the young eyes watching, giggling, from behind the tree, from the back corner of the tent. And then the kids will break off for their own entertainment, often a large mass of them led by the oldest and most bold, and they will begin to imitate in awkward, energetic fashion what they have witnessed on their reconnaissance and it will all be very exciting, the fertile smell of mowed grass in a dark and unoccupied corner of the lawn, or the empty tennis court, or the viewing deck overhanging the sheer cliff, the river below like something from a foreign land. Here the night sounds are different, the sounds of the woods, and the party seems far away. From here you can discern that the swimming pool, aglow like a luminous magical pond, is having some effect on the adults, mesmerizing them and revealing them. And you feel a bit mesmerized yourself. When you hear your father clear his throat, in the distance, across the lawn, you realize that you are still at home in your child world and that this occurrence is rare, this fantastical night. Somewhere in your subconscious you know that when you wake up in the morning, your parents will be back to themselves, the adults will be themselves, the selves they show you, and the night you are now experiencing will seem a fantastical and wondrous dream.

Her mother said: My goodness.

Said her father: My god, he's spent a million dollars on one party. What kind of man can burn money like that?

Said her husband in a mock-harsh whisper: Two drinks for your father. Tops. Any more than that and I'll end up having to throw him in the pool.

Jan Teague let these comments come and go, let them mix with the lovely music from the orchestra, until the words, useless words, were subdued by the music and the light and the faint buzz of happy people, and eventually vanished as if never spoken, an inconsistent scene edited from a movie, and what was left was the same lovely ambience: breeze, music, light, canopy of night, happy muted chatter into which she'd first entered upon rounding the corner of the house.

She said: Let's get a drink and look out over the river.

And now she stands on the viewing deck looking out over the river and the tiny blinking lights of the small community of Tipton a mile downstream and across the way. She wonders about the lives of the people who live in the small houses and trailers along the river and how this display of opulence looks from their point of view.

Her father beside her said: How much do you think this getup cost him?

He was pointing from the viewing deck to a boathouse. The boathouse was nothing fancy, smaller rather than larger, and its only distinguishing feature was that it had been built on top of a cliff, a cliff that stood impossibly above the water the boat under the house was presumably meant to float in. Leading out from the boathouse and sloping downward at a forty-five-degree angle was a massive winch. Following the track that hoisted the boat sixty yards to and from the water, she saw the dock alongside the river. An infinite number of neat wooden stairs ran parallel to the metal track that led from river to winch.

Just push a button, I guess, said her father. And down she goes. I'd have never thought you could get a boat from this cliff down to that river. Not in a thousand years. Unless you just pushed it over the side. It's a damn fine piece of engineering.

She didn't answer and neither did her mother. Thankfully Mike was under the tent mingling.

Just guess, said her father. What do you think it would cost to build something like this? That's sheer limestone they're cutting through.

Dad, she said, it's so unlike you to talk about how much this or that costs. I've never heard you like this.

I'm just curious, he said. I've never seen anything like it.

I think you're more than curious, said Jan.

Men get old and their minds turn to mortality and the money they didn't make, he said lightly.

You made plenty, said her mother. Now hush about it. We're trying to enjoy the view and it's bad form to talk about a man and his money when you're a guest at his home.

Her father pulled a handkerchief from his pocket and waved it like a white flag in front of them. He took the last sip of his drink and said, if you ladies will beg my pardon, I'm going to see if there's any gin left at the bar.

As he walked away, Jan said: Don't let him have another one.

Said her mother: I'm one step ahead of you.

Teague stood just outside the massive tent listening to J.T. and a couple of corporate sponsors discuss a possible tour of the area the next day in J.T.'s new private plane, with J.T. himself at the wheel. Around him the party felt ready to get started in full. The last of the nibblers had ruefully given up their plates to a waiter and the buffet tables, silently, invisibly, taken away. Good food and libations had copartnered to strip away the last vestiges of awe for the surroundings and people moved more surely of foot from one pocket of people to the next. Just inside the tent, J.T.'s mother and sister, dressed in come-to-town best, listened as the head of the delegation from Scotland spoke to them in a happy, animated fashion. Teague smiled. He'd heard the Scotsman's brogue—they weren't getting a word of whatever anecdote he was telling. But Mrs. Cole smiled broadly at what he said, nodding her head as Sis sipped ginger ale through a straw. And who would find whom more exotic?

A young black man in a navy suit and elaborate skull cap came up to the group, one of the managers of the exhibit from Ghana. He nodded at the sponsors and Teague but didn't smile. He pointed his empty glass at J.T. and said in a clipped British accent: Where is this famous Tennessee moonshine you have been bragging about, Mr. Cole?

Oh hell yes, said J.T. taking the young man's glass and nodding his head enthusiastically at the sponsors. The young man broke into a grin, deadpanning all along, bluffing or calling some earlier bluff of J.T.'s.

The corporate sponsors were willing. They'd been talking SEC football earlier and couldn't very well crawdaddy out of a little mountain dew now.

Teague? said J.T.

I'm from Tennessee, said Teague, raising his glass of scotch. I'll stick with the bonded.

No, no, no, Teague. This is a special brew. Got it from this old one-legged bootlegger up in Jumpoff. Apple brandy. Not just straight white lightning. It's fine.

You could still varnish floors with it I bet.

This fellow's world-famous. Our man down at the fair even tips his hat to this old codger.

Guests come first, said Teague. Get your jug. If there's any left afterward, I'll have a swallow.

That's the fellow, said J.T. I'm back in a flash.

There was a brief pause after the common denominator departed, but as usual in these situations the sporting world saved the day. As it is in Tennessee, so too in Paraguay, Indonesia, the Galapagos Islands. The corporate men broke the ice with the announcement that they'd just been discussing football and that they knew football meant soccer to the young man from Ghana. After this opening salvo, there was a brief skirmish about who would be more accompanying of the other culture's sports. The man from Ghana knew American football. Dallas Cowboys, he said with a sly smile, America's team. But the corporate sponsors, professionals in the way of deference, ultimately won out and were given a quick rundown of football and the other popular sports in Ghana: stadium sizes, vociferousness of crowd, professional vs. amateur status, how high the athletic hero pedestal, and so on.

Teague contributed as need be. His drink was getting low and an empty glass meant no alternative to J.T.'s jug. He excused himself wordlessly and headed toward safer libations. Before he reached the poolside bar, he was hailed by a female voice already ensconced at the spot where he was heading. Hello, Mr. Teague, she said on his approach.

It was Joyce, the assistant manager from the bank in Lofton.

Hello, Joyce, said Teague. And please, no more mister. Mike will do fine.

As he waited to order a drink, she introduced him to a young man who seemed less than thrilled to meet another of the male gender at this point in the proceedings.

He extended a smooth and disingenuous hand over a slumping shoulder, not really looking at Teague, looking as one does at a fly that will eventually go away of its own accord.

Marcus works for the British Embassy, said Joyce.

Very nice, said Teague, noticing for the first time the boutonniere, the polka-dot bow tie, and the cummerbund. He found himself smiling, the pain of the hunt in all its foppish glory in front of him, and then saw that Joyce smiled as well. Said Teague: So we live to fight another day.

I guess so, said Joyce. I'm glad you were there. I'm not sure I thanked you.

No need. You had it all under control. Half of banking is the pastry tray. I learned a valuable lesson today.

She smiled at this and briefly touched his shoulder as some women do, a way that Teague liked and appreciated, and then turned sharply when the young Brit hallooed the bartender as one would a speeding taxicab on a rainy night.

Thought Teague: This poor fellow doesn't know I'm safe as Grandma's afghan.

The bartender handed Marcus his drink and one for Joyce with the beginnings of a slightly dangerous smile. The smile said: Were I not on the clock, such a tone would warrant a public beating. But Marcus was already handing a drink back to Joyce. Belatedly: What's your fancy?

Scotch on the rocks, said Teague. Thank you.

Across the pool, on the patio, J.T. with his moonshine. No glassware allowed. They swigged, grimaced, laughed, and passed the jug. Sometime later that evening or early the next morning, one of the initiates would be in hasty search of a receptacle. And there, standing just behind the men, refusing the jug when offered, was April, J.T.'s mistress, tan and slender in a short yellow dress.

Teague's thought: this won't be good.

Then again, he'd been at the party for an hour now and he'd yet to spot Corrine. Sick, maybe. On vacation. Boycott. Alien abduction. Anything but a scene. And if there were a scene, someone named Cole would have to mediate, for he'd be heading for the hills.

As if the thought of a Cole could conjure a Cole, here came Roland in white dinner jacket, strolling casually across the lawn, moving in and out of the dancing tiki light, shadowed here, illuminated there, past the pool shimmering silvery blue, image of white on a pool, flickering and then gone.

Mr. Bond, said Teague, sticking out a hand, so good to see you.

With his free hand Roland picked up the lapel of his jacket and eyed it suspiciously. You think it's too much?

Not at all, said Teague. I'm always envious of the man in the white dinner jacket.

It's hard to wear as a guest. But the host has certain liberties, I think.

The host may take what liberties he pleases.

They teach things like that in the fraternity, don't they?

That and how to hold your drink.

Saying this, Teague moved his drink from the bar and brought it within seven inches of his stomach, arm bent at elbow in the proper ninety-degree angle.

Very nice, said Roland, turning to point at his brother, who was hyperbolically wiping his mouth with a sleeve and smiling bug-eyed at his mistress after another swig from the jug. The Henry City method, said Roland.

Rudimentary, said Teague, but efficient.

He's a fucking caveman, said Roland smiling. And then he was ordering a drink from the barman and grinning at Joyce all in one motion. And how are you, young lady? he said. You clean up right nice.

Though her face was in shadow, the tilt of head and quick aversion of eyes was an attempt to hide a full-blown blush.

Said Roland: I'm wondering how those farm boys down in Lofton ever let you past the county line. They must not have any sense at all.

She laughed and brushed Roland's shoulder playfully.

Farm boys is right, she said.

The thought hit Teague: not her too. But then the banter took on that of innocent flirtation, business jokey, like his crack earlier about the pastry tray. The young Brit, overtly casual, leaned against the bar.

Well, said Roland, I'm glad you could make it. I thought you mentioned that your mother was going to try and come too.

She wanted to. But she doesn't like being out so late.

Ah, well. Maybe she'd like tickets to the ballet here in a couple of weeks. That's in the afternoon. I'll be glad to arrange it, you just let me know.

Okay, thank you, said Joyce. Oh, and this is Marcus Smartt. He's in town for the fair.

Yes, said Roland, sticking out his hand to the young man who, give him credit, did manage to turn fully around for the first time and return the shake. You're with the embassy, is that right?

With a curt up-and-down thrust of chin, he allowed that Roland's observation was correct.

Well, we'll leave you two young folks to enjoy yourselves, said Roland. And Marcus, I hope you have a good time while you're in our city. You let me know if you need anything.

He turned then to Teague and asked if he had a minute.

And then the two of them were walking toward the tennis court. When they'd made it only a few steps from the bar, they passed a magician finishing up his act at one of the poolside tables. Roland slipped him a bill and pointed toward the table under the tent where his mother and sister were sitting. Give them a good show when you get a chance, he said.

Yes sir, said the magician.

As they walked, Roland said with mock hostility, man do I ever hate an Englishman.

Teague laughed.

Let me tell you something, there ain't no cockblocker like a British cockblocker. Spent three months over there in the service and every night you'd have to wade through about fifty of them to talk to one of the local gals. Hell, they even did it to each other. I'm telling you, they'd rather block your action than get their own.

All that buggery in high school, said Teague.

Buggery is right. They're a buggery bunch.

Sounds like a long three months.

Shit man, I'm wily.

They reached the court and stopped. Behind them, lightning bugs floated easily on the breeze that came up from the river, rising and then falling again, blinking on the rise, less frequently on descent. Teague put his hand on the chain-link fence surrounding the court and looked over to the viewing deck for Jan. But she must have moved on. Roland rattled the ice in his drink. He said: So how'd it go today down in Lofton?

Okay, I guess. No problems. I think Joyce could have handled it fine by herself, but I was glad to go.

Roland nodded. You play tennis?

A little.

With some of the fraternity brothers down at the club? said Roland smiling.

You know how it is. If we're not doing secret handshakes and paddling each other on the ass, we're probably playing tennis.

That's what I thought, he said, opening the gate and walking onto the court, hard rubber and top-of-the-line. Roland walked around to the far side of the taut net and Teague stood on the baseline opposite, wondering if he should mention that you should put the net down when you weren't playing, that the net would last longer if you did. Teague had had money for a good portion of his adult life, but putting down the net was as much about doing things the right way as it was about frugality. The first time he'd played at Jan's house, when they were still in college, he'd been shown by his future father-in-law how to do it.

Roland ran his hand along the net. Wish I could play more, he said. Me and J.T. have been out here ten or so times. Just knocking the hell out of that ball. Spraying it every which way. It's fun though. I think, at the risk of sounding immodest, that I'd have been pretty good if I'd ever had any lessons.

It's like golf, said Teague. Most of the folks who are good at it took lessons and played a lot when they were kids.

Teague could see a smile on Roland's face in the dim light from the party. And then applause from the tent as Josh Connor, the local singer made good, was introduced to the crowd.

You know I'm just gigging you about that fraternity stuff, he said.

Yeah, said Teague. I know. And trust me, I've never felt the need to prove I wasn't a silver spooner.

You just married one, said Roland, miming a forehand volley at the net.

I ain't all dumb.

Roland now backed up to the other baseline and executed a few sweeping backhands. His side of the court caught more of the light from the party and Teague could see him clearly. His own side was angled from the house, so that he was in shadows.

Roland said: You know how I got all this? How I got the money?

No, said Teague, I don't.

I borrowed the hell out of it, that's how.

Teague laughed.

If you don't have money and you want to have money, you have to borrow it. If you want to have a lot, you've got to borrow a lot. Me and J.T. figured that out real quick when Daddy got his bank going in Henry City. You'd see these poor small-time farmers coming in and borrowing just enough to pay off a tractor or a combine or a parcel of land they'd just added to their farm. Borrowing only what they thought they could pay off. And pay off only if everything, everything—weather, crop prices, interest rates, you name it—went their way. And them just humping it every day. Hard physical labor sunup to sundown. One day it just came to me: Shit, man, why not just borrow a lot? If you can't pay off a little, the little you need just to scrape by, if you're going to get crunched up by the interest over time and not make it, just grind along on a slow, Chinese water torture kind of death, why not just roll the dice and hope you hit it big? If you go bust, you go bust. Hell, you were probably going bust anyways. Once that theory hit me, and J.T. came to the same theory about the same time, we bought our first little bank over in Fairhope. Didn't have two nickels to our name. Just borrowed and got investors and sold the hell out of it. We sold an idea, and that idea was that we were men who were going to make you money. And from then on, we just kept building, borrowing, buying, and building.

He smashed a final forearm winner down the line then abruptly walked toward the net. En route, he stopped suddenly to kick a rock off the court. When he got to midcourt, he leaned over with his hands on the net.

He was looking intently at Teague. He said: Daddy didn't like it. He thought you only borrowed what you had the collateral for. And he didn't care anything about a fancy house or fancy cars or any of that. Could care less about coming to the banking conventions and rubbing elbows with the big shots and them thinking he's some small-timer, some hayseed banker.

Teague took the last sip from his drink then set the glass behind him. Roland seemed to be waiting for a response he didn't have.

Some folks are lucky to be satisfied with what they have. Daddy was. He had what he had and didn't need any more. You could chase that pot of gold all you wanted, good for you, whatever makes you happy, but he just wasn't going to do it.

Behind Roland the trees stood like a great wall before the river below. The light from the party hit them about midway up. Above that they remained shadowed and unrevealed.

Men like us, though, we want to be in the game. Would you agree with that?

I'm not chasing pots of gold either, said Teague. Accumulating money just to accumulate it has never had a lot of appeal to me.

Roland stood up straight from the net and took a long swallow from his cocktail. Above them a bird or bat flew over. A fast song played from the party.

I'm not talking about money for money's sake. I'm talking about being in the game. Beating *them* at *their* game. A game they don't think you've even got a right to play. I didn't like getting the high hat when I used to come up here for Daddy to the bank conventions. It stuck in my craw a bit.

Teague didn't reply. He could distinguish a batch of tree frogs from the party noise for the first time behind him.

Don't you like beating a bunch of front-runners?

Teague thought about it for a minute. Yes, he said, I always wanted to beat those fuckers.

Exactly. Me too.

Roland smiled and then Teague did too.

You think I'd have a chance for the governor's office if I ran next time around?

I think as well as the fair has gone, you'd have a good chance.

All right, said Roland. If that's the case, then how do you feel about running down to Nashville and sticking your toe in the water a bit? See if there's any buzz about who might be throwing their hat in the ring, Democrat or Republican.

Teague had been resisting phantom tennis swings the whole of his time on the court. Finally, he could resist no more, and let loose with a sweeping forehand, heavy on the topspin.

He said: It's a little early for that, I think.

I've never been known for my patience.

You sure as hell don't want to look desperate.

You mean you can't run down there and find out if there's any scuttle-butt without tipping our hand? Hell, man, I thought you were a pro.

Teague laughed. The noise from the party was reduced to that of Josh Connor's voice singing a slow song, poignant and indecipherable.

Your old friend Governor Montgomery wants to see the numbers, attendance, gate, hotel occupancy, and so on. Wants to remind everybody he made the right call by getting on board. Why don't you run down to Nashville and show him the figures yourself? While you're down that way, you can see what smoke signals are being sent from the capitol.

Teague thought about it. His mind was moving in a number of directions at once, but reaching no conclusions.

He said: All right, I can do that. But I still think it's too early to even be worrying about an election that's three years away.

Roland smiled. He was again leaning with both hands on the net. Behind him the trees stretched into the night sky and the scythe of a white moon was beginning to rise.

Roland said: Did that bank examiner have anything to say? Anything I ought to hear?

Ah, thought Teague. The sound of a shoe dropping.

Said Teague: The bank examiner seemed a little impressed, if that's the right word, that a small country bank would have so many big loans. And he seemed to find it odd that so many of the loans were from outside the region.

Roland nodded. What about our friend Joyce?

What about her?

She have any comments to make about our loan policies? About these big loans from outside the region or any of our deposits?

Teague hesitated a moment. Roland was walking casually around the net toward him. Nothing that I could tell was out of the ordinary.

Okay, good, said Roland. She's just getting broken in on the job and sometimes the new folks get a little nervous when the big numbers start popping around.

They were now on the baseline nearer the gate. Roland was smiling at him, as if waiting for him to say something. The lights on the court were streaking and inconstant.

Roland said: You got anything you want to ask me?

Listen, said Teague, I'm not sure where you're going with all this. But let's get one thing straight. If I ever have a question, I'll ask it. You got me? And if I ever don't like something, I'll quit on your ass. I thought that was implied. But enough already with the intrigue. I been around too long to put up with any of that kind of shit.

He found that he'd walked very near to Roland as he was talking and that another foot would have them eye to eye.

Roland smiled and took a step back. Then he put up his dukes and bobbed around a bit, shadow boxing against Teague and the shadow of Teague before him.

I didn't mean to get you riled up, he said. And I'd prefer tennis to fisticuffs if we have to settle anything.

Teague hung in the awkward balance between sudden anger and the realization that the source of your ire is a friend. Roland gave another boxer's bob of the head, rocking his shoulders, fists doing a cha-cha in front of his chest.

Of course, said Roland, a country boy having to play a fraternity man like yourself in tennis hardly seems fair.

Teague felt like a quickly deflating balloon.

Roland put his hands down and stopped moving. I meant no harm, he said.

All right.

Me and J.T. are doing a little shucking and jiving right now. It's nothing to worry about. We just got to keep it together for about six more months and we'll be good as gold.

Said Teague: Robbing Peter to pay Paul.

Robbing Peter, Mark, Luke, and John. And still behind to Paul. Just got stretched a bit on a couple of deals related to the fair. Nothing we haven't seen come and go before. Got a little ambitious, that's all. A little greedy, maybe. I just assumed you knew I didn't actually have any money.

Teague smiled.

I'm either rich as hell or don't have a pot to piss in. Depends on which day you ask me. And this tennis court and that house and that swimming pool, sometimes I wake up in the morning, look out the window, and think it's all a mirage.

With this, he stretched out his arms, taking in the whole of the estate and the lights and the night sky above them. I mean, am I really standing here? Tell me. Am I?

Teague said nothing.

Roland put his arms down and said: So what's the real reason you left Montgomery?

I told you. He wanted an ideologue.

Roland smiled. I never bought that one.

And you've got it wrong. He left me.

I don't believe that either. You ever gonna tell me the whole story or not?

Teague looked at Roland and then over toward the viewing deck. He thought he saw Jan, but it was another woman, blond but taller. She was walking gingerly up the steps, and he wondered why she'd walked out there alone.

He said: When people ask me about working for you five years from now, how do you want me to answer?

Roland nodded: Fair enough. He turned to see what Teague was looking at, gave a passing glance, then was back looking at Teague again.

He said: I may have to ask you to do something you don't want to do. Is that right?

We'll see. Like I said, me and J.T. are having to shuck and jive pretty hard right now. It's a short-term crunch. Just need to get the bank stock propped up until we have our legs all the way under us again. We get through this one, and it's clean sailing the rest of the way. I'm talking about three, four-generation kind of money. We get through this, and we won't ever have to shuck and jive again. I've just got to keep the dice in my hand for six months and hope Lady Luck is with me.

With a little help from me and that thing I'm not going to want to do.

I may not have to ask you. I hope I don't. And you can always say no. I won't put a gun to your head.

Teague said nothing. The blond woman on the viewing deck lit a cigarette and the orange glow waxed and waned. Teague thought soon some man would come and join her and he had a sudden envy for the intimacy of the moment they would share. To be dressed up and outside on a nice summer's night, with a drink and cigarette and alone with a woman, that was usually a very nice thing.

We make it through the next six months, Roland said, and we've got the kind of war chest where you don't have to walk hat in hand to every half-ass special interest group in the state, every half-ass millionaire contractor who wants a favor on down the road. We could finance a governor's race and not bat an eye. And have enough left over to do who knows what for the city.

Roland seemed to realize that it was not his style to pour it on this thick. He turned again and looked at the house, the lawn, the lone woman on the viewing deck. I'll ask you again, he said. Am I really standing here?

You're standing there, Teague said. And looking like you could use a drink.

Said Roland, turning on his heel and starting back toward the house: Now that's why I pay you to advise me.

For a moment Teague stood his ground, watching Roland and the shadow of Roland in the light filtering through the trees from the house as he walked away. He had the feeling he ought to go and get Jan and walk immediately to the car, never to return to anything having to do with Roland or J. T. Cole. Then Roland stopped at the gate.

If we're going to beat those fuckers, it's too late to quit now. You coming?

Teague weighed the fuckers on one hand, the mirage of a man in front of him on the other.

Yes, he said. I'm coming.

Jan came out of the bathroom and turned the wrong way. Before she knew it, she found herself in a kitchen void of guests. It felt like walking into the kitchen of a restaurant, such was her alien status there among the workers rinsing off plates and putting them into plastic trays, and the never-ending removal of garbage. The mess and frenzy behind the scenes of the smooth and glittering party outside. She was about to begin retracing her steps when Libby walked in with the caterer. Jan smiled and started to walk on, but Libby grabbed her gently by the arm as she passed. She gave a few last instructions about after-dinner drinks, then asked Jan if she had a minute. When Jan allowed that she did, Libby led her out of the kitchen, down a hall, and into a well-lit study.

Sorry to just grab you like that, Libby said. You're sure you've got a minute?

Sure, said Jan.

Won't you have a seat then?

Jan did so on a leather sofa beneath wall-to-wall built-in bookcases. Libby sat in a high-backed chair opposite, under a photo from her performing days. She looked about twenty in the picture and aware that her photo was being snapped at the time. A small smile showed on her lips as she sang. Jan pointed at it and said, where was that picture taken?

New York, said Libby. Eighteen years old and scared to death in the big city.

You don't look scared.

Libby turned to look at the photo behind her. She said: I don't, but I was.

Our mothers taught us poise if nothing else.

That's for sure.

Was it a concert?

The General Electric talent show.

How'd you do?

Libby smiled. I got lucky.

There ensued then a pause, during which Libby seemed to be weighing whether or not to broach the subject that was likely the source of the meeting.

Finally: You didn't see Corrine by chance, did you?

No, said Jan. Not tonight.

Oh good. Maybe no one did. Oh goodness, poor thing, she's a mess, a complete mess.

Jan shook her head in what she hoped was an appropriately sympathetic gesture.

I didn't know who else to talk to about it, said Libby. She came here with J.T. and then spent the next hour up in my bathroom. Right after that she stormed out.

Oh, said Jan, I'm sorry to hear that.

Libby looked at her, then straightened a magazine on the coffee table. The shiny oaken desk at the back of the office seemed comfortably sterile and clean. They might be meeting now for tea before the other members of the garden club showed up. This much seemed sure: whatever was really on Libby's mind was trying to force itself to the front, but having no easy time of it. This Corrine business was preamble.

Said Libby: She just gets so worked up. When she gets going on J.T.'s girlfriend, it's like she's a stuck record that keeps playing the same note over and over. She can't *not* think about it. I just don't understand why she can't pull herself together.

Jan looked at the desk, sparkling too brightly in the overhead light, the dust-free and new-looking books. She had the sudden impression that no one had ever sat in this room. Or if they had, it was simply to answer the nearest ringing phone. The room seemed arranged for a photographer whose appointment would be delayed indefinitely. Then she realized what this meeting was about. She measured her words. She said: Well, I think different people react in different ways to stressful situations.

Oh, I know, I know. I don't mean to sound critical. I love Corrine like my own sister. We just handle things differently, as you say. But sooner or later, she's got to run out of steam, and when she does I'm fearful of what might happen next. Roland said she barged into Mike's office this week. I guess he told you.

No, said Jan, he didn't.

Oh. Well, I just assumed he would.

Jan smiled, unsure whether her husband's way was preferable or not. Mike tends to leave his business at the door when he gets home, she said.

Libby nodded and glanced at the magazines fanned on the coffee table. She looked back at Jan and said: Roland has left that woman.

Jan returned her gaze but didn't reply.

You know the woman I'm talking about.

Yes.

Mike did tell you about the two of them.

Only because I asked.

Do you know her?

No. I've seen her, but I don't know her.

I've seen her too. She's beautiful, isn't she? And young. Younger than we are.

Near the door, Jan noticed a very small photo that she'd missed before. It was a black and white of Libby and Roland on a ramshackle dock. They looked as if they'd just come from swimming or skiing. Libby's hair was wet and Roland had his arm securely around her waist. They both smiled as one does when young, thin, and in love.

She is, said Jan. But women who have affairs with married men don't seem pretty to me for long.

I'm sorry I brought it up, said Libby. I know how Roland is. I wasn't trying to put Mike in the same boat as him.

I didn't take it that way, she said.

She thought: Libby's told no one, not a soul, about Roland and that woman. For how many years has she kept this bottled up? Something about Corrine has stirred her up. She can tell me because we have that other woman in common. We both know how strong that woman is, the gravitational pull that men feel toward her.

I guess I'm more like Corrine than I care to admit.

We all are, Jan said. The men too.

You know that woman J.T. sees is here tonight?

No, I didn't know that either.

If that woman Roland saw was at a party at my house, I probably would've spoken to her, and welcomed her as a guest.

Jan waited, unsure if she was meant to reply,

But I would have wanted to claw her eyes out.

Jan smiled. She didn't know if that was an appropriate reaction or not, but she did it anyway.

Well, Libby said, composed now, face halfway between a sardonic smile and that of the professional hostess, should we head back to the party?

Yes, said Jan. I'm having a good time.

I'm glad to hear it.

Then they rose together and began to walk out. At the door, Jan said: I love that little picture there. It's a great shot.

Oh, said Libby smiling. That old thing. Roland insisted we hang it up. It's just so ratty-looking, that old dock, our slummy-looking clothes, my hair's a wreck. So I told him he could put it in his office where no one else would see it. But you know, the funny thing is, I come in here about once a week and sit in that chair you're sitting in and look at the old picture. That's about the only time anyone is ever in here. But I'll sit in that chair for ten, fifteen minutes and look at that picture and just let my mind go where it wants to go. Sounds silly, doesn't it?

Sounds nice.

Libby smiled but didn't reply, and as they walked through the door and back toward the great throng of people, Jan knew that the Libby she'd just spoken to was with her no more.

Enough Is Enough

FADE IN

EXT: J.T.'S LAKE HOUSE

WIDE ON:

The HOUSE and the ROAD leading up to it. A MERCEDES 450 SL sits
IDLING in the circular DEAD END, thin wisps of EXHAUST against
the hazy yellow DAWN of a sleeping Saturday morning. The car faces the
closed IRON GATES head-on from about thirty feet away. Behind the
gates, a lush lawn of dewy grass, a sloping driveway. In the DRIVEWAY
a Cadillac and a RED MAZDA sports car, brand-new.

CLOSE ON:

The IDLING MERCEDES blue and stolid in the morning light, EXHAUST
FUMES thin and innocuous.

PAN TO:

The glistening RED MAZDA in the sleek white driveway.

ZOOM ON:

The RED MAZDA until the whole of the SCREEN is FILLED with sporty
red car.

CUT TO:

INT: MASTER BEDROOM OF THE LAKE HOUSE

CLOSE ON:

A bedroom BUREAU. Strewn haphazardly upon it: a man's gold watch, engraved CUFF LINKS, a pair of DIAMOND EARRINGS. A pack of Menthol 100s. A wallet. A CUMMERBUND hanging halfway off.

The sound of SNORING fills the room.

CUT TO:

The SLIDING GLASS DOOR leading out to the DECK, the tranquil LAKE below where a titmouse flitters for a moment above the lake then drops down for a quick drink. Beneath the door is a YELLOW DRESS, which lies in a SILKY pile on the floor.

PAN TO:

A CLOCK on the bedside table that reads 6:05.

Then a loud NOISE, like METALLIC SPLINTERING, followed by a much louder one, a HARSH SCREECHING of metal on metal.

J.T. SPRINGS naked out of BED.

J.T.
What the hell?

APRIL
(eyes still closed)
What? What's going on?

A car HORN is BLARING. Its persistent volume is quickly the dominant sensation in the room.

J.T. FUMBLES around the room trying to find his tuxedo PANTS from the night before. He is WIDE-EYED now, taking charge.

> J.T.
> You wait here.

And then J.T. is RUNNING through the door barefoot, bare-chested, running down the hall and out the FRONT DOOR.

CUT TO:

EXT: THE FRONT PORCH

J.T. stands in dreamlike SILENCE, oddly vulnerable-looking in his creased tuxedo pants in the morning LIGHT. Slowly, increasing incrementally with J.T.'s recognition of the scene before him, the BLARING of the HORN.

Then J.T. is racing to the sound of the HORN and trying frantically to open the DOOR of the blaring MERCEDES, which is SMASHED into the back end of the red MAZDA. Slumped against the wheel, bloodied face turned toward the window where J.T. stands, is CORRINE Cole.

> J.T.
> Oh god.

J.T. looks to the STREET as if help were available there, sees the CRASHED GATES, one of which lies across the driveway. The other dangles halfway over, held by a single bracket. The street is empty and the day is quiet save for the incessant blaring of a HORN.

> J.T.
> (banging frantically on the window of the Mercedes)
> Corrine! Corrine, honey?

J.T. runs behind the car, still calling his wife's name, and tries to open the passenger door.

>   J.T.
>   (banging on passenger door)
>   Wake up, honey!

>   (banging on passenger window)

J.T. sees high-heeled SHOES on the passenger seat. Corrine is slumped against the driver's-side door, still in her cocktail DRESS from the night before.

>   J.T.
>   Honey, wake up, wake up.

J.T. slides across the hood and runs toward the house. APRIL is at the door and he rushes past her brusquely without looking.

>   CLOSE ON:

APRIL, standing in a short ROBE, hand to mouth.

>   J.T.
>   (from interior)
>   Call an ambulance, goddammit, call an ambulance.

>   APRIL
> She's getting out of the car.

>   J.T.
>   (from interior)
>   What?

>   APRIL
> Your wife. She's getting out of the car.

J.T. rushes out the door and meets his staggering, BLOODY wife in the driveway. As he goes to assist her, CORRINE begins FLAILING at him wildly.

> CORRINE
> (connecting with solid shots to the back of J.T.'s head)
> You son of a bitch, you son of a bitch.

> J.T.
> (trying to look at her face and gauge injuries)
> Are you okay, honey? Are you hurt?

> CORRINE
> You son of a BITCH!

Corrine SWINGS wildly one last time, then FALLS in a heap on the driveway.

> REVERSE TO CORRINE'S POV:

BROKEN GLASS around her, the smashed CARS beside her. She picks up a BLOODY HAND and examines it. Glances at APRIL in the doorway, who wears a look of innocent bewilderment.

> PULL BACK TO REVEAL:

CORRINE LAUGHING.

> FADE OUT

The Setup

He was hanging his suit in the closet of the hotel room, wondering whether he should iron the shirt now or in the morning. He didn't know why he enjoyed ironing, but he did. Back when they were first married, when they were making a show of living off his teacher's salary and Jan's part-time job at the hospital, he'd iron five shirts every Sunday while watching the NFL games on their tiny black and white television. The frugal man was he. The young, frugal, serious man. The teacher of history. Now his shirts went to the laundry. Now he rotated his warm-weather and cool-weather clothing in and out of storage at the laundry. But on the road, the solitude of the road, an iron in his hand, the clean, relaxing hum of nothing important on the television in a clean and sterile hotel room, he had brief nice moments of feeling like a serious and frugal man.

Teague as Puritan?

The ridiculousness of this notion makes him turn on the television and flop on the bed. He'd iron the shirts later. He'd order room service rather than go out. He liked eating lunch alone, reading the paper and so on, but not dinner. And he'd be a knife-and-fork man all day tomorrow. The legislature wasn't in session, so he wasn't sure who he'd be able to round up for lunch and dinner. But likely there'd be a few folks hanging about, lobbyists and administrators at the least.

Would Roland have a better chance this time? Montgomery couldn't run again after two terms and there was no other Republican who looked particularly daunting on the horizon. The Democrats were a complete crap shoot at this point and Roland had the best name recognition in the state.

So Roland now or Roland five years ago? On paper, he was better now. In the flesh, Teague wasn't so sure. That he was sending out feelers this early in the game, the next election still three years away, seemed like the wrong move. Why not wait a year? Let the success of the fair sink in a bit, let other folks start talking about you first and what you've got going up in East Tennessee. Be the courted, not the one doing the courting. That was just Politics 101. But Roland couldn't wait. More and more he seemed to be pushing the pace, as if the mad dash to get the fair, the fever pitch of energy needed to obtain it and build it and sell it, was a tempo he couldn't rid himself of. A record stuck on 78. So here was Teague a year too early back in Nashville.

Teague lay on the bed, irritated by the amateurish nature of the trip. He thought: To hell with it. I'll play it the right way.

He'd done it a million times. Meet up with some folks. Get them yakking. No one could go five minutes down here without turning the conversation to politics. And sooner or later it would turn to the next governor's race. All he had to do was sit there and see what names popped out, and hope that one of the ones floated out there was Roland's. If it was, he'd have his opening. If it wasn't, well, there was plenty of time for Roland to self-float his name. Sometimes you had to do business the right way even when someone else was signing the checks. And as one of the few people ever to work in Nashville who preferred listening to talking, he'd long had a way of gleaning information without looking as if he were trying to.

He wasn't quite sure how to feel about his meeting with Governor Montgomery in the morning. When he'd called earlier in the week to propose a hand delivery of the World's Fair data, the governor said: Sure, come on down, I'll show you the house that Teague built.

Montgomery was full of it, like most of them, but who knew? Maybe, subterfuge upon subterfuge, the governor might mention who the

Republicans were thinking about running up the pole in the next election. No one, not even the governor, could resist talking politics in Nashville.

But now the phone in the room was ringing. He reached over with a casual hand and picked it up on the third or fourth ring.

Said Bennett: You think you can just sneak into town and I'm not going to know?

Well, I was hoping that was the case.

No such luck. You want to get a drink? Get a bite?

I was thinking about just getting room service.

Oh bullshit, Teague. Don't give me that just because I'm some low-level state bureaucrat. We minor cogs in the machine have feelings too. We can't all be kingmakers, you know. We're not all bringing world-class events to half-ass cities. Not all of us had daddies to send us to Vanderbilt to learn how to make a martini and speak French phrases. Some of us had to go to junior college. Some of us had to pull ourselves up by the bootstraps just to get to be low-level Kafkaesque administrative grunts.

How do I get you to stop?

Say you'll go.

I'll go.

You didn't know they taught Kafka at Tennessee's finest junior colleges, did you?

No, I didn't, but I'm glad to know now.

You reckon Big Teddy's ever read Kafka?

Are you dragging me to Rooney's?

Now he's too good for Rooney's. You've probably read the complete works of Kafka. At Vanderbilt, you probably discussed *The Metamorphosis* at fraternity galas.

Bennett, you'd have Churchill himself throwing in the towel.

Not Churchill. Churchill could hold his own, I'd have to say.

Despite never having attended a Tennessee junior college.

Well, that might be his undoing.

Might be.

You coming?

I need a little time to gather myself. After that barrage, I feel weak as a dried apple fart.

Bennett laughed, a rare and momentous occasion. He said: They didn't teach you sayings like that at Vanderbilt.

Said Teague: I'm just an old country boy at heart.

THE NET FALLS

They sat at the bar working on their second drink. After this one, they'd move over to the corner booth in the lounge area for a bite.

Bennett said: How many Vanderbilt men does it take to change a tire, Teague?

I don't know. How many?

Three. Two to mix martinis and one to call Daddy.

Do you know how many times I've heard that one?

A bunch, I reckon. Nothing ever changes down here. Same jokes. Same faces. By the way, has Montgomery confirmed he's running for the Senate? I know he hasn't announced, but what are you hearing?

I don't hear much anymore, said Teague. But from what I read in the papers and what little bits I do hear, I get the feeling that the governor is well positioned. He's done a hell of a lot of legwork in the state for the Republican Party. And people forget how good his D.C. connections are. I'm inclined to believe the yellow-dog Democrat days are a thing of the past in Tennessee. Aren't you?

Yeah, unfortunately. The Democrats can't get their heads out of their asses. You know who I keep hearing is the front-runner in the next governor's race?

Teague smiled. The look on Bennett's face, Democratic to the core, was one of intense pain. Who?

Taylor Price, Bennett said wincing.

Is he still alive?

Apparently. Or else they dug him up from that cotton patch he lives on out there in bum-fuck West Tennessee.

Teague did the math in his head. My god, he served up here when Clement was still governor.

That wasn't that long ago, said Bennett.

I mean the first go-round. Back in the fifties.

No. Are you shitting me?

I'm pretty sure. Ask Teddy.

They motioned Big Teddy over and posed the question to him: Was Taylor Price a state senator when Frank Clement was governor way back in the fifties.

Said Big Teddy: He sure as hell was. And he was ten pounds of shit in a five-pound bag.

Said Bennett: What was his drink of choice, Big Ted?

Walker Black. And soda. Lots of ice. And tight as a tick. Only tip he ever left was when he was signing on a lobbyist's tab. And ten percent then. You want more or is that enough?

Big Teddy seemed to be getting worked up, so they said it was enough. Such speech-making could tire the old master and get him off his game. No one wanted that.

Taylor Price, said Teague. That's just hard to fathom. Who else?

Bennett ran through a series of predictable names, all of whom had at least one statewide election loss already on their résumé. Then he threw out a few upstarts. Said Bennett: That Brooks kid out of Clarksville might be worth keeping his eye on.

Yes, said Teague. He's sharp. Took old Gentry to town in that congressional race. Gentry didn't know what hit him. But most people, once they get a whiff of the big time, they don't want to come back to state politics. I've known a lot of folks who went up to D.C. thinking they'd serve a term or two in Congress then come back and run for the governor's office, and I can't think of many who actually did. They get hooked on that buzz up there. You're dealing with foreign affairs and things of the world.

Plus you're that much farther away from your constituency, said Bennett. You can do whatever the hell you want to up there and no one would ever know.

Teague laughed. I guess you're right.

Bennett nodded absentmindedly. He took a sizable gulp of his drink. He placed the drink on the bar but continued to look at it. He said: I have an ulterior motive.

All right. What is it?

Valerie's meeting us down here.

Teague looked at Bennett. Then to the door. Then back to Bennett.

Are you shitting me?

No.

Bennett motioned for another round and looked as if he'd like to stick his face into the confines of the glass before him. Teague was decidedly unsympathetic. He said: I don't go for this kind of shit.

I know, I know.

I don't go for the old bait and switch.

It was unavoidable. You'd have done the same in my shoes.

No way in hell.

She cried. She begged, for Christ's sake.

No chance in hell. Zero chance of that.

Bennett took the drink from Big Teddy's hand before he could place it on the bar. This was against protocol and the Big T gave a look of fierce reproach. Bennett said, oh go to hell, Teddy.

Teddy, picking up on the tenor of things, put open palms above shoulders to say, *Okay, okay,* and moved back toward the waiters at the service side.

I saw her in the legislative plaza. Mentioned I'd heard you were coming to town. Just making conversation. You know how I get to jabbering around a good-looking woman. And that's when she said she had to see you. That it was urgent. I begged off, Teague, I swear to god, but she just wouldn't let it go. Then the tears start. And that's all she wrote.

Teague was looking at Bennett, wondering if this was sufficient grounds for striking a friend in the face.

I'm sorry, Teague. You know I'm all done when the tears start.

Teague finally took up the drink that had been cooling on the bar.

The glass felt small and very cold in his hand. He said, well goddam, this whole thing's a setup.

You reckon it's got anything to do with Roland Cole?

Teague turned to look at him. The look he gave was meant to convey that he was now conversing with someone much too stupid to be a graduate of one of Tennessee's finest junior colleges. One much too stupid to be walking the streets of the city unattended. One too stupid, say, to waste a good bullet on.

Bennett drained his drink and casually, politely, raised a finger to request another from the barman.

Yeah, he said, that's what I figured.

CHICKENS, HOME, ROOST

She walked in the door and toward where they were sitting at the bar. She didn't wave and she looked at them as she walked. Her walk was that of one who never cried, who most assuredly didn't beg.

Bennett got up to scoot down a seat and put Valerie in the middle of them, then, after giving her a quick hello, he just left in the vague direction of the bathroom. Why fake it at this point?

She placed her purse on the bar and nodded when Big Teddy looked her way. She sat down and took her cigarettes out of her purse, and instinctively Teague reached for his lighter. When she snatched a pack of matches from the carafe on the bar, he stopped short. She lit the cigarette in one fluid strike, fire and inhale, then carefully placed the smoking match in the ashtray. She inhaled once on the cigarette, then tapped it on the ashtray though there was no ash yet to tap. She was looking toward Teddy and the arrival of her drink, and her face, in profile, was that of a person waiting on an empty street on a cold night for a taxi that isn't likely to come.

Teague thought: Soon, she will have to go up in age. Soon, men her own age will be looking for the younger model.

This gave him no satisfaction.

Teddy placed the drink in front of her and she thanked him and took a sip. She seemed unusually interested in the bottles behind the bar, for that was where she continued to look. She said: I'm sorry for dragging Bennett into this.

Teague said nothing in reply. He took a cigarette from his pack on the bar and lit it.

I ambushed him in the hallway, she said with a rueful laugh. Poor thing, he never had a chance.

She said, you know this isn't my style.

WHEN THE ANSWER IS NO, IT'S BEST TO BE BRIEF

She said: He won't return my calls.

Teague was fighting the urge to say something he'd regret. What held his tongue was he couldn't decide if he was more bothered by being reduced to de facto pimp or that the image of his long-ago mistress was being deconstructed before his eyes.

He thought: I almost threw my marriage away for this?

A nasty thought, yes, and one he wasn't proud of. But sometimes the brain will go where the brain will go.

She turned to look at him. Behind her, studying the framed photos he'd seen a thousand times, Bennett drew the gaze as only a hyperactive man trying to blend into the woodwork can. He caught Teague's eyes, then walked without purpose toward the front foyer.

Will you talk to him for me? she said.

No, Teague said.

Will you just ask him to call me, goddammit?

Teague rose from his chair, stubbing his cigarette in the process. He looked at Teddy and twirled his finger, then thrust a thumb toward himself. *Put all the drinks on my tab. Include a tip. Sign my name.*

Big Teddy nodded and that was that.

THE UNINDICTED COCONSPIRATOR

His journey from bar to door was quicker than he'd imagined. In the foyer, next to the cigarette machine, Bennett.

I'm sorry, Teague.

Bennett, go to hell.

Teague went through the door. Behind him, on the steps, Bennett said: We're still friends, aren't we?

Teague kept walking. He didn't look back. When he was almost to his car, he said over his shoulder: Yes, goddammit, Bennett. But you can still go to hell.

Housecleaning

On the day after the episode at the lake, Corrine threw out:
1. Her prescriptions
2. All the alcohol in the house
3. J.T.

Teague Recalls Teague

Teague parked in the legislative plaza parking lot reserved for legislators, lobbyists, and those higher up in the government scheme of things. He'd not had a proper parking sticker on his car for years, but the attendant knew him and waved him on in every time. Since the legislature wasn't in session, he got out of the car to a hot and half-empty parking lot. Above him was the elegant capitol building with its columns and great lantern tower. It had aged well and Teague thought it befitting of a state that had produced three presidents of the United States as well as politicians like Davy Crockett, Sam Houston, Frank Clement, Albert Gore, and countless others. He'd long believed the state produced better statesmen than any other in the South and that the population had done a better job than most in promoting its best and brightest to highest office.

He went through the revolving door and down the hall where all manner of bureaucrats had their offices, the signs outside the doors formal and familiar as he passed: OFFICE OF LEGISLATIVE ADMINISTRATION, OFFICE OF LEGAL SERVICES, OFFICE OF INFORMATION SERVICES, OFFICE OF BUDGET ANALYSIS. To know the regular folks behind this Orwellian smokescreen, to know their love of tonk or home-grown tomatoes or a gin and grapefruit with a salted rim, the personal side of governmental life so hidden to the public via bureaucratic title, was a simple pleasure and one that always made Teague smile.

On most visits, he'd have made a few pit stops to see old friends, secretaries who'd let him use a phone or a desk when he needed a make-shift office back in his lobbying days, receptionists who could track down a legislative page when a copy needed to get made or he needed to slide a note to a legislator already on the House floor. But he decided to motor on. The fewer people who saw him the better if the true reason for his visit was to be kept under wraps. He'd contact who he needed to after his meeting with the governor. Had to pick and choose. For news traveled fast here, even when it wasn't news. All the old-timers up here had a certain sixth sense. They could be sitting with their feet up on the desk doing the crossword, but when something newsworthy or potentially newsworthy passed down the hall, their divining sticks would start shaking in earnest, and like the water witches they were, all they had to do was follow the stick to the source.

He passed the escalator that led to the War Memorial Building and the Tennessee State Museum. As it always did, this part of the walk reminded him of the times he brought his daughter with him to the legislative session. He'd give her a few dollars' spending money for the vending machines and snacks in the cafeteria, and usually base her out of Jack Byrd's office, who was a representative and old friend from Boys State, as he went about his day. But she essentially had free rein to roam where she would, riding the escalators, visiting the museum. So much better than school in February. Those were some of his favorite days, going to lunch downtown with Julie and legislative friends, then back to the Capitol Inn with its indoor pool shaped like a guitar. He and Julie swimming till their hands were pruned.

He breezed by the legislative cafeteria and waved at one of the ladies behind the buffet line. As he approached the group of offices for the Department of State, he had a moment's pause about running into Valerie, the State Department's director of administrative procedures. All and all he thought her title didn't quite give a true glimpse of the person. He walked on. That business the night before had been short, but no less nasty by the light of day. Pimping for Valerie? She'd asked him to do that? He thought perhaps she'd never been the person he'd once imagined. No less small, no less insecure, than anyone else. Her moxie and cool were an affect. A little money growing up, a college education, and a stylish rogue for a father had probably given any number of women the same illusion of self-possession. But he couldn't escape a nagging sense of pity, a nagging feeling that their affair had actually hurt her, stunted her, more than it had himself.

At any rate, after he met with the governor, he'd drop by Bennett's office and pop him a quick one in the nose. It seemed the least he could do.

Watch Teague walk away from the cluster of offices that is the Department of State, away he tells himself from that part of his past that is most painful, most vivid. He goes up the escalator that leads to the tunnel that connects the plaza to the capitol proper. He remembers the look of joy on his daughter's face when she realized that this was an actual tunnel, subterranean, and that they were walking *underground* to the capitol. As a high schooler visiting the capitol from Boys State, he'd wondered about this bit of architecture himself. Was it a make-do bomb shelter? A way for legislators and the governor to escape some sort of all-out attack or pending natural disaster? He is alone now in the tunnel, which is carpeted and well lit, just a long hall that happens to be underground, and then he is in the elevator going up to the capitol. He disembarks from the elevator on the second floor, though the governor's office is on the floor below. The Assembly Room of the House of Representatives is behind him and he glances once at the open door, at the multitude of shadowed desks and the large tote board of yea and nay waiting in the darkness for the firm rap of a gavel.

In front of him is the empty legislative kiosk, closed till the next session. He is flooded with memories. And always the first trip from Boys State. And what an anachronism that is, a summer camp for high school boys interested in government and public leadership. What an honor it'd been to be chosen. What feelings went through him as he walked with the other flattopped boys dressed in coat and tie despite the summer heat up the seventy-two steps of the capitol building. How many of the men who served in government he'd met there, how many who went on to collegiate glory on the gridiron or hard wood floor. He somehow doubted Boys State had the same cachet. No, Watergate and Vietnam had fucked that once and for good.

So it is with memories of his youth and the youth of his daughter that he walks the lobby. Julie stopping to stare at the nine-foot polar bear standing on hind legs at the entrance of the state museum, as he'd done on the Boys State tour so many years before. He couldn't remember what connection the polar bear had with Tennessee, other than perhaps a Tennessean had killed it. All he knew was it was the most awe-inspiring thing he'd ever seen, teeth bared, huge, and so very *other*. It was this sense of other more than anything that he'd felt on that day up from Boys State. To read about the capitol and state government in the textbooks was one thing, but this massive, high-domed lobby with the busts of presidents and governors and marble for as far as the eye could see was quite another. And outside on the capitol grounds the tomb of James K. Polk. And statues of Jackson astride his horse, wild hair and cape flying behind him, and Sergeant Alvin York taking dead aim with his sharp-shooter's rifle, and Sam Davis, the Boy Hero of the Confederacy, hanged as a spy and loyal to the end to that lost and embarrassing cause of the southern elite.

Polar bears and tombs and the stern visages of Tennessee history. He'd felt both other and innately at home. This was a place that looked simultaneously backward and forward, a constant waxing and waning between time, where the present was only temporary and of fairly little substance. This was the perspective of the historian, and one Teague felt deep in the bones.

Now Teague's shoes echo hollow on the marble floor and unnaturally loud. Looking at the busts, the marble, the dusty relics all around, he feels entombed for a moment in his past, and in his future. So without a glance at the Senate Assembly Room, the speaker's office or that of the lieutenant governor, past the House Assembly, the empty kiosk, he heads down the stairs to the governor's office and a meeting with the present.

———

The governor's receptionist said: Hello, Mr. Teague, the governor is expecting you. Then she walked him to a small waiting area and knocked lightly
on the door, cracking it as she did so and saying, Mr. Teague is here to
see you, Governor.

Teague followed the receptionist's gesturing hand into the gover-
nor's office: leather and carpet and wood and framed degrees. Governor
Montgomery came from around the desk to shake Teague's hand, saying,
Teague, you're still the best-dressed man in the state.

He motioned for Teague to take a seat, then went around to the leather
swivel chair on the other side of the desk.

They spent the next few minutes catching up on family and mutual
friends. Teague thought the office had treated Montgomery well. He
seemed fit and in his element. Nine years before, he'd had a harried look
about him, the look of someone trying to get places who is not at all sure
he'll get there. All some people needed was a little success to find themselves. Montgomery probably fit into this category, and Teague figured if
they were to start over now, he'd like him better than he had on the first
go-round. He hadn't disliked him before, not until the very end. They
just didn't have much in common. Other than that one thing. That one
thing at the end.

Thought Teague: Him? Really, him? But who cares now at this late
date? Water under the bridge, water under the bridge. Move on. Move on
down the road already.

Forcing your brain not to think of something only worked for so long,
especially if you would soon be coming face to face with that which you
wished to avoid. The man across from him seemed happy and bound
for a larger stage. Also small. A party functionary. Bland enough to be
uncontroversial, personable enough to be unthreatening. He was capable.
He was fine. The public trough was safe on his watch and no boat would
ever be rocked. The Coles had presence but no platform. Montgomery had
platform, the platform of amiable do-nothing that is the moderate Republican, but no presence. Just not quite large enough. The White House you
have your eye on requires a bigger man, one whose sharp edges have not
been completely rounded off by the political arena. Smooth and capable

will take you to this office, maybe the Senate. But the Oval Office requires personality writ large.

So, said Governor Montgomery, you have some figures for me from that World's Fair of yours?

Teague handed over the manila folder filled with the statistics to date of the fair.

The governor said: I'll look these over closely later on, after we visit. But apparently things have gone to your liking?

They have, said Teague. We're on schedule to hit most of our projections. We've already passed the twelve-million mark in attendance and should hit fourteen before we close up shop.

That's good, said Montgomery. That's great. You've really put Glennville on the map.

Well we appreciate your support. We couldn't have pulled it off without the support of the state. And I appreciate your going to bat for us.

Montgomery smiled. You know I'm going to back a winner.

Teague laughed.

This politics is a crazy business, isn't it?

It is that.

One of the state senators, I won't say who, he's from East Tennessee, though, he came up to me not long after I was elected and said: When I met the Cole brothers, I couldn't put my finger on whether they were just too slick, or just too country. Then I finally figured it out, they were just too both.

Montgomery smiled when he finished, but Teague did not.

Said Teague: They're a lot more complex than you might think.

At this, Montgomery held his hands up in a show of surrender. I never underestimated them, he said. I promise you that. And like we just said, I did support their World's Fair. I was just repeating a story I thought was funny.

I never laughed when people told funny stories on you either, said Teague. Not when I was working for you.

Montgomery paused for a moment over this. His head had snapped back a bit with that last fragment, the part Teague had put a little inflection on. Teague was looking him in the eye.

I apologize, said the governor. I meant no harm.

Teague nodded. Forget it, he said. No need to apologize.

Montgomery smiled again, then took a sip of his coffee. So, he said, if I decide to make a run at the Senate, you want to come work for me?

Teague smiled. Even odds Montgomery was putting him on. Anything to get off the misfired joke about the Coles. Mongtomery never had liked confrontation. But who knew? Maybe the question was asked in earnest.

You lost a statewide election with me, said Teague. And won two without me. Why in the world would you want me back on your side now?

I lost that first one, said the governor. You gave me my gimmick and I didn't listen. The second one, my predecessor, the esteemed Governor Hart, did you no favors handing out those pardons like they were going out of style.

I believe you'd have beaten us with or without good Governor Hart's liberal feelings about the penal system.

Sixty-one prisoners pardoned in a three-month period? Five of them up for murder? It's still hard to believe.

His rehabilitation initiatives were way ahead of their time, said Teague. Plus, you know, he was a Democrat and thus a man of the people. Old Hickory likely would have done the same.

Then invited all of them up to the White House for a hoedown.

That's right. Man of the people.

Back to the election, said Montgomery. We beat you with your idea and with an indicted Democrat holding the office.

You came up with the overalls though. That was the kicker. That made you a man of the people.

Montgomery laughed.

You are.

Teague knew that he was smiling as he said this. His sincerity would need a little work.

Yes, said Montgomery, smiling, in on the joke. I'm a man of the people. Hell, I'm practically a frontiersman. But you won't consider it? We've got a little time yet. In all honesty I do seem to have the thumbs-up from Washington. If you won't think I'm bragging, I'll tell you who called me a few weeks back.

I won't think you're bragging. Let's hear it.

The president himself, said Montgomery, smiling despite himself. And he was calling about the Senate race. He asked me to run.

That'd be hard to say no to.

I think they're trying to give a younger perception of the party. They don't want everyone associating Republicans with stodgy old men. Even though we all are, of course.

Montgomery laughed when he said this and Teague did too.

You do know, said Montgomery, that there's only been two Republican senators in this state since 1912. I'd be fighting a little history.

Yeah, but those two are both fairly recent. And I believe the wind's about to change on that one all the way around. Your president seems to be a tide that's raising all ships. I like your chances no matter who runs against you.

You think I ought to trot out the old engineering apparel again?

Oh hell yes. It's the equivalent of Crockett's coonskin cap at this point.

I find that kind of sad, said Montgomery smiling. What Tennessee has left of the frontier spirit is a pair of striped cotton overalls from an L.L.Bean catalogue.

Teague smiled at this. He remembered now what he'd liked about Montgomery in the first place. He had, in the right spots, the ability to be both utterly self-effacing and brutally honest about himself. He was a man who would look himself in the mirror and would, as often as not, give a frank appraisal. The people knew this. He was like them. He did not wow you. You did not think, oh, there goes my superior. Perhaps that was the way it was now. What we wanted was not greatness, not presence, but to feel comfortable.

Said Teague: Crockett's cap was a gimmick too, if that makes you feel any better.

I don't think that it does.

Teague smiled.

But I'm cracking out the overalls anyway.

Absolutely.

At the risk of stepping on your toes again, said the governor, I'll have to admit to being curious if Roland's considering another run at this office. Don't answer if you don't want to, obviously. I just thought you might be down here sniffing around a bit, seeing what names are already floating around.

Teague said: No, I'm just down here to deliver those reports.

Teague thought: Ah yes. The other reason I liked Montgomery. At least as a candidate. His nose is always in the air. That was the difference. The Coles walked into a room and waited to be sussed out. Montgomery walked into a room and did the evaluating. Over time, unless you were a Kennedy or Roosevelt, the latter method was the one to choose. You didn't get surprised that way. And you knew which hands to shake, which horses would never finish. He felt momentarily chagrined. Time and hard feelings had conspired to make him underestimate his former candidate.

Montgomery, lightly, smiling: Teague, I'm glad to see you, you know that. But that's a long way to drive just to deliver some pissant reports.

Teague smiled now, saying, hell, I was just looking for an excuse to get out of Glennville. I've got the fair coming out of my ears by now.

I bet. Well, now that you're here, do you have any interest in what names are being bandied about? I've never been above a little harmless political gossip, you know.

Busted. Yes. That he thought he wouldn't be was the amazing thing. He made a note to be wary about underestimating people. Especially those you've known in a former incarnation.

Sure, said Teague. Now that I'm here. Just for curiosity's sake as a voter and a Tennessean, I'd love to hear what names are being run up the flagpole.

Weather Report

Standing on the mat outside the back door, she runs a quick rough hand over her overalls to shake off what feed dust has settled there. She wipes her feet on the mat, though the farm is dry and she knows how and where to step when feeding the chickens. The four little chicks hatched last week have been named Beaker, Raker, Jilly, and Roadrunner.

The screen door lets out an ancient squeak as she enters and she closes it slowly behind her when she sees her mother on the phone at the kitchen table. She pulls three tomatoes from a side pocket and places them in the window, where several others sit catching the sun's light, filtering through the window and through the tomatoes. The smoky smell of bacon lingers in the air three hours after its cooking, and the ceiling fan thumps off-beat to the rhythms of the shifting light.

The kitchen is hot already and Sis won't stay long. Here directly she'll move to the sleep porch on the shady side of the house to listen to the news and farm report and church bulletins and birthdays and death announcements on the local radio station. As she listens, she'll work on her latest quilt, done up in the Double Wedding Ring pattern. Beside her is a scrap basket of materials that includes bits from her father's old work apron, several of his ties, Roland's American Legion baseball jersey, J.T.'s baby blanket, and other clothing mementos from the male side of the family. She's not yet decided who will receive this particular quilt for Christmas. She might wait and see which of her family lays the most specific claim. The one she made back in the winter was in the Not So Much of a Trick pattern. For it she used a sun bonnet Granny Lucy gave her on her tenth birthday, bits from her own baby blanket, ancient washrags, an old gingham dress she found in the attic that had once belonged to her mother, and scraps from some of her mother's aprons. Her mother had oohed and aahhed during the entirety of its creation to the point that Sis finally felt need to say: This one's yours, Mother. I decided that before I ever got started.

This had pacified her mother and she was allowed to work without the roar of the adoring crowd from then on.

Now her mother says into the phone: Well it just breaks my heart.

And then: I love you too, son.

When she hangs up the phone, she looks toward Sis without really seeing her. Sis glances at the clock. The news will be starting in five minutes. Her mother says nothing, but Sis senses her presence in the kitchen is expected just the same. She grabs two glasses and some ice from the freezer then pours some lemonade she squeezed this morning. When she places one of the glasses on the table, her mother sighs and says thank you. Sis looks at the clock. Three minutes until the news report. They usually give the weather toward the early portion of the show and she's wondering about rain. She heard distant thunder while out feeding the chickens, but you often got phantom thunder and heat lightning in the summer that never came to much. The vegetables could use the rain, and so could the crops. The corn is set, no amount of dry weather could spoil it now, but the soybeans are still on the fence. Plus, the dusty chicken house and the dusty yard make the chickens a grumpy and fractious lot. There was more fussing and fighting, more quick-footed chases across the yard when someone felt encroached upon. That morning, she'd finally had enough and hollered: Yall just need to settle on down. This fussing and fighting's on my last nerve. That had done the trick for a while, but by the time the feeding was over, they were back at it again. So Sis is interested in the weather report.

Her mother says: Well, that was your big brother. Corrine's finally thrown him out of the house.

Where's he going?

Oh, she says, seeming to take in Sis fully for the first time. He'll just stay at their lake house. That's why he called, wanted to let us know where to find him.

Sis says nothing. She glances again at the clock. She moved the radio from her bedroom to the sleep porch first thing this morning.

I hope and pray that Corrine will take him back. I'm just sick about it. Those poor, poor children. And poor Corrine. I wish your father was here to jerk a knot in his tail. And I've half a mind to drive up to Glennville and do it myself.

Sis takes a sip of her lemonade and reaches for an apple from the basket on the kitchen table.

Oh I pray, pray, pray that Corrine will give him a second chance. But J.T. will have to mend his ways. I don't know what all he's been doing, but I've got a fairly good guess. Do you think I should call Corrine? Do you think she'd want me to? I don't want to look like I'm prying, but I also want her to know that I'm thinking about her.

The big hand is on the hour. It's time.

Sis says, she'll call here before too long. I wouldn't worry about that. Ain't nobody around here can go too long without having to talk about something.

Then she's off to the sleeping porch, apple and lemonade in hand.

The Sun Tower: A Moment of Reflection

The Sun Dial, the upscale restaurant on the observation level of the Sun Tower, had been closed officially for an hour. J.T. sat at the table, looking through the gold-tinted windows at the nearly empty fair site below. A residual smoke from the nightly fireworks display hung in the artificial lights, giving the scene a dreamlike, cinematic quality. Roland stood at the window, drink in hand, every so often gesturing in tour guide fashion. Standing next to him was Joyce, the assistant manager from the Lofton bank. Dirty dog, thought J.T. Little brother is a dirty dirty dawg.

Moving back and forth from the table to gazing out at the fair site below were three of Joyce's friends, cute country girls, but young. He felt over that sort of thing now, after the deal with Corrine. She'd been all right after all, physically. A bloody nose and a sprained wrist were about the sum of it. But what an ugly day, a pitiful example of humanity all the way round. And him acting as ringleader.

Now he'd been given the boot. He suspected he might be given a second chance, after her feathers puffed down a bit, but he couldn't be a hundred percent certain. This time, the Monday after the incident, she'd not been angry. No shouting. No threats. No drama. Just a cold, hard look in her eyes. *You're out. Today. Get your things and get out. We'll figure out the rest later on, but I want you out of here today.*

He felt ready for the fair to be over, for the year to be over. If they could make it to the new year, they'd be okay. The loans they'd had to float and the fancy footwork to keep the bank stock propped up, well, that was some dicey business. They'd never been extended like this, never as exposed. But to hell with that. He'd thought plenty about that business. The die was cast. They'd either swing it or they wouldn't.

The girls, Joyce's friends, left to go to the bathroom. Teague sat opposite, nursing a drink and speaking when he had to, as was his wont on these late evenings. They'd started out down at the site, an official photo op with the mayor and city council in the afternoon, and then the large group had eaten here in the Sun Dial. It was City Worker Day at the fair, one of his own ideas cooked up how many years back when they were throwing everything but the kitchen sink trying to land the fair. Now here it was September and only six weeks to go before closing ceremonies. They'd done it. That was undeniable. All the logistical nightmares the doomsayers had predicted, all the shortfalls of financing, all the buildings that would not get built and the corporate sponsors who would not sign on, had been Chicken Little's sky that didn't fall.

He took a sip of his scotch. That was some satisfaction, he and Roland bringing a world-class event to Glennville. And his own Valley Industrial building, taller and grander than Roland's, had been open for several months now.

In general, though, he felt unsatisfied. The business with Corrine, the ongoing business with his mistress. He wasn't sure if this was the cause of his dissatisfaction or the manifestation of it. Whatever the case, he'd decided to break it off with April. Between April and Corrine and his family, it was no real choice. For some reason, he'd thought this sort of thing really didn't count for much at the end of the day with Corrine, that for all of her threats and upsets, she knew that he'd never leave her, that there was no one else in the world, Roland included, that he loved or respected more.

So why would he cheat and cheat prolifically on someone he loved and respected? It was a question he had no answer for. But he thought basically, at its root, it came down to an undue fondness for strange pussy.

Across the way, Teague ordered another drink. The girls, Joyce's friends, came walking out of the bathroom, their sundresses and tan shoulders glimmering in the candlelight. J.T. nodded in their direction to Teague.

He said: I'll flip you for the brunette.

Bank Vault

They'd moved from the Sun Dial. One of the country girls said she'd never been inside a bank vault before and the next thing anyone knew they were heading that way, walking up the sidewalk along Brewer Avenue, laughing and spilling into the road, Roland jiggling the bank keys in his hand as he went, Cut Worm hollering, where's that monorail you promised us, Roland?

Then the party was in the bank lobby peering into the opened vault. Johnny Boy had run up to the kitchen on the top floor and returned with a cart stocked with liquor, ice, and glasses. He stood at the entry of the vault, clanking ice into tumblers and pouring from on high, real showmanship at work here. Roland and Joyce were off near the cashier windows talking with their heads close together, the drinks in their hands almost touching at the waist. When Johnny poured and handed over the scotch highball, Teague refused.

He thought, what in the hell am I doing here?

Sometime not too long after, the country girls and most of the men were inside the huge vault, the massive door slid aside, a yawning metallic mouth opening into stack upon stack of wrapped bills, the currency looking like neatly stacked books in a library. The order and propriety and implied silence of the vault contrasted with the country girls who laughed a little too loudly. They touched the stacks of bills and made comments about what they could do with them: cars and vacations and so forth. The men smiled and talked out of the sides of their mouths, throwing back their drinks without caution. The young women pretended to stuff stacks into a blouse, into the front of a sundress. This led to Cut Worm taking a stack and motioning Johnny Boy deep, Johnny Boy going long across the lobby, Cut Worm fading back to pass, cocking his arm, the release, the tight book of bills flying across the high-ceilinged lobby and landing in Johnny Boy's outstretched arms. Touchdown! Give him six!

Roland stood smiling near the cashier windows. J.T. stood smiling from the vault. He turned to say something to one of the country girls and she laughed.

Thought Teague: I'm getting the hell out of here.

When Johnny Boy and Cut Worm walked back to the vault, they refilled their drinks before entering. From where Teague stood, it looked like one of the girls was about to take off her top in the vault. Her friends were laughing and egging her on, stacks of bills still in their hands.

Teague looked out to the street. The vault was not in plain sight, but the lobby was. Someone who happened to be out at this late hour could see people inside, could see Roland at the cashier's window with Joyce and drinks in their hands.

When he looked back to the vault, the door had been pulled to, left just barely ajar. Sporadic giggles. Flashes of a thin brown shoulder. A highball glass going from hand to hand.

Teague thought: This ship is going down.

Happy Trails

Roland stood at the cashier's window talking to Joyce. He looked down and noticed that his drink was about gone. He looked at Joyce's and saw that she was still half full. He took note of the vault door, which had been pulled shut, and was surprised that the decibel level was still as high as it was nonetheless. When he looked back to the lobby, Teague was gone.

Said Roland to Joyce: That might be it for old Teague.

Closing Ceremonies

In the past six months Glennvilleans had seen the following cultural events pass through their fair city: Mikhail Baryshnikov and the New York City Ballet, the London Symphony, the National Ballet of China, the Berlin Philharmonic, the Grand Kabuki Theater, the Vienna Boys Choir, the Radio City Rockettes, the Australian International Circus, the Royal Tahitian Dance Company, Dizzy Gillespie, Waylon Jennings, the Neville Brothers, Dolly Parton, Buckwheat Zydeco, Scruggs and Flatt, Bill Cosby, Milton Berle, and countless other symphonies, jazz artists, pop singers, bluegrass acts, folktale spinners, and comedians.

You couldn't say they hadn't entertained you.

A downtown wasteland area with a polluted creek running through it was now a clean and bright space, seventy-nine acres perfectly situated between downtown and the university and perfectly suited for retail, high-end condominiums, cultural attractions, and anything else a city hoping to make the leap to permanent cosmopolitanism might concoct.

There were now five first-rate downtown hotels where before there had been one.

The amphitheater, Federal Pavilion, and State Pavilion, were permanent buildings to be used as the city saw fit from now on.

And of course there was the Sun Tower. Cars racing past Helios and his chariot on a tight and speedy raceway, Mixed-up Merge a thing of the past.

Fourteen million visitors had visited the city in six months. Economists estimated they'd spent half a billion dollars in the local economy during their stay.

Some folks in town had made some money. Many more of them had enjoyed themselves.

Those who'd doubted the fair, those who'd been adamantly against it, had been noticeably silent these last six months. Whether they'd come around and allowed themselves to enjoy what they'd once scorned, or whether they simply sat home and pouted, Roland never really knew. It wasn't something he spent much time thinking about. It was funny, success, how it made gloating unnecessary and redundant. It was hard even to remember much of the struggle.

Now it was Halloween and the last day of the Glennville World's Fair. Roland had spent the day with Libby and the kids in one last walk about the fair site. The weather was typically pleasant and you couldn't have asked for a better day to spend outside. At the moment, his family was off grabbing a bite at the food pavilion before heading over to the amphitheater for the send-off speeches and festivities.

Walking toward the Pavilion of Appalachia, he passed a robot, or rather a man in a metallic robot outfit, handing out lapel pins in the shape of a pickle, the pickle pins a World's Fair tradition since the Chicago Fair of 1893. Reflexively, Roland touched the Helios pin on his suit jacket, the same pin he'd worn for the better part of five years. He guessed tomorrow it would go in his valet box for good. And thinking this, he felt a momentary pang at the casual ways important things in our lives can come to a close.

Then he was standing before the Pavilion of Appalachia, one of the surprise highlights of the fair. He smiled to think how dismissive he'd been when it was first proposed, thinking it ran cross-current to the global and cosmopolitan event they'd planned. Luckily, Libby and Teague had prevailed on him that a little local culture would be expected. Local? Then get some kids down here in khakis and Docksiders. And they won't be listening to mountain music on their boom boxes either.

He'd feared they'd hick it up too much like some of the Li'l Abner tourist places up in the mountains. For the world does love its Dogpatch South. But here before him were real mountain people, mountain artists, who'd spent the past six months showing visitors from around the world the finer points of rag-doll making, quilt making, chair caning, and what have you. They'd even corralled an honest-to-god moonshiner, an old-timer many times arrested, now wizened up like a dried apple and spinning yarns as the still burbled and hissed and the fluid did its loopety-loops through the plastic tubes.

And what these people could craft, and craft from, producing household necessities and art and music from so little. Such historically poor, poor people, and still the urge to create, art from apples and rags, instruments from gourds and horsehair. He thought now, on this last night of the fair, that he understood the creative urge. How it was a thing that one simply must do, regardless of situation or reception.

He stood now before the split-rail fence that surrounded the pavilion, the entirety of which was made up to look like a mountain farm: an old plow. A wooden trough. The wooden top of a well with dusty bucket on a brown-looking rope. A rickety smokehouse. In the yard, a man was coopering.

Roland walked toward the man, who was astride a shaving horse, a large pile of shavings scattered about his feet. The man pushed firmly down on the treadle with his foot to set the jaw on the stave, then pulled the drawing knife toward him in one long, steady motion, thin peels off with the stroke. When he'd finished, he released his foot from the treadle and removed the stave. He held it close to his eye and then moved it back and forth in front of his face, checking for smoothness. Something in the work didn't please him, for he placed the stave back in the jaw of the shaving horse and began the process again. Roland had stopped just short of the man, so he could watch without disturbing his work. Behind the cooper, a lady dressed in a long denim dress and brogans stirred a cast-iron pot suspended over an open fire. Lye soap. Roland wondered why they were starting projects when everything would be packed up and moved the next day. Perhaps they actually used the items they made or sold the items they made.

The smell from the iron pot was strong and pungent, and the man shaving the stave whistled a mournful mountain tune. A plug of tobacco was visible in one of the upper pockets of his overalls, a small adze hung from a loop on his overalls. A few chickens that had been added about halfway through for verisimilitude clucked fatly around the homemade wheelbarrow, the wooden rabbit trap, the moonshine still sitting like a metallic bug constructed by some impoverished Dr. Frankenstein.

Behind this patch of Appalachia was the concrete of the fair, the glowing Sun Tower, his own green shiny-mirrored building and the gold-tinted one of J.T. beside it.

He couldn't help but smile.

When he looked back to the cooper, the man had paused in his work to clean his knife with a piece of oiled cloth. The man turned and looked at him. He said: Well hello, Mr. Cole. This is a pleasant surprise.

Roland felt a moment's chagrin about being called Mister by one twenty years his senior. This was something he'd never get used to. He said, thank you. Forgive me, I've forgotten your name.

The man waved a hand to dismiss the apology. Leonard Keith, he said, standing up. He wiped each side of the blade once more on his pants legs, then placed it on the shaving horse where he'd been sitting. Then he briefly swished his hands together to brush off the sawdust, before offering a hand to shake.

Good to see you, said Roland, his standard reply when unsure if this was a first or second introduction.

The man seemed to realize Roland's predicament, for he offered: We met the first week of the fair, when we were first getting going down here. You met about fifteen of us, I wouldn't expect you to remember.

He'd said this last part with a smile, and shaking the man's rough and leathered hand, Roland felt a quick wave of nostalgia for rural humility and graciousness.

What kind of wood are you working with there, Mr. Keith?

That is red oak.

Good hard wood, said Roland.

Hard is right, the man said smiling.

But it's good for furniture, if I'm not mistaken.

You know a little about wood.

No, said Roland. But I did eat off a red oak table most of my life. The folks who bought the farm my father grew up on cleared a bunch of timber and they let Daddy have some of it. He had a local man make the table for us. We're using it still back at my folks' house.

You'll be using it in a hundred years if you live that long, said the man.

Standing there, Roland had a sudden strange memory from childhood, of being in bed but not asleep, and the comforting sounds of parents still moving about the house: the scuff and slide of his father's brush while polishing his work shoes, the clatter of plates being washed in the sink, a murmur of soft adult voices, voices that loved him, and him snug under the quilts in the four-poster bed.

The cooper said, I've enjoyed this fair of yours, Mr. Cole. I've seen every exhibit here and most of them more than once.

I'm glad to hear it, Roland said. What was your favorite?

Oh, China. That's easy. I've never seen anything like some of those jade carvings. That's some real craftsmanship there. And think of the tools they had to use to do it.

Roland smiled but said no more. A woman walked by carrying a box of rag dolls. She was dressed in a calico dress and stopped in front of the cooper, saying, I promised you one of these for that nice churn you gave me. You take your pick. That one there in the yellow dress is one any little girl would like.

The cooper looked at Roland: For my little granddaughter.

As suggested, he chose the doll in the yellow dress. Then the woman held the box in front of Roland.

You too, Mr. Cole, she said. Pick you out a nice one.

Oh no, I couldn't, said Roland.

Please, said the woman. I insist. It's the least I could do. This has been a once-in-a-lifetime experience for me. I've met people from thirty-seven countries. I'm mailing dolls all over the world now. Now you take a little doll. As a keepsake. It would mean a lot to me.

The cooper was looking up at Roland. His own doll was sitting fat-faced and jolly on top of the shaving horse. He pulled his knife from his pocket and began to clean it again.

Roland reached into the box and chose one in a blue petticoat with lacy striped bloomers on her legs. The mouth was embroidered, but the nose and eyes painted on by hand.

That's a nice one, the lady said. I named her Suzanne. But whoever you give it to can call her what they want, of course.

I'm not giving this doll to anyone, said Roland. Suzanne's going in my office. As a keepsake.

Roland could see that this pleased the woman. He said: I didn't know the faces were drawn on. I thought they usually had button eyes.

Oh, people draw them on some, said the woman. But most use plastic for the nose and eyes. Little buttons, usually. But those eyes always spooked me when I was a little girl, so I never have used them.

They're a lot more personal with the painted face, Roland said. More individual.

The woman beamed. She said, they are. They sure are.

And then they were making their goodbyes. As Roland walked away, the cooper said: You take care of that red oak table, now.

The whole fair site was benumbed with the leaf-burning smell of fall.

He thought: this was it. I won't top this.

He'd be forty-seven in a month and wondered if his best work was behind him. He thought his reserves of energy were on the wane. But how much of that was burning the candle at both ends? How much energy could he muster if he came home after work and left the nightlife to others? He'd broken it off with Valerie and that seemed for the best. This Joyce business wasn't serious, was nothing really. But it should be nipped in the bud, nonetheless. All that juggling and guilt had left J.T. looking like death warmed over. And all his life he'd learned from J.T.'s mistakes. Time to learn one more lesson: excitement or health? Take your pick. Because middle-aged men no longer get em both.

He became aware that Libby was squeezing his hand. Then she nudged him with her elbow, a nudge to say, *look over there*. He looked where he was meant to. Sitting on a bench beside the International Lake, mouth-to-mouth, oblivious to the gazes of passersby, engaged in impassioned preliminaries, a sixty-year-old knight of the round table and his sixty-year-old damsel in distress.

Nothing like young love at Halloween, said Libby.

Hey, said Roland, I'm just glad to see someone still having a good time. It was starting to feel like a funeral around here.

Libby squeezed his hand again. She was nodding her head and looking all around, trying to take it all in. She said: I still can't believe we did it.

Roland smiled.

I'm really very proud of you.

Roland had the urge to stop and sweep his wife off her feet, to hug her, to go away with her, just the two of them, on a very long vacation. That was what they'd do. Sometime in December. Hell, earlier than that. Next week. Nothing keeping him here now.

I couldn't have done it without you, he said.

The speeches were over and the crowd slowly filed out. The luminaries had not matched those of the opening. The governor had not shown after all and there was no representative from the White House. The new congressman from their district, a young guy, had shown up, a token gesture, the grunt-work glad-handing that the young politician can never avoid when people are gathering in his neck of the woods. Other than that, no real headliners on the bill. And the crowd itself was comprised primarily of locals and those who'd worked the exhibits. All in all, it'd been a dull affair, the mood of his earlier walk a portent of things to come. Everyone looked tired, everyone, it seemed, thought the time was right for going back to the life they'd known before. Roland's speech had tried to walk the line between satisfied humility and self-congratulation. Throughout, he'd tried to emphasize that it was the community and everyone who had a role in the fair, from the mayor on down to the vendors, who should give themselves a pat on the back. Still, he wondered if he'd sounded too smug. You could never tell about a speech. Intonation was so much of it. He thought, in the end, he'd probably just sounded tired. Tired words from a tired man to a tired audience. Nothing that anyone would remember one way or another six months from now. *They said we couldn't, we said we could. They said we wouldn't, and folks, the proof is in the pudding.* When he'd said this last phrase, he motioned with his arm across the entirety of the fair landscape. There was the proof. There it was. He'd finished up about all that the city could do with the renovated site and with the revitalized downtown. *Glennville is no longer walking toward the twenty-first century, but sprinting headlong toward it.*

Standing now on the stage of the amphitheater, Roland watched Expo officials and the employees and emissaries from the foreign pavilions chitchatting and laughing quietly as they made their way down the steps and into the gallery. The last laser show had just wrapped up, the last starry firework fountained in the sky. Roland couldn't decide whether to be surprised by Teague's absence or not. He'd given notice a week or so after the party in the bank lobby in a letter short and to the point: My work here is done, time to explore other career options, thanks for the opportunity, enjoyed my time, best of luck.

He'd miss old Teague, but at the end of the day, Teague never was a company man. It surprised him, in a way, he'd stuck around as long as he had. A low boredom threshold for Teague. And staying in one place for too long might give people a chance to actually know you. A tough life for old Teague. Who did he talk to? Who were his allies? The lone wolf route had some appeal in literature and lore, but not in the real world, not at the end of the day.

Standing partially hidden at the podium, he took a look around him. Near the foot of the stage, J.T. and Corrine chatted with the head of the Glennville Art Museum and her husband. They'd reconciled as he thought they would, but the old way was gone. Watching Corrine now, one saw a clear-eyed woman, supportive of her husband in public but brooking no nonsense. Old dogs and new tricks seemed to be the order of the day. J.T. said something and Corrine placed her hand on his shoulder and laughed.

A thought struck him, a funny one and ironic, and he turned nearly all the way around to see if anyone was behind him on the stage. What he discovered was that he'd been left on the dais with nothing but empty chairs. He took a deep breath. What a nice change of pace to have a few minutes to himself before the shaking of hands and the receiving of friends. His older brother seemed to intuit the humor of his situation, for when he again looked out to what was left of the audience, J.T. caught his eye and smiled. Then with slow and dramatic pacing, he made a gesture that seemed to say, *forgotten already?*

J.T. excused himself and came up on the stage with a smile. He stuck out a hand in ironic formality: How quickly they forget.

Tell me about it, said Roland.

So which was better? asked J.T. Getting the fair or winning the Henry City rook tournament when you were fourteen?

Roland laughed. The rook tourney was a definite highlight. He'd entered the all-day event at the last moment and ended up beating sixty-three adults for the first prize, the youngest person anyone could ever recall winning. The prize? Fifty baby chicks.

I don't know, said Roland. That's a tough one.

J.T. smiled.

I'm serious.

I know you are.

Those baby chicks really put Sis's collection over the top.

And fried chicken got to be a rare thing.

Roland was smiling. His brother had sensed his mood and lightened it.

It's hard to believe, said Roland, that I can't decide between that rook tournament and this fair.

Not really. Just the size of the fish and the size of the pond. I mean, you beat a townful of grown men. Men who'd played rook for thirty, forty years. That was a big damn deal.

I could play some rook.

J.T. smiled.

You remember when we first got up here and didn't know *come here* from *sic em*?

A little green, said J.T. Not long off the turnip truck.

It seems a long time ago.

It does that, little brother.

Then J.T. placed a hand on his shoulder. He said: How you feeling?

All right. A bit foggy, I guess. How bout yourself?

J.T. thought about it. He rubbed his eyes with his free hand. I feel, he said, like the host of a very good party who was too damn busy hosting to enjoy the festivities. We're going to wake up tomorrow and wonder what the hell did we miss. I don't believe I'm coming down tomorrow.

No, said Roland. Nothing sadder than watching the circus pack up and head out of town.

They were still alone on the stage. Miraculously, not a soul had come within five feet of them during the whole of the conversation.

We'll talk this weekend, said J.T. I was thinking about taking the boat out before I put up for the winter. You interested?

Sure. I might even throw out a line.

Here J.T. laughed. He patted the shoulder of Roland's eight-hundred-dollar suit. City boy, he said, I bet you don't remember how to bait the hook.

You're probably right.

They stood there for a moment more. J.T. looked over at the group of people in the front rows of the arena waiting to talk to him, talk to Roland. The crowd had mostly dispersed by now. Corrine and Libby were talking on the opposite end of the stage. When Roland saw the man and woman dressed as clowns handing out balloons in the back of the amphitheater, he started to point them out to J.T. But almost simultaneously his brother made the same observation. J.T. cut his eyes at him, smiling eyes that said, *ah yes, right on time.*

How many years have gone into the understanding of that smile between brothers? On how many occasions has it been exchanged?

Roland thought this in the moment. And then he saw that J.T. caught the calculations going on in his head, the nature and the nurture, the history, the speaking in code before you even knew you were doing it, the odd, pleasant moment of reflecting on that which is unspoken but understood. They were sibling spies. Sent out, their like and unlike minds, by their parents, their town, their kind, to see what mark they could make on the world, and to see what part of the world was theirs.

Then the moment passed. With a last pat on his brother's shoulder, J.T. walked down the stairs, greeted as he came by the mayor and assorted dignitaries who turned to hail him from the aisle.

Not long after, the clowns handed a balloon apiece to Libby and Corrine before heading out of the amphitheater themselves.

And then Roland too descended from the stage.

All Saints' Day

Jan was in the kitchen reading the newspaper when the doorbell rang. She'd not yet finished her second cup of coffee and still felt a little sluggish after staying up so late to finish a movie Mike had got started on. Staying up late wasn't her preference and she'd not loved the movie, a western, but she knew her husband had mixed feelings about skipping the closing ceremonies and thought he could use the company. She didn't know the whole of the reason for their absence, but had a decent guess. All in all, it'd been fun, but she wouldn't miss the late nights or the parties. And Mike looked run ragged. The only times she saw him were with other people around, usually a lot of other people. During their rare moments alone, she knew he was talked out, and just let him be. Yes, six months was plenty long enough, and it had been fun, but now she was ready to have the city back to its sleepy self. The doorbell rang again as she was coming into the parlor and she said, coming, coming, be right there.

The blue November day she'd observed out the kitchen window was even better when she felt the crisp dry air on her face and she couldn't help but smile as she opened the door.

But the two men in suits who waited several feet from the front stoop on the sidewalk didn't return her smile.

Janet Teague? one of them said.

Someone has died, she thought. Mike has been in an accident. Her heart felt suddenly tight and large and very fast. I'm Jan Teague, she said.

The man who hadn't spoken held a piece of paper in his hand. He was the younger of the two. Somber men, serious men, men with bad news. He said: We're from the Tennessee Bureau of Investigation. We have a search warrant to search your house.

As he said this, he pulled out a badge from the pocket of his suit jacket. Then he approached the door with both the badge and the piece of paper extended. The other man was looking off beyond the house.

Jan's legs felt quivery beneath her. She heard herself say, I don't understand. What's going on? Where's Mike?

The young TBI man now stood before her on the stoop. Here is the warrant, Mrs. Teague, he said. It gives us permission to search your house and premises. And also your automobile.

For what?

For evidence of bank fraud.

Behind the man, she saw their car, the car they'd driven in. It was parked in the driveway, grey and nondescript and so very foreign. Behind it was the blue sky and a neighbor's car entering the subdivision and making its way up the hill. She felt as if she were in a movie, in it and watching it at the same time. The movie had odd lighting, too blue, and the nondescript car in the driveway seemed to exert a gravitational pull. She couldn't stop looking at it. Then she saw the man on the sidewalk looking at her. He said: We're sorry, ma'am. But we're going to have to go in.

She felt herself backing toward the door. Where's Mike? she said. Where's my husband?

I don't know, ma'am. But we're coming in the house now.

She stepped out of the doorway without realizing she had. The men didn't look at her as they passed. She said, what's going on? What in the world are you doing?

Turn on the news, ma'am, said the man from the sidewalk as he stood in the parlor, her parlor, and pointed up the stairs toward the bedrooms to the other man. It's all over the news.

———

She followed the men from bedroom to bedroom, not knowing exactly why. What would they steal? What was there to hide? As they went through Mike's sock drawer, carefully, daintily, she sat down on the unmade bed, among the clothes that had been taken from their bureau, from their drawers, and placed her head in her hands. The men worked silently and their breathing was a background against the squeak of drawer. When she next looked up, the younger man was halfheartedly rummaging through her lingerie, his back to her, his elbows moving like a man she'd seen once in New York playing a shell game for tourists. When he pushed in the lingerie drawer, her head cleared and she no longer felt as if someone was playing a cruel trick on her. She thought, the Coles have done something. This is about the Coles. Not Mike. Not us.

She said: This isn't about us, is it?

The older man was en route to the adjoining bathroom. He stopped but didn't look at her. He said, turn on the news, Mrs. Teague.

Instead, she went to the kitchen, picked up the phone, and called Mike. When he didn't pick up his direct line, she called the secretary. Again, no answer. The phone rang and rang. She felt now for a moment like someone in a postapocalyptic movie, a survivor of some disaster that she didn't yet know had occurred. She called Mike's number again. Called again the secretary. Upstairs the men were trudging down the hall to the spare bedrooms. Thank god Julie was away at school.

The small television on the kitchen counter sat there like a patient grey bomb. Like an empty eye socket. *Turn on the news, ma'am.* When the phone rang, it sounded far away, innocuous, a neighbor's phone heard through an open window. Mike, she thought, and reached for the phone with a jerky motion.

Said her mother on the other end: Oh goodness, Jan. Have you seen? Have you seen what's going on?

No, she said.

Turn on the television, said her mother. Turn it on now.

Said Jan: I'll have to call you back.

———

Through the kitchen window, she saw the TBI men walk out of the back door of the garage and toward the pool house. The younger man tentatively tried the door and even though his back was to her, she could tell he was pleasantly surprised to find it unlocked. The tilt of his head looked pleased. The older man was circling around back of the pool house in a kind of bored amble. She could tell from here they were resigned to finding nothing. Perhaps they'd been resigned from the start and only her antenna was off and she couldn't read the signs. She got up and poured herself another cup of coffee. After the men left, if she hadn't heard from Mike, she was going to drive down to his office.

On the television, the montage of images continued, one local channel the same as the other, the producer moving the viewer from one fast-talking reporter to the next, mixing in the occasional shot from a helicopter, the stern-faced authorities walking in and out of one bank after another, stiffly and unconvincingly impervious to the jostling cameras around them. Superimposed every three or so minutes, a stock photo of the smiling gubernatorial candidate Roland Cole and a grainy candid shot of J.T. in a tuxedo and hand in hand with a woman cropped from the picture: Corrine. Running beneath the live action shots of bank buildings and the comings and goings of men carrying out boxes of files was a scrolling text rundown of the day's news, a speedy and kinetic ticker tape: *150 bank examiners from the FDIC simultaneously descend on the 36 banks owned or controlled by Roland and J. T. Cole.*

The nearly giddy news anchor added this: *According to sources, this morning's sting operation was to prevent the transfer of funds from one bank to the other within the Cole banking network, which owns financial institutions in Kentucky, Alabama, and throughout Tennessee. Again, we'd like to remind our viewers that no formal statement has been given from any of the investigating authorities. But sources close to the situation say that bank examiners from the FDIC and state Treasury Department are investigating allegations of insider loans, unsecured loans, and forged loan documents in the two-billion-dollar banking empire. The FBI and TBI have been called in to assist with the situation. All thirty-six banks are closed for the day and all bank assets have been frozen.*

When she heard the front door open, she turned off the television and went toward the parlor. Her mother's shoes clacked like castanets across the floor and she looked dressed for a cocktail party or stylish funeral. Removing her sunglasses, she said, Jan, are you okay? Have you heard from Mike? Before she could answer, the doorbell rang. She walked past her mother with a quick nod and opened the door which was only partially shut. The elder of the TBI men stood toward the back end of the porch, a deferential pose more professional than courteous. She didn't think she could hate someone she didn't know, but now, looking at the older TBI man and his weak approximation of a gentleman, she felt a kind of bile previously unfamiliar to her. She now preferred the brusque apathy of the younger man to this feigned hat-in-hand routine. How dare you? she thought. How dare you scare me like that? How dare you go through my things?

If he called her ma'am, she wouldn't be responsible for her actions.

He said: We're all through here, Mrs. Teague. We're about to take off.

She stared at the man but didn't speak.

He handed her a piece of paper and said, that's all our information if you need it. If you have any questions or comments. The page below that just says that we executed a search of the premises. You'll note at the bottom that nothing was taken from your house or premises.

Her mother stood beside her now and Jan could hear her breathing noisily through her mouth. She must have dressed and driven over like a bat out of hell. Was she expecting newsmen? Cameras? Why was she dressed like Jacqueline Onassis? No, it was just the dress of someone ready to play mother, ready to take care of business. Her mother now took in a deep breath and held it. She was shaking, bristling. Jan didn't look at the papers the man had given her, but glanced now at his partner, who was jingling car keys in his pocket.

Said her mother: You can leave now. Unless you have further business.

The man shook his head. No ma'am, we're all done.

Then good day, said her mother, shutting the door in the man's face.

A Few Questions

Teague was in his office, cleaning out the paperwork from his desk and boxing what items he meant to bring home with him. He'd given his notice that, as originally agreed upon, his duties with the Expo Commission would end with the closing of the fair. He'd had some qualms about skipping out on the closing ceremonies—he was, after all, still under contract until midnight of the thirty-first—but decided it would be easier on everyone if he just faded off into the sunset. No need to share the spotlight with Roland, it was his hour and he'd earned it. And no need to be there as a spoilsport, he'd played that role enough in the last five years. Let them have their fun with no questions asked.

Or so he'd rationalized.

He looked at a picture on his bookshelf of three couples standing in front of J.T.'s plane prior to the trip to Washington. Four people in the photo are smiling as appropriate, only Libby Cole and himself are not. Libby simply looked at the camera in a dignified fashion. A person about to embark on a serious journey, a formal person who offered no acquiescence to the command of *Cheese*. For a moment he hoped that his own reticence sprang from a similar self-possession. But when he looked closer, bringing the photo nearer for better inspection, he saw that he had indeed the beginnings of a smile, the mouth was formed in the expression of a smile, but he'd not seen fit to share his teeth with the photographer, had not deigned to fully join in the exuberant energy of the group. How stingy of you, he thought. How very typically half-ass.

He placed this photo in the box then reached for the framed item next to it. This was a shot from the front page of the *Daily Herald*. The headline read: *GROUNDBREAKING!* and showed Roland in coat and tie and hard hat. With his foot poised on the shovel, he stood ready to scoop out the first chunk of soil that would initiate the construction phase of the fair. In this one, he and J.T. are in the background. They also wear the ridiculous hard hats, and his smile is the widest of the three. He held the photo a little closer to his eye. The man in the hard hat looked like a Teague he didn't know. He looked earnest. Smiling at this realization, he pulled the airplane photo from the box and placed it on his desk next to the one at the groundbreaking. He looked from one photograph to the other, wondering, how is this the same man?

When he placed these photos in the box, he decided to finish up the packing quickly. He was between jobs now, for how long he didn't know, but there seemed plenty of time later for nostalgia and reflection. He had no hard feelings. Sometimes it was just time to move on.

When his secretary, Mrs. Goodwin, rushed in without knocking, he looked up in surprise. She stopped breathless in the space between the door and his desk and said: Have you heard?

Heard what?

The bank's closed. We're not allowed to leave. Regina down at the front desk just called me. There's men everywhere down there.

Teague pushed the box to the side of his desk and sat down in the leather swivel chair. Mrs. Goodwin was red-faced, perfectly still yet highly agitated.

He tried to sound reassuring. Now hold on, he said. Slow down. What's this all about?

She went to his window and looked out. There, she said, as if pointing out an obvious UFO to a disbeliever. Look.

Teague got up and joined her at the window. Below them on Franklin Street, car after bureaucratic car parked in front of the bank, all whites and tans and navy blues, so nondescript as to call attention to themselves. The vehicles said: *We don't fuck around.* The street had been closed and several policemen at each corner of the block diverted traffic down side avenues. On down the street, a similar menacing line of vehicles sat stolidly, bully-shouldered all bumper to bumper in front of Valley Industrial Savings and Loan. Thought Teague: This is premeditated and well coordinated. This is months, maybe years, in the works. This is multijurisdictional. They mean to bring some people down.

He had a brief light feeling in his stomach, air like a feather floating from stomach to intestines and then back up again. Beside him, he could hear the short, heavy breathing of Mrs. Goodwin. And then his adrenaline kicked in. He could feel his heart rate slowing, slower even than before his secretary entered his office. It was perhaps his one true gift: in moments of real crisis, a car wreck, an injured loved one, anything where the first reaction ought to be panic, his adrenaline produced the opposite effect. His heart slowed, but his mind was precise and anticipatory. The world seemed to be moving in slow motion.

Mrs. Goodwin, he said, let's go in the lounge and see if there's anything about this on TV.

They were in the lounge, Teague and Mrs. Goodwin and a few others from the floor, when his secretary left to answer a ringing phone. The news mirrored the gravity of what Teague had seen outside his office window. It felt very strange to be twenty-eight stories above all the bustle and stern-faced efficiency he witnessed on the television. Perhaps surreal would be the better word. On the television screen, a helicopter-camera view of the building he was standing in. Then a shot from ground level of the fleeting images of men coming and going through the revolving glass door he'd used that morning. For an instant, he considered trying his luck on one of the exit doors, catching an elevator several floors down and hitting the upper deck of the parking lot which was rarely attended. He could simply leave his car and make his way on foot, catch a taxi, and be done with this craziness for the day. But the looks of his co-workers, the fear for jobs and future written on those faces, kept him planted where he was. If the bank was truly closed for the day, they'd have to start letting the employees, especially the minor employees, leave sooner or later. Could they even keep them here legally? Or had Roland himself asked everyone to stay put? He'd give it till noon, then if he hadn't heard anything more, you could count him once and for all clocked out.

Mr. Teague, there are some men here who'd like to see you.

Teague turned to see the blanched face of his secretary looking at him from the open door of the lounge. She looked terrified. Teague smiled and stood up. Thank you, Mrs. Goodwin, I'll meet them in my office.

He walked to his office and left the door open behind him. He moved the box filled with his belongings off the desk and placed it on the floor. In a minute or so, Mrs. Goodwin tapped on the open door, seemingly at a loss for how to introduce the men or whether introductions were protocol in such a circumstance as this. She looked from Teague to the men then quickly back at Teague before turning and walking out of sight. Teague stood up and extended a hand, saying, Mike Teague, what can I do for you gentlemen?

The men approached and offered stiff, formal shakes. One of them held a thin accordion folder. The man with the folder said: I'm Agent Delk and this is Agent Harris. We're from the Tennessee Bureau of Investigation.

Teague said, have a seat, then went and closed the door. When he returned, both men were seated across from him. The one with the folder, Agent Delk, was about his age and had such an innate or affected, Teague couldn't yet tell, insouciance in his eyes that Teague surmised he must have known from a very young age that law enforcement and the carrying of a firearm were just the sort of thing he'd like to spend a lifetime doing. Teague offered this man a premeditated smile, a smile to say, *surely you don't think that steely stares are going to have an effect on me?* The other man was jowly. And even in the excitement of the day, the excitement of the present chase, whatever kind of chase it might turn out to be, his longing for retirement and quiet days on the bass boat were etched across his tanned, round face.

Teague thought: *cops.*

Said the jowly Agent Harris: I guess you've heard the commotion downstairs.

Just recently, fifteen minutes ago, said Teague. I've been watching it on TV.

Agent Harris nodded, smiled a bit. In a breezy, conversational tone, he said: What do you know about it?

Nothing. Just what I saw on TV. There was some kind of coordinated raid on all the banks. That's it. That's what I know.

Agent Delk, the young man with the folder, the man with the crafty, insolent eyes of an especially irksome teen, turned to his partner and said: It was well coordinated, wasn't it?

Agent Harris nodded slightly, a quick shake of the head. He gave the impression of wanting not to encourage the man, this tone, this tact. He said to Teague: We'd like to ask you a few questions, if we might.

Fire away, said Teague.

Agent Delk pointed at the empty bookcase behind Teague, then at one of the boxes at the side of his desk. Are you moving out?

I am.

Good timing.

I believe yesterday would have been better.

Both men smiled at this, a smile Teague returned.

So you no longer work here, for the bank?

I never worked for the bank, said Teague. My official title is Executive Vice President for the Expo Commission. Or rather, it was. Since the fair's over, so is my job.

The men said nothing for a moment. Agent Delk placed the folder on the desk. At first he placed it like a book in front of him. He left it there but kept his hand on it. Then he turned it sideways. He looked at it for a moment like this, then turned it again as he'd first had it. Satisfied, he removed his hands, then leaned back in his chair. The intent seemed to be to focus the eyes in the room on the folder on the table.

Teague made a point of smiling at this showmanship.

Agent Harris said: You never did any bank business?

Oh come on man, thought Teague. Out with it. The asking of questions for which you have answers. Is that really necessary?

Teague said: As I mentioned, I'm not a banker. On one occasion,

Roland Cole asked me to go down to one of the banks to fill in for a manager who was sick. A bank examiner was there that day and he thought the assistant manager and other employees would feel more comfortable if I was there.

Even though you're not a banker, said Agent Delk. He said this while staring at the folder in front of him.

That's right, said Teague, deciding in the last few seconds to keep his demeanor even at all costs despite the very real desire to grab Agent Delk by his five-dollar tie and repeatedly slam his face into the desk, into his beloved manila folder.

Why send a man who's not a banker down to a bank to meet a bank examiner?

This was from Agent Harris, the older man. Teague thought that if the two had been partnered long, their brand of offensive and inoffensive often proved effective. Though now Agent Harris seemed a little less sleepy, and it dawned on Teague that this was the man he really ought to be paying attention to.

Said Teague: I was under the impression that I was sent down there as a formality.

Down to Lofton?

Yes. To Lofton. The manager was in the hospital with appendicitis, I believe. The assistant manager was very new to the job. Roland thought she'd be nervous and that someone, anyone, in a suit would make everyone at the bank a little more comfortable.

Very quickly Agent Delk grabbed the folder from the desk, took the top sheet of paper from it, then placed the folder back on the desk. This was done with such speed and alacrity and obvious physical relish that Teague wondered if it was something he practiced at home.

Teague took the sheet of paper being handed him by Agent Delk. The man on the other side of the sheet said before releasing it: We've obtained these forms with permission from the state Department of Treasury and the FDIC. What we need to know is if that's your signature at the bottom of the page.

Teague looked at the sheet. It was the last page of the bank examiner's report, dated July 20. The same day as the party at Roland's. At the bottom was the bank examiner's signature. Above it was his own. He read the boilerplate above the signatures, stating that he, the bank employee of record, had been present during the examination and that to the best of his knowledge all the information that he, said bank employee of record, had given was accurate and truthful.

Yes, said Teague, that's my signature.

So you did have the authority to sign the form? asked Agent Harris.

When I was made vice president of Expo, I was also given a spot on the bank's board of directors. It was an honorary thing, basically. But I did have signatory's privileges. That was one of the formalities of getting on the board.

If you don't mind me saying, said Agent Delk, I think someone could call you a banker and not be too far off the mark.

Call me whatever the hell you like, but let's get to the point.

Teague said this without anger, and the young agent laughed in response. Whatever persona he'd adopted was now replaced with a more businesslike one. Fine, he said. Fine. We do have some questions, Mr. Teague. And we're hoping you can answer them.

With this, he drew a second sheet from the folder and passed it over the desk. That's the signatory's form, correct? The one you signed giving you the authority to sign off on bank business as an official representative of First Bank of Glennville and its affiliates?

Teague gave it a summary glance, noted the date, February 7, 1979, and his signature. You are correct, said Teague. That is the signatory's form and that is my signature.

Agent Delk nodded and began flipping through the other pages in his folder, checking to see if the order of them was still to his liking. The light on Teague's phone began to blink. Normally Mrs. Goodwin would have screened this call, but she was probably back in the lounge watching the action as it unfolded on TV. It was likely Jan calling. He debated answering, then decided against it. Better to give her all he knew in a lump, and he'd know a lot more here in a few minutes. He fought the urge to ask if there was a problem. It was rarely a good idea to rush things to a conclusion in a situation like this, though that was the common human instinct. Even bad news was preferable to not knowing, to suspense.

Agent Delk pulled a sheet from his folder and handed it across the desk. He said, this is page seven of the bank audit you signed for the bank in Lofton. You'll notice there at the bottom that ten million dollars in loans to VanCo Construction have been sold to First Bank of Glennville on July thirteenth.

Okay, said Teague. I see it.

That's one week before you went down to the Lofton bank.

Okay, fine.

Agent Delk handed over another xeroxed copy. Here is a copy of an audit done in September of FBG. You'll see on this one that a ten-million-dollar loan to VanCo has been sold back to the Lofton bank.

Teague looked at the form but said nothing.

Someone is moving money around one step ahead of the auditors, Agent Delk said. You know anything about that?

No, said Teague, I don't.

You know anything about VanCo Construction?

No.

You don't know the owner? You're sure about that? I've got a good feeling you do know.

Listen, you're not going to sit here and call me a goddam liar. If I say I don't know the owner, I don't know the owner.

Agent Delk smiled, leaned back in his chair. He said: J. T. Cole owns it. J. T. Cole is the owner, he's the silent partner. The man with his name on the stationery is Billy Phelps, but J. T. Cole is the principal owner.

Teague felt a sting of anxiety. He realized he'd not moved at all in several minutes and shifted in his seat a bit. He hated this shifting as soon as he began it. This cop would think his pregnant pause was having some effect.

Okay, said Teague. That's news to me.

The FDIC and the state Department of Treasury are interested in a number of irregularities within the Coles' banking network. I guess you heard that on the news though.

Yes.

This audit you signed for the bank in Lofton. It doesn't look good. Selling and buying back the same ten-million-dollar loan in a little over a month is unusual. Some of the boys over at the FDIC might say fraudulent. Throw in the fact that we've yet to find a single thing that VanCo Construction has ever built in its three-year existence, and that Billy Phelps, who runs a travel agency the Coles own, claims never to have heard of VanCo Construction, much less to be the owner of it, and well, a few red flags might be popping up.

Teague looked at Agent Delk and then at his partner. The older man had his fingers laced in front of him and was staring intently at his fingernails.

Agent Delk reached for the forms Teague had in front of him and Teague handed them over. He placed these in the back of the folder and handed over another sheet.

Good god, thought Teague, this could go on forever.

This is a personal note for eight hundred thousand dollars, said Agent Delk.

Teague looked at the name on the loan. This man he did know.

The loan was completed back in June of 78. The collateral used for the loan was bank stock from First Bank of Glennville.

Agent Delk paused here, but Teague said nothing. They sat in silence for a moment. Agent Harris lightly drummed his fingers in front of his chest.

The bank stock used as collateral was paid for with a cashier's check, but we can't find where the money for the cashier's check came from. It was a hefty sum, I'll say that much. More than most of our state employees have to throw around. I assume you have heard of this man, the man getting the eight-hundred-thousand-dollar loan.

I have.

Our good friend Senator Kirkwood from Memphis.

Agent Harris looked up now, looked at Teague in a frank and completely alert manner as if he'd been biding his time until just this moment.

Teague and Agent Delk started to exchange sheets of paper yet again.

At the last moment, however, he yanked back the sheet he was offering, leaving Teague's hand empty over the desk. Agent Delk then made a show of looking at the documents as he spoke.

He said: These are two loan documents. The first is a two-point-five-million note to John Dickson, a.k.a. Johnny Boy, who's listed as the co-owner of First Look Development. We have a bad feeling that First Look is nothing more than a dummy company. The same week this loan was made, Roland Cole put down, you guessed it, two-point-five million as a down payment on a small bank in Paducah. That deal never went through and we don't know where the money is now.

Agent Delk paused as if deciding what to say next. He seemed to enjoy holding the other shoe aloft, ever reluctant to let it drop.

He said: I'm not an expert on this, but this one, this one surely looks like something very close to fraud.

At last Agent Delk handed the paper over. Teague had a very bad feeling now. The day had been building to this. Agent Harris was watching him intently.

Teague took the paper and his eyes went directly to the bottom of it. There was a moment of simultaneous recognition and opaqueness, the mind recognizing the familiar and the unknown in an instant, the value of the x variable instantly known, but somehow not quite right. The brain saying, are you sure? Add it up again.

There was his name, typed and official, the date typed and official as well: July 27, 1983. Above his typed name was his name written in ink, in cursive. It was his name signed on this document.

Teague took another look. And then another. He handed the piece of paper back across the desk and said: I didn't sign this.

Agent Harris said: You didn't?

No.

Agent Harris motioned for the folder and the younger man handed it to him. He slowly flipped through the pages, patiently, luxuriously, what was the hurry, where were any of them going anytime soon?

He pulled two documents out and placed them next to this last one. Teague saw that they were the bank examiner's report and the form granting him signatory privileges. Agent Harris slowly looked from one to the other, tracing the signature at the bottom of each page carefully, methodically, with his finger, a jeweler examining the facets of a stone with his loupe, now stacking one document upon the other upon the other so that three signature lines were lined up like rungs on a ladder.

He placed the documents back on the desk then slid them sidearm and without looking over to his partner beside him.

He said: I'll have to say, Mr. Teague, that they all look pretty much the same to me.

Said Teague: I don't care how they look. I didn't sign that last form.

Agent Harris paused for a moment. Either by plan or just by feel, it was apparent that he'd be doing the lion's share of the talking from here on out. His partner was looking at him, waiting for him to go on.

Agent Harris stared at Teague. Whatever had seemed mildly avuncular about him before was gone. His manner now was straight shooter. He said: You're going to hear from the Treasury Department and the FDIC. You can just plan on that. Technically, we probably should have let them have first dibs at you. But we asked both of them and both agreed that it might behoove everyone involved, yourself included, Mr. Teague, if we were the first folks to talk to you. We're going to lay our cards on the table now.

Here the man paused. Teague couldn't tell if he was gathering his thoughts or allowing that last phrase to sink in.

He said: You ready for us to lay cards on the table?

Teague didn't reply, but made the gesture of a blackjack player requesting a hit from the dealer.

What we're interested in, said Agent Harris, what we're interested in most of all, us and the FBI. Oh, you'll be hearing from them too. Probably the IRS too. You got all kinds of initials interested in talking to you, all kinds of them. But what the TBI and the FBI are interested in is any kind of meeting you may have had that included the Coles and our good senator from Memphis. What we're interested in, very interested in, is a little thing called influence peddling. We're wondering about votes in the 78 election and loans and bank stock and that sort of thing. We're hoping you might be able to talk to us a little about those sorts of things. You say you're not a banker. Okay, fine. We've got some bank documents that have your name on them. Some of them you claim, others you don't. So the question of whether or not you are a banker, for the sake of argument, we'll just leave that question unanswered.

He stopped here, stopped, it seemed, simply to ensure he wasn't giving Teague too much to take in all at once. The man looked at Teague and nearly smiled. Agent Delk and his folder might as well have been out in the hall. It was clear now they weren't equals.

Said Agent Harris: But I do believe you have some expertise in the political arena, as they say. I believe you do get paid to work in the political realm.

Yes, said Teague. That's how I get paid.

We'd like to know what you can tell us about Senator Kirkwood and Roland Cole. I think anything you could tell us, anything helpful, will surely be in your best interest, Mr. Teague. So Mr. Teague, what do you know about loans and votes and senators and Roland Cole? Let's see your cards on the table now.

Teague felt the need to blink but suppressed it.

The man said: Mike, someone is going to get fucked on this deal. That's definite. That's an absolute certainty.

Teague said nothing. His eye went to the folder in front of Agent Delk, then back to the older man. Agent Harris was leaning over now, his chest nearly touching the desk. A small smile worked on his mouth. Teague could see him holding court at a poker table, his sad, unaggressive eyes not missing a trick. He thought in other circumstances the two of them would probably hit it off. Agent Harris had the easy style of a smart person who didn't much care if you knew it or not.

Teague said: I think I'd like to call my lawyer now.

Back Home

Her mother had been watching the television since early that morning. She'd had no lunch and had only broken away from her recliner to refill her coffee cup or to ensure, again, that the phone wasn't off the hook. *I just don't understand why one of them hasn't called me.* From what Sis could see on the television, she reckoned they were likely busy at the time and would call first chance they got.

Said her mother: I just can't believe they haven't thought to call.

Sis got up from the couch and walked toward the TV. When she got there, she said: Let's turn this off. That's Roland and J.T. they're talking about.

I know, said her mother. That's why I want to watch.

That's why I don't.

Her mother looked clearly at her now for the first time of the day. She nodded and the television was clicked shut, the shrill sounds and loud-talking reporters hushed in a moment. The house seemed to take a breath in the silence. The ice maker on the refrigerator gurgled and thunked. The wind chime tinkled thinly through the cracked kitchen window. It was cooler outside than it'd been, but the kitchen still got hot when the afternoon sun hit it. It was an ongoing debate between them, kitchen window cracked or closed when the weather began to turn cool.

Sis said: Let's run down to Bloodworth's real quick. I heard on the radio that they've got their collards in. And I want to see if they got any of that good acorn squash like we had last year.

Oh, said her mother, I couldn't go up there. I couldn't face anyone right now.

Who's there to face besides Mr. Bloodworth?

I could run into anybody. I'm sorry, I just can't make it into town today.

Well we can't just sit here all day. You're about to drive me crazy.

Her mother put the footrest down on her chair and looked absently back toward the television. I do need a few things at the drugstore, she said. I'll just wait in the car.

No, said Sis. That's not doing anybody any good. You need to get out and move around a little bit.

I just can't face anybody today.

Sis walked to her mother and put a gentle hand around her arm, the pose one takes when about to help another from a seated position. The decision had been made, Sis could tell that.

Said Sis: If they liked us before, they're still going to like us. If they didn't, then to heck with em.

Her mother nodded. Then smiled a bit. She rose from her seat and removed the shawl she'd wrapped around the shoulders of the chair. She said: What if they call while we're out?

They'll call back.

Two Weeks Later

Teague checked the clock: 8:45. He'd finally dozed off sometime after five. The guest bedroom proved no better than his own, but at least he hadn't kept Jan up. He walked to his bedroom and threw on the pants and shirt he'd left on the floor the night before. Once downstairs, he heard the familiar murmur of the local news and talk program. He came into the kitchen thinking to ask Jan to turn it up or off then remembered she was off to her exercise class. Her one bad habit: leaving the television on. He was pouring himself some coffee when a reporter said: *Reverberations from the raid on First Bank of Glennville just refuse to stop.*

That was when the phone began to ring. The rings sounded very loud and they came in a series of three, short and violent. He had turned to face the television now and a live shot of the FBG tower took up the whole of the screen. The phone continued to ring and Teague wished that it would stop. Teague couldn't hear what the reporter said because of the phone. The reporter turned to the building and made some rapid, indistinct gesture. The phone continued to ring. Who in the hell wouldn't hang up? They were now back in the studio. The female host nodded gravely. The phone rang.

Teague walked to the phone and pulled the whole of it, cradle and receiver, from the wall. The phone cord and jack and a fair amount of plaster ripped with the pull, leaving a mangled spot in the wall.

He went to the television and turned it off as the weatherman made his first jolly appearance. Then he walked with his coffee up the stairs. On the way, he decided to get dressed and get in the car and drive to Nashville.

Nashville Part III

Since the day of the raids on the bank, the day his house was searched and his talk with the TBI, Teague had met with agents from the FDIC, the state Department of Treasury, the FBI, the SEC, and the IRS. At all of these meetings his lawyer was present. The gist of each meeting was the same: Give your information on the Coles and walk away from all of this clean. Don't play ball, and take your chances with the judicial system.

Teague hadn't listened to counsel, nor to his wife or daughter or father-in-law or mother. He'd not asked his father his opinion on the matter, so his father hadn't offered it.

What Teague told the authorities was not a damn thing.

No one yet had been indicted, but that seemed only a matter of time. The doors to Valley Industrial Savings and Loan had been shut and depositors were getting vague and not-too-comforting reports of the status of their savings. If you could trust the newspaper, that money, if there ever had been any money, was not likely to resurface. First Bank of Glennville had resumed business the Monday after the raids, but most of the business they conducted was the withdrawal of funds and the closing down of accounts. The lines of people at the downtown branch and at the eight branches around the city had stretched far out the doors despite the cool weather.

If the papers were correct, the bank stock was virtually worthless.

Now Teague was on the interstate heading to Nashville on a raw and windy November day, the ringing phone of this morning a harbinger calling him west. He turned on the radio, then turned it off again. Sooner or later it would be another report on the scandal or a lame joke by a local disc jockey.

His lawyer said to just go ahead and pencil in an audit from the IRS. He'd bandied about the term *obstruction of justice* in addition to the term *bank fraud*, which was the phrase most often on the lips of the authorities.

Teague hadn't slept more than three or four hours in a single night since that first meeting with the TBI. Jan had given him back rubs, red wine, sleeping pills. She'd forced him to go to a funny movie and to play a round of golf when friends had called and offered. None of it worked. His eyes felt permanently dried out, his stomach on the fritz from coffee, from red wine, from the red wine that had transformed into highballs, from not eating.

He'd heard no word from the Coles and made no effort to call them. He was on his own, for better or worse. And this knowledge had so consumed him that he'd not thought enough about his family. It had to be embarrassing, no matter what they said to the contrary. Julie was away, but most of her high school friends still lived in the area. It had to be tough to know that your father's name was in the papers and on the news as someone who was *deeply connected to the Coles*, someone who'd had *discussions with authorities*.

The term crony had been used more than once as a tagline to his name.

His name, his name. His father's name, his mother's, his wife's, his child's.

Teague thought now of the time he took a friend to visit his grandparents in Reedsburg, down in southern Middle Tennessee where his father grew up. Eddie Hall was the friend, a boy a year older who lived four houses down. In his whole life, Teague had only looked up to one person, other than a parent or grandparent or famous person, and Eddie Hall was that person.

This idolatry had lasted about a year, then had passed. Only in college when other boys seemed to copy some of his own personal touches did Teague truly recall and understand his own year as a protégé. He thought: I did that too. That's how I was in seventh grade with Eddie Hall. And then he understood the boys in his fraternity and in his dorm who incorporated some of his phrasings into theirs, who began to dress as he did. Eddie Hall had handled his protégé with grace, had understood his role and respected it. Teague acted likewise with his friends at college. Eventually the boys would pass through their apprenticeship and find their own style and voice and their own perspectives on the world.

Eddie Hall's father was a pharmacist, so he was also rich, or what passed for rich on Teague's street. So when Teague took his pal to stay the weekend at his grandparents', he became aware, with that awful nervousness of the early adolescent, of his grandparents' very modest house, of the old-fashioned root cellar in the back, the absence of an indoor lavatory. When they entered the house, Teague felt the same pride he'd always felt in his grandparents, the same love, but also, for the first time, a bit of foreboding, the slightest apprehension.

At dinner that first night, their plates were loaded with fresh vegetables, most of which had been grown in his grandfather's garden. Tomatoes. Silver Queen corn. Cucumbers. Fried okra. Mashed potatoes. His grandmother had made her flat skillet cornbread and there was honey and sorghum on the table with which to load it down. Teague had looked at his plate, at that of his friend's. His grandparents joined them at the table. He looked at their plates as well.

He said: Why isn't there any meat?

His grandfather whom he loved, his grandfather who never said a cross word to him, who took him fishing and let him drive the car on country roads, looked at him frankly but without heat. He said: You don't always get meat at supper. Those are good fresh vegetables. That's cornbread your grandmother just made. If you don't want to eat it, you don't have to. But I don't want to hear anything else about meat.

They'd eaten in silence for a few moments after that. Teague could look at no one else at the table. And to look at his plate only reminded him of his error. He loved vegetables. He loved cornbread. He didn't care that there was no meat. He'd worried what Eddie Hall would think.

What he felt at the table was shame.

The rest of the weekend went smoothly. His grandfather took them fishing, they walked to the gas station in town for Cokes and candy bars, they explored the root cellar and looked for geodes in the gravel drive.

Teague didn't remember feeling awkward the rest of the weekend. He knew his grandfather's feelings for him hadn't changed. It was only after his grandfather died when Teague was in high school that he came to recall and reflect on the dinner with no meat. And though he had a thousand wonderful memories of his grandfather, and though he knew his grandfather likely never thought about that dinner again the rest of his life, whenever Teague thought of it, he felt the same shame. He was only a boy, a boy in that most awkward phase of life, but still he ought to have known better.

And he felt shame thinking of it now.

He rolled on toward Nashville. The wind was blowing fairly hard, and the car, especially when passing an eighteen-wheeler, was being pushed around the road. He could feel the wind's pressure on the windows, the subtle but constant whistle of air through the closed window. He kept his hands firm on the wheel and focused on keeping the car in a never-veering line, and it was like this that he rode the three hours down to Nashville.

Teague Unglued

The lights come on suddenly and a door opens onto the stage. We see the governor's office, much as it was before. Governor MONTGOMERY *is on the phone, dressed sharply if conservatively in a grey suit with red tie. Offstage, we hear a woman's voice saying,* the governor is busy right now, the governor is not taking appointments. TEAGUE *appears in the doorway and lingers for a moment, blocked by the worried-looking secretary. He is typically well dressed, but his tie is ever so slightly awry, his hair windswept or hastily combed. Gone is the cool and collected* TEAGUE. MONTGOMERY *seems to survey the scene before him in a moment's glance. With a few last words to the person on the line, Governor* MONTGOMERY *hangs up the phone. He smiles now at* TEAGUE. *The right smile. The smile of a friend welcoming a friend who is always welcome, always. With a nearly imperceptible nod, a nod to say,* it's fine, it's fine, *he dismisses his* SECRETARY *from the office.*

Governor Montgomery walks around his desk and extends a hand to Teague.

MONTGOMERY. Teague, it's good to see you. Have a seat. Can I get you a cup of coffee or something else to drink?

Teague briefly grasps the governor's hand and shakes his head no to the offered drink. As the governor goes back around his desk, Teague takes a seat in the chair opposite.

MONTGOMERY (*casually, breezy*). To what do I owe the pleasure?

TEAGUE. If you'd return your damn phone calls, you'd know.

MONTGOMERY (*with smile fading*). I'm sorry about that, Mike. It's been crazy around here lately. I was hoping to get back to you in the next few days.

Teague stands up suddenly and begins to pace around the office.

TEAGUE. Yeah, it's been a little crazy, as you say, on my end too.

MONTGOMERY. I'm sorry about all that, Teague. I really am. You have to know I hated to hear it.

TEAGUE (*approaching desk*). The last time I was here, back in the summer. Did you know this was about to go down?

Governor Montgomery looks out the window, then absently at some papers on his desk.

MONTGOMERY. That's government business, Teague.

TEAGUE. That's what I thought.

MONTGOMERY. I didn't answer you one way or another. I'm speaking in a purely hypothetical sense. If I did know, I couldn't tell you, even if I wanted to. You have to know that's how it works. But again, I'm not saying I did or didn't. (*weighing words*) I'm saying you don't have the right to ask that question.

Teague turns his back to the governor and walks to the window.

MONTGOMERY (*conciliatory*). Mike, I have a hard time believing you're involved in any of this. I can't imagine that you're in any real trouble. Or any trouble that doesn't have a fairly simple solution.

TEAGUE. I have a good idea you know exactly what kind of trouble I'm in. I think you know every damn thing the TBI knows.

MONTGOMERY. I stand by what I said. I have a hard time believing you're guilty of anything. Except maybe some poor judgment.

Teague clears his throat as if about to speak, but remains silent.

MONTGOMERY. Speaking hypothetically. Speaking as one who has read the papers and who thinks he can interpret where this thing might be heading, who the authorities are after, and how it all transpired in the first place, I'd think you'd have a pretty easy route to get your ass off the hook.

TEAGUE (*still looking out the window*). And what's your interpretation?

MONTGOMERY. They want the Coles and a few of their insiders. And they want Kirkwood.

TEAGUE. They think I'm an insider.

MONTGOMERY. You are. But not that inside.

TEAGUE. The TBI might quibble with that.

MONTGOMERY. The TBI has been known to bluff. You know that as well as anybody.

Teague turns from the window and again sits in the chair across from the governor. Montgomery smiles kindly, as if watching an old friend come to his senses.

MONTGOMERY. Senator Kirkwood has been running pretty free and easy for a lot of years now. There's been a lot of smoke around him. A lot of smoke. So far he's been able to stay one step ahead of whoever's trying to catch him. I think his time has about run out.

TEAGUE (*absently*). Maybe so.

MONTGOMERY. Speaking hypothetically, if you did know anything about the Coles and Senator Kirkwood and influence peddling or anything like that, I believe if you gave that up, your connection with this sordid little affair would be over.

TEAGUE (*leaning over the desk*). What I know about the Coles and Kirkwood is what I know about a thousand other deals. What I know about the business I'm in. And the business you're in too.

MONTGOMERY. I'm not sure exactly what you're trying to say. But you sure as hell can't put me in the same boat with the Coles and our senator from Memphis.

TEAGUE. The hell I can't. You know as well as I do you can't get a damn thing done without money, without your own money.

MONTGOMERY. You're defending Kirkwood?

TEAGUE. Hey, not everyone comes from West Nashville. And I'm pretty sure that nest egg you have for your run at the Senate didn't all come from ten-dollar donations from the Little Old Lady Republican Barbecue. And you've got your own money. You were born with money. You've had it pretty good, Lawrence, pretty damn easy. So I don't want to hear about Kirkwood. Hell, you think you're supposed to ride the bike downhill all the time.

MONTGOMERY. Now's the time to start choosing your words, Teague.

TEAGUE. How many days of your life since college have you ever worked an actual job?

MONTGOMERY (*quickly, ready to wrap things up, one talking to an inferior, a crazy man*). Did you just come here to insult me or was there something else you wanted?

TEAGUE. I came here to call in a favor.

MONTGOMERY. In other words, I owe you something.

TEAGUE. I need those fuckers off my back.

MONTGOMERY. My hands are tied.

TEAGUE. Bullshit your hands are tied. You're the golden boy up in Washington right now. They've got their eyes on you for bigger things. I know that and you know that.

MONTGOMERY. Washington's got nothing to do with this.

TEAGUE (*as with epiphany*). They're talking cabinet post, aren't they? No, no, better than that. It's better than that, isn't it? (*Teague snaps his fingers with the eureka moment*) It's a spot on the ticket. That's what it is. Everyone knows the president doesn't like who he's saddled with. Is it a spot on the ticket, Lawrence? That's been mentioned, hasn't it? Nothing firm. See how things shape up the next year. But a possibility. A chance. Am I right?

MONTGOMERY (*smiling, but with patience ebbing*). As I said, Teague, Washington has nothing to do with it. There's nothing political in this at all.

TEAGUE. Yeah, there's nothing political about jacking a Democrat who's been a thorn in the side of every East Tennessee Republican for the last eight years. You think this would have happened if the last president was still in office?

MONTGOMERY. I don't know. But from all appearances, it should have.

Montgomery rolls his chair around the desk until he's sitting side by side with Teague. He places his hand on the arm of Teague's chair.

MONTGOMERY (*quietly*). What do you owe the Coles?

Teague doesn't reply.

MONTGOMERY (*quieter still*). They fucked you, Teague. You're acting like you're mad at me. But they fucked you, I didn't.

TEAGUE. Oh, you fucked me, Lawrence. But that was years ago.

MONTGOMERY (*scooting his chair away suddenly*). That's the favor? That's why I owe you? The Coles are going to send your ass to jail and I screw your damn mistress, and what I did was worse?

TEAGUE (*turning to face Montgomery*). What you did was personal. This is just business.

MONTGOMERY (*wildly, exasperated*). Roland Cole took up with the same woman! Teague, are you crazy? Have you just gone flat crazy?

TEAGUE. That wasn't a breach.

MONTGOMERY. She was your mistress, for god's sake. Not your wife.

Teague doesn't reply to this. His face is a blank.

MONTGOMERY. Forging your name on some documents isn't a breach?

TEAGUE (*nearly smiling*). That wasn't in the newspapers.

MONTGOMERY. No, it wasn't.

TEAGUE. I'm calling in a favor I think you owe me. And it's a favor that doesn't cost you anything, doesn't cost you a damn thing.

MONTGOMERY. I can't help you.

TEAGUE. You mean you won't.

MONTGOMERY. I mean what I said.

TEAGUE. I've never asked you for a thing, not a damn thing. And this will cost you nothing. Nothing.

Montgomery stands up and pushes his chair back behind the desk. He sits down in a hard, tired fashion.

MONTGOMERY. Too big, too hot.

TEAGUE (*quietly, desperate*). I can hurt you.

MONTGOMERY. Is that right?

TEAGUE. Your golden boy halo doesn't have any tarnish on it. And I don't think you want any.

MONTGOMERY. That sounds suspiciously close to blackmail.

TEAGUE (*with urgency*). I want those fuckers off my back. I need this to go away.

MONTGOMERY. That tarnish you're talking about is your word against mine. And who the hell is going to listen to you right now? And that third party you might be thinking about, you know as well as I do that she won't say a thing. Just not her style.

TEAGUE (*standing, wild-eyed*). Lawrence, I'm asking you to help me.

MONTGOMERY. I can't do it. My advice is to tell the authorities what they want or take your chances with the legal system. So unless you have other business to discuss, I'm going to have to ask you to leave my office.

Montgomery picks up a document from his desk and begins to read it. Slowly, without looking at the governor, Teague gets up from his seat and walks out of the office.

BLACKOUT

Mystery Caller

When she got back from lunch there was a note on her desk from the receptionist. She saw the note before she even sat down and stood at the corner of her desk looking at it. The name didn't register at first, but it did have some mnemonic quality to it. The number shared the same prefix with the other offices in the capitol and legislative plaza, so perhaps that delayed the moment of recognition. The number was one she knew, but the name with it didn't match. Then she saw the first stumbling block: Michael. No one called him that. She didn't even know he ever called himself that. Teague or Mike. Usually Teague. So why Michael? Perhaps the receptionist had improvised a bit. She was new and earnest and ever professional. Perhaps Michael just sounded better to her ear than just plain Mike. No, that wasn't it. She'd write it as he told it, she'd write the message verbatim. Michael? Was he Michael now? No, that wasn't possible. If he was Michael now, he might as well be Pierre. Michael Teague? She almost said it aloud. She didn't know what to make of the alteration, the formality of it, but it gave her a feeling of things not quite orderly in the universe. And then she thought, well that's just because of what's going on up in Glennville. He's been on your mind, as well as that other fellow. The whole affair has left you with that sensation like that first rapid swoop down on a roller coaster. That's how she'd felt that first day reading the news in the paper. That's how she felt now reading the name *Michael*.

She sat down at her desk and fingered the note. Looked at the number below the name. Looked at the phone. That's Bennett's number, she realized, his office number. Michael Teague was on the premises.

She finished up some paperwork and returned a few other calls. After that she walked out into the plaza foyer toward the bathroom, more than a little expecting to run into Teague. She felt fairly ambivalent about whether she did or didn't, and when the hall was empty but for a few familiar faces, she thought no more about a chance encounter. In the restroom she made a conscious decision not to look at herself in the mirror. She'd decided not to call. Their last encounter had been embarrassingly bad.

When she got back to her office, she sat at the desk shuffling papers and trying to determine what if anything needed to get done today, but nothing she came across seemed urgent. The clock showed three now, so she still had two hours to kill. This Michael Teague business was proving more of a distraction than she'd have liked. She'd planned on stopping for takeout on her way home, reading for a while, then turning on the one television program she'd allowed herself to get hooked on at nine, a nighttime soap opera that most of the nation seemed to be watching. Ridiculous, but fun. Something to talk with the co-workers about on Friday morning. All in all, she'd planned a nice, relaxing night at home during the workweek.

Also boring.

Why not just call him back?

Curiosity and the cat. She'd heard nothing from Roland and information on what was going on in East Tennessee was proving difficult to come by. There were lots of rumors, but rumors around this joint were never in short supply.

Michael Teague? All right, then. A business call, that's what it was. The strange use of the full name, calling from a work phone, a government work phone at that. Probably in for the day and had no other option for giving a callback number. Just using Bennett's office as a home base to take care of what business he had at the capitol. Probably on his way back to Glennville by now. But when would they have had time to meet, if he was in only for the day? And how did she know the call was about a meeting?

Because no one said anything over the phone, not here in Nashville, not when you're using the name Michael Teague.

Boredom, fear of it, got the better of her. Maybe something else too. Foreboding, perhaps. Perhaps having the ball out of her court after that embarrassing display at Rooney's. That one had cost her a bit, cost her in ways she didn't like to pay. She reached for the phone, thinking: my life is very boring and soon I will either have to get used to the boredom or begin making some changes.

Maybe the change is that my threshold for boredom goes way up. But isn't that a depressing concept.

When Bennett answered, she said: I had a message from your office.

At five o'clock, she'd gone to the parking garage, found the car, and made the short drive down from the Legislative Plaza to Broadway. The Marble Lounge was not her kind of place. Too young, too trendy. The place to be if you were working downtown and on the make. But it was close and when Teague suggested it, at Bennett's recommendation she was sure, she said that it'd be okay. Now she was taking the slip from the valet and making her way to the door. The weather was less windy than it'd been that morning, but still chilly despite the sun. How rarely now she noticed the weather, how rarely she seemed to be outside. The modern woman: moving from domicile to work to restaurant to domicile.

Beat the hell out of being a pioneer woman though.

She strolled past the hostess stand without stopping and into the high-ceilinged open bar. Smoke drifted toward her from the large overhead fans and the noise off the brick walls sounded like the crash of waves against the shore. In a few minutes her ears would adjust and she'd be able to hear distinct sounds, but now it was just one long din, a face here thrown back in a roaring laugh, a set of meaningful eyes over a wine glass talking intently, in pantomime, about something gone amiss that day at work or with the love life. Wherever she looked, it was a panorama of faces, all young, all unfamiliar, in some mimetic and inaudible show of emotion. The faces and body language said it all. Why bother with words? She could tell what everyone in the place was thinking, who was complaining, who was newly in love.

She found a spot at the corner of the L-shaped bar where she could watch the door. It was probably too loud and too crowded to talk. A table in the restaurant proper would be quieter. Also more intimate. But that was a call for Teague to make. The bartender came by and took a drink order from the handsome guy beside her. He was late twenties, maybe just thirty, and dressed in a nice navy suit, his tie still zipped tightly to neck. A lawyer or lobbyist. Somebody on his way up. Suddenly he turned to her and said, can I get you a drink?

The bartender was busy and stood waiting for her answer. I'm meeting someone, she said.

That's okay. I'd still be glad to buy you a drink.

She looked at the bartender. Bombay and tonic, she said. But I'll pay for it. Just start me a tab.

The bartender nodded and walked away. Thanks anyway, she said to the young man.

Sure, he said, flashing a grin. I'll give you a rain check.

She smiled and nodded, then turned away to find an ashtray. What a cocky little grin he had. It made her a little tired to consider it.

But then she did consider it. And what such grins mean. How they were a completely uncoded suggestion. How much of life was uncoded. How much of it revolved around the boudoir. When she'd left the office, the receptionist said: You must have a hot date.

The comment startled her. She smiled but said nothing and kept walking out the door. But as she left, she thought, why would she think I have a date? What have I done differently today when leaving the office than I normally do? Then she knew. It was in the air. The young guy next to her knew something. Had she looked at him without knowing, brushed a shoulder in passing?

Teague's voice on the phone had sounded tired. Tight. She realized now she wished it had sounded differently. She knew they were all done. If the first fiasco hadn't sealed it, then the go-round with Roland had. Teague, god bless him, had principles. All the same, she wondered if he sometimes thought about her in the same way she thought about him. She could still see him, shaving in her bathroom before they were to go out, his hair damp, his nice arms, his always shy smile. When he saw her watching, he paused, razor in hand, and said: How would you feel about a handlebar mustache?

That was a time when they'd not made it out the door after all.

She wondered: With the right words, the right music, the right number of drinks, weren't all former intimates just a split second from chucking decorum and morality?

And now here was Teague, spotting her from the hostess stand and walking toward her, his face as tight and drawn as his voice had sounded two hours before. After the greeting there was an awkward moment when he didn't know quite what to do next: a kiss on the cheek, a handshake, a standing hug of a sitting person? To put the moment to a merciful end, she offered up a hand, and Teague, looking like hell, looking grateful, took it, clasped it, really, then took it with both hands, saying, thank you for meeting me, I really appreciate it.

They didn't stay long at the bar. Teague asked if she minded getting a table in the back and she said okay. As they walked past, the young lawyer at the bar gave her the smile again.

They were seated next to the large plate-glass window that looked out onto Broadway and the honky-tonks and guitar stores and pawnshops of downtown. Teague ordered a beer, which he rarely drank, and she guessed this meant he was driving back to Glennville from here.

So, said Teague, how are you?

I'm fine. How are you?

When she asked the question, she'd meant to ask it neutrally, but somehow she'd managed to emphasize the *you*. Somehow she managed to convey what she'd meant not to, namely that she'd heard Teague might be in trouble, and that looking at him now with the dark bags under his eyes and the disheveled state of his hair confirmed the rumors.

Said Teague: I've been better.

She felt herself nodding and tried to scramble for something to say.

Teague said: I guess you've been hearing about the mess up in Glennville?

Yes, she said. Just what's in the paper. It doesn't look good for Roland.

No, said Teague. It doesn't look good for Roland.

She fought the urge to ask how Roland was. The man across from her didn't look in the mood for shared sympathies.

Well, I'm sorry to hear that, she said. And I'm not prying, but I really do hope that none of this is causing you any trouble.

Teague let go with a quick, flinty laugh. A little, he said. Maybe a little.

The waiter came and delivered the drinks. Teague lit a cigarette and then held the lighter for her when she pulled one out for herself. Teague flicked the lighter shut with a rapid flip of his wrist, took a sip of his beer, then gazed out the window at a day moving into dusk. The silence now was less awkward than it should have been. She realized that Teague was in some very deep water. Everything about him showed a man about to lose his way. The rueful laugh, the admission of being in trouble. This wasn't the Teague she knew.

She thought: He looks like a man who could do anything. He looks like a man who could harm himself.

She said: Teague, you look tired. I mean really tired. You need to get some sleep.

Teague nodded.

Are you driving back to Glennville tonight? I don't think you ought to.

I've got to.

Get a hotel. Get a good night's sleep, then head out first thing in the morning.

Teague smiled. I didn't tell anybody in Glennville that I was coming down here.

She nodded. Teague as loose cannon, that was a first. He'd been a sort of wreck when they began their long and painful breakup, especially after that sorry business with Montgomery. But then it had been more confusion and anger. Not this cornered, hungry look she saw now.

Teague said: I came down to talk to some folks who I thought might be able to help.

Could they?

Yes.

Are they?

No. Not as things stand now.

She had a pretty good idea who *some folks* might be. That he wouldn't help was no surprise to her. She figured she was one of the few wrong people he'd ever got mixed up with. But he'd been young then and not yet a known entity. He'd never make that kind of mistake again.

Then the last part of what Teague said hit her. *Not as things stand now.* That was it. Teague had an ace in the hole. *She* was the ace. Whatever trouble Teague was in, she could get him out of. And her stomach went light at the thought.

She said: I can't imagine you doing anything that could get you into serious trouble. Maybe this will all pass over.

I don't think so.

She thought: Teague knows something about Roland that they want him to tell and Teague is not the type to tell. But they have something on him. And the only way to stay out of trouble and not to spill is get help from the most powerful man in the state. Who won't help. Unless his hand is forced.

So those were the options: spill what you know on Roland or blackmail Montgomery. Either option meant the end of Mike Teague as she knew him and as the world knew him. The third option, she guessed, was prison.

She said: If there's anything I can do to help, Teague, let me know. Anything. Just say the word.

Teague closed his eyes and creased his lips in a thin, sad line of a smile.

I mean it. Whatever I can do to help, I will.

When he opened his eyes, they were watery and weak-looking. He put his head down and looked at the cigarettes smoking slowly in the ashtray, the smoke spiraling toward the ceiling in barely visible wisps. He stayed like that for what seemed a long time, the watery eyes focused on some middle distance between cigarette smoke and she knew not what. The waiter approached and then backed away without Teague seeing. The noise from the bar sounded like static from a TV left on after channels went off the air. She noticed the music on the stereo for the first time, the faint trill of a jazz song. A couple walked by and the woman smiled at her, but when she looked over at Teague, the smile left her face and she hurried on by. Teague looked at the beer bottle in his hand. He fingered the label and picked at it a bit with his nail. He cleared his throat.

He looked over his shoulder absently for the waiter, then out the window again. With his head still turned, he reached up and began reflexively straightening the knot in his tie. He cleared his throat again and ran his hand through his hair.

When he finally turned in her direction, she was looking at a different man.

Said Teague: I owe you an apology for that day at Rooney's. I was very rude and I'm sorry about it.

She waved him off. No, she said, that was my fault. That wasn't one of my prouder moments.

Teague shook his head a little side to side, as if clearing out the last of some nagging cobwebs. He smiled faintly, a man contemplating a notion he found ridiculous that he'd once taken seriously.

She thought: That's it. If the bitter pill has to be swallowed, it has to be swallowed.

Said Teague: I just want you to know that I've always had a lot of respect for you. That never changed in all the years.

Well thank you, she said.

And you're as beautiful as ever.

Go on, she said. Do go on.

I could, you know.

Thank you, Teague.

Then he was standing up to leave. He reached to stub his cigarette, then came across the table to her. He bent down and kissed her on the cheek. Then he was walking out the door and across the street, and from the table in front of the plate-glass window, she watched him walk, that same long stride, that same smooth gait, down Broadway toward his car, and Glennville, and whatever was waiting for him there.

One End of the Bargain

Jan was upstairs watching television in bed when she saw the headlights in the driveway. Not long after came the slam of the back door. She threw on her robe and, as she did so, checked the clock. It was nearly ten. When she got downstairs, her husband was at the refrigerator, pulling out meat and condiments for a sandwich. She was about to speak when he turned and said, I'm sorry I didn't call.

Where were you?

I drove to Nashville.

To Nashville?

I thought I needed to talk to some people. I thought there might be a few people down there who could help out.

She came around the island that separated the breakfast nook from the kitchen. She nudged him out of the way and began making the sandwich. Why don't you pour me a glass of wine? she said.

I don't mind making the sandwich.

Just get me a glass of wine. There's an open bottle in the fridge.

He went to the refrigerator and got the bottle. He took two glasses from the cabinet and filled them both, then set one on the counter in front of where she was working. Then he stood there watching. Go, sit down, she said. I know you've got to be tired.

Her husband sat down on one of the stools at the island. She waited for him to go on, to tell her more about his spontaneous, or seemingly spontaneous, trip to Nashville. But he said nothing.

She said: I saw the phone.

Oh yeah. I'd forgotten about that. It wouldn't stop ringing.

She started to pursue'this a bit further, then didn't. She said: Do you want chips with this?

No thanks.

A pickle?

No, he said, just the sandwich will be fine. Thank you.

She placed the plate with the sandwich in front of her husband, then reached for the glass of wine on the counter. Then she walked to the table at the breakfast nook and said, why don't you sit over here with me? I want to hear about your day.

With this invitation, he took the sandwich and wine and joined her at the table. He said, there's not much to tell. I didn't get much done.

Who'd you meet with?

The governor.

And?

And nothing. He says he can't help.

Could he?

Why, hell yes.

Did you tell him what was going on, what they're accusing you of and what they want you to tell them?

He knew all that. They know exactly what's going on up here.

Then why won't he help?

Too hot. Thinks it'll jeopardize his future plans.

I never liked him.

Teague smiled, a rare occurrence these days. I remember, he said.

Eddie Haskell, she said, taking a sip of her wine.

Teague laughed. A rarer occurrence.

It began to dawn on her that the man at the kitchen table was different than the man she saw yesterday, the man she'd seen for the past few weeks. Different than the man who'd torn the phone from the wall. He looked tired, beyond tired. But he didn't look whipped. He didn't look scared. She thought: Something has happened in Nashville. He's found a way out of this like I knew he would.

She could feel herself smiling. Did something good happen in Nashville? Something you're not telling me about?

Teague looked at the last bit of sandwich in his hand, then decided he didn't want it after all. He placed it on the plate then pushed the plate out of the way. He reached for his wine and took another sip. He stood up. That wine tastes good, he said. I'm going to have a little more. Can I top you off?

She nodded yes. When he came back with the bottle, he topped off her glass first, then his own. She said: Did you see anyone else in Nashville?

No one important, he said. I mainly went to see your good friend the governor.

And he's not going to help us?

Right.

Did you find someone who could? Do you have good news? You seem happy.

Teague was again sitting across from her. He smiled. He looked like the man she'd fallen in love with so many years before. The man who knew how the world worked and how to operate in it.

Yes? she said.

I didn't find anyone that could help us, he said. And I can't say that I have good news. But I have made a decision. A final one. And it's one I can live with. So yeah, I feel better. I know how I'm going to play it.

She felt her throat go tight as he spoke. You're not going to cooperate, are you?

No.

She stood up from the table and walked without thinking to the sink. She put her half-filled wine glass on the counter, then grabbed it again and poured it out furiously. Opening the dishwasher with a jerk, she jammed the glass in, then slammed the door shut. She stood in the middle of the kitchen and said: I can't believe you.

He looked at her: Yes you can.

You owe them nothing. Nothing but scorn.

There is some scorn, he said. Trust me, I'm mad as hell.

All they want to know about is Senator Kirkwood. Just tell them what you know. Tell them it's not your name on that loan document. What do you owe Kirkwood? He's a crook. You know it as well as I do.

Her husband said: Senator Kirkwood does some good things for his district. He gets stuff done that no one else can.

So you're going to jail for him? So he can keep helping his district? That's insane. You hardly know the man.

It's got nothing to do with Kirkwood. And really, it's got nothing to do with Roland or J. T. Cole.

She was glaring at her husband. He was going to prison for a bunch of crooks who couldn't care less what happened to him.

When you pay me, he said, when you hire me on, you're not just buying my expertise. A lot of folks have expertise. What you're buying with me is my silence. That's why I charge what I do. That's why people want to hire me. If you can't trust my silence, no matter the circumstances, then I've sold you a false bill of goods. I'm charging for silence. That's my end of the bargain. And I've decided to hold up my end of the bargain just like I always have.

She felt tears welling up in her eyes, but fought them back. He was looking at her with kindness, with empathy. His voice throughout had been soft and even.

He said: I know this hurts you more than it does me. I know you're a part of this too. I know this is hard for you and embarrassing and everything else. I'm truly sorry. I hope you know that.

The tears came now. To stop herself from thinking, she said: What about your parents?

They'll be fine.

They stayed like that for a moment, then Teague laughed, a small, private laugh.

He said: Did I ever tell you about the time I got caught smoking?

She shook her head no.

He said: Hollis Raintree had snuck some of his brother's cigarettes and dared me to smoke one with him. So of course we get caught and sent to the principal's office and they call our parents. This was in grade school. So after school, I just dallied and dawdled as much as I could. I hadn't been whipped often, but I thought this might qualify. Well, I finally head home just before dark and sure enough there's Dad sitting in the den when I come in the door reading the paper. Before he could say anything, I went over and said, I'm sorry for getting in trouble, Dad. I'm sorry if I embarrassed you.

Her husband stopped here and smiled again. You haven't heard this?

She'd stopped crying. Again she shook her head no.

Dad didn't even look up from the paper. He said, you didn't embarrass me. You can't embarrass me. What you did was embarrass yourself. You're responsible for your own actions now. You're old enough to know right from wrong. If you want to embarrass yourself, have at it. But it's impossible for you to embarrass me.

She felt the beginnings of a smile form on her face. She realized she was forcing herself to do it, that to do it would make her husband feel better.

I'm sure your father will feel the same as mine, he said gently, smiling.

Oh yes, she said, laughing and crying a little at the same time. Of course he will. You'll never make it to prison, he'll kill you first. He's got a good name in this town, you know.

Oh, said Teague, standing up, I do know that. I knew what I was getting from the very beginning when I married the emperor's daughter.

He walked over, but stopped when they were face to face.

He said: Did you know what you were getting?

She said nothing as he put his arms around her. But putting her face against his chest, she moved her head up and down.

Thanksgiving Week

J.T. stood at the stove prepared to flip the eggs he was frying. The biscuits were warming in the oven as the sausage cooled on a plate spread over with a paper towel. On the kitchen table sat a bowl of sliced cantaloupe and honeydew melon. You could never tell when Corrine wanted to eat heavy or light, so he'd prepared for either occasion. He'd already fed the boys and seen them off to school. The older boy could drive now so Corrine's days of playing chauffeur were basically at an end.

He'd used the pretext of fetching the paper as the rationale for following the boys out to the driveway in his robe. That they had to go to school where everyone was talking about their father and uncle and had not once complained about it, well, it all left him a little emotional. The time had gone by in a blur. He'd missed their formative years, that was all there was to it, and now they were more men than boys. At least with Sarah he'd not been so busy when she was in early adolescence. But with his sons, what they got was a kiss some nights before bed and the occasional weekend on the boat.

Despite their crazy parents, despite the spell when he'd driven Corrine about plumb crazy, they'd hung in there. Good grades, pretty good ball players on the school teams. Not a lick of discipline problems. That was Corrine. She'd done it solo.

As he set a plate over the skillet to keep the eggs warm, he couldn't stop the memory of that morning's wave goodbye from his sons. The elder had saluted, a quick snap of the hand, a light gesture trying to make his father smile as he prepared to go in reverse all the way to the road simply for the fun of it. The younger had waved slowly all the way down the drive. He hadn't smiled for the longest time, then seemed to realize that what his father needed to see was a smile. J.T. could see him muster it up, the smile, as sleepy as he was, for the younger was a night owl like his mother and wouldn't really wake up till noon. J.T. realized it as he was doing it: he's faking a smile, he's forcing himself to smile. The boys are worried about me.

And all these last few weeks he'd been getting up to get their breakfast and get them off to school because he was worried about them. Or so he told himself. Turning off the eye on the stove, he acknowledged the real reason for his new morning schedule. He needed the boys. Needed their vitality. Their moxie. Their teenage cool. He needed time with people who didn't look at him differently than they had before.

And his sons had seen through him.

He checked the biscuits, almost done, and lowered the temperature of the oven. When he got upstairs, Corrine was in the bathroom, so he went to the window to look out at the driveway and yard. The yard had been raked once in late October but could use another go-round. The brown leaves windblown against the trees and on the driveway and scattered about the lawn wouldn't do. He wasn't going to let the house go, or the grounds either, for that matter. They were going to keep up appearances. There'd be no white flags raised.

This thought cheered him. He'd call the lawn man and they'd get the damn lawn raked today. And the sun rising over the trees like the head of a yellow cat promised an unusually bright November day. He thought: I'm going flying today. A beautiful day for flying. This cheered him as well and he said, Corrine, your eggs are getting cold downstairs.

Through the closed bathroom door, with water running from the sink, she said, I'm not eating any eggs today. My god, J.T., are you trying to fatten me up for market?

He smiled at this and came to the bathroom door. Knocking lightly, he said, do you care if I come in?

I'm not dressed, came the reply.

Say no more, he said, opening the door and coming up behind his wife. She was standing at the sink, nude but for her house slippers, rinsing her face. He placed his hands on her hips and pressed up against her, kissing lightly about the neck. Corrine turned off the water as he did so and stood up full in front of the mirror. Her eyes were closed as he kissed along her neck and shoulders. When she opened her eyes and smiled at him in the mirror, he stood back a bit to get a better look of the whole of the backside. He patted that backside.

Said Corrine: You see anything back there you like?

You mean this little troublemaker right here?

She gave the little troublemaker a quick sashaying motion as reply.

I'm already looking forward to my conjugal visits.

That's not funny, she said.

They were looking at each other in the mirror. He realized he'd overplayed his hand. He said, I'm just kidding. I'm not going anywhere.

Corrine didn't reply but continued to look at him in the mirror, wanting to be further convinced.

He said, let's just let the lawyers do their thing.

With this she reached behind with both hands and pulled him closer. They were still back to front and watching themselves in the mirror. She began to undo the sash to his robe. She said: I'd do it. I'd come for conjugal visits. Every time we could.

J.T. bent down to kiss her again on the neck. He said: I never doubted it for a minute.

He got to the office and parked in the cool damp of the parking garage, dreading the trek from here to his office. The looks of employees and customers that greeted him now were getting harder and harder to take. In the immediate days after the raid, he'd come through the main lobby as was his custom. For a week straight, the security man in the lobby had walked him to the elevator with the same daily question: How's it looking, Mr. Cole? When will we know if our money's safe?

On the day after the news came out that Valley Industrial was insolvent, the security guard kept his seat when J.T. entered the lobby, hadn't spoken, hadn't bothered to look at him.

When he entered the empty elevator it was with a sigh of relief. He pressed the button and hoped for a solitary trip to his floor. He didn't know how they'd let things get this screwed up. You couldn't just keep doubling up. It was crazy to think your luck would hold indefinitely. It was actuarially impossible. He saw himself, the self he was just months ago, and thought, who was that guy? Who the hell did he think he was? Who the hell thinks they can roll the dice indefinitely? How much money did you need?

But it wasn't about the money, really. It was the action. They simply couldn't push themselves away from the table.

Now they were busted. Bankruptcy, sooner or later, was inevitable.

You could come back from being busted. Plenty of men had. Most of his friends in construction and oil had gone bust, had made and lost several fortunes. But that was a different field, a different game. Bankers weren't supposed to be wildcatters.

Halfway up to the executive suites, a young man got on the elevator. This was the floor where the architectural firm was. The young man had a smile on his face when the doors opened, as if he were thinking of something humorous from the night before or some joke about to be played on a friend. But as soon as he saw J.T. the smile vanished and he looked at his shoes. Morning, J.T. said.

The man kept his eyes averted as he pushed the elevator button. When the elevator opened a moment later, he got off hurriedly and didn't look back.

J.T. wondered: Did he lose his money too? His parents?

When he got to his own floor, he was thinking, I'm going to have to stop coming in here. I can sign the papers for the lawyers from the house. I can return my calls from the house. Then he thought: that's the coward's way out. You've got to take what's coming to you. You earned it, it's yours.

He spoke to Sally, his secretary, and got his messages and mail. She offered to bring him a cup of coffee, but he declined. He'd get it himself. It was Monday of Thanksgiving week, so he told her, you just plan on taking Wednesday off. I know you're traveling to Arkansas, so you might as well get on the road early. We can get by here without you for a day.

Sally thanked him. She'd not invested in Valley Industrial and her checks still cleared, so she could still look him in the eye.

He walked to the coffee room and poured himself a mug, wandered over to the open door of the conference room. Phone calls and mail, mail and phone calls. And all of it lawyers. What of it couldn't wait?

He found the plush carpet and picture windows of the conference room comforting, quiet and serene, and walked to the corner window that looked out over East Glennville. This was the industrial side of town and the working portion of the river, the same view he'd had in the FBG building. His new office faced west, toward downtown, the university, the great sprawl of the suburban middle class, and offered, cornered as it was, perhaps the best view of the river in the city. Better even than Roland's, who claimed to prefer his own serenely perched four stories lower.

He'd call Roland and see if he wanted to go for a spin in the plane. They could fly over to Asheville and get some chili at the airport diner. They'd done that once and met an old-timer who regaled them with tales of WWII pilots from the area and the stunts they'd pulled when they were fresh back from the Pacific and not readily adjusting to civilian life. It was a beautiful flight over the mountains, and the landing at the small airfield was still pretty tight, you had to bank it around the rim of the mountains and come in with an elongated U-turn. It was his favorite place to land and the day had bloomed perfect for flying.

He found that he'd been staring at the William Glenn Fort below, from whence sprang modern Glennville. He tried to imagine what this area must have looked like then. How forested? What kinds of trees? What route was there to the river? What route heading over the mountains toward Asheville and the North Carolina piedmont? It was the only frontier settlement for two hundred miles and he thought how large it must have looked, how impressive. To see it from the river or to come across it on horseback, nothing but wilderness and then this two-story house surrounded by the twelve-foot timber walls of the fort, must have been quite a sight. One would have to think: This here is a new deal. This thing here is going to redefine the landscape.

He could conceptualize how the terrain might have looked, but not visualize it. Try as he might, he couldn't erase the highway looping around the rough-cut walls and sentry posts, the innumerable faceless buildings and businesses that dotted that terrain around the timber walls, the cars zipping heedlessly by. It looked old and small. Forgotten. He checked the parking lot for cars and saw a couple. Often school buses would be parked there, it was a favorite local field trip, but there were none today.

A depressing sight.

Above the fort, above the industrial city, spread the blue sky of a day not meant to be spent indoors. Great Thanksgiving weather. Weather this time of year so hard to predict, some Thanksgivings a beautiful fall day like this, others freezing cold, with the crunch of frozen ground under your boots.

When he was a boy, his father had traded out a calf for a little 410 shotgun that Jet Peters's wife once used and had surprised him with it on his ninth birthday that August. The following Thanksgiving, he and Roland were allowed to go hunting with their father for the first time. J.T. could carry his gun, but unloaded. Roland would trudge along empty-handed.

They were hunting on Duncan Wainright's land about ten miles out of town. He and Roland were dressed like their father and Jet. They looked like hunters, he noticed that first thing. Canvas pants to keep the burrs at bay. The much-coveted canvas hunting coats with the game pouch sewn in the back and the big double pocket up front for the shells. Pockets now filled with shells for their daddy and Jet.

The field was wet with frosted dew and the world was still in that grey milky time before winter sunrise. Despite the cold, he felt happy and attentive, eyes glued to the backsides of the dogs as they walked, anxious to see them point. Ahead was a stand of blackjack oak, which made the shooting tougher, but often proved thick with birds. The tops of wooden posts could be seen before the woods, a fence that'd once marked this field from the others. He knew quail often nestled in beside a row of fence where they had easy access to food in the field and also the protection of the woods should they need it. So more and more his eyes went toward the stand of trees, half a mile or so in the distance.

He wanted nothing more than to fire his gun, fire it for real, at a covey of quail taking flight. Roland had asked to carry his gun and he said, okay, if Daddy says okay. Their father and Jet spoke rarely, only the occasional call to a dog of *whoa*. When he'd asked his father about Roland holding the gun, his father nodded and said, no pointing, though, Roland. You hold the gun in the proper position, like a hunter.

As they walked heavy-legged behind the men, he couldn't help but watch the intense look on Roland's face. He marched directly behind their father, directly in his shadow. Their mother had long teased him about aping their daddy, and the truth was this mimicry bothered J.T. a bit. He wondered if perhaps Roland didn't do it simply to curry favor. But now, out of their father's sight, he was mimicking not just his walk but the way he held the gun, higher than Jet Peters did, tight and alert. Jet, he noticed, watched only the bird dogs. His father, on the other hand, kept the dogs in his peripheral vision, his eyes scanning for a covey that might be spooked out from afar, before they'd been flushed proper. Now here was Roland scanning the horizon as he walked.

He thought: Brother's not copying Daddy to get Daddy's attention. He doesn't even know he's doing it.

And then Roland had looked at him, almost as if he knew he was thinking about him, and smiled. It was a smile to say *thank you for sharing your gun,* a smile to say, *this is fun, isn't it?*

Not long after Roland returned the gun, when they were almost to the fence line before the woods, Little Pearl began running with her nose to the ground, her slim, elegant body zigzagging across the field. Daddy said, I believe Little Pearl's struck bird.

As she got closer to the fence line she slowed to a creep, sweeping her head and raising her legs slowly and very high, like a small child sneaking up on someone.

Then she froze on point, a sudden statue, right front paw frozen in midair, tail an iron rod behind her. Head high. Ears pricked.

J.T. felt like he hadn't taken a breath in a long time. He'd never seen anything so wondrous as a dog frozen on point. He thought he knew Little Pearl, thought he knew all their dogs, but this was something he'd never imagined. Roland was somewhere behind him, but he couldn't see him or hear him. His father and Jet walked slowly past Little Pearl toward the fencerow.

And then the quails flushed, an eruption in the lank brown weeds, and it seemed for a moment as if the earth below their feet had taken flight. In later years, he'd never hear a helicopter without thinking of a flushed covey, the whirring, choppy rhythm steady and sudden at the same time. The guns boomed in front of him, then the echo off the woods and the mountains a mile behind them. Roland was standing beside him now.

His father told the dogs to *hunt dead*. He said this in a normal speaking voice, but it sounded like another shot in the sudden silence. Little Pearl remained on point. His father said: Little Pearl, hunt dead. Still she held the point, her white head with the lone spot of lemon, tail like a quill in the air.

Daddy said: Jet, there's more quail in there.

And right as he spoke came the second round. It was smaller than the first and J.T. could pick out individual birds now. He watched their father pick one, sight it, follow it for the briefest moment, and then the gun's report.

Little Pearl, hunt dead.

And only then did the dog head off, nose to ground, tail swishing behind her.

Daddy smiled then. He walked closer. Behind him the sun had just begun to rise over the blackjack oak. His boots crunched as he came. He said: You boys just saw something special. You know what I'm talking about?

J.T. saw Roland nod his head. He nodded too. He said: Little Pearl.

That's right. Little Pearl is special. She always wants to do her best. She doesn't know how to do anything but her best.

J.T. nodded. He thought Roland was probably nodding too, but didn't look over to see.

Daddy said: For people, it's a little tougher. No person is always at their best. What's important is that you try to do your best. And to know when you are and when you aren't doing your best. That's what's important. Being truthful to yourself.

He stood there looking at his young father. He'd forgotten that it was cold and that the new gun felt heavy in his hand. He understood that Little Pearl was special, that she was the best. But that his father didn't love Little Pearl because she was the best, but because she always gave her best. His father was smiling at them. J.T. could tell that he was proud of them and thought they probably tried to do their best, like Little Pearl. He could tell that his father enjoyed their company. He could tell also, and this is what left him feeling a bit light-headed for the rest of the day, that his father knew that they wouldn't always do their best. But that he would love them anyway.

His father took a knee between them and placed the butt of his gun on the ground. J.T. could feel his father's hunting vest rubbing up against his own. There were burrs on the thigh of his pants. In nearly a whisper, he said, now watch Little Pearl gather those birds.

He turned slowly from the window and walked back to his office. He was dialing Corrine before he knew what he wanted to say and when she answered, he said, are you sure you won't go flying with me today?

I don't know why you bother asking.

I'm a persistent person, he said.

Delusional is more like it.

You want me to pick anything up on the way home? What are we taking to the farm for Thanksgiving?

I think I've got it all. You might pick me up a little brown sugar for the sweet potatoes, if you're just wanting to run by the grocery. Otherwise, I can get it tomorrow.

I'll get it, said J.T. Anything else? We got milk? Bread?

We're stocked up.

All right. Well I guess I'll be honking at you here in a bit when I fly over.

I'll be waiting, she said.

I might just parachute out and land in the yard.

Go ahead, you crazy thing. There's nothing you can do to surprise me.

Nothing? Not a thing? You've seen it all in twenty-four blissful years of matrimony?

Well if you're home on time and remember the brown sugar, that would be a surprise.

Now that's just sassy. You been drinking that sassafras tea again?

I got to go, J.T. I've got squash casserole in the oven.

I'll be home by six. As a special surprise.

I won't be holding my breath.

You lay off that sassafras tea though.

Said Corrine: Honey, I just brewed me a fresh pot.

Then she was hanging up the phone and J.T. was grinning, the receiver still in his hand. He punched the button for Roland's extension. When Roland answered, he said, let's go flying.

Roland laughed.

Let's head over to Asheville and get some of that chili.

I can't do it. I'm supposed to meet with the lawyers later on today.

Oh fuck the lawyers. Let em earn their money for a change.

I can't go. I wish I could. It's a good day for it.

What's the weather supposed to be like for Thanksgiving? This going to hold out?

I think it's going to cool down some, but it's supposed to be clear.

You want to go hunting?

Sure. Let's get the boys and go.

I'll call Jet. He was after me this summer about going. Thinks he's found himself a bird dog.

Thanksgiving morning or Friday?

I don't care. Maybe keep with tradition?

Suits me. It's funny you called. I've been thinking about Daddy all day.

Me too. Thanksgiving, I guess.

I'm sure that's what it is.

You got a birthday coming up too. Hard to believe you'll be forty-eight.

Nice try.

Oh, forty-seven. That's right. You got shells? Or anything else you need? I might run a few errands this evening. I can run by Hoskin's while I'm out by the airport.

Yeah, get me some shells if it's no trouble.

No trouble. You sure you can't sneak out.

I probably could, but I'd just as soon wrap this shit up before we head down to Mother's.

All right, I understand. I'll see you down there Wednesday night then.

I'm looking forward to it.

So am I.

He placed the receiver in its cradle and started for the elevator. En route he decided not to come in the next day and said his goodbyes and Happy Thanksgiving to Sally as he walked past her desk. Over his shoulder he asked her to call the airport and tell them to get his plane ready. He punched the button for the elevator, then thought better of it and opened the door to the stairs. He made it down the thirty-three stories at a dizzying pace, passing one person heading up from the second floor who went sideways in the stairwell as if in alarm at his approach. Howdy, he said, slowing, then coming to a stop. He was a little short of breath and realized he had an idiotic grin on his face. The man gave a brief nod in response then J.T. again was on his way. He thought, I must look like a kid who just got out of school for summer vacation.

In the car he loosened his tie, then took it off completely and flung it in the backseat. He fiddled with the radio until he found an up-tempo song he liked. He pulled onto Franklin then took a quick left onto Brewer. As he made his way down the steep incline, he glanced into his rearview mirror. What he saw was the shimmering silvery green of his brother's building reflecting off of the golden-tinted windows of his own, quick flashes of color and light like sun flashing sea. He found the image briefly optimistic, then a little poignant. Then he decided to think of it no more. And as he passed the empty World's Fair site on his right, he didn't bother to look at the work crew disassembling a pavilion, the still-turning Rubik's Cube, the dull gaze of Helios peering out over the city.

At Glennville Island Airport, he drove directly onto the tarmac, where his plane waited. The lineman, a boy of eighteen or nineteen, stood on one of the wheels cleaning the window on the pilot's side. He waved when J.T. honked and then J.T. drove the car past the rows of hangars until he found his own. His was the only plane on the tarmac and as he walked to the small terminal, he thought: Everybody else got off early. The runway with its huge painted numbers looked like a concrete football field before him and the orange wind sock hung limp on its pole. He checked the weather from the phone in the lobby and since it was clear from here to Asheville, he didn't bother to file a flight plan. He poked his head in the pilot's lounge to see if anyone was playing poker, he thought he might sit in for a few hands when he got back, but the lounge was empty. Too nice out to be shuffling cards.

He bought a Coke and candy bar from the vending machines then walked out the back door and onto the tarmac. The lineman was still standing on the wheel and when he saw J.T. out of the corner of his eye, he popped open the door before hopping down. J.T. had seen this lineman at least once before and looked at the name tag on his coveralls before saying, thank you, Luke.

The boy nodded and smiled. It all looks good, Mr. Cole. I believe you're ready to roll.

Good, good. I appreciate it.

Hadn't seen you in a while, the boy said, shielding his eyes from the sun.

J.T. moved a little toward the plane to get the boy's eyes out of the sun and the boy shifted accordingly. Yeah, he said, I know it. It's a sin to own a plane and not get to fly it any more than I do.

Especially one as nice as this one.

You like it?

Sure I do. But I love that Dassault Falcon 20.

Yeah, that's a nice one. But it's primarily for business, you know. And it gets old always having to line up a pilot. This is the way to go. Just hop in and fly when the mood strikes.

He thought the boy might have winced a bit at the mention of business. But he couldn't be sure.

I bet that Falcon's cool though.

It's not bad, J.T. said smiling.

The boy nodded, smiling away. He seemed to be jetting off somewhere in the Falcon.

Said J.T.: I was wondering how the Fly-In went last month.

Pretty good. Had a couple fly up from Texas.

That's a long way to fly for a pancake breakfast.

Hey, they're good pancakes, the boy said smiling.

I know it. And I shouldn't be talking. I'm fixing to fly to Asheville for some chili. Come on and go with me. I'll have you back in a couple of hours.

I'd love to. Got to work though. Mr. Larkin might not like it if I was to sneak off.

Luke, life's too short to always be following the rules.

The boy's face betrayed him. He stammered a bit before spitting out: I wish I could, Mr. Cole.

J.T. smiled. People were used to seeing him on the news and in the paper. But to see him in person was like viewing a boogey man not that scary, a ghost not quite dead. The boy before him was nearly blushing.

J.T. said: I know you got to work, Luke. I was just pulling your leg.

The boy made an effort toward a smile.

You're taking flying lessons, aren't you?

Yes sir.

They ain't cheap, are they?

No sir, the boy said, smiling now, relieved. They're right pricey.

J.T. reached into his wallet. He had four one-hundred-dollar bills and a twenty. He slipped out a hundred and held it out to the boy. Here, he said, this will help a little with the lessons.

The boy didn't move. He seemed to be worrying that his comment was being interpreted as a tip solicitation. Or perhaps that the money offered was of the illegal variety.

Luke, he said, you don't have to fly with me. But you do have to take the tip. That's nonnegotiable. Buy your mom a turkey, throw it out the window, I don't care. But I do wish you'd take it. I appreciate your hard work around here.

The boy took the bill with a shy smile and quickly tucked it into the breast pocket of his coveralls. Behind him the languid orange wind sock was vivid against the grey of the airfield. Vivid too against the unkempt and colorless fields that bordered the runway down to the river and the embankment jutting out over the water. On the other side of the river the trees were either grey or brown-leaved and the brilliance of the sky seemed incongruous in comparison. It was unusually warm and J.T. took off his windbreaker. It'd be cool in the plane once he was up there flying, but he'd rather be a little cool than the opposite.

Luke, he said, I'm going to bring you a quart of the best chili you ever had.

Then, holding on to the wing, he took one long step up and was sitting in the pilot's seat.

The Lineman's Perspective

Luke was walking toward the row of T-hangars nearest the terminal. When things were a little slow, it was his habit to quickly sweep the portal when a plane had just been taken from it. Occasionally he'd even bring the hose out. The plane was idling smoothly behind him, a soothing sound. He hoped someday to own his own, but knew that was a far stretch down the road. The only sound he preferred to an idling airplane engine was the sound of a plane taxiing down the runway, the ever increasing hum of wheels, less and less bumpy-sounding as she went, followed by the sudden silence of takeoff.

So, though he'd heard and seen twenty-plus takeoffs on this day, he couldn't resist poking his head out from the One Hangar when he heard the plane begin to taxi in earnest. As it came to the end of the runway, he heard that lovely moment when tires are no longer rubbing pavement. But then another sound as the plane came over the river. A quick cough, sudden but weak.

For a moment there was no sound. Even when the plane hit the water, it was surprisingly quiet. There seemed not another person alive on the planet, so quiet was it now.

And then, without knowing he was doing it, he was sprinting down the runway and toward the river and the shiny wing of a plane that was about to disappear.

Falling Action

Early One Morning, December

Roland sat in the reception area, waiting for his attorney to arrive. He'd met the receptionist, keys in hand, at the door and walked in with her. She'd seemed a little confused by his presence, seeing as it was only eight-thirty and the office wasn't due to open until nine. I'm a little early, he'd offered. In fact, he'd been sitting in his car since eight, with the motor running on this cold December day, and the exhaust from the tailpipe curling up in the rearview as he checked for signs of life in the empty office building. Now he sat, mug of coffee next to him on the end table, flipping through a news weekly but unable to concentrate enough to actually read. He checked the clock on the wall for the twentieth time then the watch on his wrist. It was the same watch Teague had recommended he not wear in the commercial and thinking of this made him feel a little rueful. He'd not slept at all that night and had finally just given up and gotten out of bed, afraid he was keeping Libby awake with his tossing and turning and trips to the bathroom for water. As he made his way down the steps, carrying his suit and shoes to dress in the kitchen, he'd already made his decision.

What part J.T.'s death had in his decision, he didn't know. He wondered what part of his sitting here now could be chalked up to simple, base superstition, his brother's accident a harbinger of ill will, some sort of cosmic payback for unchecked ambition, unchecked pride. He didn't consider himself a superstitious man, but here he was, tossing the idea around as he'd done off and on since he'd first gotten the call from the airport. Why they called him first and not Corrine, he didn't know, other than that antiquated notion of sparing the women from bad news for as long as possible.

So it had fallen to him to tell Corrine. As soon as he got off the phone with the man from Island Airport, he told Libby, then out the door he went. It didn't seem right to tell Libby and then leave her alone like that, but he felt he had to tell Corrine right away before it had sunk in, while he still had the courage. Seeing his wife's face drop like that had been enough. He'd called over his shoulder, I'll call you from J.T.'s. We'll get together over there in a bit or I'll bring Corrine and the kids over here. I'll call you and we'll figure it out.

Said Libby to his back: I'm just so sorry, Roland.

He nodded without stopping. He'd tell Corrine as quickly as possible before she heard it on the radio or from someone else. He would not think of his brother or the absence of his brother until he'd done his duty. On some level, he felt the absence already, felt it expanding within him, expanding throughout the world he inhabited. On some level, the thought crossed his mind: First Daddy, now J.T. I've no more men around me.

When he got to the house, one of the garage doors was still up. The boys had probably forgotten to close it behind them. He saw his nephew's car in the garage, then Corrine's.

He thought: J.T.'s car is still at the airport.

He found this notion strange and couldn't quite get his mind around it. And then he was knocking on the side door that the family used and entering in the same motion. Corrine had come to greet him and was smiling when she rounded the corner from the den. But when she saw his face, the smiling stopped.

He stood in what they called the mudroom, where the boys were to take off their shoes before entering the house. He'd forgotten to shut the door. He said: Corrine, I've got some bad news.

Corrine said: I knew that damn thing would kill him.

They stood looking at one another. He turned to close the door behind him. When he was again facing Corrine, he had the thought that he ought to go and hug her. Normally this would have been instinctual. A hug was their typical greeting. But something in her face held him back. Then he realized what it was. She's angry, he thought. She's furious.

I should have known that once he straightened his ass out, he'd have to pull something like this.

Roland thought he ought to defend his brother. But then his brain cleared for the first time since the phone call. With Corrine, hurt was anger, anger was hurt.

He said, can I get you anything? Can I do anything?

The questions were ridiculous. He said them for himself, to find some measure of escape from the awful rage across his sister-in-law's face, the awful and undisguised hurt. It hurt him to look at her.

He went to her, wrapped her in his arms, where he could no longer see the rage, but only feel it in her body. He was thinking, why won't she cry? When will she cry?

The cursing came first. That S.O.B. That S.O.B. And then they could cry.

And all the time he was worried the boys would come in before he had the chance to compose himself. He thought it was his duty to tell the nephews, that it would be too hard for Corrine. He was the eldest Cole now, the eldest in the male line. He thought he should be the one, though he dreaded it, dreaded it even more than telling Corrine. It was hard enough losing a father when you were grown, but to be a boy?

She said: Let's sit down. I think I will take some water. Get me some water and tell me what you know then I'll stop crying and tell the boys. The boys are upstairs watching TV.

When he protested and offered to break the news, Corrine only shook her head and said: No, I'm going to tell them. Then I'll call Sarah up at school.

But get me that water first, Roland. I do think I'd like a glass of water.

———

And now Booth Langley, his lawyer, was entering the waiting room, smiling a surprised smile at him, an exaggerated and mock smile of surprise. Why Roland, he said. Come in. Do come in.

Roland sat down in a leather wing chair on one side of an oval coffee table and Booth sat down opposite. You need a refill on that coffee? he said.

Roland shook his head and looked about the table for a coaster.

Said Booth: Just put it on one of those magazines. I don't know where all the coasters get to. I believe the cleaning lady may be starting up her own collection.

Roland placed his mug on a copy of *Field and Stream*. He took a mint from a holiday bowl then couldn't spot a trash can for the wrapper. Booth was sitting across from him, his grey hair left long and a little curly in the back in the style of a more genteel era. It was a moment before he realized that Booth was waiting for him to state his business. I'm sorry, Booth, he said. I'm just over here dillydallying.

Booth waved him off. I've got all the time in the world, he said. What's on your mind?

Let's plead.

Booth took a cigarette from a silver box on the coffee table and searched around in his suit pocket for a lighter. He offered the box to Roland, but he shook his head no. Fishing the lighter out and flicking it in the same motion, he ignited the cigarette and took a long, luxurious puff. He closed his eyes for a brief moment. It's hard to beat the first cigarette of the day, he said.

Roland smiled.

So you're ready to deal?

I am.

You're sure?

Yes.

Do you mind if I ask why?

I don't mind you asking, but I'm not sure I can give you a satisfactory answer. I'd say some of it has to do with J.T. But that's probably not all of it. I haven't been sleeping well. I feel like shit. I don't know. Is a guilty conscience not a good enough reason?

Booth smiled. Depends on what kind of deal you can strike.

That's why I'm here. What kind of deal do you think I can get?

Booth stood up and paced around the room, smoke from the cigarette curling behind him. He said: You want it shucked or unshucked?

Roland smiled despite himself. He hadn't heard that one in years. He wondered: How often do I come across one of us? A man about my age, a successful man, who can dip down to *fixing to* one minute and talk macroeconomics the next. He could name twenty, thirty men across the city who could modulate diction as situation fit, as mood fit. They'd cobbled their way through a college education: GI Bill. Athletic scholarship. Working two jobs. But when they got together, it was a chance to let their hair down and revisit some of the sayings they'd heard on the square and at the barbershop as boys. It was a way, he realized, of keeping that vernacular alive, a code that said, we're in the city now, but you and I both know where we *come* from.

Said Roland: Might as well have it unshucked.

Booth said: Five years minimum. That's a bare-ass minimum. But eight to ten is a realistic possibility.

Even if I say what they want me to say?

You talking the TBI too?

I don't give a rat's ass about the TBI. If they had anything, they'd have already jumped. They're just trying to leverage what the Feds have, right?

I think so.

That Kirkwood business, hey, that's just politics. That's politics Memphis-style and has been for a hundred years. Everybody knows that. The TBI knows that. And the FBI knows that too. TBI is just trying to use this to pin Kirkwood down. He's been a pain in their ass for a decade now. But there was a Kirkwood before Kirkwood. And there'll damn sure be one after he's gone. Am I right?

Yes.

Roland said: Four men were at that first meeting. One of them is dead. Two are me and Kirkwood. And we're not talking. Mike Teague is the fourth. If he was going to talk, and he has every reason to, he would have by now. Teague's not going to talk. I'd bet my life on it.

You might be betting some of it if you try and strike a deal without cutting the TBI in.

With TBI cut in, what's the best deal I can get?

Eight minimum.

And cutting the TBI out?

Five minimum.

I'll wager on those three years. If Teague hasn't talked by now, he's not going to. TBI's got nothing but some bank stock with Kirkwood's name on it. We've got a facsimile of the cashier's check he used to pay for it.

Said Booth: And where that cash came from for the check, you've no way of knowing.

Exactly.

Booth sat down, took another long drag of the cigarette, then stubbed it in the ashtray in front of him. You sure you don't want to take your chances in court? You can't ever tell how a trial will turn out.

I'm sure.

Five years is a long time.

It sure as hell is.

And it could be eight.

I'm not putting my family through any more of this. My brother's dead, my wife's miserable. I'm miserable. Let's take our medicine and move on.

So you're going to admit to bank fraud?

He nodded.

And forging the names?

Yes.

Okay, said Booth. You still want it husk and all?

At this late date? Absolutely.

Have you thought about what it's going to be like afterwards? After you say you're guilty? Your life will never be the same.

It's already not the same.

You'll be a pariah in this town. In the whole state. People won't remember the fair or what you've done downtown. What they'll remember is *bank fraud*. And when you walk down the road, the word crook is going to be on the tip of every tongue. I'm talking about for the rest of your life. That's what's going to happen if you plea-bargain. I just want to make sure you've thought it out. What the cost will be to your wife and kids.

Roland nodded. He pointed toward the silver box with the cigarettes and when Booth nodded, he reached over and took one. Booth passed over his lighter and Roland fired the cigarette. He said: I appreciate it, Booth. I really do. I've thought about it.

Booth nodded.

Then Roland stood up. He said: When you call the special prosecutor, the first thing I want you to say is that Teague didn't do a damn thing.

Booth smiled.

That's the truth.

Said Booth: You seem to think I care what's true and what's not. I'm just here to represent my client.

Fine, said Roland. Good deal. And as soon as you're done with the prosecutor, I want your second call to be to Mike Teague's lawyer.

February

Outside his kitchen window, the grey remnants of the weekend snow lay like rubble from a demolished frozen city. The snow on the cover of the pool had mostly melted and water pooled in a few low spots where the heavy blanket had pulled the tautness slack. He'd have to go out later on, tomorrow maybe, and pull it tight again. It was strange, he thought, how starkly the grey world outside contrasted with the kitchen Jan had recently painted lemon yellow. He'd not liked the color at first, found it hard on the eyes. But in February, when Glennville stayed grey, the sky less a thing overhead than an enveloping presence, he could see the benefits of brightness and light and the promise of spring.

He poured himself another cup of coffee and considered the long walk down the driveway to get the newspaper. What he needed to do was go downtown and get a *New York Times*. That was the way to kill a winter day. Maybe pick up a couple of books at the bookstore. He'd fallen out of the habit of reading and thought it something he ought to get back to.

It was odd to think that he was now looking for ways to spend his time. The legislature had convened the second week in January and he'd made three trips to Nashville already. The trips were exploratory mostly and involved a little consulting work with some lobbyist friends of his. He had the feeling that his friends in Nashville were inviting him down less for his expertise, and more to get him back in the swing of things. The next round of elections was just around the corner. Montgomery looked to be the man to beat in the Senate, but talk of a former senator, eight years retired, kept rearing its head. Where there was smoke there was often fire, and at this juncture in the election season most of the smoke was sent by the candidates themselves. Little floating rumors to a friendly newspaperman just to see if any kind of groundswell might get started. The proverbial toe in water.

And with the Montgomery vacancy, the governor's office would prove a real free-for-all. It was anyone's guess at this point which candidate either party would run up the flagpole. He'd had a few meet and greets with some of the men considering a run, but they seemed to be meeting with him more as a favor to mutual friends than truly interested in his services. Though his name had been cleared, the whole bank business still seemed a little raw. He thought he could see it in the eyes of the folks he met with in Nashville. It was a gossip-run place, and the thinking was, again, where there's smoke . . .

He'd nearly vowed to go ahead and shower and shave and get out of the house for the first time in nearly seventy-two hours when the phone rang. He waited for Jan to answer, the phone was never for him this time of day, never for him at all it seemed these days, but she must have been in the shower. As he walked toward the ringing phone, he glanced at the clock on the stove: ten-fifteen. And still in pajamas and slippers. Hello, he said.

Mike, said a silvery baritone voice, this is Booth Langley. How are you?

I'm fine, Booth, what can I do for you?

Roland was wondering if you might be willing to meet him for lunch.

Does his phone not work?

Teague, I'm just the messenger here.

I don't deal with intermediaries, Booth. And I haven't for a hell of a long time. If your client has something to say, he seems damn well capable of doing it himself.

I'll pass along the message, Mike.

Teague hung up the phone and walked up the stairs to his bedroom.

He kicked off his slippers, forcefully, idiotically, and waited for Jan to get out of the shower. Then the phone rang again. He looked at it on the bedside table. He let it ring. From the bathroom, the shower was shut off and Jan yelled *telephone*, as loudly as she could, thinking him still downstairs.

I hear it, said Teague.

Well, get it, Jan said. Mother's supposed to call me about that birthday party for Dad.

Teague walked around the bed and picked up the phone. He offered a monotone greeting.

Said the voice on the other end: Teague, this is Roland Cole.

Halfway

I understand if you don't want to see me.

No, said Teague, I'm fine. I'm bored as hell. Where?

Roland suggested Melvin's and Teague said okay. As they were hanging up, Roland said: If you're going to come armed, I'd prefer knives to guns.

Now Teague was stepping over grey puddles in the parking lot of Melvin's, an old time burger joint on the far north side of the county, fifteen miles or so from downtown, an area known as Lake City. A hundred years ago, it'd served as a vacation spot for the well-to-do of Glennville. A man-made three-acre lake right off of Highway 9 had been the inspiration for the first word in the town's title. Paddleboats to rent and ducks to feed. The second word had been ambitious at the time of its christening and more than a little ironic for most of the twentieth century. But with annexation and the spreading strip malls, there wasn't much point in differentiating Lake City from the expanding city to its south.

It was nearly one-thirty and the lunch crowd had long since cleared out. The warmth of the restaurant hit him right away, that and the sizzle and smell of burgers on a grill. He spotted an empty booth in the back. The same red and white tiles he remembered as a boy, the soda fountain, all unchanged. Framed photos on the walls of Lake City baseball teams recently sponsored, all sporting MELVIN'S across the chest. And black and whites from the glory era of the college football team. Unhelmeted and crew-cut stars with knees raised in a jaunty and unrealistic move, stiff-arms out, faces a photographer's suggestion of openmouthed and wide-eyed intensity. He'd mimicked the same poses on photo day at the high school, the hair flattopped and perfect, the face a boy Doc Blanchard juking in the backyard. His wife and daughter were good for a belly laugh every time the photo albums were brought out at his folks' house. On the back wall, Melvin's through the years, the cars in the parking lot changing as you went, the haircuts of the patrons.

He was sitting in the booth when Roland walked in the door. Roland in the flesh was quite different than Roland as mere conceptualization. He felt a mix of sudden emotions, which would take time to untangle. Roland was nearly to him when he scooted out of the booth, stood up, and offered a hand to shake. It was the way a man greeted another. To not stand and shake hands wouldn't have entered Teague's mind, but Roland smiled at the gesture nonetheless. A complicated smile, showing mostly relief. But something else as well. Teague couldn't put his finger on it. Post-despair?

Thanks for meeting me, he said taking the hand and firmly shaking it several times. I really do appreciate it.

They sat down and each reached for the menus sandwiched between the salt and pepper shakers and the metal napkin holder. Roland's back was to the restaurant and before he opened the menu, he craned his neck around to have a look. This place doesn't change, he said. As the words were coming out of his mouth, he placed the menu back from where he got it. Burger, fries, and a Coke, he said. What else are you going to get at Melvin's?

Teague agreed, but continued to make a show of studying his choices. He found it hard to look at Roland, so drawn was his face and dark the circles under his eyes. He was wearing jeans as well, and a sweater, and Teague found the whole effect disarming. This despite the fact that he was dressed in slacks and a sweater himself. We spend so much time in suits, he thought. To be seen like this was like seeing a policeman out of uniform, your doctor in tennis shorts.

Roland was studying a photo above them of Lang's Dome, one of the highest peaks of the Appalachian chain. Roland said: Did you ever hike up there?

Once, said Teague. When I was in high school.

Was it tough trucking?

As I recall, you can get pretty close by car. And then you've got a pretty short hike to the top. Less than a mile. It's damn steep though.

Roland nodded. I always meant to get up there, he said. It's a shame how little I've taken advantage of the mountains.

That's the way it is. If it's in your backyard, you just take it for granted. I don't get up there often enough either. We did it a fair bit when Julie was little. We used to go up to the Hyatt during the winter every now and then so Julie could swim in the indoor pool.

We did that, said Roland. That was a neat deal. With that waterfall and all.

It was, said Teague.

Roland studied the wall at Teague's back then turned to look at the soda fountain. He was drumming his fingers on the table as he did so. Man, he said, Daddy sure loved this place. Whenever we were headed to Glennville, it was either the last stop going in or the first stop heading back to Henry City. Burger and a strawberry milkshake for him.

Teague nodded from his menu as a reply.

This was a big Henry City place, said Roland. We'd always run into two or three families we knew making the trip to Glennville.

He laughed suddenly and Teague looked up. I just realized something, he said.

Teague waited for what was to follow before he understood that Roland was talking primarily to himself. An incredulous smile was upon his face and he was nodding his head as if in further agreement with his initial discovery.

He still wasn't exactly looking at Teague when he said: We were all stopping here so we wouldn't have to go into any strange restaurants in Glennville. This was like our last little Henry City oasis before we hit the bright lights of the big, big city.

He laughed again at this thought. His tone was wry, pleased to reconsider his yokel self and yokel brethren steeling themselves for the tumult of urbanity. He glanced at Teague a moment then turned back toward the soda fountain, squinting to see next year's schedule behind the counter. As he did so, Teague realized how unlikely it was he'd be on this side of the free world come football season.

They get through September, they ought to be in good shape.

I think you're right, said Teague.

You understand these people who get all worked up over it?

No, said Teague. I never did. And I've been around it all of my life.

Imagine letting a football game ruin your weekend.

It never did mine.

No, said Roland. Me neither. I mean if I was playing in the game, sure. But a grown man getting all worked up over it? Over a bunch of college kids playing ball? It's damn embarrassing.

Teague laughed. I know, it is.

The waitress showed up as they were discussing the strange phenomenon that is the southern football fan. She did a quick double take when she glanced down and saw Roland, then concentrated on taking their orders. Two young men sat at the counter and an elderly couple had the booth at the door. Otherwise the place was empty. The bell in the window rang with a new order and a hand reached out to grab it. *Two burgers and fries* came the call to whoever was on the grill. The waitress popped two bottles of Coke from behind the counter and gave the radio a slight increase in volume before heading their way. An old Hank Snow song followed her out and save for that and the scrape of spatula on steel, the room was silent.

Teague had his Coke in hand and was watching the waitress as she headed back to the counter when Roland said: It may not mean anything to hear how sorry I am, but I did want to tell you.

Teague took a sip of his Coke and looked at the man across the table.

Roland returned the look briefly then glanced out the window. In a low, distant voice he said: We just got our ass in a jam. We got greedy.

And then we got sloppy. And then we were arrogant enough to think we could pull it off.

Teague thought: What reply am I supposed to give to this?

On those deals where we signed other people's names. On those forged signatures. That was just to buy us some time. We'd been swirling money long enough and pulling it off, that we thought if we could just hold on for another six months, we could make it all good. And we couldn't just keep putting our own names on all these phony loans. It would have raised too many eyebrows.

Teague looked Roland in the eye, then looked toward the counter, the window where their food would soon pop up.

We hold on for six more months, and the money for those loans is there. Those loans are paid in full. And no one ever knows that Mike Teague's name is on there. We weren't trying to make you an accessory. We just needed names. Hell, we used every bank officer we had on some of those loans. Some of them knew about it. Others didn't.

Teague was looking at his place mat, a laminated map of the state of Tennessee marked with landmarks and old heroes. Davy Crocket. The Hermitage. W. C. Handy. Reelfoot Lake.

Said Roland: I'm not trying to make an excuse. It was a shitty, shitty thing we did. I'm just trying to tell you how it went down. And to say I hope it didn't hurt you too bad.

Teague looked at Roland now. It wasn't a hell of a lot of fun, he said. I'll say that about it.

Roland nodded. I'm sure, I'm sure of that.

I was sorry to hear about J.T.

Roland nodded and looked again toward the parking lot. He lifted his Coke and tapped it gently a few times on the table. He looked about to say something, but couldn't quite get it out.

Then the bell rang to say *order's up*. Teague watched the waitress grab two rolls of silverware and stuff them in her apron, then take the plates from the window. The song on the radio was King of the Road and the waitress mouthed the words as she came their way.

———

They'd spoken little while they ate, only the occasional comment about the superiority of thin fries to thick and the like. Neither was able to finish his burger. When each had pushed his plate toward the center of the table, Teague said: So how do you like Montgomery's chances for the Senate?

Pretty good, I'd say. Don't you think?

Some folks are worried about Woodson since he's already held the office.

Too old, said Roland. That big cigar routine of his is from another era. Plus he's just not telegenic.

Roland put a little extra emphasis on this last word and offered a faint smile.

Yeah, said Teague. You're right. Montgomery's got D.C. in his corner too. And how does Woodson help the Republicans nationally? He doesn't. So I'd say it's smooth sailing for Montgomery unless he gets caught with a dead hooker or a live boy.

Roland smiled at that old saw. He said: I remember when we had a friend in the White House. That's a nice ace up the sleeve.

It sure as hell is.

Roland shifted in the booth. He looked out the window and then back to Teague.

At the risk of bringing it up again, he said, I was a little surprised the governor didn't help you out. It was obvious they were just pressing you to get to me and our friend in Memphis.

He's a good politician. What's the upside?

Roland thought about this for a moment. Not a hell of a lot, he said. Friendship and loyalty, I guess.

Teague smiled at this.

Roland said: That must sound ironic.

A little.

At a nearby table, the waitress was filling ketchup bottles and Roland waved her over and asked if she could take their plates. She took the plates and set them on the table behind her. When she asked about desserts, Roland said: Oh yes. Absolutely. You can't come to Melvin's and not get a milkshake. Give me a chocolate. Extra thick.

The waitress looked at Teague. She was a woman of few words, but had the art of nonverbal communication down to a science. Strawberry for me, said Teague.

Get it extra thick, said Roland.

Taking his server's cue, Teague agreed to this suggestion by nodding and flashing a *ditto* finger at her.

They both watched her walk behind the counter and pull out two mixers, then the milk from the glass-doored refrigerator. They heard the slide of the floor cooler top and soon her arms could be seen scooping. The ice cream must have been hard because her shoulders were tensed and she gritted her teeth as she worked.

Roland said: Do you mind if I ask you a question?

Go ahead.

You don't have to answer if you don't want to.

All right.

Why didn't you just tell them what they wanted to know?

Teague glanced at the place mat in front of him. Elvis Presley. The Grand Ole Opry. John Sevier. Chickamauga.

He said: Maybe I just hadn't yet. Maybe I was biding my time to see how things played out. If prison was really looking me in the eye, I might have sung like a canary.

Roland said: I don't think so.

I guess we'll never know.

Roland nodded to this. He'd press it no further. He said, well you're a good man, Teague. If you ask me, you deserve better friends than me and the good governor.

Yall were paying me, said Teague. That always complicates the nature of friendship.

All the same. All the same.

Teague reached for the straw holder, took one out, and unwrapped it. As he was doing it, he realized he'd probably use a spoon instead.

Hey, said Roland, can I ask you one more question? It's a little personal, maybe. But maybe not. It's something I've wondered about quite a bit. And I can't believe I haven't asked you before.

Have at it, said Teague.

Why didn't you ever run for office? I mean you've obviously got the ability and you seem to have a certain amount of civic interest. So why didn't you ever run? I think you'd have been a good leader.

Maybe, said Teague. I'm not so sure. The main thing was I never could find enough people I was interested in leading.

Roland laughed. That sounds slightly misanthropic.

I guess it does. Well let me rephrase. I just didn't think I had the energy to convince a bunch of people that I had their best interests at heart. I guess I was just waiting to get drafted by the people.

It don't work that way.

No, said Teague, it don't. That's why all you get is salesmen. You've got to be a seller and you've got to sell it on TV. That's too high a price for me. I'd rather sell watermelons like old Tuck Shelton. You remember those commercials?

Roland laughed. Oh hell yes, of course I do. And I remember when he buried the man in his grocery store parking lot in the Plexiglas coffin with the tube down in it so the man could breath.

Oh yeah, said Teague. Sure. You could see down in it. See the man.

Right, exactly.

They were smiling at the memory of the local huckster when the waitress brought the milkshakes. She set the shakes down and slid the check on the table between them without a word. Roland reached for the check and pulled it to him, then put straw to shake.

This shake's as good as I remembered, said Roland.

Yeah it is, said Teague.

Roland took a couple more sips then pushed his milkshake away, three-quarters of it still in the glass. He took a napkin from the holder and ran it across his mouth.

He said: Booth Langley says that since I'm pleading guilty, no one will remember what I did with the fair or what we did downtown. That in twenty years when I walk down the street all anyone is going to remember is *bank fraud*.

Teague had been sipping on his milkshake without spoon or straw.

Now he stopped. He pushed the drink to the side.

You think that's so?

I don't know, said Teague.

Yeah, me neither.

Said Teague: History is funny the way it gets written and then revised. What people say in five years won't be what they say in twenty. And what they say in twenty won't be what they say in a hundred. If it makes any difference, I think you made the right decision to come clean. And I'm talking about for you, not for me.

Roland didn't reply to this.

Teague knew what he ought to say. It was what he was thinking. To not say it would be stingy and small.

He said: Roland, you did a lot of good things for the city.

Roland nodded. He took their glasses and reached across the aisle to place them on a nearby table. He then reached for another napkin to wipe the wet rings on the table where the glasses had been. Then he placed the napkin with the dirty glasses. The waitress was on her way over as he did so. He nodded in thanks and watched her walk with the glasses back to the counter. When she was back behind the counter, he turned to Teague.

He said: A little old lady came up to me at the cleaner's last week. I'd just paid and was turning to go. I didn't even see her behind me. But it turns out she was waiting for me. She must have seen me come in because she already had her dry cleaning in her hands. Anyway, I say hello as I'm walking out and she says, don't you hello me, you crook. My daughter lost ten thousand dollars in that Valley Industrial of yours.

Roland's eyes were very intense as he spoke and he was looking directly at Teague.

Said Roland: She grabs me by the arm, this old lady. And says, I just want to know how you sleep at night.

Teague said nothing, he reached for the unused straw on the table.

I told her, not very well. And then she followed me to my car, talking all the way.

Teague shook his head. There was nothing that anyone could say to this.

Hell, said Roland. I don't blame her. How could I blame her?

Then he took the check and walked to the register to pay. Teague grabbed first his coat and then Roland's from the booth. He waited at the door for Roland to place the tip on the table. When Roland approached he handed him his coat, which was leather and much too thin for this weather. Said Teague: How's Libby?

They were standing at the door as Roland put on his coat. The restaurant was now empty but for employees. The schedule on the door indicated that lunch was not served after two. It was now half past. She's fine, said Roland. She'll be all right. She's as tough as they come. Hadn't blinked once through all of this mess. Hell, J.T. and I both married gals a lot tougher than we are.

Teague had his hand awkwardly on the door. He said: Well please send my regards. Jan and I always thought the world of her.

Thank you. I'll pass that along.

Teague opened the door and held it for Roland. The air was wet and heavy with cold. He wondered if it might snow again. The weatherman had hinted at the possibility. Roland came through the door and nodded his thanks to Teague. He made a motion with his head toward the restaurant but didn't look back. Melvin's, he said. Halfway between home and ambition.

Then he stuck out a hand to shake and said, thanks for meeting me, Teague. It meant a hell of a lot.

And then he was walking to his car through the puddles and not breaking stride as he went.

The River Speaks

Some Time Later

Jan Teague walked toward one of the department stores in the Parkview Mall, hoping to find a bathing suit for her husband to take to the annual Fourth of July family reunion. Getting him to shop for shorts and other summer casual clothes proved nearly impossible year after year. He was old-fashioned or just perverse in thinking that men looked a little ridiculous in short pants unless they were playing tennis or out on the boat. And he was especially picky about bathing suits, invariably finding them too short, too long, too baggy, too tight, too loud and so on. She didn't think she could survive another summer of complaint about *tight inner netting*, so this time she'd buy three or four and take back which ones didn't make the cut. One way or another, in cut-off dress pants if need be, he was going on her brother's boat this Fourth of July. And waterskiing too.

She made her way slowly down the corridors of the store. The humidity had finally kicked in a week or so back, and nowhere in town was as cool and refreshing as the mall. Her mother's birthday was coming up and maybe she could find a present. She looked at some earrings first and was just moving down to the bracelets when she heard her name called from across the aisle.

Turning, she found the lady at the cosmetics counter smiling her way. The woman was wrapping up a makeup demonstration with a customer and held up a finger to say, *be done in just a minute*. Jan hadn't the foggiest. Then it hit her. The hair was shorter and the face a little more angular, as if she'd been exercising or being careful about what she ate. This and the salesperson's smile and cosmetics frock had combined to make Corrine seem much younger than she was.

She'd have to wait and that was all there was to it. Back at the jewelry case, eyeing but not seeing the bracelets before her, she reminded herself not to overcompensate. The cheery and bright routine was a transparent guise. She'd discovered that firsthand when Mike had his trouble and his name was always in the paper. Coming across anyone who wasn't an intimate in the grocery store, she'd receive a steady dose of awkward avoidance of her husband's troubles. Brevity had been the essence as well. *Well, I've got to run. Good to see you, so good to see you.* As if whatever she had was catching.

When she looked up from the jewelry case again, the customer at the cosmetics counter was gone and Corrine was putting her equipment away.

Well hey there, Corrine, I almost didn't recognize you back there.

Corrine turned, smiling, and briefly gripped Jan's hand across the counter.

It's the haircut, she said, with a mockingly dainty swish of her hair. It's shorter. And highlights are a girl's best friend, you know. I'm always surprising people back here. I get these scrunched-up-looking faces looking back at me, wondering who in the heck is hollering at em.

Corrine laughed a little at this game she played and Jan realized how silly her earlier discomfort had been. If anybody could cut through fake cheer and unwanted sympathy, here was that person. A lifetime with your dukes up would surely give you that talent.

So how long have you been working here?

Corrine paused to count the time in her head. Going on five months, she said. I like it.

Good, said Jan. Good good.

Idle hands, you know. Once I sold the house and found the condo, I had to find something to do. I was driving the boys crazy.

She laughed as she said this and Jan did too.

They said, you've got to get out of the house. And I knew they were right, but it was just so hard to get started. Then one day it dawned on me that here in a few years I'd be on my own, the boys would be off to school. That was all it took. I said, you got to get going, man. You're not going to end up one of those old widow ladies getting your hair done on Tuesday just to go to church on Wednesday night. So I went out and got a paper and started looking through the want ads. And now here I am.

As she spoke, Jan couldn't help but wonder how she'd react under similar circumstances. Even if Mike died, even if he lost all of his money, she wouldn't have to sell the house, wouldn't have to work in a department store. This knowledge didn't comfort her or make her feel guilty. It was simply a fact.

She said: They say it's good to stay active.

Corrine smiled.

We were so sorry to hear about J.T.

Thank you, said Corrine. I appreciated the card.

The card had not been sent immediately after the funeral, but several months later. After Mike had been cleared. She'd gone back and forth about whether to send one immediately, but just couldn't force herself to do it.

And how's Libby?

I think she's doing okay. She's living down in Charleston with her mother. They'd been talking about getting a place down there for a number of years to be close to her. So Libby just went on down. They still haven't sold their house though.

Jan knew this. It was mentioned every so often in society columns in the newspaper. Not many people in Glennville could afford such a place, and since the house was in Libby's name, it couldn't be foreclosed upon during the bankruptcy. Libby was going to get a reasonable price and good for her.

When Corrine asked about herself, Jan stuck to Julie's recent movements and news and their plans for the Fourth of July. She didn't mention Mike. To do so would move to thoughts of business, and of that business, and neither of them needed that.

Well, said Jan, I'm glad you like your job. You seem really happy.

Oh, Corrine said, waving a hand in front of her in a gently dismissive fashion. It's just temporary. A gal's got to make more money than this.

I've been studying for my real estate license. Taking night classes and all that jazz. I'll be taking the exams later on in the summer. Can you imagine someone my age still having to take tests? I wake up sometimes in a cold sweat and I'm dreaming about Miss Joy Bell Murphy's tenth-grade geometry class.

Jan laughed. Oh, you'll do fine, she said. And you'll be a great realtor. I know that for sure.

I do think I'll enjoy it. I've always liked looking at houses and I'm hoping I might have a knack for describing them, showing people how you could fix them up and where furniture could go and so on. You know us Henry City gals are known for our sophistication.

Jan laughed again and said: I know you'll be great at it. When you get your license and get set up, send me some cards and I'll pass them along to people when I hear they're going on the market.

I'll do that. Thanks.

It was then that a customer came up to the other side of the rectangular counter. She had the look of someone ready to buy, and Jan said: Well, it was sure good to see you.

It was good to see you too, said Corrine. And then she turned to the customer with a smile and said, may I help you, ma'am?

Jan bypassed the jewelry counter as she left. She had some other things to do later in the day to get ready for their trip. Walking away, she remembered an English class she'd had in college. The professor had quoted a writer who said there were no second acts in American life. She'd taken the quote at face value at the time, but with age and experience, she'd found it not to be so. The truth was there were second acts, and third acts, and possibly more. She'd known women who'd fallen apart after divorce and the attendant economic spiral. Others soldiered on, adjusting their lifestyles, often making a new set of friends, often, very often, with women in the same boat they were. Like flocked to like and always would.

She turned to look once more at Corrine, gently tilting the woman's chin with her finger to get the light. Then, checking her watch, she headed toward the escalator and the men's department and what bathing suits she might find there.

Offertory

FADE IN

INT: A SMALL CHURCH PACKED FOR SUNDAY SERVICE—DAY

The congregation is on their feet. Light filters in from the STAINED-GLASS windows, sporadic beams dancing about the pews in a RAINBOW of colors. The shards of LIGHT never stay in one place long, but are always SHIFTING, on a hand, a singing face, skipping, a stone on the lake, across the opposite wall.

CLOSE ON:

STAINED-GLASS WINDOW

Through the window the SHADOW of a large tree in the full leaves of summer. The tree moves this way and that with the breeze, the shadow of LIMBS blocking, then releasing the radiant LIGHT outside.

PAN:

Row upon row of singing FACES.

UNTIL CLOSE ON:

MRS. COLE singing without hymnal in hand.

REVERSE TO MRS COLE'S POV:

Behind the pulpit is the small CHOIR, dressed in heavy purple ROBES despite the season. The members are male and female and range in age from sixteen to seventy. In the back of the small-tiered bleachers is SIS, farthest from the minister's lectern in front of them. She sings in a perfunctory manner, making little attempt to show that the languid tempo and unwieldy lyrics of the hymn are not to her liking.

THE REVERSE:

MRS. COLE smiles despite herself at Sis's displeasure with the song.

REVERSE:

The MINISTER as he steps to the lectern for the offering prayer.

> MINISTER
> (with arms gently raised)
> Bless the gifts and the giver.
> May both bring glory to Thee.

He returns to his seat on the pulpit. The unseen ORGANIST begins the Offertory. Against the soft musical interlude we hear the faint sound of CHANGE CLATTERING in collection PLATES.

WIDE ON:

THE SANCTUARY. Three ushers walk the aisles, silently gathering the PLATES as they move down the short rows. The congregation drops CHANGE and donation ENVELOPES into the plates without a word. After their offering, they look a little awkward for a moment and gaze toward the front of the PULPIT at the CHOIR.

MRS. COLE'S POV:

As the Offertory comes to a close and the CHOIR stands. There is a pause between the organ interlude and the next song, the GLORIA PATRI. The first line of the song to follow is relatively slow and dignified. However, with the phrase *as it was in the beginning* the TEMPO changes very quickly and is quite FAST and UPBEAT. The song slows again on *World without end*, and Amen is really stretched out. It is the kind of song that SIS will like, the two changes in tempo, the clean simplicity of the lyrics. As the chorus and congregation wait for the opening bars, SIS glances quickly toward the ORGANIST, eager to begin.

CHORUS

Glory be to the Father
and to the son
and to the Holy Ghost;
As it was in the beginning, is now, and ever shall be,
World without end. A-men. A-men.

CLOSE ON:

SIS, who ends the song with a tight-lipped smile.

FADE OUT

The Long Way Home

Teague was driving back from the golf course early in September, the trees along the road holding their green, the sky above blue and high with the approach of fall. He'd played a nice round on his favorite course in the state, Bernard Hills, the oldest country club in the city and possessing one of the best layouts anywhere around. Once it'd been Glennville's most prestigious, but as the city's demographics slowly shifted from east to west, Riverside Country Club had supplanted it as the choice of the elite. Playing Bernard Hills these days meant any tee time you wanted and little waiting to hit the ball, the members primarily of the older set and those few well-to-do who still lived over the river.

The day had been satisfying on all accounts and he'd decided to take the long way home in order to prolong the residual good feeling that comes from a day of clean strikes on balls, the ball flying off the head of the club in a clean hiss, the sweetness of a good strike versus bad felt all the way through the body. He'd crossed over the river on the old Douglass Street Bridge and taken the road that ran parallel to the river and past the homes of old Glennville. The road was winding and little used and as he took the turns, his clubs rattled vaguely in the trunk.

It was in such a mind, restful and contented as the air conditioner blew upon the dampness of his golf shirt, that he came around a curve and realized with a start that Roland Cole's house lay half a mile up the road. What he found shocking was that he'd taken this road home without the first thought of who used to live on it. He didn't know what this forgetting foretold, other than he'd moved on and moved on much more thoroughly than he'd ever have imagined.

As he approached, he made sure to slow the car. Jan would want a report on its present state. Such things worried her, the fact the house hadn't yet sold worried her, so he wanted to get a good look. She still had no time for Roland, but Libby and her present circumstance were another matter. Unfortunately, another car came up behind him, so he either had to resume speed or pull into the driveway. He chose the latter.

The gates had been left open. Perhaps the realtor left them open all the time now. Whatever the case, they were flung open, a two-foot SKY atop one, a two-foot LAND upon the other.

Someone had recently cut the grass, but the clippings, a foot deep, ran in long uneven furrows the length of the massive lawn. In the middle of the yard, a tiny FOR SALE sign, like a faint flare in an empty ocean. And the bricked-over mailbox was now spray-painted in the university colors. School pride reaching far and wide. Looking at the huge empty house, he couldn't help thinking about the two great buildings he'd see when he got back on this road and headed through downtown, how they'd be shining in the sun. And then down Brewer Avenue he'd pass the fair site, abandoned but for lanky weeds and building debris and the hasty and flimsy chain-link fence surrounding Helios and his chariot. Yes, the pre-fair inertia had returned to the city, and returned threefold. The old guard was back in charge of the money in the city and money again was tight. Unless, of course, you had it coming in.

He thought of Roland's public apology in the paper to his parents and old teachers and the whole community of Henry City. They had, he said, taught him right from wrong. And he'd let them down in a most profound way.

It was profound indeed, one of the largest bank failures in U.S. history. And people throughout the city and region had lost part or all of their savings.

J.T. was dead. Roland in prison. Their wives and family left to pick up the pieces as they could.

He checked the road for cars, then sped to the top of the long drive. He parked as discreetly as he could, but someone who wanted to take a really good gander from the road would still be able to see the car and him getting out of it.

When he slammed the door behind him, the sound carried, loud and hollow at the same time. He walked down the stone path and through the overgrown shade garden. He'd never seen the garden but by artificial light and was surprised how well it blended into the wooded area behind it. The decorative pond had been drained and the small fountain with the slim Venus atop it was beginning to turn a little green. In the absence of its sound, Teague noticed for the first time the fountain's quiet bubbling. Every other time he'd walked this path he'd been with a crowd, usually a boisterous one after several highballs at a downtown restaurant, hearing the gentle gurgling of the fountain without knowing he had.

How strangely the brain worked.

He walked into the backyard and past the swimming pool and its leaf-strewn cover. Past the tennis court and memories of a late-night discussion.

Another example of not hearing what was there.

When he got to the deck, his loafers thumped against the boards, echoing, or seeming to, in the silence of the day. A lone shingle had peeled off the gazebo. And the deck was splintered in a few spots. But otherwise things looked no worse for wear.

On the observation deck, he found that the sky overhead was as hard as a sheet of blue marble, and the land below, and the river below, seemed separate and disconnected.

He felt very much beneath the sky, very obviously above the murky water below.

A small creature, bird or chipmunk, skittered in a rustling of dry leaves out from under one of the steps leading down to the boat dock and into the brush beside it. The elaborate winch that ratcheted the boat from boathouse to water some sixty yards below was now a rusty metal scar, jagged and ill-sewn into the side of the cliff. The land here was not meant for boat ramps, was meant to be impenetrable, unassailable, land to water, or water to land. But here was the winch. And not two years before a boat had been affixed to it. And, presumably, would be again.

Looking at the winch bothered him, so Teague looked down to the water. He tried to remember the last time he'd been this far upriver, but couldn't recall it. Probably as a teen in one of his friends' johnboats, tooling up the river in search of new fishing spots and unexplored islands. He thought next time he was on the water, maybe when Jan's brother brought his boat up, he'd suggest a trip up this far. He'd like to see how the deck and the observation point looked from the water. How well could it even be seen?

Below him the water lapped against the cliff, against the two-tiered dock. Some large craft was recently past, and the residual waves, ever smaller but constant, came and then came again. He looked up river and down for boats, but saw none. Hardly any breeze blew and what did barely flipped the leaves of the maples that lined the back edge of the lawn. Here and there wily cedar trees made a go of it in the crevices of the cliff. Amazing trees. How little they needed for a foothold to get started. How little they needed to survive.

He supposed that survival was what it was all about. Persistence. Indomitability.

All right. Fair enough. But persistent and indomitable as you might be, the end result was still the same. The jig would be up someday.

Perhaps there were some who could just pack mule it through and play it safe until the time came to retire and then start your life. But that wasn't the way he'd been wired. He'd gambled when he quit teaching. The bureaucracy of public schools had been some of it, but if you were going to marry the rich girl, you had to make your own money. No way around that. And you couldn't be bankrolled by the emperor either. By wits or guile or luck, the nut you made had to be your own or there'd be no harmony in the home. That was fact. That was natural law. Then when that gamble seemed to pay off, he'd nearly lost it all on a woman. Risked too much. Made bad bets. Somehow he'd survived that, even though he'd not deserved to. Then he'd tempted prison and his father's and his family's good name after that. Why? Why'd he gotten involved with the Coles in the first place? Maybe the excitement of doing something big for the city. But that wasn't all of it. Not all.

Now here he was. What he knew was that it wasn't over. Cashing in your chips? Then you don't get to play. Then you're just going to work and mowing the lawn. Life was risk. To ignore that fact was naïveté or sticking your head in the sand. The key was to pick your spots. Too few gambles or too many were both losing propositions. He knew what he was now. A hired gun. An insider. And once you were inside, once you were behind that great curtain of Oz, there was never a way to get back out again. He didn't know how much longer he'd work, but what work he'd do would be in that field. Maybe he'd find a man worthy of his talent, maybe he wouldn't.

The breeze picked up.

The branches of the trees swayed, the undersides of the leaves showing briefly, then gone, and then again. The scraggly cedars bent with the wind. Some small unseen branch scraped against wood somewhere on the steps, or on the railing behind. Little waves in the river crested for a moment, showing white. Across river, a farmer pulled a hay baler and the dust flew up and caught the wind in sudden, surprising gusts. The sky above Teague was the blue glass top of an aquarium, the river a thing that slowly moved.

The wind was blowing on the water and on the hay in the field.

Blowing too on the dampness of his shirt.

And with a chill, with a sudden and painful piercing of humility, Teague realized what a lucky man he was, and what a lucky man he'd always been.

Acknowledgments

Thanks to Starling Lawrence, the quintessential writer's editor, for his keen eye and keener ear. I'm especially grateful for his support of the conceptual elements of the book and for his assistance in melding concept to form. The book as it appears here is greatly enhanced by his talent.

Thanks to Michael Lewis for kindly putting me in touch with Norton. His generosity of spirit is something for which I'll always be grateful.

My two earliest editors were Frank Majors and Allen McDuffie, who read early drafts and many of them. Their help with characterization and plot was most invaluable and a great deal of the credit for this book should go to them.

I am grateful to David Jeffrey and Bob Hoskins, my chain of command at James Madison University, for going to bat for me and for their continued support of my work. Thanks also to JMU for a summer grant.

Thanks to Chris Vescovo for a variety of things and for always lending a sympathetic ear. I also appreciate the support of Mom and Stan; Nina; Molly May and Nydia Parries at Norton; my copy editor, Dave Cole; my agent, David McCormick; and his assistant, Gillian Linden.

Thanks to Ted Sabarese for the author's photo and to the following for either reading portions of the manuscript, providing some sort of assistance, or answering a myriad of questions: Bo Creech, Bob Sterchi, Lucy and Larry Majors, Andy Burton, David Coffey, Steve Glassman, Steve Elkins, Jeff Novinger, Rob Schutt, Doug Majors, Bryan Hudson,

Barry Paige, Eric Jaegers, Rose Gray, Judy Good, and keeper of the lexicon, Wade Anderton.

Finally, I'd like to thank my lovely wife, Christy, who edits all of my books and makes them all possible, and my children, Tessa Rane and Maxwell, two great kids who make me proud every day.

My father, a Nashville lobbyist for nearly four decades, was the best teacher of politics that any man could have. But a debt of gratitude is owed to several books for further enhancing my knowledge of the political arena. Anyone interested in how things get done at the local, state, and national levels would be well served by the following: Robert Caro's series *The Years of Lyndon Johnson*, Joe Dodd's *World Class Politics*, and V. O. Key Jr.'s *Southern Politics*.